MODERN KOREAN FICTION

MODERN KOREAN FICTION

AN ANTHOLOGY

Bruce Fulton and Youngmin Kwon

COLUMBIA UNIVERSITY PRESS NEW YORK

COLUMBIA UNIVERSITY PRESS WISHES TO EXPRESS ITS APPRECIATION FOR ASSISTANCE GIVEN BY THE PUSHKIN FUND TOWARD THE COST OF PUBLISHING THIS BOOK.

Columbia University Press
Publishers Since 1893
New York Chichester, West Sussex

Library of Congress Cataloging-in-Publication Data
Fulton, Bruce.
Modern Korean fiction : an anthology / Bruce Fulton and Youngmin Kwon.
p. cm.
Includes bibliographical references.
ISBN 0-231-13512-2 (cloth : alk. paper) — ISBN 0-231-13513-0 (pbk. : alk. paper)
1. Korean fiction—20th century—Translations into English. 2. Short stories, Korean—Translations into English. I. Kwæon, Yæong-min, 1948– II. Title.
PL984.E8F85 2005
895.7′30108′0904—dc22

2005041378

Columbia University Press books are printed on permanent and durable acid-free paper.
Designed by Chang Jae Lee
Printed in the United States of America
c 10 9 8 7 6 5 4 3 2 1
p 10 9 8 7 6 5 4 3 2 1

CONTENTS

PREFACE

In the 1990s modern Korean fiction, theretofore enjoying a scant presence qualitatively if not quantitatively in English translation, began to appear with increasing frequency in the English-speaking world. Several important fiction writers have appeared in at least one volume dedicated to their works alone, and most have been anthologized and/or published in journals (see "Suggestions for Further Reading" at the end of this volume). Korean women writers, their voices traditionally muted both at home and in translation, are receiving long-overdue recognition. All of which may lead the prospective reader to ask why there should be a new anthology of fiction writing from modern Korea. An answer to this question requires some background.

This anthology was conceived in 1992 at the inaugural meeting of the International Korean Literature Association at the Center for Korean Studies of the University of Hawai'i at Manoa. At that time the sparseness of modern Korean literature in acceptable translation made painfully obvious the need for readily available volumes that would offer comprehensive coverage of Korean literature. In the case of Korean fiction from the modern period—that is, fiction dating from the late 1910s—there was no readily available anthology devoted to fiction alone.

This anthology attempts to meet that need and several others as well. For one thing, existing anthologies, unless devoted specifically to women, are weighted heavily toward male authors; we have attempted more balanced coverage. Second, we have tried to match authors with translators who have already served them well in translation. Third, we have attempted representative coverage of contemporary voices, including writing from the 1990s. Fourth, we have attempted to include voices of important authors thus far little represented in translation, such as Yi T'aejun, Ch'oe Chŏnghŭi, Yi Hoch'ŏl, Ch'oe Illam, and Ch'oe Inho. Fifth, we have included a story from the Democratic People's Republic of Korea (North Korea). Finally we aim to fulfill the long-standing need of the Korean literature field and the interested general reader in the English-speaking world for a volume of translations that are faithful to the original, that stand on their own as literature in English, and that convey the distinct voices of different authors rather than the single voice of the volume editor/translator.

As with any anthology, this one has gaps and omissions, for the usual reasons of space limitations and lack of quality translations of certain authors. Those who would wish for novel extracts will, we hope, be satisfied by our inclusion of two selections from major linked-story novels: "Knifeblade" from Cho Sehŭi's remarkable *Nanjangi ka ssoaollin chagŭn kong* (1978, trans. 2006 *The Dwarf*) and "The Old Hatter" from Yi Munyŏl's *Kŭdae tashi nŭn kohyang e kaji mot'ari* (1980, You can't go home again). Regrettable also is the impossibility of including extracts from any of the multivolume novels that collectively constitute one of the major achievements of modern Korean literature, such as Pak Kyŏngni's *T'oji* (1969–1994, part 1 trans. 1996 *Land*) and Hwang Sŏgyŏng's *Chang Kilsan* (1983–1984, Chang Kilsan). On a more positive note, several more novels are available now in English translation, an improvement over the situation in 1992; some of these appear in the list of suggested reading at the end of the anthology.

This anthology and its companion volumes published by Columbia University Press are the fruit of the vision of the late Marshall R. Pihl of the University of Hawai'i, who was acutely aware of the need for a selection of Korean literature in translation that would be useful as a teaching tool. Marshall's untimely death in 1995 deprived us of a general editor for the project as well as one of our best and most versatile translators.

We are indebted also to the Department of Korean Language and Literature at Seoul National University, which in an unprecedented display of trans-Pacific collegiality in the Korean literature field invited several colleagues outside of Korea to participate in the preparation of a series of Korean anthologies of Korean literature (published by Haenaem ch'ulp'ansa in Seoul). Many of the works in that series appear in translation in this volume and its companions from Columbia University Press. Sustaining both the preparatory meetings in Honolulu and Seoul and the translation of the works appearing in these volumes was a very generous grant from the Samsung Cultural Foundation in Seoul. Our thanks are due as well to Jennifer Crewe, Editorial Director at Columbia University Press, and her staff, who have shown admirable patience during the long gestation of these anthologies.

INTRODUCTION

The title of this volume—*Modern Korean Fiction*—necessarily begs the question of what, precisely, qualifies as modern, as Korean, and as fiction. The task of defining fiction, first of all, is scarcely less challenging than that of defining *literature*, the difficulty of which may be appreciated by anyone who has read, say, the introductory chapter to Terry Eagleton's *Literary Theory*. Perhaps the best we can do here is to point out that among Yi Kwangsu's many contributions to the development of modern Korean literature was his attempt to divest the Sino-Korean term *munhak* of its connotations of scholarship and science and instead to understand it in terms of the English word *literature* in its modern sense of imaginative and creative writing. This marked a fundamental rupture with the traditional understanding of literature, and especially fiction, among Korean literati and was hence a milestone in the evolution of literary theory in modern Korea. Moreover, in conceiving of literature as an independent artform, Yi may be said to have aestheticized the traditional Korean concept of literature, and thereby fiction.

Another way to approach the question of defining modern Korean fiction is to try to imagine oneself modern, Korean, and a writer of fiction. What would this mean now, at the outset of the new millennium? It would mean, first of all, that one has experienced at least one wave of modernization (industrialization, either export-led, as in the Republic of Korea [South Korea], or self-sustaining, as in the Democratic People's Republic of Korea [North Korea]),

We acknowledge with gratitude the contribution of David McCann to this introduction.

and perhaps a second wave as well (the establishment of an industrial infrastructure during the period 1910–1945, when Korea was a Japanese colony). And it would mean that one's parents or grandparents likely experienced a third wave of modernization as well—the enlightenment movement that swept East Asia at the turn of the twentieth century.

It means, second, that one lives with some 70 million other Koreans on a comparatively small neck of land jutting from the northeast Asian landmass. To be sure, people of Korean ancestry inhabit other parts of the world. Are those individuals Korean? For a people who continue to wrestle with the question of what constitutes Korean national identity, such a question assumes a significance that for other peoples and in other circumstances it might not seem to warrant. More to the point, if one is of Korean ancestry, lives in Japan, China, the United States, Mexico, Kazakhstan, or elsewhere, and writes fiction in the language of that nation (and perhaps in Korean as well), is one producing Korean fiction?

Third, if one is modern, Korean, and involved with fiction, then one either produces fiction or else studies and critiques it. In South Korea today, one normally does one or the other, not both. The producer of fiction may be male or female, but the odds are about nine to one that the scholar-critic is male.

How do these three essential factors interact? Although we continue to debate the meaning of *modern*, most of us agree that what is modern marks a break with what is traditional, or premodern. Does this mean, then, that the practitioner of modern Korean fiction differs in fundamental ways from practitioners of premodern Korean literature? (We shall return to the question of who studies and critiques fiction.) To answer this question we need to draw some contrasts between practitioners of premodern Korean written (as opposed to oral) literature and practitioners of modern Korean fiction. Among the former, we can make one distinction on the basis of gender. The male practitioner typically studied literature as a prerequisite for the national civil service examination, wrote primarily or (if before the mid-1400s) exclusively in classical Chinese (*hanmun*), favored poetry over prose, and was honored in death by the publication of his *munjip*, or collected writings; he is likely known to us by name. In the rare cases in which he left us attributed fictional works he did so ostensibly for purposes of entertainment (Kim Manjung's *A Nine-Cloud Dream* [Kuun mong, ca. 1689] is often cited as an example). The female practitioner, on the other hand, wrote primarily or exclusively in the Korean script (*hangŭl*), circulated her writing—often in the form of long, admonitory poems to her daughters—only within the family, and has not left us a *munjip;* her works are likely anonymous.

And what of practitioners of modern Korean fiction? An early-modern practitioner, say one who debuted in the 1920s, was commonly male, often went to high school and/or college in Japan, and kept body and soul together working for a newspaper or literary magazine. (*Early-modern* [*kŭndae*] is the conventional designation for the period 1917–1945; the period from 1945 on is termed *contemporary* [*hyŏndae*].) A present-day example is either male or (increasingly) female, usually has a college degree (increasingly, in Korean literature or in creative writing), and either is a full-time writer or works in a field such as publishing or education. Both the early-modern and contemporary writers of fiction have almost always made a formal debut in the Korean literary world by capturing a prize in a newcomers' competition sponsored by one of the Seoul dailies or by appearing in one of the nation's numerous literary journals.

One essential difference, then, between premodern writers and modern fiction writers is that the former most likely considered literature one of several fields to be mastered in the course of becoming a scholar-bureaucrat. Although one may have attached his name to the literature he produced, it was probably not crucial to him to have done so. And heaven forbid if someone had offered him compensation for his work. Practitioners of modern Korean fiction, on the other hand, often produce work for hire. Once they have made their formal literary debut and been acknowledged by the nation's powerful literary establishment, they will likely be asked to contribute not only fiction but also poetry, essays, or criticism to a legion of literary journals, anthologies, festschrifts, conference volumes, and the like. These requests may very well account for the majority of one's literary production.

But there is also an important continuity between premodern writers and modern fiction writers. The former were often concerned with the vagaries of life and politics at the royal court. They were also concerned with depredations, domestic or foreign, taking place on the Korean peninsula. Though they were clever enough to cloak blunt details in learned allusions befitting someone of their erudition, the discerning reader (who else were their works meant for?) would understand from their poems and perhaps from their occasional fictional narratives how the prevailing political winds blew inside the court or out. The reader would perceive that a feminine speaker professing undying love for her lord in fact represented the male writer's unswerving loyalty to a monarch who has spurned or banished him. Likewise, practitioners of modern Korean fiction have grown to maturity with the realization that literature in their nation is an important means of bearing witness to events beyond their (or the nation's) control; the notion that their writing, despite the camouflaging necessitated by the powers-that-be, should be solidly grounded in the realities of the times; and the belief that fiction writing is essentially a serious undertaking, and one with ethical overtones. Writers will not be condemned for didacticism.

Having suggested what it might mean to be modern, Korean, and a writer of fiction, we should now ask how the contents of this anthology amplify this meaning. The volume begins with two stories from the 1920s, Hyŏn Chingŏn's "A Lucky Day" (Unsu choŭn nal, 1924) and Kim Tongin's "Potatoes" (Kamja, 1925). These stark sketches of desperate people in straitened circumstances have a strong flavor of nineteenth-century Russian or French realism—which should come as no surprise, considering the access young Korean students in Japan had to those literatures in Japanese translation. Other anomalies: Hyŏn, arguably the father of modern Korean short fiction, had already, in his story "A Society That Drives You to Drink" (Sul kwŏnhanŭn sahoe, 1921), abandoned the possibility that young Korean intellectuals could work together to modernize their land. For his part, Kim, one of the modernizers of the language of modern Korean letters, turned later in his career to historical fiction.

In their short fiction, these two, along with Yŏm Sangsŏp, are credited with introducing psychological realism to Korean fiction. And yet earlier, in the first decade of the twentieth century, in a transitional narrative form known as the new fiction (*shin sosŏl*), this very accomplishment had been substantially achieved by Yi Injik in novels such as *The Devil's Voice* (Kwi ŭi sŏng, 1906–1907). Are the stories of Hyŏn, Kim, Yŏm, and their contemporaries truly modern? Did they mark a distinct break with the past? Or are they seen more properly as accents in a broad literary phrase that segues between premodern or transitional fictional narratives and fiction of more recent decades?

The difficulty of such questions suggests to us the dubiousness of attempts to demarcate modern Korean fiction either by decades or by watershed political events. Instead it seems to make more sense to attempt to note the cadences in modern Korean literary history and to understand those cadences in dynamic terms. We therefore wish to think of groups of writers and works that, in retrospect, seem to lead up to or away from a primary accent in the flow of fictional works over a given interval. Such an approach may be our way of trying to impose some sense of disorder on Korean literary history, which has tended to try to make periods plain and sequential, and has divided the writers and works within them according to overly reductive, ideological contrasts.

What, then, are some of the cadences with respect to which modern Korean fiction seems to arrange itself? Let us resist, first of all, the temptation to start at the beginning—traditionally represented by Yi Kwangsu's novel

Heartlessness (Mujŏng, 1917)—and listen instead to the voices of fiction writers in present-day South Korea. These voices are often female, their accents sharp, and the structural underpinnings of their compositions unsettling. Until very recently modern Korean fiction has been gender-specific (and poetry even more so). Women writers labored under the designation *yŏryu chakka* ("female writers"), and their acceptance by the overwhelmingly male literary establishment was based on the usual criteria of (1) historical awareness and (2) utilization of tried-and-true themes (in their case, subject matter deemed proper to women) but also on the extraliterary criterion of adherence in one's lifestyle to traditional Neo-Confucian gender-role expectations.

Until recent decades women who flouted those expectations found themselves ostracized by the literary establishment. Today women writers enjoy a wider range of creative options. Single women writers write stories about single women writers (and compose poems that subvert traditional gender-role expectations). The symphony of a divided nation is compressed into the sonata of a woman writer divided in her allegiances to a predominantly female readership and an overwhelmingly male literary power elite, a writer coming to terms with a consciousness of self unconditioned by traditional obligations to father, husband, or son. The voices may be polyphonic—see Ch'oe Yun's novella "There a Petal Silently Falls" (Chŏgi sori ŏpshi han chŏm kkonnip i chigo, 1988)—and historical detail may be embedded in a nonprogrammatic context, as in that author's "The Gray Snowman" (Hoesaek nunsaram, 1992). Not surprisingly, this predominant swell of the present day, like those of earlier literary movements, has as a counterpoint the rearguard action of male writers and critics concerned about the "feminization" of Korean literature.

If the fictional production of the present day represents a swell in the evolution of modern Korean fiction, is there an ebb in the stories that follow the demarcating year of 1917? In terms of fiction, the tone of those early years is decidedly muted, the outlook constrained. The theme of life in a colonized land admitted of few variations. Instead of harmony there was a cacophony of voices—pure versus socially engaged fiction, class-conscious as opposed to bourgeois writing, cultural nationalism versus accommodation to Western influence, urban-centered experimentation in contrast with rural-centered traditional lyricism.

Pure literature and socially engaged literature are alternating refrains throughout the modern period. The enlightenment agenda of Yi Kwangsu's *Heartlessness* and his other long fictional works derives from the premodern literatus's didacticism, his sense of moral obligation to instruct the people. *Heartlessness*, serialized in a daily newspaper and then published in book form, was a logical medium for the message. In reaction to Yi's proselytizing tendencies there emerged the *Creation* (Ch'angjo) coterie of Kim Tongin and his colleagues, centered in a literary journal of that name and dedicated to art-for-art's-sake. Art-for-art's-sake fiction in these early years often consisted of highly realistic still lifes, slices of deterministic life that reflected the bleak mood resulting from the crushing by the Japanese of the Korean attempt for national autonomy expressed in the March 1, 1919, Independence Movement.

Then in 1925, with the formation of the Korean Artist Proletariat Federation (KAPF), formed primarily by writers who had been attracted to socialism during their studies in Japan, socially engaged fiction takes on a political ideology to complement the enlightenment ideology of Yi Kwangsu. For the next ten years, except for intervals of silence following police raids on the KAPF membership, authors such as Yi Kiyŏng, Im Hwa, and Han Sŏrya wrote of socioeconomic inequities, the downtrodden proletariat and peasantry, and the class struggle. Sympathizing with the views of the KAPF writers but not joining their ranks were fellow travelers (*tongbanja*) such as Ch'ae Manshik, Yi T'aejun, and Yi Hyosŏk. Ch'ae would use satire to outline the incongruities of a society that urged its citizens to invest in an education but, because of an economy distorted by the needs of the colonial masters and increasingly by the demands of the Pacific War, failed to provide them with suitable jobs. He would also, as in "My Innocent Uncle" (Ch'isuk, 1938), satirize resourceless socialists who failed to act upon their ideals. Yi T'aejun would write of personal idiosyncrasy rather than societal incongruity, sketching individuals, like the protagonist of "Crows" (Kkamagwi, 1936), whose quirks made them outsiders in their highly structured society. And Yi Hyosŏk would concentrate initially on the dismal lives of the urban proletariat before returning to the countryside of his origins to record the timeless rhythms of rural life in stories such as "When the Buckwheat Blooms" (Memil kkot p'il muryŏp, 1936).

With the forced dissolution of KAPF in 1935 the social-engagement refrain of pre-Liberation fiction dies out, except in the clever satires of Ch'ae Manshik and the introspective stories of writers such as Han Sŏrya and Kim Namch'ŏn. In its place, in the mid- to late 1930s, there swelled a crescendo of short fiction that evinces storytelling skill and artistic creation: accounts of the clash between tradition and modernity (Kim Tongni's "The Shaman Painting" [Munyŏdo, 1936] and Chu Yosŏp's "Mama and the Boarder" [Sarang sonnim kwa ŏmŏni, 1935]); modernist vignettes of urban life (Pak T'aewŏn's *Streamside Sketches* [Ch'ŏnbyŏn p'unggyŏng, 1936–1937]) and antic protagonists (Yi Sang's "Wings" [Nalgae, 1936]); adolescent sparring between the sexes (Kim Yujŏng's "The White Rabbit" [Ok t'okki, 1936]). In such stories the drumbeat of issue and problem heard in socially engaged fiction yields for the most part to development of story line and delineation of character.

The imperial Japanese war effort brought discordance and then silence to Korean literary voices. With the prohibition late in the colonial period of publication in Korean, writers were forced to either publish in Japanese or remain mute. Authors such as Hwang Sunwŏn continued to compose in Korean, but the premieres had to await Liberation in 1945. The "post-Liberation space" (*haebang konggan*), an interlude lasting until the establishment of separate regimes in northern and southern Korea in 1948, was marked by medley as writers of socialist and nationalist persuasions scrambled to form choruses of similar voices. The ideological divisions initiated during the period 1945–1948 set in motion a migration of approximately a hundred writers from southern to northern Korea and a lesser number from north to south, most of them seeking a more harmonious social and intellectual climate for their compositions. The departure of the former group of writers, those who moved from south to north, represented a burning of bridges: their works were banned in South Korea until the advent of democratic presidential elections in 1987. During that period the voices of Yi Kiyŏng, Yi T'aejun, and Pak T'aewŏn—to mention just three of these *wŏlbuk* ("gone north") writers—were removed from the South Korean literary repertoire.

Korea after the Korean War was a traumatized land: approximately 2.7 million Koreans lost their lives during the civil war, and millions of family members found themselves stranded indefinitely on separate sides of the demilitarized zone established by the 1953 cease-fire (which at the time of publication of this volume has yet to be replaced by a peace treaty between the two Koreas). Korean fiction of the 1950s was in tune with these times, dirgelike stories and novels featuring a variety of walking wounded, victimized aesthetes, and inspired rebels, to use the nomenclature offered by Kim Chong-un in the introduction to his anthology *Postwar Korean Short Stories*. The protagonist of Chŏn Kwangyong's "The Bandmaster" (K'ŭraun chang, 1959), a promising cellist during the Japanese occupation reduced to playing in nightclubs and numbing his regret with alcohol, represents a generation of shattered hopes.

If the fiction of the postwar was played adagio, then the brash stories of a brace of newcomers, Kim Sŭngok and Ch'oe Inho, are scherzo. These two, representing a new wave of writers born near the end of, or shortly after, Liberation in 1945, were educated in their own language, unlike the generation of their parents (educated in Japanese) and that of their grandparents (taught if at all from classical Chinese texts). Exercising an imaginative power not seen since the fiction of Yi Sang in the 1930s, Kim and Ch'oe write lively, descriptive narratives that occasionally blur the boundaries between reality and illusion. Other members of this diverse group known as the *Hangŭl* Generation, such as Yi Ch'ŏngjun, write of the creative process, whether in literature, photography, or art, or compose allegories of Korea's recent political history. Still others—Hwang Sŏgyŏng and Cho Sehŭi are good examples—expose the social ills associated with South Korea's economic strategy of export-led industrialization since the 1960s. And then there are writers such as Cho Chŏngnae and Yun Hŭnggil, who examine the psychological and political impact of the territorial division of the nation.

The richness of Korean fiction of the 1970s and 1980s is due in no small part to the work of two very different women writers, O Chŏnghŭi and Pak Wansŏ. O composes chamber pieces, focused portraits of nameless individuals from broken families; the style is at once placid and intense, normality often masking perversion. Pak is a vocalist, a storyteller of such empathy as to give readers an almost palpable sense of intimacy. If writers dating from the colonial period such as Kim Myŏngsun, Ch'oe Chŏnghŭi, and Kang Kyŏngae pioneered modern Korean women's prose writing, then O and Pak made the breakthrough, empowering the growing constellation of women writers who occupy center stage in Korean literary circles today.

Korean fiction of the 1990s looked both forward and back. Yi Munyŏl, as critically and popularly successful as Pak Wansŏ, looked to Korean history and tradition for answers to the dilemma of a society increasingly vulnerable to the economic and cultural challenges of globalization and interdependency. Ch'oe Yun also resorted to history, albeit more recent, but was more concerned with the spiritual legacy of traumatic events and with the foibles of contemporary Koreans. Kim Yŏngha, the youngest author in this anthology, is a writer for the new millennium, his fictional works visual, fast-moving, and visceral.

The future of modern Korean fiction is uncertain. Will today's younger writers revert to the form of their predecessors and adopt the tried-and-true method of composing variations on such familiar themes as the division of the nation, the confrontation between tradition and modernity, and South Korea's checkered social and political legacy? Will they continue to embrace traditional modes of writing, or will they forswear them in favor of more experimental approaches? Will strident voices be accepted as well as mellifluous ones? Can the fiction of North and South Korea find harmony with each other? These are some of the questions that confront Korean fiction as it enters the twenty-first century.

MODERN KOREAN FICTION

1. HYŎN CHINGŎN

Hyŏn Chingŏn was born in Taegu in 1900 and was educated there, in Japan, and in Shanghai. He spent much of his working life with the *Shidae ilbo* and *Tonga ilbo* newspapers. He died in 1943.

Hyŏn first appeared in print in 1920 with the story "Hŭisaenghwa" (Sacrificial flowers), published in the literary journal *Kaebyŏk*. This story was soon followed by other works of fiction, such as the autobiographical "Pinch'ŏ" (1921, The destitute wife) and "T'arakcha" (1922, The degenerate), that depict the problems faced by an intellectual class whose society struggles to modernize. The story translated here (Unsu choŭn nal, 1924) and "Pul" (1925, trans. 1974 "Fire") are perhaps his two best-known stories. The latter depicts a child bride driven to distraction by the nightly sexual demands of her husband. Both can be read as allegories of occupied Korea. "Sul kwŏnhanŭn sahoe" (1921, trans. 1997 "A Society That Drives You to Drink") is a passionate if somewhat overstated account of enlightened minds trying to overcome factionalism and other vestiges of traditional Korean society.

In 1926 Hyŏn collected these and other stories in his *Chosŏn ŭi ŏlgul* (Faces of Korea). These slices of life in colonial Korea are peopled almost uniformly by individuals oppressed by forces beyond their control. This volume established Hyŏn as one of the fathers of Korean realist fiction, along with Kim Tongin and Yŏm Sangsŏp. Toward the end of his career he produced historical novels such as *Muyŏng t'ap* (1939, Muyŏng Pagoda). An edition of his collected works was published in 1988.

A LUCKY DAY

There was an unfriendly murkiness in the sky that suggested snow, but the snow did not come, only a frozen rain that kept dripping, dripping down.

Today was the first lucky day in a long time to come the way of Kim Ch'ŏmji, a rickshaw man who worked on the city side of Tongsomun. It began with the woman in the house opposite who wanted to go downtown. He took her to the tram-stop, and then, in the hope of getting another fare, he wandered around the depot, turning imploring eyes on each person who got off a tram, until finally he got a fare to Tonggwang School, a man dressed in Western clothes who looked like a teacher.

The first run was thirty *chŏn*; the second, fifty *chŏn*. Not a bad omen to start the day! Kim Ch'ŏmji had been in such utterly bad luck that he hadn't seen the sight of money for ten days, but the jingle now of three ten-*chŏn* nickel coins, followed by five more, falling into the palm of his hand was almost enough to bring tears of joy. For him, today, the value of this eighty *chŏn* was inestimable. Not only would he be able to slake his thirst with a drink, but he would be able to buy a bowl of *sŏllŏngt'ang* for his ailing wife.

His wife had been racked by a cough for more than six weeks. And in circumstances where even a bowl of millet was difficult to get, it goes without saying that she had had no medicine. It wasn't that medicine was completely out of the question. To some extent at least Kim Ch'ŏmji was being true to his belief that if you give medicine to get rid of the demon of disease, the demon will get to like it and keep coming back for more. For this reason he hadn't had a doctor look at her, and so he didn't really know what was wrong with her. However, her condition was obviously serious in view of the fact that she was lying down all the time, quite unable to turn on her side, much less get up.

Her condition had become worse ten days ago when a bowl of millet she ate lay on her stomach. Kim Ch'ŏmji had just got his hands on some money after a long lean spell. He bought her a little millet and a ten-*chŏn* bundle of wood, and then the damn woman, in Kim's own words, had been completely reckless. She had thrown the whole lot into a pot to boil, but before the fire turned red hot, too impatient to wait for it to cook, the damn woman dispensed with the spoon and began scooping up the half-cooked millet with her hands. Acting as if she feared someone was going to take it away from her, she began stuffing it into her mouth till her cheeks looked like a pair of fist-size tumors. By evening she was complaining of a tightness in her breast, her stomach was cramped, her eyes were wide and staring; she was having a fit. Kim Ch'ŏmji was really angry.

"Goddamn woman! It would be your luck! Sick when you don't eat, sick when you do! What's to be done now? Can't you look straight?" he cried, and he slapped her once across the cheek. Her eyes came back a little into line, but there was a wet film clinging to them. Kim Ch'ŏmji's eyes were burning, too.

The patient, however, didn't go off her food. For three days she badgered her husband for *sŏllŏngt'ang*.

"Damn woman. Can't even eat millet and here she is wanting beef soup! Stuff herself again and have another fit," he ranted.

Inwardly, however, he had felt bad that he couldn't buy it for her. Now, though, he would be able to buy her the *sŏllŏngt'ang*. He would also be able to buy food for the three-year-old child howling with hunger by her sick mother's side. Kim Ch'ŏmji, eighty *chŏn* tight in his fist, had a feeling of plenty.

His good fortune didn't end there. Coming back out the school gate, wiping the mixture of sweat and rain that was running down the back of his neck with a greasy Japanese cotton handkerchief, he heard behind him a cry of "Rickshaw!" Kim Ch'ŏmji took one look at the person who had stopped to call him and guessed it was a student from the school. The student got straight to the point.

"How much to South Gate Station?" he asked.

The boy was probably a boarder at the school going home for the winter holidays. Probably he had made up his mi[illegible] go today, but with the rain and having baggage as well, he had bee[illegible] know what to do until he spotted Kim Ch'ŏmji. Otherwise [illegible]g out after a rickshaw man, shoes trailing behind, ge[illegible]f it was only a cheap cotton uniform?

"South Gate Statio[illegible]ould it be that he was reluctant to s[illegible]ain gear? Or might it be that he was [illegible] not at all.

It was just that he was a little afraid of this strange good fortune that seemed to be rushing in upon him. And there was also the fact that his wife's request, as he left the house this morning after getting the call from the woman across the street, was still nagging at him. There was an imploring light in the sick woman's eyes, eyes that were unusually big and sunken, the only living things in her fleshless face.

"Don't go out today. Please, for my sake, stay home. I'm so sick. . . ." Her voice was a murmur like the buzz of a mosquito, her breathing labored.

Kim Ch'ŏmji made light of it.

"What are you saying? Whipped you should be, talking nonsense like that! Who do you think will feed and look after us if we sit here holding onto each other?" he said, but as he made to rush off, the sick woman reached out her hand as if to hold him.

"I wish you wouldn't go, but come back early," she said, her thin, throaty whisper following him out.

Now, the instant he heard that his fare wanted to go to the station, his wife's convulsively trembling hands, her exceptionally big eyes, and her face on the point of tears danced before Kim Ch'ŏmji's eyes.

"Well, how much is it going to be to South Gate Station?" the student asked, looking impatiently at the rickshaw man's face, and then as if talking to himself, he mumbled, "There's a train to Inch'ŏn at eleven; is the next one at two in the afternoon?"

"You'll have to give me one *wŏn* fifty."

The fare came out abruptly, before Kim Ch'ŏmji realized it himself. He was shocked by the staggering sum of money, even though it came from his own lips. What a long time it had been since he had even asked for a fare as big as this! The opportunity to earn this money overrode his concern for his sick wife. Surely nothing would happen today? This bit of good luck was more than double the first and the second together. He felt he couldn't afford to pass it up, no matter what.

"One *wŏn* fifty is too much," the student said, shaking his head.

"The distance alone is more than fifteen *li*, and it's reasonable to pay a little more on a rainy day like this," the driver said, and a joy that could not be hidden flowed across his face.

"All right, I'll give what you ask," the generous young customer agreed. "But let's go quickly," he said and hurried off to change his clothes and get his things.

Kim Ch'ŏmji's legs felt strangely light when he got the student aboard. He went at a run; it was almost as if he were flying. And the wheels turned so fast it was like sliding on skates along ice. Actually the rain falling on the frozen ground had made it slippery.

The driver's legs soon grew heavy. This was because he was coming near his own house. Renewed anxiety weighed on his chest. *Don't go out today: I'm so sick.* The sick woman's whimpering echoed in his ears. Her deep-sunk eyes seemed to glare at him in reproach. He could almost hear the wailing of the child. And he seemed to hear a gasping sound, a struggle to draw breath.

"What's the matter, we'll miss the train."

The impatient cry of the passenger barely got through to the driver. Reality returned abruptly: Kim Ch'ŏmji, hands still holding the shafts of the rickshaw, was crouched down in the middle of the road—he had pulled up.

"Yes, yes," Kim Ch'ŏmji said, and he broke into a run again. The farther he got from his house the more life came back into his gait, as if the brisk movement of his legs was the only thing that could make him forget the ceaseless flow of anxiety and worry in his mind.

When Kim Ch'ŏmji delivered his passenger at the station and he actually got that staggering one *wŏn* fifty into his hand, he had no thought for the fifteen *li* he had splashed through in the rain. He was as grateful as if he had got the money for nothing, as happy as if he had become a millionaire overnight. Several times he bowed deeply to his young customer, who was young enough to be his son.

"Have a good trip," he added respectfully.

The trip back in the rain with an empty, rattling rickshaw didn't bear thinking about. The sweat of labor had run cold, and there was a chill welling up from his soaking clothes that he could feel in his famished stomach and that gave him a heightened awareness of both the satisfaction and the anguish of one *wŏn* fifty. There was no strength left in his gait. He was huddled up as he left the station, and he felt as if at any moment he might fall down and not be able to get up again.

"Damn rain! Rattling an empty rickshaw back in this rain! Why does this bloody rain have to keep battering me in the face?"

Kim Ch'ŏmji was violently angry, grumbling and complaining as if in defiance of someone. At this stage a new, bright idea flashed into his mind. This is no way to do it, he thought. If I circle the area and wait for a train to come, I could get another fare. He had been so lucky today, who could say he wouldn't have another stroke of luck? He felt absolutely sure good fortune was waiting for him; he would have been willing to bet on it. However, he couldn't stand in front of the station because he was afraid of the regular rickshaw men. So, he did what he had often done before: he parked the rickshaw at a point between the tramlines and the footpath, a little way from the tramcar depot opposite the station, and circled the area to survey the situation. A train came after a little while, and quite a crowd poured out in the direction of the tramcar depot. A woman caught Kim Ch'ŏmji's fare-searching eye. She looked like a former *kisaeng* or a playgirl student; she had a Western hairdo and wore high-heeled shoes and a cape thrown over her shoulders. He stole up beside her.

"Rickshaw, ma'am?"

Student or not, she put on an exceedingly haughty expression for a moment. Her lips were sealed tight; she didn't spare Kim Ch'ŏmji a glance.

"I'll bring you a lot cheaper, ma'am, than the boys in the station. Where are you going?"

Kim Chŏmji was nothing if not persistent. He laid his hand on the Japanese wicker bag she was carrying.

"How dare you pester people like this!" she thundered, and she turned away.

A tram came. Kim Ch'ŏmji glared spitefully at the people who boarded it. But his instincts had not been wrong. When the tram, loaded to the last, began to move, there was one man left behind. Judging by the huge bag he was carrying, it looked as if he had been put off by the conductor because his bag was too big for the crowded tram. Kim Ch'ŏmji pulled over beside him.

"Rickshaw?"

There was some stubborn haggling over the fare before Kim Ch'ŏmji agreed to bring him to Insa-dong for sixty *chŏn*.

All day long, when the rickshaw grew heavy, Kim Ch'ŏmji's body felt strangely light, and when the rickshaw felt light, his body grew heavy. This time, however, anxiety ate right into his mind. A view of the house kept shimmering in front of his eyes, so that now he couldn't think of more good luck. His legs felt like stumps of trees, as if they did not belong to him, and the only way to keep them going was to drive them on and on, abusing them, racing steadily forward. His pace was reckless enough to worry passersby: how could that damn rickshaw man be so drunk and still stay on his feet in this muck?

There was a somberness in the overcast, rainy sky that made it seem as if it were already close to dusk. He slowed down passing Ch'anggyŏng Gardens to catch his breath. Step after step, the nearer he got to home, the more he felt a strange calm penetrating into his mind. This calm was not coming from any sense of security, rather it was springing from a fear born of a vivid realization of the imminence of accumulated misfortune. He was writhing, trying to prolong the time, at least a little, before he collided with calamity. He wanted, if possible, to hold on for a long time to the joy of earnings that amounted almost to a miracle. He craned his neck, searching in all directions. He gave the impression that he was completely powerless to do anything about his legs, which were racing toward his own house, that is, toward certain calamity, and would someone, anyone, grab him, save him?

Just then his friend Chisam emerged from a roadside drinking establishment. Chisam's wrinkled, fat face was a purple glow, and jet whiskers covered his cheeks and chin, offering a striking contrast to the appearance of Kim Ch'ŏmji, whose face was wizened and sallow, with furrows cut across it here and there, and a skimpy beard that amounted to no more than a few inverted pine needles of stubble beneath his chin.

"Hello, Kim Ch'ŏmji! On your way back from the city, I see. Made a lot of money, I presume. How about standing me a drink?" cried the corpulent Chisam at the sight of his skinny friend. His voice was soft and gentle, in contrast to his bearing. Kim Ch'ŏmji was indescribably glad to see his friend. He was as grateful as if Chisam were a benefactor who had saved his life.

"You seem to have had one already, you look in good form yourself today," Kim Ch'ŏmji said, a smile spreading across his face.

"I'd have my drink whether I was in good form or not. But what happened to you? You're like a drowned rat. Come on in here and dry yourself."

The drinking house was warm and comfortable. The clouds of steam rising whitely into the air whenever the lid of the fish pot was lifted; the beef broiling on the gridiron; dressed meats, liver, soybeans, pollack, lentil pancakes . . . the disorderly arrangement of side dishes on the table—it all brought an unbearable burning hunger to Kim Ch'ŏmji's stomach. If he followed his inclinations, he would have gobbled down everything edible there and still not be satisfied. Ravenously hungry, he decided to start with something that had a little body to it. He ordered two warm meat pies and a bowl of fish soup. At the taste of food, his famished insides became more and more empty, demanding more and more food. He gulped down a second bowl of soup, with bean curd and loach, as if it were water. As he set to his third bowl, the two double portions of *makkŏlli* being warmed for them were pronounced ready. Drinking the rice brew with Chisam, he felt his empty stomach suddenly fill out and a warm glow came to his face. He knocked another double straight back.

Kim Ch'ŏmji's eyes were growing bleary. His cheeks bulged with two pieces of rice cake, large pieces cut from the gridiron, and he ordered two more doubles. Chisam looked at Kim Ch'ŏmji a little dubiously.

"More! We've had four each already. That'll come to forty *chŏn*," he warned.

"What a bloody man! Is forty *chŏn* big money? I made a pile today. This was a real lucky day."

"How much did you make?"

"I made thirty *wŏn*. Thirty *wŏn*. Why shouldn't I pour this damned liquor . . . it's all right, it's all right. It doesn't matter how much we drink. I made a pile today."

"Ah, you're drunk, you've had enough."

"You think this is enough to make me drunk? Come on, drink up!" he cried, pulling Chisam's ear. Then he turned on the boy who was pouring the *makkŏlli*, a boy of about fourteen with cropped hair.

"Pour, you little bastard," he shouted at the boy.

The boy giggled and looked questioningly at Chisam.

The drunken man read the look and thundered in anger, "You little bastard, you'd lay your own mother, you think I've no money."

He fumbled in his waist pocket, took out a one-*wŏn* note, and threw it angrily at the boy. A few silver coins jingled and fell in the process.

"Look, you're dropping it. Why are you throwing money all over the place?" Chisam said, beginning to pick up the money.

Kim Ch'ŏmji, drunk though he was, opened his eyes wide to see where the money had gone. He looked down at the floor, and then as if shocked by the depravity of what he was doing, he shook his head and gave vent to an even greater anger.

"Look here, you dirty sons-of-bitches! You think I've no money. I should break every bone in your bodies." He took the money Chisam had gathered and flung it away. "Blasted money, damn-blasted money," he cried. The coins struck the wall and fell into the bowl where the *makkŏlli* was being warmed, emitting a jingling cry as if getting a deserved beating.

Two more doubles were filled and emptied in one motion. Kim Ch'ŏmji licked the *makkŏlli* on his lips and beard. Stroking his pine-needle stub of a beard, he shouted as if greatly pleased with himself, "Another! Keep pouring!"

After yet another double, Kim Ch'ŏmji slapped Chisam on the shoulder and burst into boisterous laughter, laughter so loud that the eyes of everyone in the establishment were drawn toward him. He laughed all the more.

"Look, Chisam, I'll tell you a funny story. I took someone to the station today, you see?"

"So?"

"Once I was there, I didn't want to come back empty, so I was hanging around the tram-stop wondering how I'd get a fare, and there's a lady, or maybe a student—it's hard to know a *kisaeng* from an ordinary girl these days—standing there in the rain wearing a cape. I ease up beside her, ask her does she want a rickshaw and try to take her bag. She brushes away my hand, wheels violently around and shouts 'Why are you pestering people like this?' There's warbling for you," Kim Ch'ŏmji cried with a laugh, and he gave a very good imitation of a warble. Everyone laughed.

"Beggarly old bitch, who'd she think she was talking to? Hadn't even dignity in her moaning."

Laughter swelled all around, but Kim Ch'ŏmji began to snivel before the laughter faded away.

Chisam was at a loss. He looked hard at the drunken man.

"Laughing and kicking up a racket one minute, crying the next. What does it all mean?"

Kim Ch'ŏmji kept sniveling.

"My wife's dead," he said.

"What? Your wife dead? When?"

"What do you mean, when? Today of course."

"You're crazy. Don't be telling lies."

"Why would I lie, she's dead, really . . . me drinking, she lying there lifeless . . . I deserve to be killed, to be killed." Kim Ch'ŏmji burst into loud wailing.

Chisam's face showed that the pleasant mood had been broken.

"I can't tell whether the man is telling the truth or lying. Come on, we'll go to the house," he said, pulling the crying man's arm.

Kim Ch'ŏmji broke away from Chisam's grip and began to laugh soundlessly through tear-filled eyes.

"Who says anyone's dead?" he cried, greatly elated. "Why should she be dead? She's as alive as alive can be. Using up good food. I fooled you."

He clapped his hands and laughed like a child.

"I don't know whether you're really out of your mind or not. I mean, I heard your wife was sick," Chisam said, and as if he felt a certain apprehension, he urged Kim Ch'ŏmji to go home again.

"She's not dead, I tell you, she's not!"

But there was something in the angry conviction of Kim Chŏmji's shout that betrayed an effort on his part to believe she wasn't dead. They had one more double each, rounding out the one *wŏn*, and came away. A nasty rain was still dripping, dripping down.

Drunk though he was, Kim Ch'ŏmji bought some *sŏllŏngt'ang* and arrived home. *Home* was a bit of an exaggeration. Actually, it was a rented house—not all of the house, mind you, but a tiny servant's room, separate from the rest of the house, for which he paid one *wŏn* a month in addition to drawing water for the main house. Had Kim Ch'ŏmji not been affected by drink, he would have trembled before the awful silence that dominated the place when he put his foot on the threshold, like the silence of the sea after a rainstorm has passed. No racking cough could be heard, no tortured breathing even. Only one sound broke the gravelike silence, not breaking it really, rather giving it added depth: the lonely, ominous sound of a child sucking its mother's breast. Perhaps someone with sensitive hearing might have guessed that the sound was entirely a sucking sound, that there was no gulping sound of milk being swallowed, that the child was sucking an empty breast.

Perhaps even Kim Ch'ŏmji recognized the ominousness of the silence. If not, it was rather odd that as soon as he stepped onto the threshold he began to shout, "Damn woman, her husband home and she doesn't come out to meet him. Goddamn woman!"

The shout was mere bluster to dispel the sinister fear that was suddenly bearing down on him.

Kim Ch'ŏmji threw the door open. A nauseating stench—the smell of dirt beneath the reed mat, the smell of stool and urine from unwashed diapers, the smell of all sorts of dirty clothes, the smell of stale sweat from the invalid—pierced his drink-blurred nostrils. The drunken man began to yell at the top of his voice as soon as he entered the room. He didn't even take time to put the *sŏllŏngt'ang* down in the corner.

"What a bloody woman! In bed night and day, is that all you want to do? You can't even get up when your husband comes!"

And as he shouted he drew a vicious kick at her legs. But it wasn't human flesh he was kicking; it felt like the stump of a tree. The sucking sound changed to a whimper. The child let go the nipple it had been sucking and began to cry. The child's face was all puckered; it was dry crying, no tears came. Even the whimpering sound seemed to come from the child's belly, not its lips; crying and crying till no sound could come from its throat, and it seemed not to have the strength to cry again.

When Kim Ch'ŏmji saw he was getting no results from kicking, he fell on his wife's head and began to pull and shake her magpie's nest of hair.

"Damn woman, say something, talk! Are you dumb, Goddamn woman!"

There was no reaction.

"Oh, God, look at her, she won't say a thing."

Still no reaction.

"Oh, God, no answer, she really must be dead."

Suddenly he noticed that her eyes were staring straight up with only the whites showing.

"Your eyes, your eyes! Why won't they look straight at me, why are they staring at the ceiling, why?" he cried. No other sound could come from his throat.

Then the tears of the living spotted and wet the stiff face of the dead like hen's droppings. Kim Ch'ŏmji was like a man gone mad as he rubbed his face against the dead woman's.

"I brought you some *sŏllŏngt'ang*," he muttered. "Why won't you eat it, why won't you eat it? . . . Unbelievable, today of all days! And my luck was in. . . ."

Translated by Kevin O'Rourke

2. KIM TONGIN

Kim Tongin was born in Pyongyang in 1900 and died in Seoul in 1951. Like many other young Korean intellectuals of his time, he received his higher education in Japan. It was there in 1919 that he and other advocates of art-for-art's-sake literature founded the influential but short-lived journal *Ch'angjo* (Creation). In so doing, Kim and his colleagues took a stand against the didactic literature of social engagement championed by Yi Kwangsu—a contest that in various incarnations has survived in Korea to this day.

A brilliant, iconoclastic aesthete, Kim was one of the most public figures of the first generation of modern Korean writers. At the same time, he is one of the fathers of modern Korean fiction. He helped make literary Korean more colloquial, and, perhaps influenced by the European writers he read in Japanese translation—Zola, Maupassant, and Turgenev, among others—he pioneered the tradition of realism that was to become paramount in twentieth-century Korean fiction. He also wrote historical novels and was a prolific essayist and critic. "Potatoes" (Kamja), first published in *Chosŏn mundan* in 1925, is probably his best-known story.

POTATOES

Fighting, adultery, murder, theft, prison confinement—the shanty area outside the Seven Star Gate was a breeding ground for all that is tragic and violent in this world. Before they arrived there Pongnyŏ and her husband were farmers, the second of the four traditional classes—scholar, farmer, tradesman, and merchant.

Pongnyŏ had always been poor, but she had grown up with the discipline of an upright farm home. Of course, the strict, traditional discipline of a gentleman-scholar's household disappeared after the family fell in the world to the rank of farmer, but a sort of clear yet indefinable family code still remained, something other farming families did not have. Pongnyŏ, who had grown up in this environment, regarded it as perfectly normal to bathe naked in the stream in summer with the girls from the other houses and to run around the district with nothing but trousers on; still, when she did, she carried in her heart a sort of vague sense of refinement in regard to what is called morality.

At fifteen, Pongnyŏ was sold to a widower in the area for eighty *wŏn*, and she became, so to speak, his wife. The bridegroom—*elderly husband* would be more accurate—was twenty years or so older than her. In his father's time, the family had been farmers of some standing with several *majigi* of land, but in the present generation the property had begun to diminish, a little here, a little there, till in the end the eighty *wŏn* with which he bought Pongnyŏ was his last possession. He was an extremely lazy man. If he got a tenancy on a field on the recommendation of an elder in the area, all he did was sow the seed. Subsequently he did no hoeing, and no weeding, either; he left the field as it was; and when it came autumn, he gathered in the crop with typical lack of care, saying, "This was a bad year." He never gave any of the crop to the owner of the field; he kept everything himself. The upshot of it was he never held the same field two years running. After a few years, he lost the sympathy and trust of the people to such an extent that he couldn't get a field in the area.

Thanks to her father, Pongnyŏ managed to get by one way or another for three or four years after the marriage, but even the old man, although he still had a bit of the gentleman-scholar about him, began to look with distaste at his son-in-law. So Pongnyŏ and her husband came to lose trust even in her father's house.

Husband and wife discussed various options, saw there was no alternative, and finally came inside the walls of Pyongyang to work as laborers. The man, however, was an idler; he couldn't even make a success of laboring. He would go off to Yonggwan Pavilion with his A-frame on his back and spend the whole day looking down at the Taedong River. How could even laboring work out?

After laboring for three or four months, husband and wife managed with a bit of luck to get into servants' quarters in a certain house. But before long they found themselves thrown out of that house too, for although Pongnyŏ worked hard looking after the master's house, nothing could be done about her husband's laziness. Day in and day out, Pongnyŏ would look daggers at her husband, trying to drive him, but you can't throw off lazy habits like you throw a scrap to the dog.

"Clear away those sacks of rice."

"I'm sleepy. Clear them away yourself."

"Me, clear them away?"

"You've been shoveling rice into you for twenty years or more, can't you do that much?"

"You'll be the death of me yet."

"Cheeky hussy!"

Rows like this were frequent. Finally they found themselves thrown out of that house too.

Now where to go? There was no help for it; they ended up being pushed into the shanty area outside the Seven Star Gate.

Taking the area outside the Seven Star Gate as a whole, the principal occupation of the people who lived there was begging. As a secondary occupation they had thieving and—among themselves—prostitution, and apart from these occupations there were all the fearful, filthy crimes of this world. Pongnyŏ entered the principal occupation.

Who is going to be generous about feeding a nineteen-year-old woman in the prime of youth?

"A young thing begging! Why?"

Pongnyŏ countered such remarks with the excuse that her husband was on the point of death, or something similar, but the people of Pyongyang were hardened to this sort of excuse; their sympathy could not be bought.

Pongnyŏ and her husband were among the poorest of those living outside the Seven Star Gate. Actually there were some good earners among these people, some who came back every night with as much as one *wŏn* seventy or eighty gripped tightly in their fists, all in five-*ri* notes. Then there were the exceptional cases: people who went out earning at night and in a single night made forty *wŏn*, enough to start a cigarette business in the area.

Pongnyŏ was nineteen and her face was on the pretty side. Following the example of the other women in the area, she could have gone now and then to the house of a man earning even moderately well and made fifty or sixty *chŏn* a day. But she had grown up in a gentleman-scholar's house: she couldn't do that kind of work.

Husband and wife continued on in poverty; at times they went hungry.

The pine grove at Kija's Tomb was swarming with caterpillars. The Pyongyang city administration decided, as if it were bestowing a favor on them, to use the womenfolk of the shanty area outside the Seven Star Gate to pick these caterpillars. The women of the shanty area all volunteered, but only fifty or so were chosen. Pongnyŏ was one of them.

She worked hard, placing the ladder against a pine tree, climbing up, grabbing a caterpillar with the tongs, and dropping it into the insecticide. Then she repeated the operation. Soon the can would be full. She got thirty-two *chŏn* a day in piece wages.

After she had picked caterpillars for five or six days, Pongnyŏ discovered something peculiar. A number of the young women spent their time prancing around under the trees, chattering and laughing, not picking any caterpillars, and they were earning eight *chŏn* a day more than those who were actually doing the work.

There was just the one overseer, and not only did he make no comment about the women playing around, sometimes he played with them.

One day Pongnyŏ took a break for lunch. She climbed down the tree, ate her lunch, and was about to climb up again when the overseer came looking for her.

"Pongne, hi Pongne!" he called.

"What is it?" she asked.

She put down the insecticide can and the tongs and turned around.

"Come over here a minute."

Without a word she went over to the overseer.

"Hey, would you, um . . . let's take a look over there."

"What do you want to do?"

"I don't know, you have to go first. . . ."

"All right, I'll go. . . . Sister!" she shouted, turning toward the other women. "You come too, sister," she said to one of them.

"Not on your life!" the woman replied. "You two going off real nice. What fun is there in it for me?"

Pongnyŏ's face turned a deep red. She turned toward the overseer.

"Let's go," she said.

The overseer set off. Pongnyŏ bowed her head and followed.

"Pongnyŏ will be made up from now on!"

Pongnyŏ's downturned face grew even redder as she heard the banter behind her.

From that day on, Pongnyŏ was one of the workers who got more wages and did no work.

Pongnyŏ's moral attitude, her view of life, was changed from that day forward.

Till now she had never thought of having relations with a man other than her husband. It wasn't something a human being does; she knew it as the type of thing only an animal does. Or if you did it, you might fall down dead on the spot. That was how she saw it.

This was indeed a strange business. She was a human being too, and when she thought of what she had done, she discovered it wasn't at all outside the boundaries of human behavior. In addition, she did no work, made more money, and there was the intense pleasure: this was more gentlemanly than begging. . . . Put in Japanese, it was the grace of three beats to the bar, that's what it was. And this wasn't all: she discovered, for the first time, a sort of confidence that she was actually living a life befitting a human.

From then on, she took to putting powder on her face, just a little at a time.

A year went by.

Pongnyŏ's plan for getting on in life progressed ever more steadily. Husband and wife now came to live in not such severe want.

The husband, stretched out on the warmest part of the floor, would give his silly laugh, implying that in the long run this was a good thing.

Pongnyŏ's face became more beautiful.

"Hello, friend. How much did you make today?"

Whenever Pongnyŏ saw a beggar who had the air of having made a good deal of money, she would question him like this.

"Not a whole lot," the beggar would answer.

"How much?"

"Thirteen, fourteen *nyang*."

"You did well. Lend me five *nyang*."

If he made excuses, Pongnyŏ immediately hung on his arm and pleaded, "Surely you'll lend me the money—I mean, with all I know about you?"

"My God, every time I meet this woman, there's trouble. All right. I'll lend it to you. In return, eh? You understand?"

"I don't know what you mean," Pongnyŏ would giggle.

"If you don't know, I'm not giving."

"Ah, I know. Why are you going on like that?"

Pongnyŏ's personality had reached this point.

Autumn came.

On autumn nights, the women in the shanty area outside the Seven Star Gate would take their baskets and steal sweet potatoes and cabbage from a Chinese vegetable garden. Pongnyŏ also made a practice of stealing sweet potatoes and whatever else was available.

One night Pongnyŏ had stolen a bag of sweet potatoes; she was getting to her feet, about to go home, when suddenly a black shadow standing behind her grabbed her tight. When she looked, she saw it was the owner of the field, a man called Wang. Pongnyŏ couldn't get a word out; she stood there, looking down foolishly at her feet, not knowing what to do.

"Go up to the house," Wang said.

"If you say so. Sure. What the hell!"

Pongnyŏ gave a swish of her bum and followed Wang, her head high in the air, and her basket swinging in her hand. About an hour later she came out of Wang's house. She was about to step out of a furrow and onto the road when someone called her from behind.

"Pongne, isn't it?"

Pongnyŏ turned in one movement and looked. It was the woman next door, a basket tucked under her arm, groping her way out of the dark furrow.

"Is it you, sister? Were you in there too?"

"Were you in yourself, missus?"

"Whose house for you, sister?"

"Me? Nuk's house. How about you, missus?"

"I was in Wang's. How much did you get, sister?"

"Nuk's a miserly devil. I only got three heads of cabbage."

"I got three *wŏn*," Pongnyŏ said with an air of pride.

Ten minutes later Pongnyŏ was laughing with her husband: she laid the three *wŏn* in front of him and told him what had happened with Wang.

From then on, Wang came looking for Pongnyŏ as the occasion demanded. He would sit there for a while with a foolish look around his eyes; Pongnyŏ's husband would get the message and go outside. After Wang had gone, husband and wife would set the one or two *wŏn* down between them, clearly delighted.

Pongnyŏ gradually gave up selling her favors to the neighborhood beggars. When Wang was busy and couldn't come, Pongnyŏ sometimes went to his house looking for him.

Pongnyŏ and her husband were now among the rich of the shanty area.

Winter went and spring came around again.

Wang bought himself a wife, a young girl, paying a hundred *wŏn* for her.

"Hmm," Pongnyŏ said, laughing up her nose.

"Pongnyŏ will be jealous for sure," the young wives of the area said.

Pongnyŏ snorted. Me, jealous? She denied it strongly every time, but she was helpless before the black shadow that was growing in her heart.

"You devil, Wang. Just you wait and see."

The day for Wang to bring the young girl home drew near. He cut his long hair—until now he had been very proud of it. At the same time a rumor spread about that this was the new bride's idea.

"Hmm." As always Pongnyŏ laughed up her nose.

Finally the day arrived for the new bride to come. Gorgeously decked out, she rode in a palanquin drawn by four men and arrived at Wang's house in the middle of the vegetable garden outside the Seven Star Gate.

The Chinese guests in Wang's house kept up a racket till late in the night: they played weird instruments and sang songs to weird tunes. Pongnyŏ stood hidden behind one corner of the house, a murderous look in her eyes as she listened to what was going on inside.

Pongnyŏ watched the Chinese visitors going off around two o'clock in the morning. She entered the house. Her face was powdered white.

The bridegroom and the bride stared at her in amazement. Pongnyŏ scowled at the way they were staring at her; her look was frightening. She went up to Wang, caught his arm and pulled. A strange smile ran on her lips.

"Come, we'll go to our house."

"We . . . tonight we have work to do. I can't go."

"Work? In the middle of the night? What work?"

"All the same. What we have to do . . ."

The strange smile that had hovered around Pongnyŏ's lips suddenly disappeared.

"You good for nothing! Who do you think you are?"

Pongnyŏ raised her leg and kicked the ornamented bride in the head.

"Come on, let's go, let's go!"

Wang shook with trembling. He flung off Pongnyŏ's hand. Pongnyŏ fell in a heap. She stood up immediately. Her raised hand held a reaping hook that gave off a cold glint.

"You dirty Chink! You bastard! Strike me, would you! You bastard! Ah, God, I'm being killed."

Sobs wrenched out of her throat as she brandished the hook. Outside the Seven Star Gate, in the middle of the isolated field where Wang's house stood all alone, a violent scene took place. But the violence was quickly ended. The reaping hook that had been raised in Pongnyŏ's hand suddenly passed to Wang's hand, and Pongnyŏ, blood spewing from her throat, collapsed where she stood.

Three days went by and still Pongnyŏ's remains did not get to the grave. Wang went to see Pongnyŏ's husband several times. And Pongnyŏ's husband went to see Wang a few times. There was a matter to be negotiated between the two.

Pongnyŏ's body was moved in the night to the house of her husband. Three people sat around the corpse: Pongnyŏ's husband, Wang, and a certain herbal doctor. Wang, saying nothing, took out a money bag and gave three ten-*wŏn* notes to Pongnyŏ's husband. Two of those notes went into the herbal doctor's hand.

On the following day, Pongnyŏ, declared by the herbal doctor to have died of a brain hemorrhage, was loaded off to a public graveyard.

Translated by Kevin O'Rourke

3. YI T'AEJUN

Yi T'aejun was born in 1904 in Ch'ŏrwŏn County, Kangwŏn Province. He made his literary debut in 1925 with the story "O Mongnyŏ," published in the *Shidae ilbo*, a Seoul daily. In 1929 he became arts editor at another daily, the *Chungang ilbo*, and in 1939 he was appointed managing editor of *Munjang*. In 1933 he joined the Kuinhoe (the Circle of Nine), and in 1945 he organized and cochaired the central committee of the Chosŏn chakka tongmaeng (Chosŏn Writers' Alliance). By the time he migrated to North Korea in 1946, he had published some seventy stories. Little is known about his life in the North.

Yi is one of the more accomplished stylists of twentieth-century Korean fiction. His spare prose style is shown to good effect in stories such as the character study "Talpam" (1933, trans. 1998 "An Idiot's Delight") and "Poktŏkpang" (1937, The realtor's office). No less a writer than Kim Tongni took Yi as his mentor, and when Kim made his literary debut in 1935 with "Hwarang ŭi huye" (trans. 1998 "A Descendant of the *Hwarang*"), he chose to have the story published in the *Chungang ilbo*, where Yi worked, rather than in the more prestigious *Tonga ilbo*. Yi's works, along with those of the other *wŏlbuk chakka*—those authors who moved to North Korea after Liberation in 1945—were until 1987 proscribed in South Korea.

"Crows" (Kkamagwi), one of Yi's best-known stories, first appeared in the January 1936 issue of *Chogwang*. A somewhat precious story, it reflects a youthful aestheticism occasionally seen in pre-Liberation fiction by writers ranging from Na Tohyang in the early 1920s to Hwang Sunwŏn in the late 1930s. The impecunious young writer who finds a haven in the villa is of the generation of starving intellectuals portrayed with such devastating accuracy in Ch'ae Manshik's "Reidimeidŭ insaeng" (1934, trans. 1998 "A Ready-Made Life"). Many of Yi's characters, in fact, are failures, pessimists, or victims of nostalgia, unable to adapt to changing circumstances. As such, they are representative of an age of increasing suppression of native cultural pursuits under the Japanese colonial occupation.

Among Yi's last published stories are two in which he attempts to come to terms with life in colonial Korea: "Sŏgyang" (1943, The setting sun) and "Haebang chŏnhu" (1946, Liberation before and after).

CROWS

The lamp was new and the glass shade didn't yet smell of kerosene. There wasn't much to clean, but from habit he breathed on the shade and held it up against the dusky evening sky. The glass was sensitive to his warm breath, and it clouded over at once.

"Well—it's quite a bit colder now. . . ."

As he wiped the shade, he looked the garden over; he still wasn't accustomed to the sight of it. At the base of the mossy stone steps were enough leaves to bury your feet. The maples were already half bare, and some trees, virtually stripped of leaves, stood lank and gangly, in contrast with the junipers, firs, and other evergreens. He finished cleaning the lamp, yet remained for a time observing these lonesome trees standing mutely in the recesses of the garden like so many prisoners of war with upraised arms. Finally he returned to the small guest room he had selected in the outer wing of the villa.

The villa belonged to a friend. He himself, an author who clung to an idiosyncratic style that limited his popularity, had been living in a student boardinghouse, paying some twenty *wŏn* a month for a room of his own. But even this arrangement hadn't been affordable. And so as a last resort he had taken a room for the time being in this summer house, which would be empty during the winter. He could use the room of his choice till July of the following year, his friend had told him. The groundskeeper had shown him one room after another, but all were designed for summer use: they faced north, they received little light, they were too spacious, and there were too many windows. In the end, he had come upon the outer wing of the house and decided to take this small room that would normally have been occupied by servants.

Though a room for the help, it didn't compare unfavorably with the rooms in the main part of the villa. A late riser wouldn't have liked it in summer because it faced east, but in winter it could well be brighter than the other rooms—and warmer too, for it featured a double sliding door and a double window. What's more, the door to the storage loft sported a painting of "the four gentlemen"—the plum, orchid, chrysanthemum, and bamboo—and the casing for the sliding door bore an Eastern still life. Imprinted on these paintings were the artists' seals, but his knowledge of these men did not extend beyond their names. Outside above his door hung a board inscribed with "Ch'usŏng Pavilion" in the style of Chosŏn calligrapher Ch'usa Kim Chŏnghŭi, and left and right, at the end of each eave, hung a brass wind-bell with a fish clapper whose turquoise patina gave it a hoary air. When he slid the door open, the panorama seemed no less impressive than what he could see from the main guest room. Water Pavilion stood gracefully at the foot of the hills, and below it was a pond covered with maple leaves and desiccated lotus fronds. When his eyes traveled up the hill from the pond, he saw the miniature rockbed hill and the curving path through the grass. This view seemed best from his room. Looking up, he could see the eastern sky, expansive as the sea but concealed in part by a massive old fir. The crown of this decaying tree resembled a set of antlers and was speckled white with bird droppings. Observing this quiet scene at his leisure, he felt nestled in antiquity.

It had been some time since he had lit a kerosene lamp. When he touched the flickering match to the wick, dense smoke and vapor steamed up the small shade, and then finally the lamp began to brighten. The gradual brightening of the lamp brought to mind from long ago the image of his family sitting around in a circle. For him, the flame of a kerosene lamp evoked many such memories.

He lay down and soon was enthralled by the profound silence. He began to call up faces from the distant past. And then from somewhere very near he heard cawing. He quickly rose and opened the door. There was still some light outside. He heard more caws. A closer look revealed that they came not from birds on the wing but from three black crows hunched up on the dead branches of the fir.

"Crows!"

They weren't as pleasant to look at as magpies or doves. But he didn't feel it necessary to wish them ill out of hand, just for their black color and the strident call that nature had given them.

Just then the groundskeeper appeared.

"What about your meals, sir?" the man asked.

He would be all right, he replied. He'd make do with milk and pastries, and if he wanted something more traditional, he'd go into town for a meal. To avoid further questions, he asked the groundskeeper about the crows.

"Quite a few of them around here," came the answer. "And that's where they live, right there in that tree."

"Is that so? Well, I guess I'll have myself some friends," he said with a smile, his voice trailing off.

"Down there's where we keep the pigs, and they usually have plenty of scraps, so I think those crows are going to stay put."

As he said this, the groundskeeper took a step toward the fir and pretended to shy rocks at the crows. The birds flinched and seemed about to fly off, but then they looked down toward the two men and instead resettled themselves on the branches. Their calls now were different from before—not *caw* but something like *gar*, the *r* sounding as if it would never end.

The groundskeeper left.

He slid the door shut and sprawled out again on the heated floor.

He was hungry, and his hunger called to mind a theory he had once read about sleeping habits. Sleeping through the night, a certain scholar had proposed, was a custom handed down from the time before fire was discovered, when people had nothing to do at night. Otherwise there was no reason for people to have to sleep all those hours. He himself wanted to believe that this theory applied as well to hunger, that filling one's stomach three times a day without fail was not a matter of necessity. Back when the human population was still small, things to eat were near at hand in bountiful nature. The act of eating was a custom received from those times. There seemed no other reason people had to eat as many as three meals a day according to schedule. In the case of sleeping, ancient custom imposed no great inconvenience. But how burdensome to have to observe the custom of eating three meals a day! And wasn't this how people came to believe that we live to eat, and not vice versa?

"To live in order to eat! Scrambling frantically for the next meal, eyes bloodshot—is that all there is to life?! What an insult to human nature."

He smiled bitterly and tried to dismiss the gnawing in his stomach, the dry thickness in his mouth, the recurring image of a lavish meal. These were merely the fitful vestiges of worthless customs, he told himself.

He then recalled something Renoir was supposed to have said: An artist will pick a flower rather than buy a loaf of bread. "But what if he's hungry?" he asked himself. "Well, if he's half starved, he might steal or kill for food. But if he's a writer he won't give up writing," he answered. "The first thing you have to do," he now told himself, "is take that aggravating custom of thinking you're hungry, and put it out of your mind. Now look, you have a brand-new bottle of ink, filled to the brim like a well at dawn, and a nice, thick pile of blank manuscript—a dozen bundles."

"The cost of rice is always going up," his former landlady used to mumble perfunctorily as she briskly paced the breezeway outside his door. "And I'll have to stock up on coal. . . ."

But she was miles away now, and he thought only of turning up his cozy lantern and writing in this villa room, now enveloped in thick darkness and the faint sound of the wind-bells. He was giddily happy, as if he were meeting a former lover, as if he were suddenly clothed in silk, as if suddenly he had some flesh on his bones.

He fed the kerosene lamp each evening, he polished the glass shade, and then he listened to the crows while awaiting dusk. When the mystery of the night began to emerge like so many soft whispers from the recesses of the room, he would rise carefully to his knees, raise the lamp lid as respectfully as if it were something worn by an honored guest, then light the wick. And when the flickering light had taken, he would withdraw to the warm part of the floor, there to sit or lie as he pleased, all alone, reading, thinking, or writing till deep into the night. And so he always slept late. Some mornings he would walk up to the well behind the main guest room to wash, and the sound of the noontime bell would carry over the hills to him.

But on this particular day a bad dream had rent his slumber, frightening him awake, and he saw it was already light. The angular limbs of the fir appeared in outline on the rice-paper panels of the sliding door, like the pheasant's plumes you might see ornamenting a flagpole, and the glaring sun seethed so that he half expected to hear it hiss. Released from his chaotic dream, curious about awakening early for the first time at the villa, he shook his head and slid the door wide open. The draft that crossed the sill was as bracing as cold water. Rubbing his eyes with his bony hand, wondering how lovely the morning might be, he looked outside. Dazzled by the sunlight full in his face, his eyes searched for Water Pavilion, the pond, the path through the grass, then came to rest on the threadlike coils of the path—for he had discovered there the shadow of a woman.

Was he still dreaming? He rubbed his eyes again. It was a woman, all right, there in the flesh, but she was motionless. Flustered, he shut the door to a crack, then peeked out.

The woman basked in the sun for the longest while, as if in a reverie, and then, observing a bird that had come down from the hills to light on a nearby branch, she languidly began walking. She wore her hair up. Her jacket was of shiny, yellowish silk; a reddish brown sweater was draped across her back, the sleeves hanging down in front like the arms of a child riding piggyback. Beneath her slender waist, the hem of her jade-colored skirt rippled like gentle waves. She held a single scarlet maple leaf. Apparently she was out for a stroll on this still morning.

Who could she be?

His curiosity was aroused, as if he had come across a beautifully bound new book. As he watched her form pass close by beneath the terrace, his glance came to rest on her forehead, clean as an unused envelope, and gently traced the corners of her eyes, as if he were writing cursive letters. Her face, with its pinched lips and sharp nose tip, told him she didn't lack pride.

What was she doing there?

Again the next morning he awoke earlier than usual. He peered toward the pond, but there was nothing resembling a human form in front of the pond or along the path through the grass. He felt somehow depressed, as if he had just released to the sky a bird he had captured.

That afternoon he raked leaves, and as he was burning them in the stove he noticed someone below the terrace. He swept his hair out of his eyes, and saw she was the woman from the previous morning. She wore the same clothes, was just as quiet, and looked no different but for the tinge of red now showing in her face. She looked up and then stopped at the sight of him, but didn't turn away—it was as if she knew him.

Flustered, he swept his hair back again and rose from his squatting position.

"Aren't you Mr. —," the woman ventured.

"Yes."

Instead of following up, the woman quickly lowered her head. The color in her face had reached the base of her ears. The only sound was the crackling of the leaves burning in the fuel hole of the stove.

"How did you know?" he asked.

The woman looked up again, but instead of replying she struggled up the stone steps beside him, smiling bashfully.

His hands trembled as he fed another pile of leaves into the fuel hole.

"I saw your name on the gate."

"Uh-huh. . . ."

"I'm one of your readers. I guess I've read most everything you've. . . ."

"Really? I'm flattered."

As he nervously rubbed his hands, he looked at her eyes. They were tired and a bit hollow, like a lake that has dried up in autumn, but they shone with a cold, wintry luster.

"Did you make that fire all by yourself?"

"Um-hmm."

"I come over here every day. I feel like it's my own garden. And in the morning—"

"Yes! It's a nice big garden."

"Very nice. . . . Now don't neglect your fire on my account."

"Oh, I won't. . . . Do you live around here?"

"Over there—on the other side of the stream."

The woman was too bashful to say more that day, and she returned home.

Sometime later he walked out to the main road and gazed beyond the stream. The hillside opposite was layered with tile-roof houses and thatched huts. He couldn't possibly guess which one the woman had entered.

That evening he asked the groundskeeper about her.

"She's an invalid," the man replied.

"But she didn't look that ill."

"That's the way it is with consumption," said the groundskeeper. "She came here for the cure. She gets winded easily and can't go up in the hills, so she always visits the pavilion here."

Consumption! He felt sympathy for her, sympathy unlike what he would feel for a healthy person. Those lovely lips that conversed so gently and decorously—the mere thought that they probably radiated a sinister bacillus dejected him.

He took pleasure, though, and a certain amount of consolation, in being able to greet the woman in the garden from the next morning on; he wanted to talk with her about his indigent craft. And so, when she arrived outside his room he would venture to remark on the chill of the wind. But each time she would reply that she was fine where she was and then perch herself on the edge of the breezeway, not forgetting to frequently cover her nose and mouth with her handkerchief.

One day, finally, he issued a direct invitation: "You know, I wouldn't mind if you came inside."

Seeing it had been an effort for him to say this, the woman blushed faintly, but then, as if she wanted to make things perfectly clear to him: "I have a contagious disease." She gave a wan smile.

"I know. But I still wouldn't mind if you came in."

Finally, as if carried on the crest of some delicate emotion, she threw a glance toward the distant heavens and gingerly entered his room. It was twilight. "Twilight in an east-facing room." Her limpid eyes and white teeth were particularly distinct as she said this.

"Have you ever considered writing a story about a young woman who's facing death, like me?"

"Never! But why the concern with death? You're not that ill."

"I can't help it. It keeps cropping up in my mind."

She looked toward the ceiling, a faint smile on her face, then fell silent for a while before resuming with another gentle smile.

"When I first became ill, I was quite happy. . . ."

He wasn't sure how to take this.

"Everybody did things for me. My friends brought flowers. And I had so many plans—many more than when I was healthy. I'd say to myself, 'Now the very first thing you have to do when you're better is write everybody and apologize for anything you might have done wrong'—oh, I had all these wishes. . . . I was so thankful I'd fallen ill. . . ."

"And now?"

"I'm scared. At first I thought death might be quite lovely. I was happy to know I could plunge into a lovely death, just as I could romp around in a flower garden whenever life became vexing. But now that I'm looking death in the face I'm always frightened—even in my dreams. . . ."

The crows cawed, their calls coming from the same direction as always—doubtless the dead limbs of that fir, he thought.

"Those are my friends calling," he said, determined to block with his smile the ominous sound of the crows.

"Your friends! I like everything around here, but not those creatures. It's as if they're reminding me of death."

"Now what makes you want to say that? Some birds are white, some birds are black; some have nice, clear calls, some have harsh, rough calls. Depending on a person's taste, I think it might even be possible to have affection for crows."

"You sound just like healthy people who can't be bothered with thoughts of death—their minds are too beautiful for that. I find those birds frightening. I feel as if a wicked man is following me in disguise and he's up to no good—it gives me the creeps. Maybe when I die, those creatures will swoop down and perch right in front of me. . . ."

He didn't know what to say.

"Back when I thought death was lovely, there seemed no happiness like that of dying."

She covered her mouth and nose with her handkerchief and observed the darkening panels of the sliding door, a faraway look in her eyes. Perhaps she thought she had gone on too long.

That night he was terribly depressed. The young woman had entered his room for the first time, and had left behind the few words she had spoken, together with the warmth of her body and the organisms that infected her.

What could he say to comfort her? Was there really no cure for her disease? How could he help the woman see death as a flower garden, as she had before?

He considered this awhile, leaning askew against the wall. Suddenly he had the strange sensation that something was rustling inside his head. But after pressing a hand to his forehead, he realized the sound was coming from the storage loft. He opened the loft door to find a couple of mice. After shooing them away, he produced from the loft a piece of bread that was hard as a wood chip. With his other hand he took out a rabbit dropping he had found on the hill behind the villa. It was round as a pill, light as a dried leaf. He smiled. These days his own production wasn't much heavier. The words of Thoreau came to mind: "People too can't help smelling of grass." The humblest insect would be content with clear dew and fragrant grass. But not people—not for as long as they lived. Such was their sad fate, it occurred to him.

What can I say to give her new hope?

He became absorbed in such questions, and then suddenly he came face to face with his own passion:

I'm going to fall in love with her!

Surely, he told himself, she couldn't have had a lover. Who would vest his love in that disease-ridden chest of hers?

He spread out his palms on the floor where the woman had been sitting. But he felt only the chill of the laminated surface; her body heat had long since dissipated.

"Sorrowful maiden," he silently called to her, "if you must die, then die loving me. Sadder still to die alone than to die leaving a lover behind. . . . You've struggled so long with the germs that have infected you, my beloved—you couldn't have had a lover."

The rice-paper panels of the inner door trembled in the wind; he slid the outer door shut and lowered the flame in the lamp. And then he thought of Poe's doleful poem "The Raven" and tentatively called out in a plaintive tone, as Poe himself might have in summoning the departed spirit of his lover: "Lenore? Lenore?" He imagined Poe's lover meeting her end happily, pitiable yet lovely in death, with nothing for a shroud but the poet's worn overcoat. He felt an urge, a passion greater than Poe's, to draw the consumptive woman to him in a warm embrace. He pictured Poe in his lonely study poring over old books; a storm rising, the wind throwing open the door; the call of an unseen raven from a dark wood; the departed spirit of his lovely Lenore with her scattered tresses, softly entering to occupy a corner of the room.

"Oh, my Lenore! You couldn't have had a lover. I will give you my love, and watch over you in death, your mournful lover."

The night was ever so long, he lamented as he longed for dawn.

But the morning sky was thick with cloud, and a fierce wind swirled. There was a scattering of snow flurries. He pictured the woman in a greenhouse, head tilted up as she looked out at the world, her face delicate as a flower blossom from a gentle clime—there was no hope of her appearing in weather such as this.

"Oh, poor girl! How sad if you were to die loveless, lying in a gloomy room on such a cloudy day. My poor Lenore!"

It snowed some three days, and then came a three-day blizzard, followed by several overcast days and more snow. Finally the weather cleared and the days were warmer. One afternoon when snowmelt flowed like rain over the eaves, this poor young woman of his appeared. Her face was more pale, and the mask she wore over her mouth seemed in his eyes an emblem of mourning. She entered his room, and as she talked, he noticed she had difficulty keeping her eyes open.

"I've had a couple of coughing fits where I spit up blood—it was awful."

"But—"

"The doctor said it comes from my windpipe, but I know it's from my chest—he must think I'm stupid."

"But don't you think he knows better?"

"He's not being honest with me. And it's not just him—it's everyone. When my back's turned they talk about me dying—I know they do—but when they see me they start pretending. They treat me like I've got a foot in the grave—it makes me sad. They're giving me a taste of how lonely it is to die."

Her voice quivered.

"But . . . even now . . . if by some chance . . . there were someone who loved you with all his heart, wouldn't you believe that one person?"

She closed her eyes without a word and didn't open them.

"If there were someone who felt not the least dislike for your illness, someone fully prepared to accompany you to your fate . . . ?"

"I don't think someone like that would be human. I do have someone who loves me, but. . . . He loves me passionately, and he still comes often to see me."

He didn't know what to say.

"To show me he really loves me, to show me he's the one person who isn't the least displeased that I've caught this disease I detest, he drinks the blood I cough up—and one day that amounted to half a cup or so. But do you think that makes me feel any better?"

He remained silent. All he felt was dejection.

"Oh, he's so close to me, drinking my blood and all, but he's perfectly healthy, and he's perfectly ready to go on living. When his hair grows good and long he goes to the barber, and when his shoes wear out he has a new pair made. Day in, day out, all he does is go to the university library and study for his degree. His way is so different from mine. All I think about are hearses, graves, and such."

"Why do you dwell on those things?"

"Because I don't get genuine sympathy from anyone. Oh, I know sympathy is a natural human impulse, but I don't think people can really be sympathetic."

"Why do you say that?"

"Well, if a person's ill, you really can't show sympathy for her if you don't have the same illness. But then you can't just make up your mind you're going to develop that illness, be just as ill as she is, and die at the same time. If someone's sure to die, people can try to keep her in the dark—'Oh, it's all right, you're going to be all right'—but that will only isolate her all the quicker."

"What kind of hearse do you think about?"

He realized this was a blunt question, but he hoped he might thereby find a way inside her universe.

"One thing I positively don't want is an old-fashioned Korean hearse. And I don't want one of those gold-colored motor hearses you see these days. What I fancy is a white carriage drawn by a team of white horses. And I just can't get attached to the idea of Korean graves, either. In the West, cemeteries are like parks—they're beautiful, so I'm told. But where in the Korean landscape can you have the feeling that you're looking at someone's final resting place? Since they can't keep the coffin in the house, they have to cover it with dirt, and when the dirt washes away in the rain, all you can grow there is grass—where can you find enough earth to grow or plant a flower? Koreans must be the only people who lack feeling for those who are dying. When a family member dies, they wail their heads off inside the house, and outside the gate they leave bits of rice cake and other food to appease the spirits, but all that does is draw crows. . . ."

He remained silent.

"Sir, why do you live like this all by yourself?"

Painfully aware of his foolishness in supposing the woman had no lover, he chided himself instead of replying. He could only envy the young student who had taken this divine woman for his love, a woman who in her extreme despair hadn't the slightest worldly desire.

Twilight was fast approaching. The strident cawing hadn't yet started from the top of the fir below the pond, but they could hear the crows pecking away with their fierce beaks at the deadwood.

"The crows are back, aren't they?" she said.

"Do you really dislike them so much?"

"Yes. They scare me. I feel as if their stomachs are filled with evil things. I had a dream where I saw a charm, a knife, a bluish flame—all inside a crow's stomach. Please don't laugh at me. I'm afraid my common sense deserted me some time ago. . . ."

He chuckled. But at the same time he had an idea: he would kill a crow, open it up, and show her that the insides were no different from those of any other bird. That way he could rid her of her irrational fear of crows, and lessen her fear of death as well.

After she left, he took the path up the hill behind the villa, and there he cut down an ash tree and bent one of the branches into a large bow. He then fashioned some arrows from a stand of sturdy bush clover, wedged some large, sharpened nails into the tips, shot several arrows for practice, and set about luring the birds to his window. He scattered beans on the snow, and finally the crows flew down to peck, all the while looking about with their subtle eyes. As the more distant feed was eaten, they gradually approached his door, pecking at the nearer beans and all the while tensing as if they would take wing at any moment. Holding his breath, he positioned an arrow, resting the tip in a hole in the door panel, took aim at the nearest bird's flank, pulled back the bowstring as far as he could, and let fly.

There was a flapping of wings, and the crows flew off, cawing, to the top of the fir—all except one, which fell to the ground, the arrow embedded in its wing joint. He quickly pulled on his shoes and gave chase. But before he could hold the bird down with his foot, it jumped up and managed with its two legs and one sound wing to half-fly, half-hop to the grass, scattering glistening drops of blood on the snow. Panting, he ran after the crow. To all appearances a wicked creature, it was, after all, only a bird. Having lost the freedom of the sky, it now found itself cornered. It fell upside down into the drain leading to the pond and was stuck there cawing, its eyes covered with tiny fireballs of blood. Its pincerlike beak opened wide and its head perked up. Other crows dropped from the fir and flew about in low, menacing circles, as if bespeaking an intention to reclaim their lost family member.

Despite his rising fear, he hefted a stone and threatened the crows above while chasing down the wounded one, which had risen from the drain. With all his might he kicked the bird in the gullet. The kick dislodged the arrow and sent the bird some ten yards distant; its caws were now reduced to squeaks. He was about to kick the bird again, but by then it had ceased to regard him as an enemy and could only struggle with its impending death. His heart throbbed as he observed the black bird's death agony while trying to imagine what the end would be like for the consumptive young woman. It was a sad business.

Presently he returned to his room, and later he had the groundskeeper hang the dead bird by its neck from a maple tree. As soon as the young woman appeared, he would dissect the crow with surgical skill, showing its abdomen to contain only simple aviary innards no different from those of any other winged creature. He could then prove its stomach held no such thing as a charm, knife, or bluish flame.

But the weather turned even colder; for ten days the sun's warmth was absent. Over a month passed, but the young woman was nowhere to be seen. The weather moderated, the snow on the pond melted, and the crow's carcass became soft enough to dissect—but the young woman failed to appear.

One afternoon, when the weather was colder again and the roads were sprinkled with tiny pellets of dry snow, he was on his way home with a few groceries; a magazine had just bought a piece he had taken great pains to finish. Arriving at the road to the villa, he noticed a pair of black motorcars and a gold-colored hearse parked on the broad expanse of grass across the stream.

His heart fell. He looked up toward the villa, and there crouched atop the fir tree, as before, were a few crows, observing the scene.

"She's dead, isn't she?" he murmured to himself.

The coffin, draped with black linen, had already been loaded into the hearse. The groundskeeper appeared among the villagers surrounding the hearse, and approached him.

"That lady passed away—the one who used to visit our pavilion all the time."

He removed his hat and looked toward the hearse.

"The man getting into the car to the rear was her fiancé," the groundskeeper continued.

He silently watched this young man who spent so much time in the university library studying for his degree. The young man took a seat in the car, and presently produced a white handkerchief with which he dabbed his face. And then the two cars silently eased into motion behind the hearse and departed. The snow had changed to large flakes that began to pour down thick and fast. Before long the tire tracks were completely covered.

There was nothing particularly unusual about the cawing of the crows that evening. But from time to time their call was the *gar* he had heard before, the *r* sounding as if it would never end.

Translated by Bruce and Ju-Chan Fulton

4. KIM TONGNI

Kim Tongni was born Kim Shijong near the city of Kyŏngju in 1913 and was educated there and in Taegu and Seoul. He made his literary debut as a poet, but soon switched to fiction. He died in 1995 after a long and distinguished career, which included teaching positions at Seoul's Sŏrabŏl College of Arts and Chungang University.

One of Kim's central concerns is the clash between tradition and modernity in Korea. "Munyŏdo," translated here, frames the contest as a struggle between a mother's shamanistic beliefs and her son's faith in Christianity. First published in the journal *Chungang* in 1936, this story continued to claim the author's imagination: Kim revised it several times, made it the title of a 1948 story collection, and developed it into a novel, *Ŭlhwa* (1978). Kim's debut story, "Hwarang ŭi huye" (1935, trans. 1998 "A Descendant of the *Hwarang*"), has a similar theme. A penetrating sketch of an old-fashioned, down-at-the-heels Confucian "gentleman," it also portrays the bustle of Seoul in the mid-1930s. Among his other important stories are "Hwangt'ogi" (1939, trans. 1977 "Loess Valley"), a study of primordial passions, and "Yŏngma" (1948, trans. 1993 "The Post Horse Curse"), which depicts a young man's wanderlust in the light of native folk beliefs.

Kim is thought of by critics and literary historians as a writer who more than most captured in his fictional works the ethos of the Korean people. Kim himself advocated a humanistic worldview that combined what he saw as Western rationalism and Eastern intuitiveness.

THE SHAMAN PAINTING

I

Low hills slumbering on night's distant horizon. Broad river winding black across the plain. Sky spangled with stars about to rain down on hills, river, and plain as this night approaches its climax. On the broad, sandy riverbank under a large canopy a crowd of village women held in thrall by a shaman's magic dance for a lost soul, sadness and hope in their faces and a weariness that tells of coming dawn. In their midst the shaman caught up in the ecstatic throes of her dance, spinning weightless in her swirling mantle, pure spirit freed of flesh and bone. . . .

This painting was made before I arrived in this world, around the time my father married. Before this, people looked on our family, with its wealth and lineage, as one with "good pedigree." The manor was always alive with literati gentry, and we had what was said to be one of the best collections of precious calligraphy and antiques in the country. This love of art was handed down along with the family's wealth from generation to generation, father to son to grandson.

Grandfather was not the kind to concern himself with the material condition of the estate, and he kept up this family tradition even after our family's fortune had begun to wane, around the time he turned over authority as head of the family to Father. He continued welcoming others who shared his love of the arts, as if the good times had never ended. And so there was always one or another itinerant high-born poet or wandering low-born artist enjoying a few days or months of his hospitality in the gentlemen's quarters.

It was around that time that a peculiar-looking stranger appeared at our door. He came at dusk, I remember, on the day the apricot tree by the vegetable patch in the yard had just blossomed—one of those days in early spring when the gritty loess wind blew from dawn to dusk. About fifty or so he seemed, small of build. With no long coat he was improperly attired for the road; on his head sat a straw commoner's hat held down by an old silk kerchief tied from the top down round his chin. One got the impression that he had been traveling a long time with no special place to go. In his hand he held the reins of his donkey, and on that donkey sat a girl with a very pallid complexion, about sixteen. The two looked like a rustic servant escorting his master's daughter.

It was not till the next day that the man got around to introducing the girl. "I thought we might visit your lordship because people say this young one here—my daughter—they say she is quite good with a brush. . . ."

"What's your name, dear?" Grandfather asked. She simply looked at him a moment with those big almond eyes, and Grandfather later recalled the girl's intriguing face, whiter even than the white clothes she wore, and at the same time tinged with a shadow of sorrow.

"Well then, how old are you?"

But that one glance was all she was prepared to give, and she remained silent.

Her father answered for her. "My daughter's name is Nangi, sir, and she is sixteen." Then he lowered his voice. "She can't hear too well, you know."

Grandfather nodded. He asked the girl's father to stay a few days and let him get a better look at what the girl could do. So father and daughter stayed on for over a month, daughter painting and her father recounting to Grandfather the sad details of the girl's hard life.

On the day they left, even when Grandfather gave the unfortunate pair some very expensive silk and a generous sum of money for the road, the face of that silent girl seated on the pony was filled with the very same grief that appears with tears. . . .

But now, let me tell you the story that they left behind with the painting, the one Grandfather called "the shaman painting."

2

About a half-hour's walk outside the walls of Kyŏngju, ancient Shilla's capital, there is a tiny village. Some knew it as Yŏmin, and to others it was Chapsŏng. At any rate, in one isolated corner of this village lived a sorceress whom people called Mohwa. They called her this because it was the name of the place she had come from.

Mohwa's house was quite unlike the others in this hamlet. This house hid deep in the weeds that crowded a large yard encircled by a long rock wall, which was crumbling in places like the ancient fortress wall that snaked along the mountain ridge nearby. The roof of this old house was blackened from one end to the other with shingle mushrooms that gave off a revolting stench of humus. One corner of the decrepit dwelling was in a state of impending collapse. The flourishing jungle that surrounded the house was overrun with all sorts of vines and herbs, and nameless grasses and weeds grew so high a person could get lost in them. This jungle was fed throughout the year by pools of old rainwater covered with black-green algae. In the nocturnal world beneath all this vegetation worms as big as snakes slithered and frogs as hoary as toads prowled, and except for these creatures no living thing—no human anyway—seemed to have lived there for decades, even centuries.

The shaman Mohwa lived with her daughter Nangi in this weary, run-down haunted house. The solitary pair had little to do with anyone from the outside. Practically their only visitor was Nangi's father, who had a seafood shop on the coastal road a few hours' walk from Kyŏngju. They said Nangi was the only thing of any meaning in his life, and she was so dear to him that he could not bear to be away from her for very long, so in the spring and fall he would come visiting with precious foods from the sea like tasty bundles of dried kelp and seaweed. Until Mohwa's son Ugi returned after several years away, mother and daughter had no other visitors to their goblins' den except for the occasional woman, from town or from afar, who wanted Mohwa to exorcise a demon or summon the spirits for protection.

On these rare occasions that someone came to ask Mohwa to perform a rite, the visitor would peek in the outside gate and call, "Mohwa, you in there? Mohwa . . . ?" and when there was still no answer, come into the yard and call a couple more times. Then she might approach the house, maybe lean with one hand on the low, narrow porch and reach over with the other to open the door . . . but just then the door would open and peeping out would be the young girl Nangi, staring at the visitor without a word. The girl might have been painting all by herself and then, when she heard someone calling, dropped her brush in surprise and blanched with fear, and finally crept to the door, trembling from head to toe.

It was always like this, Nangi sitting alone all day at home and Mohwa spending all day outside. Mother was up and out the very moment the sun breached the ancient fortress wall, and it was not till that sun sank behind the west ridge that she could be seen coming back home, tipsy, with some peaches in a knotted wrapper, slowing now and then into her dance, intoning in her doleful chant,

> Daughter, my daughter, Mr. Kim's daughter,
> Sea Kingdom Flower Spirit, my daughter Nangi . . .
> Let me into the Dragon King's Palace

Twelve gates all locked
Open up, open up you twelve gates.
Please open up. . . .

"Had one today too, Mohwa?" the villagers greeted her, and she smiled and clasped her hands in front and twisted her shoulders demurely, "Yes, on my way home from the market," and then bowed politely. When she was not doing an exorcism or summoning the spirits she was usually at the wine shop.

She liked drinking so much and Nangi liked peaches so much that she came back drunk every day, in midsummer always with a few peaches. "Daughter, daughter, my little daughter . . . ," calling Nangi with this chant all the way into the house. And Nangi would attack one of these luscious peaches and gobble it up, just as she used to go so hungrily for her mother's breast when she was much younger.

To hear Mohwa tell it, Nangi was an incarnation of the Sea Kingdom's Flower Spirit. In a dream Mohwa had a visitation from the Dragon Spirit, who ruled the Sea Kingdom, and he gave her a peach to eat. Nangi was born seven days after this. Now the Sea Kingdom's Dragon Spirit had twelve daughters. The first was Moon, the second Water, the third Cloud, . . . and so on till the twelfth, Flower; these daughters were betrothed to the Mountain Spirit's twelve sons—Moon to Sun, Water to Tree, Cloud to Wind—each pair betrothed and to be married in their turn, but Flower, the last daughter, who had a romantic sort of nature, could not wait her turn and grabbed Bird, the eleventh brother and darling of Flower's elder sister Fruit, so the bereft Fruit and the twelfth brother Butterfly complained so pitifully to the Dragon Spirit and the Mountain Spirit that the Dragon Spirit got angry and punished Flower by making her deaf and then banishing her from the Sea Kingdom, which of course turned her from Flower Spirit into an ordinary peach blossom, and though she bloomed in rich hues every spring by the river and in the forest, and Bird Spirit came every spring to perch on her branches and sang plaintively over and over of his love for her, all that is left now of the Flower Spirit is her deaf and dumb reincarnation Nangi.

At times Mohwa would be in the wine shop drinking, or dancing with the male shamans, when all of a sudden she would stop, then run off as if she were losing her mind. When they shouted "Now what's got into you!" she would yell back at them over her shoulder as she hurried off: Nangi was calling from home. The Dragon Spirit, who was after all the Great Mother and Nangi's first and real parent, had entrusted Mohwa with Nangi for only a while, and Mohwa knew that if she did not take care of this girl she would feel the fury of the Spirit's wrath.

Nangi was not the only incarnation around. Mohwa might pounce on anyone she came upon, admonishing, "Don't forget now, you're an incarnation of the Tree Spirit," or "I hope you know you're a son of the Rock Spirit." And then she reminded them to pray often to the Seven Stars Spirit or the Dragon Spirit, who had given them all they had.

There were times that she saw everyone and everything as if they were the spirits themselves. It was not only to the grownups that she demurely twisted her shoulders and bowed in respect; even children awed her, and upon occasion even a dog or a pig would be the object of her embarrassing demonstrations. Cats too, and frogs, and worms, or a lump of meat, a butterfly, a potato, an apricot tree, a fire poker, a clay pot, a stone step, a straw shoe, the branch of a jujube tree, a swallow, a cloud, wind, fire, rice, a kite, a gourd ladle, an old straw cattle-feed pouch, kettles, spoons, oil lamps . . . and so on and so forth. When she was in this mood every thing she chanced to meet became her neighbor, no less worthy of being a spirit than her neighbors who happened to be human and whom she exchanged glances and greetings with, and talked and fought with, even envied and cursed.

3

From the day Ugi came back home Mohwa's goblin den began to seem more like a place where people lived. Nangi, who used to hate to set foot in the kitchen, now came up with an occasional meal for Ugi. And at night now, a paper lantern hung from the corner of the sagging tile roof and provided a faint glimmer of light where there used to be only the black gloom of the yard and the stars far above.

Ugi was born of a relationship that Mohwa had with some man when she still lived in Mohwa Hamlet, before her spirit took possession of her. Even when Ugi was still very young everybody around remarked what a precocious one he was, but Mohwa was so poor she could not send him to the classics primer school that most of the children in the village went to. When he turned nine, though, an acquaintance of Mohwa's got a temple to take him in as a novice. After that there was no news from him at all until that day ten years later when he appeared again out of the blue.

Nangi was his half sister. When she was around five, before Ugi left and she got sick, she was always calling his name and tagging along after him everywhere he went. It was soon after Ugi went off to the temple that Nangi took to her bed with her sickness. She came out of it three years later unable to hear much at all, though no one was ever able to tell exactly how bad her hearing was.

For a while after Ugi left she would stammer to her mother, "Wh-where is Ugi?"

"Temple," Mohwa would shout. "Studying in the temple."

"Wh-what temple? Wh-where?"

"Chirim. Very big. . . ."

That was not true, though. Mohwa herself had no idea what temple Ugi was at, but she did not want to admit it. So she just said the first thing that came to her.

One day, arriving home from the market, Mohwa found a beautiful eighteen-year-old boy in the yard. When she was finally able to make out who the lad was, she panicked, and her booze-darkened face blushed an even deeper shade of scarlet. She turned to bolt, but then stopped, then shuffled a moment in hesitation—and abruptly turned back toward him. Those long arms on her long willowy frame spread open, then she ran to Ugi and embraced him like a big hen drawing her chick to her breast.

"Who can this handsome young man be? Whoever . . . ? Oh my son, my dear son!" She let the tears flow, oblivious to everything around her. "Look who's here! My son!"

"Mother!" Ugi buried his cheek in his mother's shoulder. "Mother. . . ." And he cried too, long and hard.

Before Mohwa came back home Nangi had been sitting by herself in the family room when this strange young man opened the door and looked in, and he scared her so bad her heart stopped and she sat there pinned in the corner unable to utter a sound, unable even to show her fear except in her violent trembling. Nangi saw the boy had Mohwa's slender waist and her long neck, and she guessed who he might be. But that beautiful face that gave him such a noble countenance did not belong to a person who had undergone the lonely rigors of working in a temple for several years. She had seen a clear resemblance to Mohwa, yet it was only now that she was fully able to comprehend this young man was truly her lost Ugi. When she saw her mother smothering this boy in her embrace and sobbing "My son, my son!" through her streaming tears, she felt the tears coming to her own eyes. This young man that was able to bring out such tender feelings from this crusty sorceress had to be her brother, Ugi, and an indescribable thrill ran through her.

Within a few days, though, Ugi had become an unsolvable riddle to his mother and Nangi. When he was about to eat, or go to bed, and then again when he got up in the morning, he never neglected to mumble some strange long incantation. And at times he would pull a small book from his breast pocket and bury himself in it.

On one of these occasions Ugi saw Nangi's puzzled expression and a smile lit up his beautiful face. "Here," he offered, opening it up and showing it to her, "you can read it too." Though it was not all that easy for her, Nangi could read—she had already been through the classic *Tale of Shim Ch'ŏng* a few times—but this was the first time she had ever seen that word *Bible*, there on the cover. Ugi saw her puzzled look and that whole exquisite face of his lit up in one big beatific smile.

"Do you know who made you?"

Though Nangi could not hear what he said, she was able to get the general idea through his gestures and the expressions on his face. But what he really meant—well, this was difficult, something she had never thought of before.

"All right then, do you know what happens to you when you die?"

She just stared in reply.

"It's all here, right in this book." And then he pointed at the sky. The only word she could just barely make out was *God*.

"God is the one who made us. And it's not only us He made, He made everything on the earth and in the sky. And we return to Him when we die."

It was not long before this god of Ugi's roused Mohwa's suspicion, even revulsion. Four days after he arrived, when he was just about to say his prayers over the food she had put in front of him, she ventured, "I never knew they had that stuff in Buddhism." Apparently she was thinking that he had been in the temple all those years and that this was some sort of arcane Buddhist practice.

"No, Mother. I am not a Buddhist."

"Well then, what else is there besides Buddhism?"

"Mother, I ran away from that temple because I could not abide seeing another Buddhist."

"Couldn't abide . . . ? Buddhism is the Way. So what are you, a Taoist, some Taoist immortal maybe?"

"No, Mother, I am a Christian."

"Christian?"

"They call it Christianity up north. It's a new religion."

"So you're one of that Tonghak cult?"

"No, not Tonghak. Christian."

"Sure, sure. In this Christianity or whatever you call it do they do this incantation every time they sit down to eat?"

"That is no incantation, Mother. I was offering a prayer to God."

Her eyes bulged. "God?"

"Yes. It's God who made us."

His mother blanched. "Oh my, the boy's gone and got possessed by some drifter demon!" And that was the end of her questions.

The next day Mohwa went to the house of someone possessed by one of those drifter demons, who latch on to one victim and torment him for a while till they get chased off to another victim. She had taken care of this demon with her rice-water cure and had just returned home. Ugi saw how worn out and disheveled she was, and asked, "Mother, where have you been?"

"Pak Kŭpch'ang's. I did them an exorcism."

Ugi silently thought to himself for a while, then asked, "And does the demon leave when you tell it to?"

"Well, the man has returned to his senses so it must be gone," she replied in a tone that wondered what sort of silly question he was going to come up with next.

Until now in this area she had conducted countless exorcisms and cured hundreds, even thousands possessed by every sort of demon, and not even once had she ever doubted the power of her spirits or her power to use them. Chasing away those drifter demons came as naturally to her as offering a cup of water to a thirsty person would to you or me. And Mohwa was not the only one who believed this. The one who asked for her services, and all those related to the one possessed, thought the same way. It was simple: When you got sick, you went to Mohwa before you went to any doctor. Everyone knew that Mohwa's exorcisms and conjurations worked a lot faster and were far more effective and far cheaper than any medicine or needle they had in any clinic.

Ugi, bowed in thought, now raised his head and looked straight into his mother's eyes. "Mother, that is a sin—it is Jesus who does that sort of thing, not people. Look, right here in Matthew, chapter 9, verses 32 and 33: If we bring the deaf mute to Jesus he will cast out the evil spirit and the dumb shall speak again and. . . ."

But before he was able to finish Mohwa got up and went over to the altar she always kept in the corner of the family room.

> Great spirits,
> rulers of heaven and earth,
> north, south, east, and west,
> above and below,
> what you've made to fly flies,
> what you've made to crawl crawls.
> No more than beasts in human clothes are we,
> tenuous lives hanging by a thread.
> In your bosom we find protection;

you guide us along the righteous way,
grasping good and spurning evil.

Mohwa's eyes gleamed like jewels, and her whole body began to tremble violently, as she rubbed her hands in prayer.

House Spirit gives us land, Hearth Spirit gives us fire,
Family Spirit gives us good fortune, Seven Stars Spirit
gives us life,
and Maitreya protects this tenuous life.
Lead us along the righteous way,
the broad and level way.

As soon as she finished her wild prayer the spirit who now possessed her grabbed the dish of rice water from above the altar, took a mouthful, and sprayed the demon in Ugi with it head to toe. Then "Shoo–o–o–o–o!" she shrieked at him,

Shoo, demon!
You're in Yŏngju here, place of the gods,
at Piru Peak, highest of all—
Too high for the likes of you!
Sheerest cliffs, fifty fathoms of blue sea—
Too deep for the likes of you!
A sword in my right hand, torch in my left,
Out, evil spirit, on your way.
Shoo and away with you!

Ugi, stunned at Mohwa's frenzied raving, bowed his head in a short prayer. And then, without another word, he got up and left the house.

Long after Ugi had gone, Mohwa went on ranting as she sprayed the demons from every corner.

4

Ugi decided it was about time to find out if there were any Christians in the area. Mohwa thought he would be back soon, but the sun set and the night deepened without his return. Mohwa and Nangi slumped gloomily in a corner of the family room waiting for him to come back.

"Is that Jesus demon book here somewhere?" she asked Nangi. The child shook her head, she did not know, but wished at the same time that he had left it with her, that thing he called the Bible and Mohwa called the Jesus demon book because she was sure Ugi was possessed.

Ugi was thinking the same way about them. He believed this demon of Mohwa's had probably gone and possessed Nangi too, had even struck her dumb. But he remembered: "In his time, Jesus cured people possessed by the devil and rendered deaf and dumb," and determined with all his heart that he would pray to the Lord as much as it took to get Him, through Ugi, to cure his mother and little sister.

> When Jesus saw that the people came running together, he rebuked the foul spirit, saying unto him, "Thou dumb and deaf spirit, I charge thee, come out of him and enter no more into him." And the spirit cried, and rent him sore, and came out of him: and he was as one dead; insomuch that many said, "He is dead." But Jesus took him by the hand, and lifted him up; and he arose. And when he was come into the house, his disciples asked him privately, "Why could not we cast him out?" And he said unto them, "This kind can come forth by nothing but praying and fasting." [Gospel of Mark, chapter 9, verses 25–29]

And so Ugi believed that if he only prayed persistently, God would chase the demons out of his mother and little sister. Straightaway he wrote a letter to Reverend Hyŏn and Elder Yi in Pyongyang, who had taught him about Jesus.

> *Dear Reverend Hyŏn,*
> *Through the bountiful grace of God I have found my mother. However, since the word of our Lord has not yet spread to this area, so many here are possessed by the devil and they worship idols. Without a church—as soon as possible—these people will never hear the Good News.*
>
> *I am embarrassed to tell you this, but both my mother and sister are possessed by demons. One demon has turned my mother into a sorceress and another has stricken my sister deaf and dumb. As Jesus instructs us in Mark's gospel, chapter 9, verse 29, I am praying to Him very hard to chase away these demons, but it is very hard to pray here without a church. I sincerely hope that a church will be built here as soon as possible.*

It was this Reverend Hyŏn, from America, who had clothed, fed, and educated Ugi. In the summer of the year Ugi turned fourteen the boy had announced at the temple that he was going to Seoul and then quit his life as a novice, but instead of going to Seoul he wandered here and there through the country, and in the autumn of the year he turned fifteen he found himself in Pyongyang. That winter he met Elder Chang, and Elder Chang introduced him to Reverend Hyŏn.

A couple of years later, when Ugi told Reverend Hyŏn he was going to have to try to find his mother, the minister sat him down and told him, "Within three years I will be returning to America. If at that time you wish to go with me, you're very welcome to."

"Thank you, Reverend. I would like very much to go with you."

"All right, then. Go find your mother, and return as soon as you can."

But the house he found his mother living in was of a totally different world from the one he had known with Reverend Hyŏn. In place of those bright, cheery sounds of hymns and the organ and voices reading the Bible and the happy, smiling faces of people sitting together at a table of wholesome food and giving thanks to the Lord, here was this forlorn crumbling wall surrounding a yard of twisting vines and tangled weeds crawling with frogs and worms around a stale old house suffocating under a roof creeping with dark-green shingle mushrooms, and every time he saw these two women in the midst of all that—mother possessed by the sorceress demon and daughter possessed by the deaf-mute demon—Ugi immediately wondered whether he himself had not been bewitched into that goblins' den.

A while after Ugi finally came back home one day from meeting the Christians in the area, Nangi started to change. All day long Ugi could sense this girl with her lithe body, smooth skin as fair as paper, languishing in the corner without a word, without a smile, following Ugi's every movement with her big gleaming eyes. Then when night came and the paper lantern glowed dimly from the roof corner and Ugi went out for some air, Nangi would stroll into a dark corner of the yard and watch him. Before long the blood-starved mosquitoes started swarming round her with their mad singing, and she flew from them to Ugi for protection. Her lips sought his neck, and her ice-cold hands startled him as they found his breast; he pulled her hands away, and she backed off some but then, whole body trembling, moved in again. After a while Ugi took her hand and led her into the light of the lantern, both of them confused and embarrassed at what was happening to them.

From the time Nangi started behaving this way Ugi grew paler by the day, and in his face showed the confusion that was working inside him. After a couple weeks of this he abruptly left home, without a word of where he was going or when he would return.

Two days after he left, in the middle of the night, Mohwa woke, sat up, and let out a long sigh. She looked at Nangi, lying next to her, and shook her awake. In a voice heavy with gloom she asked, "When did Ugi say he was coming back?" When she saw Nangi had nothing to say, she grumbled, "How can we expect him to come back if you don't have his supper ready like I asked you to?"

Every day that he did not come back she got more anxious. In the middle of the night she would suddenly get up and go to the kitchen, set aside the dinner tray they had prepared for Ugi, pour some more mint oil into the ritual lamp saucer and light the wick. She raised her hands above her head and then bowed.

> Our own Household Spirit, our own Seven Stars Spirit,
> our own Hearth Spirit. . . .

She rubbed her palms together in supplication and bowed again, then straightened and began to work slowly into her dance to beckon the spirits.

> I pray to you, and to the Guardian Spirit of this family
> I pray.
> Heaven has its stars, the sea has its pearls,
> and this house has its prince,
> Precious as gold and silver, beautiful as jade, child of
> auspicious star.
> We pray for him to the Birth Spirit for long life,
> to the Seven Stars Spirit for glory,
> to the Family Spirit for good fortune,
> to the Dragon Spirit for virtue,
> to the Hearth Spirit for enlightenment,
> to the Homesite Spirit for talent.
> Stars in the heavens, pearls in the sea . . .
> Birth Spirit, Hearth Spirit won't refuse
> to come and cast out the Jesus demon,
> craving fire demon 10,000 *li* from the west.

Now she was ranting, wheeling and whirling madly about.

> He burns, look at him burn—whoosh! whoosh! he burns,
> the fire demon up in flames!
> And when he's finished burning, my child of auspicious
> star is sitting over his Ashes,
> unscathed, shining like gold and silver.

Yes, Birth Spirit is on his way,
here comes Hearth Spirit!

The commotion in the kitchen would waken Nangi, and she would get out of bed and go to the door that connected the family room and the kitchen. She would peep through the hole in the window paper, holding her breath, enthralled, and then before she knew what was happening her whole body began to twitch and tremble. Soon she jumped up, possessed by her mother's spirit. She took off her upper clothes. Then her lower clothes. One step in tandem with her mother, then another, and one more, and soon she was with her mother step for step, gesture for gesture, chanting the same lyrics to the same notes to the same rhythm, daughter in the family room, mother in the kitchen. And then at dawn after one such night, when Nangi returned to her senses she found herself off her sleeping mat and spread out on the bare floor, completely naked, now a sorceress.

One day around this time Mohwa was on the porch trying on a new pair of shoes that she had been given to wear for her next ritual. She looked up, and there was Ugi, a smile on his face. The mother put down her shoes and got up, and, just as when he had returned the first time, beckoned him with outspread arms, then wrapped them around Ugi's slender form, enfolding him like a big mother bird protecting her chick. And she wept. She uttered not a word of resentment, not a sound other than the quiet sobs of her relief and happiness. That usually ghostly ashen face now glowed with warmth, and in place of the crudity of the possessed sorceress showed the wholesome bearing of a mother.

"Well, uh . . . ," said the uncomfortable boy as he extracted himself from her embrace, "I think I'll get some rest now."

After Ugi went to his room Mohwa went back to the porch. For a long time she sat there, legs spread out in front of her, head hanging, lost deep in thought. And suddenly it came to her. She raised her head with an "Ah . . . !" got up, and went into the house and started rummaging for something among Nangi's paintings.

Later, in the middle of the night, Ugi's hands sought the Bible that he always slept with at his breast, and when they found nothing there he began to stir from his sleep. At the same time a muffled chanting teased his slumbering consciousness. He woke, sat up, and looked for his Bible, but no, it was not there. Then he noticed that his mother was not there either, where she usually slept between Nangi and himself. An ominous premonition chilled him. And there, that sound again, clearer now, a ghost's wailing babble from the very bowels of the earth—a witch's incantation. Without another thought he was up and peering through the hole in the paper window of the door to the kitchen.

Jesus demon, craving fire demon 10,000 *li* from the west!
Torch in my right hand, sword in my left.
Vagabond, you drifter, no way to escape,
Dash here, blocked by the Mountain Spirit.
Dart there, Dragon Spirit waits.
Up to the Seven Stars—
they block your every probe.
Break through the clouds? Ride the wind?
Cloud Spirit, Wind Spirit, they're already there.
Down to the Dragon Palace—all Twelve Gates locked.
Rattle the first, four devas jump out,
fierce eyes flashing, iron maces high.
Pound on the second, firedog mates pounce:
Male spits flame, female spits hot coals.
Bang at the third door and water dogs spring out,
Male's bark douses the flame,
Female's bark douses the coals.

Mohwa was in her sorceress outfit, a mantle over white garments. She rubbed her palms together as she bowed and danced in languid, beckoning moves. On the hearth the ritual flame in its offering dish was burning clean on its wick in mint oil, and above this was a tray with one offering dish of water and another of salt. To the side of this Ugi detected a blue curl of smoke rising from a flame's dying flicker on the thick cover of his Bible. One corner of the cover had already turned to ash, along with the pages inside.

That eerie scornful grin on Mohwa's face showed a crazed determination to meet the Jesus demon's challenge. She swung by the tray and picked up some salt out of the dish and sprinkled it on the black ashes, which had now stopped smoking. Her voice was hard with hatred.

There you go, Jesus demon, craving fire demon 10,000 *li*
from the west,
to our village shrine to get some money for the road,
to Kwanu's shrine to take your leave.
Bells on your ears, keep in step,
ding-a-ling one-two, ding-a-ling one-two!
Cross the mountains, cross the seas,

move onward, forward.
And once you go, you'll never return,
your feet will be too sore.
The flowers may be back next spring, not you;
in that leanest month your hunger will keep you there,
10,000 *li* away in the west.

Deranged babble from a witch's brew, her song sent a shiver of revulsion through Ugi. His heart was wrenched by that coy coaxing in those eyes hard and cold as gems and those lurid gestures in rhythm with the swinging folds of her mantle. He could bear it no longer and, like one struggling out of the throes of a nightmare, he burst out with a cry and in the next instant bounded blindly outside and around to the kitchen door, kicked it open, and made for the dish of water on the offering tray next to Mohwa to save his Bible. But Mohwa whirled round at him, and before he could reach the dish the big kitchen knife in her hand flashed him a warning to back off. She waved it tauntingly in his face, between him and his Bible, as she stepped slowly back into her dance.

Shoo, demon. . . . Get out!
You can't fool me,
craving fire demon 10,000 *li* from the west.
You're in Yŏngju here, place of the gods,
at Piru Peak, highest of all—
Too high for the likes of you!
Sheerest cliffs, fifty fathoms of blue sea—
And a patch of thorny ash for your feet.
This is no place for you.
A sword in my right hand, torch in my left,
Away, you drifter demon from the west.
Shoo–o–o–o! And away with you!

And she slashed at Ugi's face. He felt the blade cut the edge of his left ear and he grabbed the water dish from the tray, throwing the whole thing into Mohwa's face to bring her to her senses. Then he saw that he had knocked over the ritual flame and the paper door was burning so he jumped up on the hearth to stop it. Mohwa, her face dripping water but burning with rage, followed Ugi up onto the hearth swinging her knife, and Ugi, trying to smother the spreading flames, felt the blade slash his back. He straightened, turned, and fell straight into his mother's arms and the last thing he saw was the ghost-white face of a fiendishly grinning witch.

5

The wounds from Mohwa's frenzy still showed on Ugi's head, neck, and back, and with each day he grew thinner until he was just skin and bones with two sunken eyes. But it was not his wounds that made him so sick.

Mohwa nursed him with all her energy, running here and there day and night to see to his every need. Sometimes in desperation she pulled him up and squeezed him to her breast. But he did not respond. Of course she fed him all kinds of medicines, performed every rite she knew, and recited her most eloquent incantations over him. But Ugi did not get better.

The more Mohwa devoted herself to Ugi the weaker became the spirit that possessed her. When someone asked her to do an exorcism or summon the spirits she usually declined—she had to nurse her son. The few times she consented to perform a rite they said later that the spirit was not with her like it used to be.

Around this time a preacher came to the county seat and a small church was built. Evangelizing teams were dispatched to every village and Christianity spread like wildfire. And one day the word reached even Mohwa's village in the person of an American missionary.

"Brothers and sisters, thanks be to the Lord for letting us meet. God created each and every one of us, he loved us so. Yet we are all sinners; in our hearts lurks only wickedness. And to save us from our wicked selves Jesus offered himself up to be nailed to that cross. Thus only belief in Jesus Christ will save us. We must glorify him with joyful hearts. And now, let us pray to the Lord our God."

They said it was more fun to watch this American with his weird blue eyes and his parrot's beak than it was to watch a circus monkey.

"And he doesn't charge a thing. Come on!"

They gathered in droves.

Elder Yang, who had brought the missionary here, paid a call at every household. As a sign of the changing times, he was accompanied by his wife, granddaughter of a respected patriarch of the town. He exhorted the villagers, "Believing in shamans and fortune-tellers is a sin before our Father, the one and the only Master of heaven and earth. What power has the shaman? She prays and grovels to a rotted old tree, to a deaf and dumb stone image of the Maitreya Buddha. What power has the fortune-teller? This one who cannot see what is right in front of him and gropes his way with a cane claims to guide a person with eyes that see. The almighty who put us on this earth is the absolute one and only Heavenly Father. And what then did our Father tell us? 'Thou shalt not have strange gods before me.'" And he poured forth endlessly on how God's only son Jesus cast out every demon, healed the leper, the cripple, and the deaf, and about how Jesus rose from the dead and ascended into heaven only three days after he died on the cross.

When Mohwa overheard any talk about these preachers she sneered, "Worthless drifter demons." Disdain their derision and slander as she might, though, it hurt deeply, and she banged her large gong and she banged her small gong and ranted . . .

> Shoo, demon! Away!
> You leech off my people,
> the poorer the better for you.
> But you know Mohwa, so you'd better listen.
> If you don't vanish right now I'll wrap you and all your
> descendants in the hide of the White Steed Spirit
> and throw you into an ash briar patch,
> into a boiling cauldron,
> into the fifty-fathoms deep blue sea.
> Your grandchildren and their grandchildren,
> they'll never again see the light of day,
> and never beg again.
> Away, demon, get away while you can!
> Burn the road up with your feet;
> Shoo you, 10,000 *li* back west,
> A ball of fire on your tail,
> A bell on each ear, ding-a-ling ding-a-ling. . . .

But the Jesus demon was not driven away; in fact, his followers multiplied. Worse, he began taking possession of those who had come to Mohwa for her magic, until no one came anymore.

In the meantime a revivalist had arrived in town. They said he had the skill to cure an illness with a prayer and so everybody in the county started to flock here. He laid his hands on the head of the sick and intoned, "It is your sins that are causing you to suffer so," and prayed over them. They told far and wide of women who had their female maladies washed away with their sins, of the blind who saw again, the crippled who walked again, the deaf who heard, the dumb who spoke, and the paralytic and the epileptic and all those others who, depending on the strength of their faith, had their sins washed away and their afflictions along with those sins.

Day after day the women placed their silver rings and gold rings in the offering box on the dais at the preacher's feet. Contributions poured in. They said the show Mohwa put on could not begin to compare with this one.

"So our phonies from the West have brought their magic show," Mohwa sneered. Her own patron spirit had given her, and not these scoundrels, the power to summon the spirits and exorcise demons. But where she saw the spirits—in the old tree, the rock, the mountain, the river—they saw only craven idols. And in her they saw an enemy: "Believe in the sorceress and the fortune-teller and you sin in the face of our one and almighty God the Father!" When those Jesus demons put on one of their drum-beating, pipe-squealing anti-superstition parades and slandered Mohwa and her gods, Mohwa went off by herself and danced and chanted to the rhythm of her gongs:

Shoo you, 10,000 *li* back west,
You drifter demon.
A ball of fire on your tail,
A bell on each ear, ding-a-ling . . .

6

As fall turned to winter that year Ugi got even worse.

Mohwa watched her son waste away a little more every day. At times, faced with her utter powerlessness, she broke down and mourned in a trembling voice, as if her heart were going to break, "Poor thing, you poor thing, what's happening to you? Come from so far away to find your mother, and look what you get for it!"

When Ugi saw this helpless grief he held her hand and, through his tears, said quietly, "Mother, don't fret yourself so. When I die I will go to our heavenly Father."

Mohwa might ask him if there was anything he wanted, but he would only shake his head quietly. Now and then, though, when his mother went out and he was alone with Nangi, he clutched her hand and uttered, "If I only had my Bible. . . ."

The following year, four days before Ugi finally departed this world, the one he had longed so to see again arrived from Pyongyang. As soon as the American missionary was led into the yard by the village's Elder Yang he winced at the desolate scene and the fetid stench. "How on earth can Ugi live in such a place?" he wondered to himself.

Ugi's eyes lit up as soon as he saw the man. "Reverend Hyŏn! You're here!"

The missionary's face flushed crimson and his brow knitted against the tears that wanted to come. He took Ugi's emaciated hands in his own, closed his eyes, and said nothing for a while, trying desperately to control the emotions that were overwhelming him.

Elder Yang attempted to ease the strain. "Ah yes . . . yes now, Reverend Hyŏn, isn't it all thanks to this brave young man's distinguished service that the church in Kyŏngju was established so quickly!" He went on to review how Ugi had pleaded for a church in his letter to Reverend Hyŏn, how this letter got Reverend Hyŏn to approach the Taegu Presbyters Council and propose construction of a church, and how Ugi at the same time rallied the faithful in Kyŏngju to present a united appeal to the Council, with the result that construction had progressed faster than anyone could have hoped.

After a few whispered words with Ugi, Reverend Hyŏn got up, promising to come back with a doctor. Ugi asked him, "Reverend, please, get me a Bible."

"Of course, of course. But in the meanwhile you can use this one," and he pulled his own Bible out of his bag. Ugi took it and clasped it to his breast. His eyes closed and two tears formed, like drops of dew.

7

Just as in the past, ancient frogs and other creeping things prowled the entangled weeds in Mohwa's yard. Now that Ugi was gone the house was back to normal.

But Mohwa was not performing any rites in public now and spent all day every day banging away on her gongs and dancing with her spirits in her decaying, dilapidated house in the weeds, and people were saying she had gone mad. Her kitchen was now a perpetual ritual site, hung with five-colored streamers and Nangi's ritual paintings of the Mountain Spirit, Seven Stars Spirit, and many others. She had stopped eating, as if she had forgotten how, and her face turned sallower day by day even as the flame in her eyes burned hotter. And every day the spirits that possessed her ranted and raged to the furious beat of her gongs.

> Going, Jesus demon, 10,000 *li* back to the west.
> A ball of fire on your tail,

A bell on each ear, ding-a-ling-a-ling.
Shoo demon, off with you.
And if you don't go I'll wrap you and all your descendants
    in the hide of the White Horse Spirit,
throw you into an ash briar patch,
into a boiling cauldron,
into the blue sea fifty fathoms deep.
Shoo, demon! Shoo–o–o–o!

Once in a while a neighbor, remembering how much Mohwa used to enjoy drinking, dropped by with a jar of local brew. "How you can bear such a loss, that dear boy. . . ." To which Mohwa would only mumble, "Taken off by that Jesus demon . . . ," and put an end to the conversation with a long sigh.

Her neighbors mourned that she had completely lost her mind. "She was so good. Will we ever see her do another rite?"

Before long, though, word spread throughout the area: Mohwa was going to conduct one more rite, her last. The daughter-in-law of some rich gentry family in the county seat had thrown herself into the river, where the current had carved a deep pocket in its bed. Legend had it that the black fathomless depths of these slowly turning waters that locals called Yegi Pool took for themselves one person every year without fail, and deep in the bowels of this pool quietly stewed the sufferings and secrets of generations. The family wanted to send the tormented soul on to her rest, so they had pressed Mohwa with two silk outfits to use in conjuring up the soul, and she had consented to do just this one last service. At the same time, the rumor went, Mohwa was going to restore her own daughter's hearing.

"Hmph. Now we'll see who's for real—that Jesus demon or the spirits," she asserted.

The rite was to be held on the sandy beach near the pool where the young woman had drowned herself. The big night finally came, and the people turned up in droves, out of both curiosity and expectation. They came from over the mountains and across the river with a mixed sense of excitement and nostalgia.

The beach swarmed with taffy vendors, rice cake vendors, and drinking stalls and food stalls equipped with their awnings and their mats, and in the center of this was the big canopy where Mohwa would summon her spirits to help rescue the young woman's lost soul. Silk lanterns like green, red, yellow, blue, and white flowers had been strung all over the tent, and lined up under these lanterns was an array of offering tables, one for each spirit that would be called upon. There was the table for the Host Spirit, with its rice cake steamer, jar of wine, and carcass of a pig. There was a table for Chesŏk, guardian spirit of the drowned woman's family, with its bowl of uncooked rice, spool of thread, plate of tofu, and skewer of dried persimmons. There was a table for the Maitreya Buddha with apples, pears, and mandarin oranges, snowy white rice cake, cooked vegetables, vegetable soup, salted fish, and hard honey cakes. There was a table for the Mountain Spirit with twelve kinds of wild herbs, a table for the Dragon Spirit with twelve different seafoods, and a table for the Lanes Spirits with one dish for each of a variety of foods. There were a few more large and small offering tables, and a table for Mohwa, with just one bowl of plain water.

Tonight Mohwa's face was suffused with a dignified and serene countenance that had not been there before. People gabbed how, for a woman who was mourning her son as if he had died only the day before and was at the same time bearing every abuse and insult imaginable from these Christian interlopers, she had assumed quite an air of dignity. This was the face they knew from long ago, of that shaman ennobled by a few nights' vigil under the light of the moon. She did not gad about and fawn over everyone as she used to, nor did she make a big fuss about every detail; she only stood there quietly, waiting. At one time, surveying the sumptuous offering tables with contempt, she sniffed at her assistants, "Lowlifes, thinking a few offering tables is all you need."

When the women who gathered there saw this new Mohwa they started whispering that a new spirit possessed her.

"It's the spirit of that young lady," they grudged.

"Will you just look at that stoic composure, so demure—kind of prissy if you ask me—and when was Mohwa ever that pretty. That young woman's spirit has got into her all the way."

Others gossiped among themselves of how tonight Nangi would speak again, and still others debated the rumor that Nangi was with child, whoever the father was. And all of these women were eager to get answers tonight to all these questions buzzing about.

Mohwa's spirit began by recounting, in a more plaintive voice than anyone ever heard from her, all that had happened to Lady Kim from the day she was born till the day she drowned in Yegi Pool. Then the sorceress moved into a frenzied dance accompanied by the fiddle, flute, and bamboo oboe, and it was not too long before she lost herself to an ecstatic trance steeped in the anguish of the dead woman's soul. Her human body metamorphosed into pure rhythm, uninhibited by skin or bone, only a phantom of fluid motion. The blood of the mesmerized spectators pulsated in harmony with the folds of the shaman's mantle undulating in tempo with her racing blood. The stars turning in the heavens and the water flowing in the river paused in witness.

Yet, as the night wore on, the young woman's soul was not responding to Mohwa's invocation. Her male assistants and her apprentices had tied a rice bowl to the spirit line made from pieces of the young woman's clothes, thrown it into the pool, retrieved it a few times, but in the bowl they could not find the strands of hair that would announce the soul's recovery.

With an anxious look one of Mohwa's assistants whispered in Mohwa's ear, "We can't fetch her spirit. Now what?"

Mohwa showed no concern at all. As if she had expected this she calmly took up her spirit pole and walked to the edge of the pool. The male shaman with the spirit line maneuvered the rice bowl here and there in the water in the directions indicated by Mohwa's spirit pole. Mohwa called to the dead soul.

> Rise, rise up,
> thirty-year-old wife of Master Kim from Wŏlsŏng.

She stirred the water with the spirit pole and continued in a voice now husky with emotion.

> When you were born under that auspicious star,
> offerings were made to the Seven Stars Spirit.
> You came into existence like a flower blossom,
> and you were cared for like a precious gem.
> But then you jumped into these dark waters,
> deserting your parents, your infant child,
> so even the Dragon Spirit turned from you.
> When your skirt ballooned 'round you as you hit the
> water,
> what on earth were you thinking?
> That you were mounting a lotus blossom?
> That you would float on to eternal life?
> Oh no, you're just a water demon,
> hair let down like a scraggle of hemp.

Mohwa followed the spirit pole a little deeper and then a little deeper into the river. The turning water took one fold of her mantle and twisted it round her, left the other bobbing on the surface. The dark waters covered her waist, covered her breasts, rose higher, and higher . . .

> Going, I'm going now,
> a farewell cup of white dewdrop wine and I'm gone.
> Young lady, gone before me, call me to you.

Her voice began to fade and her thoughts seemed to stray.

> Nangi, my daughter, dressed in your mourning white,
> when it's spring on the river's bank and the peach
>   blossoms bloom
> come and ask after me.
> Ask the first branch how I am,
> ask the second. . . .

And that was the last anyone could make out, because the pool took Mohwa, along with her song, to itself.

Her mantle floated on the surface for a while, but soon that was gone too. Only the spirit pole floated there, turned a while, then flowed on with the river.

Ten days after Yegi Pool took Mohwa, a small man said to be running a seafood shop in a back lane in a town on the east coast came up to the old goblin house, riding a donkey. Inside he found Nangi lying in bed, eyes sunken in her ghost-pallid face, still suffering the agonies of the shaman initiate.

The little man made her some rice gruel. It was not until she had eaten a spoonful that she fully recognized him, and uttered, "Fa . . . Father . . . ?" Whether Mohwa had actually given the girl her speech back, as the rumor had prophesied, this was the first time in years that anyone heard the girl speak anything that could be understood.

Ten more days passed. Out in the yard the little man pointed to his donkey. "Up you go now." Nangi silently did as her father bade her.

After the man and his daughter left the house, no one came there again. And now, at night, in that jungle of weeds, those swarming mosquitoes are the only sign of life.

Translated by John Holstein

5. KIM YUJŎNG

Kim Yujŏng was born in 1908; it remains uncertain whether his place of birth was Ch'unch'ŏn or Seoul. He studied at what is now Yonsei University in Seoul. He left us with some thirty stories, most of them published in 1935 and 1936, and perhaps a dozen personal essays. The playfulness of some of the stories masks a profound sorrow: at an early age Kim lost his parents and then contracted tuberculosis. He died in 1937.

Many of Kim's works have rural settings and are characterized by wit and irony. "Anhae" (1935, trans. 1998 "Wife") is an inspired, uninhibited monologue, rife with scenes of domestic violence, narrated by an unlettered, sexist woodcutter who is not afraid to poke fun at himself. In bringing alive the character of his wife as well as himself, and in evoking familiar Korean ballads, this man gives us a taste of the *kwangdae*, the narrator of the traditional oral narrative *p'ansori*. There is little else like this story in modern Korean fiction. In stories such as "Tongbaek kkot" (1936, The camellias), Kim writes with affection of Korean farming villages and the foibles of their denizens. Other works are more serious. The budding sexuality implicit in "Tongbaek kkot" is more overt in "Sonakpi" (1935, Rain shower). Later stories, such as "Ttaengbyŏt" (1937, trans. 1994 "The Scorching Heat"), are gloomy in the extreme. Whatever the tone, the writing is rich and earthy, for Kim had an excellent command of native Korean vocabulary.

THE WHITE RABBIT

Night and day I had that rabbit on my mind: I wanted it to grow to maturity as quickly as possible so it could start making babies, but how could I do it?

This rabbit was a treasure delivered to me from God.

One fiercely cold morning I was still wrapped in my warm cocoon of sleep when I felt Mother shaking my arm to wake me up. Even those times when I knew I was oversleeping, I got annoyed when someone tried to wake me, and I poked her with my elbow. I was about to tell her to leave me alone when I heard her say, "You don't want this rabbit?" as if to say all right then, we'll forget about it.

Still half asleep, I wondered if Father had been craving the taste of meat, long denied us, and so had bought a rabbit to eat. If so, I thought, then Mother must want to feed me some. I turned sleepily and opened my eyes, and lo and behold, there bundled up in my mother's skirt was a rabbit the size of a fist, white as jade.

Flustered, I rubbed my eyes and sat up.

"Where did you get it?"

"Cute little thing, isn't it?"

"I'll say. But tell me where you got it."

"When I went out to rinse the morning rice I saw it curled up on top of our cooking stove. Probably belonged to someone else and got away."

Mother rubbed her hands over the brazier, beaming with happiness. Ever since we moved here to Shindang-ni, we had had nothing but suffering. But the rabbit had come to *us* among the four families living in the house—perhaps this was a sign that with the new year our luck would change. Mother let out a deep, sad sigh. For my own part, I felt entitled to a private hope. Maybe this cute, white rabbit, passing others by to find me, was a sign that I could be happy. I took the white rabbit from my mom's skirt, held it to my lips, rubbed it against my cheeks, and pressed it against my chin.

It was really cute, a beautiful animal. Taking no time for breakfast, I was about to walk out the door when Mother grabbed my arm.

"You're not planning to give it to Sugi, are you? You're not supposed to give away good fortune that has come to your home. Give it to me."

I stumbled out the door, ignoring her attempts to stop me. I cut through the back alley to where Sugi's family lived and discreetly called her outside (whenever we met, the two of us stood outside trembling because we were scared of her parents; of course we were not allowed inside).

"Here, I want you to take good care of this rabbit."

So saying, I produced the little cutie from inside my coat and handed it to her.

Just as I had expected, Sugi's narrow eyes rounded large in amazement. She scooped it up, and the next thing you know she was kissing it and rubbing it against her cheeks just as I had. But she was pressing it too hard to her chest.

"No, no, no, you're going to crush it if you do that. You're supposed to hold a rabbit by its ears, like this."

I couldn't leave without first teaching her the proper way to handle a rabbit. As I watched Sugi standing there, holding the rabbit by its ears like I showed her, I thought how wonderful it would be if this were my house and Sugi were my wife. Sugi had asked me to buy her some women's socks. It had been a month since I said I would, and the thought of not being able to do even that for her made me feel pathetic.

"When this little guy gets big, we'll find it a mate and get lots of babies. Then we can sell them and the money will start rolling in," she said.

But when I held up the rabbit I couldn't tell whether it was a boy or a girl. This worried me a bit.

"We have to know what it is before we can find it a mate!" I complained.

"Oh, yeah." Sugi blushed a little, but then covering her embarrassment with a smile, she ventured, "We'll know once it grows up!"

"Sure! Take good care of it now."

From then on, I went to check on the rabbit every day. And I was delighted to hear that every day it seemed to have grown.

"Is it still eating well?" I would ask.

"Yes," Sugi answered proudly. "I was feeding it leftover radish soup, but today I gave it some cabbage and it ate it all up!"

I thought that as long as it didn't get sick and just ate well, everything would be all right.

Sure enough, Sugi soon reported, "Now it's running around and even going outside to poo."

And then one day a look in those big black eyes told me that finally the rabbit was fully grown. Now we'll have to find it a mate, I thought. As I returned home I agonized about not having any money. No matter how I mulled it over, I could think of no way to come up with the dough. Should I pawn my coat? Then what would I wear? As I vacillated among my few options, almost a week passed without my visiting the rabbit. And then one day at dinner, I was shocked to hear my mother complain furiously,

"Kŭmch'ŏl's mom said that Sugi ate that rabbit!"

The reason my mother was so upset was because of the time I had nagged her to set up a marriage between myself and Sugi; I had been rejected. Her family had insisted that she was still too young, but in fact they were scheming to marry her off to a family with money. Mother was aware of all this and hated them for it.

"I knew it! How would the likes of them know how to treat such a cute animal?"

"They ate the rabbit?!"

Furious, I ran out. Try as I might, I just couldn't understand this. Sugi had made a rainbow-striped vest for that rabbit with her own hands. There was no way she could have eaten it.

But when I called Sugi outside and asked her to bring me the rabbit, she didn't respond. Her face got redder and redder, and as I looked at her I realized that the rabbit had indeed been eaten. And if that was the case, it was easy to see that the little tease of a girl must have had a change of heart about herself and me. Unless she had forgotten our mutual pledge to live together some day, she would never have allowed the rabbit that I valued so much to be killed and eaten.

I glared at her with big, round bunny eyes.

"I've come for my rabbit. I want it back."

Sugi was almost in tears. "It's gone." She lowered her head. "My dad did it—he didn't tell me." She seemed awfully ashamed of herself.

In fact, Sugi had been sick and hadn't been able to eat for three or four days. Sugi was a wage earner for her family, working at the tobacco factory. Her father had grown desperate when he realized that she was ill and not taking food. The family was in no position to buy meat to strengthen her, and so without her knowing, her father had slaughtered the rabbit and fed it to her.

But I didn't know this at the time. Instead I hated Sugi as she stood there silently—was she so hungry that she had to eat my rabbit?

"Bring out the rabbit. I'm taking it back," I told her again.

"I can't—I ate it," she finally confessed.

Tears filled her eyes and began streaming down her face. And then she fumbled inside her skirt, held out the purse I had given her when we secretly got engaged (I hadn't had the money to buy her a gold ring, but I had to get her *something*, and so I bought the purse at a night market for 15 *chŏn*), and offered it to me, turning her head away as if she didn't care.

Wretched girl. Go on—eat my white rabbit and pout like that. What do you expect me to do? But I knew that I would look ridiculous if I carried on like that. I hastily lifted up Sugi's blouse and stuck the purse back in her skirt and then hurried home, afraid she might chase after me. She had eaten my white rabbit, and now, even if her father objected and even if she'd lost interest—sooner or later she would have no choice but to become my wife!

Lying under the covers considering all this, I finally realized what a godsend that rabbit had been.

No doubt about it—you belong to me now!

Translated by Sena Byun

6. YI SANG

Yi Sang was born Kim Haegyŏng in Seoul in 1910 and was trained as an architect. During his short literary career he showed an interest first in poetry, turning out highly idiosyncratic and experimental pieces in both Japanese and Korean that also use mathematical notation, especially the "Ogamdo" (1934, trans. 1995 "Crow's-Eye Views") series, and then in fiction. In the fall of 1936 he journeyed to Tokyo, where he soon ran afoul of the authorities and was imprisoned. He died of tuberculosis in a Tokyo hospital in 1937.

Yi Sang was a writer far ahead of his time. While his debt to Western and Japanese modernism is evident, scholars have also investigated the influence of traditional Korean literature on his work. Since the 1970s his critical reputation has soared. (For an excellent portfolio on this gifted artist, including some of his drawings, translations of his poetry, fiction, and essays, and literary criticism on his work, see the 1995 issue of *Muae* [New York].) Critical writing on Yi Sang has proliferated in recent years, and in 2001 an annual journal devoted to his work was established.

Several of Yi Sang's stories feature an antic, self-deprecating narrator, interior monologues, and staccato narration. "Hwanshigi" (1938, trans. 1998 "Phantom Illusion") is a good example. "Nalgae," the story translated here, was first published in 1936 in *Chogwang* and is his most widely read work. Whether it is read as an allegory of colonial oppression, an existential withdrawal from the absurdities of contemporary life, an extended suicide note, or the degradation of a kept man, it is strikingly imaginative.

WINGS

Have you heard about "the genius who ended up a stuffed specimen"? I'm cheerful. At moments like this, even love is cheerful.

Only when the body crumples in exhaustion is its mind bright as a silver coin. Whenever *nicotine* sinks into the worm-ridden coil of my intestines, a clean sheet of paper is ready in my head. On it I line up *wit* and *paradox* like paduk stones.[1] Sick with despicable common sense.

Once more I draw up plans for life with a woman. One who's become clumsy at lovemaking, who's peeked at the peak of knowledge, that is, a kind of schizophrenic. To be in receipt of just half—which would be half of everything—of such a woman, that's the life for which I'm drawing up plans. I'll dip but one foot in that life and like two suns we'll stare away at each other, giggling and giggling. Maybe everything in life was so bland I couldn't put up with it anymore and just quit. *Goodbye.*

Goodbye. It might be good for you now and then to experience the irony of devouring the dishes you dislike most. *Wit* and *paradox* and . . .

To devise a counterfeit of yourself would also be worthwhile. Depending on ready-mades never seen before, your artifice will be all the more nifty and lofty.

The 19th century—block it off, if you can. Dostoyevsky's vaunted mind is about to go to waste, it seems. Calling Hugo a chunk of French bread, who said that?—I think it a well-made remark. But why be tricked or worse by life's *details*, or even its model's? Don't suffer misfortune. Please, since I'm trying to inform you . . .

(When the *tape* tears blood appears. I believe the wound will heal soon. *Goodbye*.)

1. *Paduk*: A board game better known in the West as Japanese *go*.

Emotion—a certain *pose*. (Whether I'm only pointing out an element of that *pose*, I wouldn't know.) When the *pose* advances to attention, emotion immediately cuts off its supply.

After looking back upon my unusual development, I established my views on life.

A queen bee and a widow—among the truly many women in this world, is there one who is not essentially a widow? No! Does my theory that every woman in her daily life is a "widow" somehow insult the entire sex? *Goodbye.*[2]

Now, about "No. 33"—one gets the feeling that its layout resembles that of a brothel. Eighteen households are lined up shoulder to shoulder at that one address, their sliding doors exactly the same, the shape of their fireboxes the same. And all the people in those households are young like blossoming flowers. The sun never comes in. Because they pretend it doesn't. They hang a wire across their sliding doors and drape stained bedding over it to dry, a convenient excuse for blocking out the sunlight. They nap inside these dark rooms. Do they sleep at night? I wouldn't know. I have no way of knowing since, day or night, I'm always asleep. The days of the eighteen households at No. 33 are ever so quiet.

But only during the day. When dusk falls, they gather in their quilted bedding. Then the lights go on and the eighteen households begin to shimmer. As the evening deepens, there is the constant clatter of sliding doors. Things get busy. Various smells emerge. Grilled herring, dark *Tango* foundation, rice rinsings, soap . . .

But it is the households' name plaques that really make one nod. Though there is a so-called front gate for the eighteen households, it stands in a remote corner of the compound. It might as well be a walkway since it is never shut and allows all sorts of peddlers to enter or leave any hour of the day. Indeed, the residents don't come out to the gate to get their bean curd: they just slide their doors open and buy it right in their rooms. So it's meaningless for the eighteen households of No. 33 to bunch their name plaques together at this gate. They've developed the habit of posting them above their sliding doors instead, next to signs like "The Hall of Eternal Patience" or "The Hall of Many Blessings."

2. Here ends the part of the text that, in its original version published in *Chogwang*, is surrounded by a rectangular rule indicating that it is a separate note or letter.

The affixing above our sliding door of my—no! my *wife's* name card, one-quarter the size of a playing card, must be seen as following this custom as well.

But I don't mix with any of the people here. In fact, I don't even say hello. I have no desire to greet anyone except my wife.

The reason? It occurred to me that by exchanging greetings or associating with anyone but my wife, I may hurt her reputation. That's how dear she is to me.

As for why my wife is so dear to me, it's because I know that she is the daintiest, most beautiful woman in the eighteen households of No. 33, just like her name card. A flower blooms in each of the eighteen households, but she is a particularly beautiful one who brightens every corner of this sunless, tin-roofed lot. And so I guard that one blossom—No, "I" survive by clinging to it, leading an existence that was nothing if not indescribably awkward.

Every part of my room—Not a house. There is no house.—pleases me. The room's temperature suits my body's and its degree of dimness is agreeable to my eyesight. I never hoped for a room cooler or warmer than mine. Nor have I wished for one that is brighter or cozier. I have always been grateful to my room, which seems to constantly maintain these conditions for me alone, and I am delighted that it may be for the sake of this room alone that I was born into the world.

Not that I was calculating whether I was happy or unhappy. That is, I had no reason to think of myself as happy, but then again, I had no reason to think of myself as unhappy. Everything was okay as long as I wasted each day in utter idleness.

To lounge around in a room that hugs my body and mind like comfortable clothes, free of such worldly calculations as happiness or unhappiness, is an absolute convenience and ease. One might even say it is the ideal state. I liked being in such a state.

Counting from the main gate, this ideal room of mine is precisely—the seventh. This is not unrelated, of course, to the *Lucky Seven*. I have cherished this number like a medal. A room partitioned into two by a sliding door: who would have known it was a symbol of my fate?

The outer room does get some sun. In the morning a patch of sunlight the size of a square wrapping cloth enters; it leaves in the afternoon small as a handkerchief. Mine, of course, is the inner room, the ever sunless half. The sunny room my wife's, the sunless room mine—I cannot recall who decided it, she or I. But I have no complaint.

The moment my wife goes out, I steal into the outer room and lift up the east-facing window. When I do, the sun streams in and shines upon her makeup stand, speckling the array of colored vials and making them glow; to view this is my favorite amusement. I take out a tiny magnifying glass and play with fire, scorching the sheets of *chirigami*[3] that only my wife uses. I refract the sun's parallel rays and gather them at a focal point until it heats up, singeing the paper and giving off wisps of smoke. It's only a matter of seconds before a hole appears in the burning paper, but the suspense is so pleasurable that it almost kills me.

When I get tired of this game I take out my wife's hand mirror and play with it in various ways. A mirror is of practical use only when it reflects one's face. At all other times it is nothing but a toy.

Pretty soon I get tired of this game, too. My playful spirit leaps from the physical to the psychological. Tossing the mirror aside, I draw close to my wife's makeup stand and gaze at the assortment of cosmetic vials lined up in a row there. The vials are more captivating than anything else in the world. Selecting just one, I gently remove its stopper, bring it to my nose, and inhale lightly, almost holding my breath. When the exotically *sensual* fragrance pervades my lungs, I feel the soft, autonomic shutting of my eyes. The perfume is definitely a fragment of my wife's scent. I replace the stopper and think for a moment. Which part of my wife's body gave off this smell? . . . It's not at all clear. Why? Her scent is most likely the sum of all the different fragrances arrayed here.

My wife's room has always been lavish. In contrast to the simplicity of my room, where not a single nail protrudes from the walls, there are hooks all around her room just below the ceiling, gorgeous skirts or blouses hung on each one. The varied patterns are pleasing to the eye. From snatches of her skirts I conjure again and again the whole of my wife's body and the various *poses* it can strike, and then my heart always misbehaves.

Yet for all that, what clothes do I have? My wife has not given me any. The single corduroy suit I wear has served as my pajamas, casual clothes, and dress suit all combined. And regardless of the season a single *high-neck sweater* serves as my undershirt. They are all black. I suspect that it is so my clothes won't look too disgusting even if they are washed as seldom as possi-

3. Japanese word for facial or cosmetic tissue.

ble. Wearing soft long trunks with elastic bands around the waist and both thighs, I play without making a peep.

By and by, the handkerchief-sized sunlight departs, but my wife does not return from her outing. A bit drained by these trifles and thinking that I should leave my wife's room before she returns, I go back to my room. My room is dim. I pull the quilt over my head and take a nap. My never-folded bedding welcomes me back almost as if it were part of my body. I sleep well, sometimes. But when my whole body feels so ragged, it is impossible to sleep. At times like this I pick a topic to investigate, any topic. Inside my clammy bedding I have invented such a variety of things and penned many a treatise. I also knocked out a decent number of poems. But these, like detergent, dissolve without a trace in the sluggish air that overflows my room the moment I fall asleep. When I wake up I am nothing but a suit of nerves again, like a pillow stuffed full of buckwheat husks or cotton scraps.

And so there's nothing I hate more than bedbugs. Even in winter, bedbugs keep showing up in my room, a handful each time. The one worry I have, if I have any at all, concerns these hated bedbugs. I scratch the itching bites until they bleed. They sting. No mistaking the profoundly pleasant tingle. I fall into a deep slumber.

Even within this tucked-in life of contemplation, I never pursued anything constructive. There was just no need to. If I were to come up with a constructive idea I would definitely have to consult with my wife, and if I consulted with her I would definitely get scolded, a prospect more annoying than frightening. Rather than try working as a fairly competent member of society or listen to my wife's lectures, I enjoyed being lazy, like the most slothful animal. If only it were possible, I would have gladly thrown off this meaningless human mask.

I felt estranged from human society. I felt estranged from life. Everything simply discomfited me.

My wife washes her face twice a day. I don't wash mine even once. At around 3 or 4 at night, I usually go to the outhouse. On clear moonlit nights I might stand listlessly in the yard for a while before coming back in. So I almost never come across anyone from the eighteen households, but nonetheless recall the faces of most of their young ladies. None of them can equal my wife.

The first time my wife washes her face, at around 11 a.m., she does it rather perfunctorily. But the second time, around 7 in the evening, she devotes much more care to it. At night my wife slips on nicer, neater clothes than what she wears during the day. She goes out during the day and also at night.

Has my wife been holding down a job? I have no idea what it is. If she were like me and did not have a job, then she wouldn't need to go out—but she does. Not only does she go out, she also has many visitors. When my wife has visitors, I have to lie in my room all day under the quilt. No playing with fire. No sniffing at cosmetics. On days like this I make a point of moping around. Then my wife gives me money. A 50-*chŏn* silver coin. I liked that. Since I didn't know what to use it for, I would always toss it down by my pillow and soon enough there was quite a heap. Spotting this one day, my wife bought me a coin bank in the shape of a safe. After I dropped all the coins in one by one, she took away the key. I think I continued to put silver coins in the bank once in a while even after that. What's more, I was lazy. Could the fact that a fancy new ornament popped up from her hairdo like a pimple not long thereafter mean that the coin bank has become lighter? In the end I did not pick up the coin bank by my head. I was too lazy to even want to pay attention to such things.

On days that my wife had guests, I couldn't doze off like I did on rainy days, no matter how deeply I burrowed into my blankets. At such times I investigated why my wife always has money, why she has so much of it.

My wife's guests don't seem to know that I'm on the other side of the paper door. They don't hesitate to indulge with her in the kinds of games that even I would find difficult to attempt. However, one could see that a few of her visitors were relatively well mannered; on the whole, they didn't stay much past midnight. But there were others of very shallow cultivation, the type who usually ordered food. Replenished by the food, they continued to enjoy themselves, generally without incident.

I first set myself to the task of investigating the nature of my wife's vocation, but this was hard to accomplish from my limited vantage point and knowledge. In the end, I may never find out what her vocation is.

My wife always wears brand-new socks. She also cooks. I've never seen her cook but she delivers meals to my room every morning and evening. Since there is no one else besides me and my wife in our home, it is clear that she is the one who prepares these meals.

But my wife has never called me over to her room. I always ate and slept alone in the inner room. The food was terrible, the side dishes skimpy. Like a chicken or puppy dog, I silently gulped down what she gave me, although not always without resentment. I grew completely pale and began to waste away. My strength dwindled visibly with each passing day. Due to lack of nourishment, my bones began to stick out all over. They ached so much that I had to change position dozens of times each night.

Hence, wrapped up in my blankets, I investigated the provenance of all that money my wife has at her disposal and the kinds of dishes served in the outer room, basing my research on what escaped through the space between the door's sliding panels. I could not sleep.

Suddenly I understood. Understood that the money my wife uses must have been left her by those puzzling visitors, who I had thought were utter buffoons. But why they would leave her money and why my wife would accept it were notions of Civility completely unfathomable to me.

Is it nothing more than mere Manners? Perhaps some type of payment? The fee for a service? Or did they look upon my wife as a pathetic character in need of pity?

Whenever I try to think about these matters, my mind just ends up more and more muddled. The only conclusion that I ever manage to reach before falling asleep is that the entire subject is absolutely aggravating, but I never ask my wife about it. I leave everything alone, not only because I don't want the bother, but also because I'm like a new man who has clean forgotten about it all by the time I wake up.

When the guests leave or when my wife returns from one of her trips out, she changes into something lighter and visits me in my room. She lifts up the quilt and tries to comfort me by offering my ear a few of her always-rejuvenating phrases. With a smile that is neither sneering nor bitter nor callous, I gaze at my wife's beautiful face. She beams a smile back at me. But the trace of sadness that strays across her face does not escape my notice.

My wife should be able to see that I am hungry. Still, she never gives me leftovers from the outer room. No doubt this is out of her deep respect for me. Though famished, I did enjoy the feeling of security this thought gave me. No matter what my wife chattered about, nothing lingered in my ear. There were only the silver coins that she left by my head, faintly glimmering in the lamplight.

How many coins could there be in the bank? I wondered. But I did not try weighing it in my hands. All I did was continue to slip coins through the buttonhole-shaped slit, wishing for nothing, praying for nothing.

Why my wife leaves me money is as unsolvable a mystery to me as why guests leave her money. Even though I did not exactly dislike the fact that she left me money, the only happiness it afforded me was the slight, fleeting sensation that lasted from the moment my fingers touched a coin until it vanished into the bank's slit.

One day, I took the bank and threw it in the latrine. I didn't know exactly how many coins were in it at the time, but there were definitely a lot.

Thinking of the earth rushing at lightning speed through vast and infinite space, and of my existence on it, I had been overcome by a sense of futility. I wanted to jump off as soon as possible, before the industrious earth had time to give me vertigo.

After all these musings inside my bedding, even dropping coins into the bank had become a chore. I began to wish that my wife would use the bank herself. I waited for her to take it to her own room; after all, she was the one who needed the bank and money, which had been utterly meaningless to me from the start. But my wife didn't take it. I thought about taking it to her room myself, but she had so many visitors these days that the opportunity did not present itself. I had no choice but to toss it into the latrine.

With a sad and heavy heart I awaited my wife's scolding. But she never questioned me or said anything about it. What's more, she went on dropping coins by my head! Pretty soon, there was another heap of silver.

Was there nothing else that motivated the movement of money from the guests to my wife and from my wife to me—besides "pleasure"? I resumed my research from inside my bedding. If it is pleasure, then what sort of pleasure? I continued to probe. But there was no way to answer these questions by means of under-cover investigations. Pleasure, pleasure . . . To my own surprise, it was the only topic in which I felt any interest.

My wife, of course, has always kept me in near-captivity. I have no basis for complaining. Nonetheless, I wanted to experience the presence and absence of this thing called pleasure.

During one of my wife's evening outings, I snuck outside. Once out, I exchanged the silver coins, which I had made sure to bring with me, for paper bills. It amounted to a whole 5 *wŏn*. I put the money in my pocket and wandered around and around just to forget what I was after. Being back on the streets after so long could not help but excite my nerves to an astonishing degree. Soon I was tired. Still, I persisted. As the night wore on, I drifted aimlessly through street after street, forgetting my objective. As for the money, of course, I did not spend a single *chŏn*. I didn't even dare to entertain the thought. It appeared that I had already lost any capacity for spending money.

The fatigue became almost impossible to endure. I barely managed to find my way home. When I cleared my throat with an embarrassed cough outside the sliding door, worried that my wife might be with a guest but knowing that I couldn't get to my room without passing through hers, the door banged open and the faces of my wife and an unfamiliar man looked out at me. I faltered a bit, blinded by the sudden outpouring of light.

It wasn't that I didn't see my wife glaring at me. I simply had no choice but to ignore it. Why? I had to go through her room. . . .

I pulled the quilt over my head. The most unbearable thing was the pain in my legs. Under the quilt, my chest was throbbing and I thought I would faint for sure. I hadn't noticed it while walking around, but I was panting severely. Cold sweat drenched my back. I regretted going out. How nice it would be to forget my tiredness and immediately drift off to sleep. I wanted to sleep, soundly and for a long time.

I lay there on my stomach for a while and the pounding clamor in my chest slowly subsided. This modicum of relief made me feel as though I could live again. Turning myself over, I looked squarely up at the ceiling and gave my legs a long stretch.

It was inevitable, however, that the pounding in my chest would return. Through cracks in the sliding door, I caught snatches of hushed, barely audible conversation in the outer room between the man and my wife. In order to sharpen my hearing I opened my eyes. And held my breath. By then they had already gotten up and straightened out their clothes, and I thought I heard him donning his hat and coat as he got up. Then there was the sound of the door sliding open, his shoes being set out, and a thud as he stepped down into the yard, and after that the sound of my wife following him in rubber slippers that first squeaked, then glided along, as their footsteps disappeared toward the front gate.

I had never seen my wife act like this. My wife never whispers to anyone. Cocooned in my quilt in the inner room, I may have sometimes failed to catch the drunken disquisitions of tongue-twisted guests, but never have I missed a single word spoken in my wife's measured voice, which is neither loud nor weak. Even when her words should have offended me, the simple fact that they were delivered in her calm, unperturbed voice was always enough to reassure me.

The thought that there must be some unusual reason behind this change in my wife's attitude distressed me, but I was so tired that I resolved not to do anymore under-cover research this evening. I waited, but sleep did not come right away. Neither did my wife, who had gone out to the front gate. When I did finally drift off, it was into a fitful sleep. Through a baffling maze of street scenes, my dream continued to wander.

I was violently shaken awake. My wife, back from sending off her guest, had latched onto me and was shaking me. My eyes popped open and I stared into her face. There was no smile on it. I rubbed my eyes a little and examined it more closely. Anger flashed in the corners of her eyes and her delicate lips were trembling. I could tell that it was the kind of anger that would not easily subside. I just shut my eyes, waiting for a bolt of lightning to strike. Instead I heard the crisp swish of my wife's skirt as she took a few vexed breaths, and then the door sliding open and shut as she returned to her room. I turned over again, pulled the quilt over my head, and crouched there like a frog; even in my hungry state, I regretted the night's outing once again.

Under the blanket, I begged my wife's forgiveness. I said: There's been a misunderstanding. . . .

I was under the impression that it was really late. I swear to you it didn't even occur to me that it was still before midnight. I was exhausted. I shouldn't have walked around like that after being inside for so long. That was the only mistake I made, if I've made any at all. Are you asking me, Why did I go out in the first place?

I wanted to see what it would feel like to take the 5 *wŏn* that had materialized by my head and give it away to someone, to anyone. That's all. But if you say that was also my mistake, so be it. Don't you see how sorry I am?

Had I been capable of spending the 5 *wŏn*, I would not have returned home before midnight. But the streets were too chaotic and there were too many people swarming about. Who could I grab and give the 5 *wŏn* to? I hadn't a clue. All I managed to do was exhaust myself in the process.

Most of all I wanted to rest. I wanted to lie down. That is why I had no choice but to come home. It was truly unfortunate that I miscalculated the hour and returned before midnight. I feel terrible about it. I will apologize as many times as I have to. But what good are my apologies if in the end they can't make my wife see how she's misunderstood me? How exasperating it all was.

After fretting away a whole hour like this, I finally kicked off the covers, stood up, opened the sliding door, and careened into my wife's room. I had almost no consciousness to speak of. The only thing I can remember is grabbing the 5 *wŏn* out of my trouser pocket and thrusting it into her hand as I tumbled face-down onto my wife's bedding.

The next morning when I woke up, I was in my wife's room, in her bedding. For the very first time since taking up residence at No. 33 I had slept in her room.

The sun was high up in the window and my wife was no longer by my side, having gone out early. Then again, had she? Maybe she went out last night after I lost consciousness. But I did not want to investigate such matters. My whole body felt so ragged that I did not have the strength to lift a finger. A patch of sunlight, smaller than the size of a wrapping cloth, dazzled my eyes. In it, countless dust particles danced riotously like microbes. My nose suddenly felt all congested. Closing my eyes again, I buried myself under the quilt and set to work on taking a nap. But the provocative scent of my wife kept teasing my nose. Twisting and writhing, retracing my memory of the vials arrayed on her cosmetics stand and the suffusion of fragrances once they're opened, I waited helplessly for sleep that would not come.

Reaching the end of my endurance, I kicked the covers off, sprang to my feet, and returned to my room. My cold meal, the feed my wife left me before going out, was laid out neatly there. I was famished. But when I scooped a spoonful into my mouth, it felt chill like cold ashes! I put the spoon down and went back under my quilt. Even though I had deserted it for a night, my bedding welcomed me all the same. I pulled the covers over my head and this time slept a long, deep sleep. Good—.

When I wake up, the lights are already on, but it seems that my wife hasn't returned yet. No, maybe she did return, but went back out again. How would I know? What use is mulling over such things again and again?

My mind is much clearer now. I try thinking about last night's events. I cannot explain the pleasure I felt when I fell over and put the 5 *wŏn* in my wife's hand. It thrills me like nothing ever has before that I may have discovered the secret psychology behind the guests leaving my wife money and my wife leaving me money. I grin happily to myself. What a clown I was not to have known about such matters until now. My shoulders rise and fall in a dance.

And so I wanted to go out tonight as well. But I have no money. I regretted giving my wife the 5 *wŏn* last night all at one time. I also regretted dumping the coin bank into the latrine. In senseless disappointment, I put my hand in my pants pocket where the 5 *wŏn* had been and fished around from sheer habit. To my surprise, something came into my hand. Though it was only 2 *wŏn*, the amount didn't matter, just as long as there was something. I felt so grateful for so little.

I took heart. I put on my only suit and, forgetting my hunger and shabby appearance, set out for the streets again, swinging my arms. As I walked on, I anxiously prayed that the swift arrow of time would quickly overtake midnight. Giving my wife money for the privilege of sleeping in her room was all fine and good, but how terrifying it would be to return home too early by mistake and be subjected to her glare. As the day waned, I wandered the streets aimlessly, looking at every clock that I passed. But today I wasn't tired. I only felt impatient with the dawdling pace of the hours.

I headed home after making sure that it was past midnight on the Kyŏngsŏng railway station clock.[4] This time I encountered my wife and her man talking together by the front gate. Pretending not to notice, I slipped past the pair and entered my room. My wife followed me in. She then did something she had never done before: sweep the room in the middle of the night. When I heard her lie down a short while later, I slid the door open again, went into her room, and thrust the 2 *wŏn* into her hand. She darted several glances at me as if it were truly strange that I had once again returned home without spending money, but let me sleep in her room without protest. I didn't want to exchange this joy for anything else in the world. I slept very comfortably.

The following morning as well, when I awoke my wife was nowhere to be seen. I returned to my room and laid my tired body down for a snooze.

When my wife shook me awake, it was once again after the lights had come on. She beckoned me to her room. This kind of thing had never happened before. With a smile fixed on her face, my wife was leading me by the arm. Naturally, I grew uneasy, suspicious that a major conspiracy was lurking behind her smile.

Yielding to her wishes, I allowed myself to be dragged into her room. A humble dinner was waiting for us there. It suddenly struck me that I hadn't eaten for two days. Just a few moments ago, I had been lolling about, not even sure if I felt hungry.

It was clear to me now. Even if a bolt of lightning were to strike me the moment I finished this Last Supper, I would have no regrets. Human society is so uninteresting that I couldn't have stood it much longer anyway. Everything is a nuisance, but sudden calamity is a joy!

My mind thus at ease, I sat across from my wife and shared the bizarre dinner. The two of us didn't chat. We never do. After finishing the meal, I just got up and went over to my room without saying a word. My wife did not detain me. Back in my room, I waited, leaning against the wall with a cigarette dangling between my lips, thinking to myself all the while that if lightning is going to strike, let it strike now!

Five minutes! Ten minutes!—

4. Also known as "Seoul Station." "Kyŏngsŏng" is the Korean pronunciation of "Keijō," the Japanese name for Seoul.

There was no bolt of lightning. Little by little, the tension began to slacken. Before I knew it, I was thinking about going out again and wishing I had some money.

But I definitely do not have any money. Even if I were to go out today, what happiness would I find when I return? I was completely at a loss. In a fit of rage, I pulled the covers over my head and rolled from side to side. The meal I'd just eaten kept surging back up my throat. I felt nauseous.

Why can't money, any amount would be fine, suddenly pour out of the sky? It was so cruel and sad. I knew of no other way to obtain money. I think I wept a while under my quilt, wondering why I have no money. . . .

Thereupon, my wife came into the room again. Startled, I held my breath and squatted down like a toad, afraid that the lightning might finally strike now. But the words that trickled out from between her parted lips were gentle. And affectionate. She said that she understood why I was weeping. Isn't it because you have no money? she asked. The question left me dumbstruck; I was amazed that she could peer so clearly into my heart. It even spooked me a little. At the same time, I felt cheered by the thought that she might be planning to give me money; why would she say these things otherwise? Rolled up in a blanket, not even daring to lift my head, I waited for my wife's next move. Presently, she said, "Here"—and dropped something near my head that had to be a paper bill, judging by the light fluttering sound it made. She then whispered in my ear that today I could come home even later than I did yesterday. That won't be difficult, I thought. I was glad and thankful for the money.

In any case, I set out. Since I am somewhat night-blind, I decided to keep, as much as possible, to well-lit streets. I came to Kyŏngsŏng railway station and dropped in at the *tearoom* in a corner of the first- and second-class waiting hall. The *tearoom* was a big discovery for me. First of all, no one I know ever came here. And even if they did, they would soon be on their way. I made a mental note to pass time here every day.

I also liked the fact that the station clock is probably more accurate than any other clock. I mustn't run into trouble by relying on just any old timepiece and returning home too early.

Sitting in a booth across from no one at all, I sip hot *coffee*. Even in their mad scramble, travelers still seemed to relish their cup of *coffee*. Quickly emptying their cups, they stare a moment at the wall as though pondering something before taking off. There's something sad about it all. I found this air of sadness to be more real and appealing than the irksome atmosphere of *tearooms* outside in the city. The occasional whistle of a train, shrieking one moment, roaring the next, was closer to my heart than even the music of Mozart. I read many times over, backward and forward, the names of the few dishes scrawled on the menu. They became jumbled and vague, like the names of my childhood friends.

I don't know how long I sat there, my mind drifting off, but I noticed that the customers had quietly dwindled in the meantime and cleaning up had commenced around the room. I guessed that the shop must be closing. But it's only a little past eleven! There's no refuge here after all! Where should I go until midnight? I left the place, beset with all these worries. It was raining outside. I had no raincoat, no umbrella, and the pelting rain seemed intent on making me suffer. But given my freakish appearance, I couldn't very well loiter in the hall. So I set forth without a plan, muttering to myself that it's just rain after all.

The cold is unbearable. My corduroy suit is getting wet and before long every thread is soaked and clinging to my skin. I was going to kill time by roaming the streets until I could no longer bear traipsing around in the rain, but now it's so cold I can't take it any more. My body shakes and my teeth chatter from the chill.

Hastening my steps, I kept turning ideas over in my head. How could my wife possibly have a guest on a nasty night like this? I thought it highly unlikely. I have to go home. If I'm out of luck and my wife has a guest, I will make my plea. And if I do, I am bound to be forgiven because anyone can plainly see how hard it is raining.

I rushed home and found my wife with a guest. Benumbed by the extreme damp and cold, I had forgotten to knock. And so I ended up seeing what my wife would prefer me not to see. Smearing the floor with big, muddy footprints, I stamped across my wife's room into mine, peeled off the dripping clothes, and crawled under my covers. I was shaking and shivering. My chills were getting worse each moment. It was as if the ground were still collapsing beneath me. I lost consciousness.

The next day when I opened my eyes, my wife is sitting beside me with a look of considerable concern on her face. I've caught a cold. In addition to the chills, my head aches, my mouth is filled with bitter drool, and my limbs are heavy and slack.

After pressing her palm against my forehead, my wife says that I better take some medicine. It should be a fever suppressant, I thought, since I could tell from the icy touch of my wife's hand on my forehead that I am running quite a fever; just then, she gives me some warm water and four white tablets. She says that I will be fine once I take the pills and sleep it off. I lap up the pills she gave me. The slightly bitter taste leads me to guess that they are aspirin. Pulling the covers over my head again, I immediately lapse into a deathlike slumber.

I was sniffling and feeling weak for several days. While laid up, I continued to take the pills faithfully. My cold went away in the meantime but a bitter taste, like that of sumac bark, remained in my mouth.

Gradually, I started wanting to head out again. My wife, however, told me not to go out. She said that I should take the medicine every day and stay in bed. Wasn't it my useless outings, she asked, that gave me a cold in the first place and caused her so much trouble? She had a point. So I vowed not to go out, and resolved to continue taking the medicine and building up my strength.

Buried all the time under my quilt, I slept day and night. It was curious that I was always so drowsy that I could not keep myself awake, but I firmly believed that even this was a sign that my body was becoming sturdier than ever.

I must have spent a good month this way. One afternoon, I decided to take a look in the mirror because my shaggy hair and beard had grown unbearably itchy. I went over to my wife's room while she was out and sat down before her vanity stand. What a sight I was. My hair and beard were a tangled mess. Resolving to get a haircut today, I took the opportunity to unplug the cosmetic bottles and sniff them in no particular order. From among those briefly lost fragrances wafted a bodily scent that practically made me squirm and writhe. Silently, I called out my wife's name: "Yŏnshimi!" . . .

For the first time in a long while I played the magnifying-glass game. Played the mirror game, too. The sunlight through the window was quite warm. I'd forgotten that it was already May.

Getting up for a big stretch, I tossed my wife's pillow on the floor and plopped back down to rest my head on it. Reclined like this, I wanted to show off to God what a comfortable and happy life I was leading. I had no dealings whatsoever with the outside world. It seemed that not even God can praise or punish me.

The very next moment, however, something truly strange caught my eye. It was a box of Adalin sleeping pills. I found the pills under my wife's vanity stand and it struck me that they looked just like aspirin. I opened the box. Exactly four tablets were missing.

I remembered taking four aspirin in the morning. I had fallen asleep immediately afterward. Yesterday, the day before yesterday, and the day before the day before yesterday as well—I had been helplessly sleepy. Even though the cold was gone, my wife continued to give me aspirin. Once a fire broke out next door but I was too knocked out to even notice it. No wonder I've been sleeping so soundly. I took Adalin for an entire month, believing all the while that it was aspirin. I could hardly believe it!

Suddenly everything grew dim and I felt faint. I put the Adalin in my pocket and set out from the house. When I came to a hill, I started climbing. For the very sight of the human world disgusted me. As I walked I made every effort to banish from my thoughts anything related to my wife, because I could have easily fainted right there on the path. My plan was to pick a sunny place somewhere, set myself down, and take my time studying the situation in regard to my wife. Until then, the only kinds of things I thought about were a muddy roadside ditch, golden forsythias in bloom the likes of which I had never seen before, skylarks, and tales of stones hatching eggs. Luckily, I did not faint on the road.

There was a *bench*. I sat upright on it and ruminated about aspirin and Adalin. But try as I might, my head was so cluttered that I could not organize my thoughts. Less than five minutes passed before I got cross and tired thinking about it. From my pocket, I took out the Adalin I had brought along and chewed up the remaining six pills all together. There was a funny taste to them. I stretched myself out on the *bench*. What possessed me to behave like this? No way to know. I simply wanted to, that's all. I fell into a deep slumber right then and there. Yet in my sleep, I could still faintly hear the ceaseless burbling of water between rocks.

When I woke up the day was already very bright. I had slept there the whole day and night. The surrounding landscape looked jaundiced. But even at such a moment, thoughts of aspirin and Adalin flashed like lightning through my mind.

Aspirin, Adalin, aspirin, Adalin, Marx, Malthus, *matroos*,[5] aspirin, Adalin.

For a month, my wife had fed me Adalin, tricking me into thinking it was aspirin. The discovery of the Adalin box in my wife's room was incontrovertible proof of this.

Why did my wife need me to sleep all day and night?

And what was she up to while I slept?

Was she trying to kill me, little by little?

But on second thought, maybe what I had been taking the whole month was aspirin after all. Maybe it was my wife who used the Adalin to dissolve the worries that kept her awake at night, and if so I am truly sorry. How terrible of me to harbor such grave suspicions about her.

5. Yi Sang uses here the Korean word *madorosŭ*, a transliteration into *hangŭl* of the Dutch word *matroos*, meaning "sailor."

And so I rushed down the hill. My legs almost buckled beneath me and I felt so dizzy that I could barely walk homeward. It was nearly eight o'clock.

I intended to confess every one of my misbegotten thoughts and seek my wife's forgiveness. But in my haste I forgot again to announce my presence.

And what a disaster that was. I ended up seeing exactly what I should never have laid eyes upon. Stunned, I quickly shut the sliding door and, to still the dizziness coming over me, put my head down and shut my eyes for a moment. As I stood there leaning against the post, the sliding door clattered open and my wife, all her clothes in disarray, leaped out and grabbed me by the throat. My head swam and I collapsed on the spot. My wife pounced upon my prostrate body and tore wildly at my flesh with her teeth. The pain was excruciating. Since I didn't have any will or strength to resist, I just lay there flat on my stomach and waited to see what would happen. A man came out, swept my wife up, and strode back into the room. My wife was the very picture of demureness and docility in his arms, and I felt a surge of hatred at the sight. It filled me with bitterness.

My wife rails at me: "What do you do all night? Run around robbing people? Drop in on whores?" What a cruel and unfair accusation. I was so completely flabbergasted, I couldn't even open my mouth to speak.

Isn't it you who tried to kill me?! I wanted to scream, but who knows what harm will befall me if I rashly voice such a wild accusation? Though it was all terribly unfair, silence seemed to be the best policy for the moment, and so I got up, dusted myself off, and without knowing why, quietly took out the few *wŏn* and change left in my pants pocket, furtively slid open the door, and gently placed the money down inside the threshold. Then I bolted out.

Although I was nearly hit by automobiles several times on the way, I managed to reach Kyŏngsŏng Station. With an empty seat for company, I wanted something to drink that would chase the bitter taste from my mouth.

Coffee—. Yes, that's it. But as soon as I set foot in the station hall, I realized that it had somehow slipped my mind that there wasn't a single coin in my pocket. Everything began to spin around me. All I could do was stand around somewhere in listless confusion. Like a walking corpse, I paced back and forth, this way and that. . . .

I wandered around and around, I didn't know where. But when I found myself a few hours later on the roof of Mitsukoshi,[6] it was almost noon.

6. Mitsukoshi was the name of a major Japanese department store in downtown Kyŏngsŏng.

I plopped myself down somewhere and tried reflecting on the twenty-six years of my life. No title for it emerged from the morass of my memory.

I asked myself again: Do you have any ambition for your life? But I didn't want to answer Yes or No. Just trying to recognize my own existence was difficult enough for me.

Instead, I bent over and gazed at some goldfish. How handsome they were. The small ones and the big ones, each in their own way, were all full of zest and pleasant to watch. In the radiant May sunlight, the goldfish cast shadows upon the bottom of the bowl. Their fins mimed the gentle waving of handkerchiefs. Trying to count them, I remained hunched over for a long time. My back became warm.

I also looked down at the turbid streets. Weary lives swayed languidly there, exactly like the fins of the goldfish. Tangled in a sticky, invisible web, they could not break free. I realized that I too would have to drag this body along, disintegrating from hunger and exhaustion, and dissolve into the grimy flow.

Coming out, I suddenly thought about something else. Where my steps were leading me now . . .

At that very instant, my wife's head dropped before me like thunder. Aspirin and Adalin.

There's been a terrible misunderstanding between us. Surely my wife couldn't have been feeding me doses of Adalin instead of aspirin? How ludicrous. What reason could she possibly have? Did I go around stealing and whoring day and night? Nothing could be further from the truth.

My wife and I are a pair of cripples destined to be out of step with each other. There is no need for me to assign a *logic* to my wife's behavior or mine. No need to justify it either. Isn't it enough to keep moving through this world, endlessly limping along with whatever truths and misunderstandings in our tow?

But now the only difficult thing for me to decide was whether I should trudge back to my wife. Should I go? And if so, where?

At that moment, the noon siren wailed: *Tuu–u*—! People extended their four limbs and flapped around like chickens, while all sorts of glass, steel, marble, money, and ink seemed to rumble and boil up—right then, the noon reached the zenith of its dazzling splendor.

All of a sudden, I feel an itch under my arms. Aha! The itching is a trace of where my artificial wings had once sprouted. Wings that are missing today: pages from which my hopes and ambition were erased flashed in my mind like a flipped-through dictionary.

I want to halt my steps and shout out for once:

"Wings! Grow again!
"Let's fly! Let's fly! Let's fly! Let's fly just one more time.
"Let's fly once again!"

Translated by Walter K. Lew and Youngju Ryu

7. YI HYOSŎK

Yi Hyosŏk (1907–1942) is one of the talented group of young Korean writers whose flame burned brightly in the 1920s and 1930s, only to be extinguished by the time of the Pacific War. Much of his early fiction concerns the urban poor and the destructiveness of city life. This concern, together with a flirtation with socialism in the late 1920s and early 1930s, produced stories such as "Noryŏng kŭnhae" (1930, Along the Russian coast). By the mid-1930s he was taking inspiration from the Korean countryside where he was born. Works from the late 1930s, such as the novel *Hwabun* (1939, Pollen), reveal an eroticism that has drawn comparisons with D. H. Lawrence.

"When the Buckwheat Blooms" (Memil kkot p'il muryŏp), first published in 1936 in the literary journal *Chogwang*, is his best-known story. Set in the Kangwŏn-Ch'ungch'ŏng border area that the author knew so well, it depicts the lives of rural peddlers and the colorful sights and sounds of market day—still a feature of Korean villages and towns. Its rich language, vivid descriptions of rural Korea, and masterful plot development have made it a favorite of readers and critics alike.

WHEN THE BUCKWHEAT BLOOMS

Every peddler who made the rounds of the countryside markets knew that business was never any good in the summer. And on this particular day, the marketplace in Pongp'yŏng was already deserted, though the sun was still high in the sky; its heat, seeping under the awnings of the peddlers' stalls, was enough to sear your spine. Most of the villagers had gone home, and you couldn't stay open forever just to do business with the farmhands who would have been happy to swap a bundle of firewood for a bottle of kerosene or some fish. The swarms of flies had become a nuisance, and the local boys were as pesky as gnats.

"Shall we call it a day?" ventured Hŏ Saengwŏn, a left-handed man with a pockmarked face, to his fellow dry-goods peddler Cho Sŏndal.

"Sounds good to me. We've never done well here in Pongp'yŏng. We'll have to make a bundle tomorrow in Taehwa."

"And we'll have to walk all night to get there," said Hŏ.

"I don't mind—we'll have the moon to light the way."

Cho counted the day's proceeds, letting the coins clink together. Hŏ watched for a moment, then began to roll up their awning and put away the goods he had displayed. The bolts of cotton cloth and the bundles of silk fabrics filled his two wicker hampers to the brim. Bits of cloth littered the straw mat on the ground.

The stalls of other peddlers were almost down, and some groups had gotten a jump on the rest and left town. The fishmongers, tinkers, taffymen, and ginger vendors—all were gone. Tomorrow would be market day in Chinbu and Taehwa, and whichever way you went, you would have to trudge fifteen to twenty miles through the night to get there. But here in Pongp'yŏng the marketplace had the untidy sprawl of a courtyard after a family gathering, and you could hear quarrels breaking out in the drinking houses. Drunken curses together with the shrill voices of women rent the air. The evening of a market day invariably began with the screeching of women.

A woman's shout seemed to remind Cho of something.

"Now don't play innocent, Saengwŏn—I know all about you and the Ch'ungju woman," he said with a wry grin.

"Fat chance I have with her. I'm no match for those kids."

"Don't be so sure," said Cho. "It's true that the young fellows all lose their heads over her. But you know, something tells me that Tongi, on the other hand, has her right around his finger."

"That greenhorn? He must be bribing her with his goods. And I thought he was a model youngster."

"When it comes to women, you can never be sure. . . . Come on now, stop your moping and let's go have a drink. It's on me."

Hŏ didn't think much of this idea, but he followed Cho nonetheless. Hŏ was a hapless sort when it came to women. With his pockmarked mug, he hesitated to look a woman in the eye, and women for their part wouldn't warm up to him. Midway through life by now, he had led a forlorn, warped existence. Just thinking of the Ch'ungju woman would bring to his face a blush unbefitting a man of his age. His legs would turn to rubber, and he would lose his composure.

The two men entered the Ch'ungju woman's tavern, and sure enough, there was Tongi. For some reason Hŏ himself couldn't have explained, his temper flared. The sight of Tongi flirting with the woman, his face red with drink, was something Hŏ could not bear. Quite the ladies' man, isn't he, thought Hŏ. What a disgraceful spectacle!

"Still wet behind the ears, and here you are swilling booze and flirting with women in broad daylight," he said, walking right up in front of Tongi. "You go around giving us vendors a bad name, but still you want a share of our trade, it seems."

Tongi looked Hŏ straight in the eye. Mind your own business, he seemed to be saying.

When the young man's animated eyes met his, Hŏ lashed Tongi across the cheek on impulse. Flaring up in anger, Tongi shot to his feet. But Hŏ, not about to compromise, let fly with all he had to say.

"I don't know what kind of family you come from, you young pup, but if your mom and dad could see this disgraceful behavior, how pleased they would be! Being a vendor is a full-time job—there's no time for women. Now get lost, right this minute!"

But when Tongi disappeared without a word of rejoinder, Hŏ suddenly felt compassion for him. He had overreacted, he told himself uneasily; that wasn't how you treated a man who was still but a nodding acquaintance.

"You've gone too far," said the Ch'ungju woman. "Where do you get the right to slap him and dress him down like that? To me you're both customers. And besides, you may think he's young, but he's old enough to produce children." Her lips were pinched together, and she poured their drinks more roughly now.

"Young people need a dose of that now and then," said Cho in an attempt to smooth over the situation.

"You've fallen for the young fellow, haven't you?" Hŏ asked the woman. "Don't you know it's a sin to take advantage of a boy?"

The fuss died down. Hŏ, already emboldened, now felt like getting good and drunk. He tossed off almost at a gulp every bowl of liquor he was given. As he began to mellow, his thoughts of the Ch'ungju woman were overshadowed by concern for Tongi. What was a guy in my position going to do after coming between them? he asked himself. What a foolish spectacle he had presented!

And for this reason, when Tongi rushed back a short time later, calling Hŏ frantically, Hŏ put down his bowl and ran outside in a flurry without thinking twice about it.

"Saengwŏn, your donkey's running wild—it broke its tether."

"Those little bastards must be teasing it," muttered Hŏ.

Hŏ was of course concerned about his donkey, but he was moved even more by Tongi's thoughtfulness. As he ran after Tongi across the marketplace, his eyes became hot and moist.

"The little devils—there was nothing we could do," said Tongi.

"Tormenting a donkey—they're going to catch hell from me."

Hŏ had spent half his life with that animal, sleeping at the same country inns and walking from one market town to the next along roads awash in moonlight. And those twenty years had aged man and beast together. The animal's cropped mane bristled like his master's hair, and discharge ran from his sleepy eyes, just as it did from Hŏ's. He would try as best he could to swish the flies away with his stumpy tail, now too short to reach even his legs. Time and again Hŏ had filed down the donkey's worn hooves and fitted him with new shoes. Eventually the hooves had stopped growing back, and it became useless trying to file them down. Blood now oozed between the hooves and the worn shoes. The donkey recognized his master's smell, and would greet Hŏ's arrival with a bray of delight and supplication.

Hŏ stroked the donkey's neck as if he were soothing a child. The animal's nostrils twitched, and then he whickered, sending spray from his nose in every direction. How Hŏ had suffered on account of this creature. It wouldn't be easy calming the sweaty, trembling donkey; those boys must have teased it without mercy. The animal's bridle had come loose, and his saddle had fallen off.

"Good-for-nothing little rascals!" Hŏ yelled. But most of the boys had run away. The remaining few had slunk off to a distance at Hŏ's shouting.

"We weren't teasing him," cried one of them, a boy with a runny nose. "He got an eyeful of Kim Ch'ŏmji's mare and went crazy!"

"Will you listen to the way that little guy talks," said Hŏ.

"When Kim Ch'ŏmji took his mare away, this one went wild—kicking up dirt, foam all around his mouth, bucking like a crazy bull. He looked so funny—all we did was watch. Look at him down there and see for yourself," shouted the boy, pointing to the underside of Hŏ's donkey and breaking into laughter.

Before Hŏ knew it, he was blushing. Feeling compelled to screen the donkey from view, he stepped in front of the animal's belly.

"Confounded animal! Still rutting at his age," he muttered.

The derisive laughter flustered Hŏ for a moment, but then he gave chase to the boys, brandishing his whip.

"Catch us if you can! Hey, everybody, Lefty's gonna whip us!"

But when it came to running, Hŏ was no match for the young troublemakers. That's right, old Lefty can't even catch a boy, thought Hŏ as he tossed the whip aside. Besides, the liquor was working on him again, and he felt unusually hot inside.

"Let's get out of here," said Cho. "Once you start squabbling with these market pests there's no end to it. They're worse than some of the grown-ups."

Cho and Tongi each saddled and began loading his animal. The sun had angled far toward the horizon.

In the two decades that Hŏ had been peddling dry goods at the rural markets, he had rarely skipped Pongp'yŏng in his rounds. He sometimes went to Ch'ungju, Chech'ŏn, and neighboring counties, and occasionally roamed farther afield to the Kyŏngsang region. Otherwise, unless he went to a place such as Kangnŭng to stock up on his goods, he confined his rounds to P'yŏngch'ang County. More regular than the moon, he tramped from one town to the next. He took pride in telling others that Ch'ŏngju was his hometown, but he never seemed to go there. To Hŏ, home sweet home was the beautiful landscape along the roads that led him from one market town to the next. When he finally approached one of these towns after trudging half a day, the restive donkey would let out a resounding heehaw. In particular, when they arrived around dusk, the flickering lights in the town—though a familiar scene by now—never failed to make Hŏ's heart quicken.

Hŏ had been a thrifty youth and had put away a bit of money. But then one year during the All Souls' Festival he had squandered and gambled, and in three days he had blown all of his savings. Only his extreme fondness for the donkey had restrained him from selling the animal as well. In the end, he had had no choice but to return to square one and begin making the rounds of the market towns all over again. "It's a good thing I didn't sell you," he had said with tears in his eyes, stroking the donkey's back as they fled the town. He had gone into debt, and saving money was now out of the question. And thus began a hand-to-mouth existence as he journeyed from one market to the next.

In the course of all his squandering, Hŏ had never managed to conquer a woman. The cold, heartless creatures—they have no use for me, he would think dejectedly. His only constant friend was the donkey.

Be that as it may, there was one affair, and he would never forget it. His first and last affair—it was a most mysterious liaison. It had happened when he was young, when he had begun stopping at the Pongp'yŏng market, and whenever he recalled it he felt that his life had been worth living.

"For the life of me, I still can't figure it out," Hŏ said to no one in particular. "It was a moonlit night. . . ."

This was the signal that Hŏ would begin yarning again that night. Being Hŏ's friend, Cho had long since had an earful of what was to come. But he couldn't very well tell Hŏ he was sick of the story, and so Hŏ innocently started in anew and rambled on as he pleased.

"A story like this goes well with a moonlit night," said Hŏ with a glance toward Cho. It wasn't that he felt apologetic toward his friend; rather, the moonlight had made him feel expansive.

The moon was a day or two past full, and its light was soft and pleasant. Twenty miles of moonlit walking lay before them on the way to Taehwa—two mountain passes, a stream crossing, hilly paths along endless fields. They were traversing a hillside. It was probably after midnight by now, and it was so deathly still the moon seemed to come alive right there in front of you, its breath almost palpable. Awash in moonlight, the bean plants and the drooping cornstalks were a shade greener. The hillside was covered with buckwheat coming into flower, and the sprinkling of white in the gentle moonlight was almost enough to take your breath away. The red stalks seemed delicate as a fragrance, and the donkeys appeared to have more life in their step.

The road narrowed, forcing the men to mount their animals and ride single file. The refreshing tinkle of the bells hanging from the donkeys' necks flowed toward the buckwheat. Hŏ's voice, coming from the front, wasn't clearly audible to Tongi at the tail end, but Tongi had some pleasant memories of his own to keep him company.

"It was market day in Pongp'yŏng, and the moon was out, just like tonight. I'd taken this tiny little room with a dirt floor, and it was so muggy I couldn't get to sleep. So I decided to go down and cool off in the stream. Pongp'yŏng then was just like it is now—buckwheat everywhere you looked, and the white flowers coming right down to the stream. I could have stripped right there on the gravel, but the moon was so bright, I decided to use the watermill shed instead. Well, I want to tell you, strange things happen in this world. Suddenly, there I was in the shed, face to face with old man Song's daughter—the town beauty. Was it fate that brought us together? You bet it was."

Hŏ puffed on a cigarette, as if savoring his own words. The rich aroma of the purple smoke suffused the night air.

"Of course she wasn't waiting for me, but for that matter she didn't have a boyfriend waiting for her, either. Actually she was crying. And I had a hunch why. Old man Song was having a terrible time making ends meet, and the family was on the verge of selling out. Being a family matter, it was cause enough for her to worry too. They wanted to find a good husband for her, but she told me she would have died first. Now you tell me—is there anything that can get to a fellow more than the sight of a girl in tears? I sensed she was startled at first. But you know, girls tend to warm up to you more easily when they're worried, and it wasn't long until—well, you know the rest. Thinking back now, it scares me how incredible that night was."

"And the next day she took off for Chech'ŏn or thereabouts—right?" Cho prompted him.

"By the next market day, the whole family had vanished. You should have heard the gossip in the market. The rumors were flying: the family's best bet was to sell the girl off to a tavern, they were saying. God knows how many times I searched the Chech'ŏn marketplace for her. But there was no more sign of her than a chicken after dinner. My first night with her was my last. And that's why I have a soft spot in my heart for Pongp'yŏng, and why I've spent half my life visiting the place. I'll never forget it."

"You were a lucky man, Saengwŏn. Something like that doesn't happen every day. You know, a lot of fellows get stuck with an ugly wife, they have kids, and the worries begin to pile up—you get sick of that after a while. On the other hand, being an itinerant peddler to the end of your days isn't my idea of an easy life. So I'm going to call it quits after autumn. Thought I'd open up a little shop in a place like Taehwa and then have the family join me. Being on the road all the time wears a man out."

"Not me—unless I meet her again. I'll be walking this here road, watching that moon, till the day I croak."

The mountain path opened onto a wide road. Tongi came up from the rear, and the three donkeys walked abreast.

"But look at you, Tongi," said Hŏ. "You're still young—you're in the prime of life. It was stupid of me to act that way at the Ch'ungju woman's place. Don't hold it against me."

"Don't mention it. I'm the one who feels silly. At this stage of my life, I shouldn't be worrying about girls. Night and day, it's my mother I think about."

Downhearted because of Hŏ's story, Tongi spoke in a tone that was a shade subdued.

"When you mentioned my parents at the tavern, it made my heart ache. You see, I don't have a father. My mother's my only blood relation."

"Did your father die?"

"I never had one."

"Well, that's a new one."

Hŏ and Cho burst into laughter.

"I'm ashamed to say it," said Tongi with a serious expression, forced to explain himself, "but it's the truth. My mother gave birth to me prematurely when they were in a village near Chech'ŏn, and then her family kicked her out. I know it sounds strange, but that's why I've never seen my father's face, and I have no idea where he is."

The men dismounted as they approached a pass, and fell silent while climbing the rough road. The donkeys frequently slipped. Hŏ was soon short of breath, and had to pause time and again to rest his legs. He felt his age every time he had to cross a pass. How he envied the young fellows like Tongi. Sweat began to stream down his back.

Just the other side of the pass, the road crossed a stream. The plank bridge had been washed out during the monsoon rains, so they would have to wade across. The men removed their loose summer trousers and tied them around their backs with their belts. Half naked, they presented a comical sight as they stepped briskly into the stream. They had been sweating a moment ago, but it was nighttime and the water chilled them to the bone.

"Who the devil brought you up, then?" Hŏ asked Tongi.

"My mother did. She had no choice but to remarry, and she opened up a drinking house. But my stepfather was a hopeless drunk—a complete good-for-nothing. Ever since I was old enough to know what's what, he beat me. We didn't have a day's peace. And if Mother tried to stop him, she'd get kicked, hit, threatened with a knife. Our family was one big mess. And so I left home at eighteen, and I've been peddling ever since."

"I always thought you were quite a boy for your age, but to hear all this, it sounds like you've *really* had a hard time."

The water had risen to their waists. The current was quite strong, the pebbles underfoot slippery. The men felt as if they would be swept off their feet at any moment. Cho and the donkeys had made quick progress and were almost across. Tongi and Hŏ, the younger man supporting the older, were far behind.

"Was your mother's family originally from Chech'ŏn?" asked Hŏ.

"I don't think so. I never could get a straight answer out of her, but I've heard say they lived in Pongp'yŏng."

"Pongp'yŏng . . . What was your dad's name, anyway?"

"Beats me. I never heard it mentioned."

"I suppose not," mumbled Hŏ as he blinked his bleary eyes. And then, distracted, he lost his footing. His body pitched forward, plunging him deep into the stream. He flailed about, unable to right himself, and by the time Tongi had called out to Cho and caught up to Hŏ, the older man had been washed some distance away. With the sodden clothes on his back, Hŏ looked more miserable than a wet dog. Tongi lifted him easily from the water and carried him piggyback. Soaked though he was, Hŏ was a slender man, and he rested lightly on Tongi's sturdy back.

"Sorry to put you to this trouble," said Hŏ. "I guess my mind's been wandering today."

"It's nothing to worry about."

"So, didn't it ever seem to you that your mother was looking for your dad?"

"Well, she's always saying she'd like to see him."

"And where is she now?"

"In Chech'ŏn—she went there after she split up with my stepfather. I'm thinking of moving her up to Pongp'yŏng this fall. If I put my mind to it, we'll make out somehow."

"Sure, why not? That's a swell idea. Did you say this fall?"

Tongi's broad, agreeable back spread its warmth into Hŏ's bones. And then they were across. Hŏ plaintively wished Tongi might have carried him a bit farther.

Cho could no longer suppress a laugh.

"Saengwŏn, this just isn't your day."

"It was that donkey colt—I got to thinking about it and lost my balance. Didn't I tell you? You wouldn't think this old fellow had it in him, but by God if he didn't sire a colt with the Kangnŭng woman's mare in Pongp'yŏng. The way it pricks up its ears and prances about—is there anything as cute as a donkey colt? There are times I've stopped at Pongp'yŏng just to see it."

"Must be some colt to make a man take a spill like that."

Hŏ wrung a fair amount of water out of his sodden clothes. His teeth chattered, he shivered, he was cold all over. But for some unaccountable reason he felt buoyant.

"Let's hurry to the inn, fellows," said Hŏ. "We'll build a fire in the yard and get nice and cozy. I'll heat up some water for the donkey, and tomorrow I'll stop at Taehwa, and then head on to Chech'ŏn."

"You're going to Chech'ŏn, too?" asked Tongi, his voice trailing off in surprise.

"Thought I'd pay a visit—haven't been there in a while. How about it, Tongi—you and me?"

As the donkeys set off again, Tongi was holding his whip in his left hand. This time Hŏ, whose eyes had long been weak and dim, couldn't fail to notice Tongi was left-handed.

As Hŏ ambled along, the tinkle of the donkeys' bells, more lucid now, carried over the dusky expanse. The moon had arched far across the heavens.

Translated by Kim Chong-un and Bruce Fulton

8. CH'AE MANSHIK

Ch'ae Manshik—fiction writer, playwright, essayist, critic—was born in Ŭmnae, a coastal village in North Chŏlla Province, in 1902. Like many of the intellectuals of his generation, he studied for a time in Japan, then returned to Korea to work at a succession of writing and editorial jobs. He died of tuberculosis in 1950.

Ch'ae is one of the great talents of modern Korean literature. His penetrating mind, command of idiom, utterly realistic dialogue, and keen wit produced a fictional style all his own. The immediacy of some of his narratives produces a strong sense of a storyteller speaking to his listeners.

Often pigeonholed as a satirist, Ch'ae was much more. Long before the appearance of such satirical sketches as the story translated here and "Misŭt'ŏ Pang" (1946, trans. 1994 "Mister Pang"), set during the American military occupation, Ch'ae had written "Kwadogi" (1923, Age of transition), an autobiographical novella about Korean students in Japan testing the currents of modernization that swept urban East Asia early in the twentieth century. In other early works, such as "Segillo" (1924, In three directions) and "Sandungi" (1930, Sandungi), he dealt with the class differences that are so distinct in Korean society past and present. In these earlier stories Ch'ae is concerned as well with the plight of the unemployed young intellectuals turned out by the modernization movement—young men such as P, H, and M in "Redimeidŭ insaeng" (1934, trans. 1998 "A Ready-Made Life"), who perpetually make the rounds of publishing houses, pawnshops, and cheap bars. Ch'ae was also at home depicting the rural underclass, so long suppressed as to be almost incapable of autonomous action, in stories such as "Ch'ajung esŏ" (1941, On a train). *T'aep'yŏng ch'ŏnha* (1938, trans. 1993 *Peace Under Heaven*), on the other hand, is a pointed treatment of traditional Korean etiquette in the person of one who thrived materially but wasted spiritually during the Japanese occupation. It has been acclaimed as one of the great Korean novels.

Ch'ae's later works are somewhat bitter and introspective. In these stories the author's wit is tempered by the spiritual turmoil of having to come to grips with the role of the artist in a colonized society. "Minjok ŭi choein" (1948–1949, Public offender), for example, is a semiautobiographical apologia for those branded as collaborators for their failure to actively oppose Japanese colonial rule. "Maeng sunsa" (1946, trans. 1999 "Constable Maeng") is a caustic portrayal of a member of the Korean police force during the Japanese occupation. "Ch'ŏja" (1948, trans. 1993 "The Wife and Children") portrays a man who finds himself out of political favor after Liberation. The man's exile from his family echoes not only premodern Korean history, in which victims of factional infighting in the capital were frequently banished to the countryside, but contemporary history as well, with its record of house arrests of dissident politicians. In this and other works Ch'ae also offers keen insights into the long-standing oppression of Korean women.

"My Innocent Uncle" (Ch'isuk) first appeared in the *Tonga ilbo*, a Seoul daily, in 1938.

MY INNOCENT UNCLE

My uncle? You mean that fine gentleman who married my father's cousin, the man they put in jail when he was younger on account of that darned socialism, or scotchalism, or whatever you call it, the one who's laid up with tuberculosis?

Don't get me started on him. It's beyond me how a man like that can . . . Brother!

He's got himself a fine row to hoe!

Sure, he had all those years of schooling, college too, but what's he got to show for it? He idled away his shining youth, his reputation's ruined because he's an ex-con, god-awful disease inside him, stretched out eyes shut night and day year round in a tiny rented room that's dark as a cave.

A house? Land of his own? No way! He's so poor you could wave a three-fathom stick around him and not a straw would catch on it.

Thank God for my aunt. She's so kind and gentle. She does piecework sewing, goes to other people's houses and does their wash, sells cosmetics—all so she can serve her dear husband. But what she makes from such miserable work is barely enough for them to scrape by.

However you look at it, the gentleman would be better off dead. But no, he's not about to die off.

My poor aunt. She should have turned her life around when she was younger. God only knows why she puts up with these troubles—must be she's hoping that after all the damned suffering she's gone through she'll have better luck later on.

She's been neglected by him going on twenty years now.

Sighed away twenty years of her sorrowful youth, and now it's too late. She sits at the bedside of that living corpse, caring for that fine gentleman just because he's her husband, wearing herself out going around trying to make a living—it's just plain pathetic.

And what did she do to deserve it? Everybody talks about fate—well, why don't they do something about it? Old-fashioned Chosŏn women! When are they going to wise up?

My aunt would be a lot better off if that fine gentleman would just up and die.

She's good-hearted and has a nice touch at what she sets her hand to, and I imagine she could take care of herself and live comfortably just about anywhere.

Let's see, she says she got married when she was sixteen, and that's when I was three, which means it's been a good eighteen years she's been neglected. Well, eighteen years, twenty—what's the difference?

My uncle was young when they got married and he spent a good ten years knocking around Seoul and Tokyo—"studying," you know—and when he was grown up enough to develop a taste for women he asked my aunt for a divorce, sent her packing to her family, and turned his back on her. . . . How generous of him.

No sooner did he finish his studies and come home than he went nuts over that damned scotchalism and got himself another woman, one of those "educated women," you know? I've seen her a few times and that puss of hers is not about to catch anyone's attention. Beats me how a woman who looks like that can be someone's mistress. They say pretty women are jilted but ugly women aren't, and it's a fact that if you stack up my aunt against that woman, then my aunt is prettier by a long shot.

Well, eventually that fine gentleman got nailed by the police and was a jailbird for five years. During that time my aunt's family and her in-laws were completely ruined and she had no one to depend on.

What was she supposed to do? It was just a matter of time till she starved.

Well, she ended up with me, though she said she didn't much like the idea, but she needed someone to provide for her, and she had to wait for Uncle's release, and I was the only one she had in Seoul. That was—let me see—the year before Uncle got out.

I was just a kid then, but I played all the angles right and soon I had myself a job at Mr. Kurada's.

I wish I could count all the times I told my aunt she ought to remarry. Even to a young guy like me, it was pitiful and embarrassing to see her like this.

While all this was happening a better opportunity came my way. I knew a man named Mr. Mine who sold bananas cheap in front of the Mitsukoshi Department Store, and he was a good person all right. My Japanese boss knew him well, too. This Mr. Mine was always telling me he'd like to live with a "Chosŏn *okam*," and he kept asking me to fix him up.

Mr. Mine didn't have much in the way of savings, but he was capable of supporting a family. And so I asked my aunt if she wouldn't be more comfortable living with such a person. I asked her more than that, but darned if she didn't turn a deaf ear and tell me to stop coming out with such unseemly talk.

That aside, I've done more than my fair share behind the scenes to take care of Aunt, right up to the present day, and that's no lie. Besides, I was kind of obligated to her.

You see, when I was seven I lost my parents. I had no place to go, but fortunately my aunt took me in and brought me up. This was after my uncle turned her loose and she went back to live with her parents.

Because back then, at least, they weren't so hard up. My aunt thought I was the most precious thing, but so did my great-aunt and great-uncle—they didn't have any other children.

I lived there till I was twelve.

Went through fourth grade, too.

Who knows, maybe if those three hadn't had such sour luck I'd have stuck around and maybe I'd be in college now.

I didn't forget that obligation, but I reckon I've paid it off.

Still, my aunt comes by from time to time and tells me she's bad off, out of food. To be honest, I find it kind of aggravating.

If I cave in to her every time, how am I supposed to get on with my life? So most times I just tell her flat out no.

But there are times, Western New Year for example, when the least I can do is send her a pound of meat, or else drop by her place for a chat—things like that.

In any event, for one whole year my aunt worked as a maid for Mr. Kurada's family and got five *wŏn* a month. That's not much, but she managed to save it all, and in her spare time she took in sewing and earned a little money on the side, and by the time she left the Kuradas, the mister and missus were impressed enough with her to give her a seven-*wŏn* bonus, and in these various ways she put together close to a hundred *wŏn*.

With that money she took out a small room and bought a few household items, and then it happened that her dear former hubby-poo was set free and she took him in.

I went with Aunt the day he was let out, and—I can hardly believe this myself—the moment he came out from his cage the sight of her waiting for him brought tears to my eyes.

And that bitch of a mistress he used to dote on—you suppose she showed her mug? Hell, no. What do you expect? They're all like that.

My uncle looked every which way, wondering if the other woman had come. That's how little sense he has. There was no woman, not even her shadow—just Aunt and me.

As he climbed into the taxi he spit up blood. Seems he started doing that about a month and a half ago in his cage.

After the taxi dropped us off we practically had to carry him piggyback the rest of the way home, the guy being half dead and all. But from the moment we laid him down inside, Aunt looked after him around the clock, and what with all her bustling and attentiveness he showed a gradual improvement until now he's got his life back. What a makeover, I'll tell you—like a toad turning into a dragon!

You can never underestimate a wife's devotion.

And that's the way it's been for a good three years now. But if someone had said to me, "Be nice to your uncle and I'll bring your parents back to life," I would have said, "No thanks!"

And now, you know what? If that fine gentleman my uncle had any kind of a conscience, don't you think he'd say to himself, "Well now, I ought to get myself back into condition real quick, make me some money fast, make my wife nice and comfortable, and repay her for all she's done for me, to atone for my sins"?

Thing is, he won't ever be able to make it up to her, even if he carried her around on his back all day long so her feet wouldn't get dirty.

It's time for him to come to his senses. Whatever it takes. And if he can't get a government job or work for a company because of his prison record, well, he's got no one to blame except himself, so he ought to roll up his sleeves and do some manual labor—that's the least he could do.

Now that would be worth seeing—a college graduate doing drudge work. But what else can he do, you know?

All of which makes me shudder to think what might have happened if my great-uncle's family hadn't gone under and I'd graduated from technical school or college and ended up like my uncle. Good thing I went the way I'm going now, without spending all that time studying.

Fact is, that fine gentleman with all his education, the best he can do now is day labor. Look at me, though—I barely made it through fourth grade but my future's bright. Compared with me, he's worse than an errand boy.

But drudge work's the last thing on his mind. Now that he's showing some signs of life, you wouldn't believe the nonsense that fine gentleman's cooking up.

That damned scotchalism is his worst enemy, and yet he can't give it up. He's nuts about it.

Is it supposed to put food on your table? Is it supposed to make you famous? Or maybe in the end it just makes a jailbird out of you.

Damned scotchalism, it's just like opium. Once you get a taste of it you're hooked.

But once you figure out what it really is, it's not very exciting, not much flavor to it. The ones who do it are a bunch of crooks. A bunch of crooks up to no good.

Now somewhere in the West, some lazybones who didn't like to work got together in a nice sunny place and figured out ways to goof around and still make a living. My landlord gave me a detailed explanation.

"What it is, these rascals get together and debate. One of 'em will say, 'Well, in this world there are rich people and poor people, and it's just not fair. Everyone's born with eyes, a nose, a mouth, and a throat, and with two arms and two legs, and yet this person is rich and lives well and that person is poor—what kind of nonsense is that? It's only right that the rich ought to share and share alike with us poor folks.'

"And someone else says, 'Yeah, that's the ticket! Yeah, that's telling 'em! Share and share alike.'"

Hey now, that's a pretty persuasive message. I'll bet it gets a lot of people worked up.

With that kind of nonsense you can see why I think those people are out-and-out crooks.

Some people get rich because they're born in the right place at the right time, or else they work hard. And some people are poor because they were born in the wrong place at the wrong time, or else they're lazy. That's the way things are—the way the world turns. Where do people get off saying it's unfair? Those that figure on stealing what's someone else's are crooks pure and simple.

But it's more than that. If those crooks make good on what they say, then the lazybones will only get lazier; they'll take what belongs to the rich folks and live off that, and then the world will be full of thieves. Tell me, though—what happens when the rich people have had everything taken away from them and there's nothing more to eat? It's doomsday, that's what.

If farmers sit around doing nothing and rob what other farmers have harvested, and if weavers sit around doing nothing and rob what other weavers have woven, then where's the grain and fabric supposed to come from? The world's doomed!

And you know darn well they don't realize that damned scotchalism's sending the world to ruin. Some of those poverty-stricken suckers—the lazy ones that don't like to work—got blinded right off the bat by the idea of robbing what they need from the rich, and then every Yi, Kim, and Pak of 'em joined in.

That's exactly what happened to the Russkies.

You want to know how? Simple: the farmers stopped producing grain and tens of thousands of people are starving to death. Well, any fool could have predicted that.

What did they expect! That's what happens when people go *yippie!* thinking they got themselves a quick fix.

Heck—in no time those worthless practices spread practically around the world, made waves in the home country too. Then a bunch of Chosŏn guys who don't know any better got carried away and tried to jump on the bandwagon.

But now it's strictly prohibited here, so it's been pretty much reined in and there's hardly anyone left who's committed to it.

And I say well done. If it's such a great thing, then tell me, why is it prohibited here and why do those fellows get pinched and locked up as if they're mortal enemies of the state?

If it's good and beneficial, then of course the government's going to promote it. And if you do well at it you'll get an award, right?

Take motion pictures; sumo wrestling; comedy shows; Japanese festivals; the All Souls ceremony; doing calisthenics to the radio, things like that—all of them are beneficial and so they're encouraged by the government, right?

What's a government for, anyway? Well, it tells us what's good and bad and what's right and wrong, and it directs us to do this or that, and so it tries to help each of us live comfortably according to our lot.

Now what would happen if their damned scotchalism wasn't prohibited and they could do whatever they wanted? Can you imagine the state of the world now?

I'll bet a lot of people have gotten screwed over. Good thing it didn't happen to me. I can just imagine everything getting totally messed up.

Now here's my idea. My boss has taken a shine to me, and because he trusts me it looks like in just ten years or so he'll stake me a considerable amount of money and set me up in a different business. Based on that, in just thirty years' time, when I've reached the big six-oh, I'll have put together a good hundred thousand *wŏn* from my business. With that much money I'll be as rich as a thousand-sack-of-rice-a-year man—that's rich even by Chosŏn standards. I'll be living high on the hog and you better believe it.

And there's something else my boss said. You see, I'm going to take a young lady from the home country for my wife. My boss said he'd take care of everything—he'll pick out a nice, well-behaved one and fix me up with her. Women from the home country sure are swell.

Me, I wouldn't take a Chosŏn woman if you *gave* me one.

The old-fashioned ones, even though they're well behaved, are ignorant, and people from the home country won't keep company with them. And the modern ones are all full of themselves just because they've had some schooling, so they won't do. So, old-fashioned, modern, doesn't matter—when it comes to Chosŏn women, forget it!

A wife from the home country—that's only for starters. I'll change my name to home-country style, same with house, clothes, food, I'll give my children Japanese names and send them to a Japanese school here.

Japanese schools, they're the thing. Chosŏn schools are dirty—just perfect for turning out rotten kids.

And I'm going to kiss the Chosŏn language goodbye and use only the national language.

Because once I've taken up home-country manners I'll be able to put together a lot of money, just like a home-country man.

That's my plan, and a road's going to open wide to me. At the end of that road I'll be a two-hundred-thousand-*wŏn* rich man, and I'm working hard to follow that road. Heck, is it any wonder I get the creeps from those bloodthirsty lunatic scotchalists who are going to be the ruin of the world? It's awful just to hear about them.

What do you expect me to do about something that's going to screw up the world? All my efforts'll go down the drain. And you call that justice?

You know, everything my boss says makes sense.

If you figure that common theft, extortion, or swindling is a form of robbery, then the only thing you lose is money, so these aren't such serious crimes. But that damned scotchalism or whatever you call it is going to mess up the world and throw the whole country into chaos—it's simply unforgivable, he said.

Forgiveness! If it was me, I'd sweep up the whole lot of 'em and show 'em no mercy. . . .

Frankly, when I think about this, that fine gentleman my uncle is a very wicked man. You think I'd visit him if it wasn't for my aunt? No I wouldn't, even if he didn't have that bad disease—I'm no Catholic, you know. And I'm not about to get choked up when he dies.

It would be one thing if he'd repented for his sins and washed his dirty mind clean, but he'll always be like that—can't expect a tiger to change his stripes.

He really gets my dander up, and the occasional times I drop by, if I happen to be sitting across from him I'll make a point of attacking him with spiteful words; I'll pick on something he says and drive him into a corner.

I sure taught him a lesson last time. But get a load of what he told my aunt afterward: that rascal—meaning me—has fallen into bad habits and gone completely bad and turned into a good-for-nothing!

Brother! To hear that made me speechless!

People sure are different, but where does he get off saying I've gone bad and turned into a good-for-nothing! You could give that gentleman ten mouths and still he'd come up with something like that!

If I was him I'd wait until all the mutes of Chosŏn could talk before I said a word. He must think that what he says actually makes sense!

So that's his excuse for a lecture, huh? I'll bet he figured that if he told me that to my face I'd turn the tables on him and give him a hard time, so he decided to be sly about it and go through my aunt instead.

Amazing, isn't it? Good thing God made people's noses with two holes, so we can snort at stuff like that!

So what if I didn't get nice and educated like him? So what if I bounced around running errands and working as a clerk? I may not look like much, but I've gotten two commendations for being a model worker, and people praise me to the skies, saying I'm intelligent, skillful, and well mannered. I'm a young man with a bright, shining future, and in his eyes I've turned into a good-for-nothing rascal?

Yeah, right! Let me see if I've got this straight. He's saying that since he's right in what he does, then I'm all wrong?

And so if I was like him and got involved in that damned scotchalism and dropped dead, or became a jailbird and an ex-con and got tuberculosis, then I could practically say I didn't go bad and didn't turn into a good-for-nothing!

Huh! The very idea . . .

There's a saying that the man who doesn't know his rear end stinks blames others, and guess which fine gentleman that seems to fit?

And in fact that's how it was the day I taught him a lesson and then he said those things to my aunt.

It happened to be my day off, and I had something to talk about with my aunt, so I dropped by, but my aunt had left to do some sewing for a wedding. That fine gentleman my uncle was the only one home, and as usual he had found his way to the warm spot on the heated floor to lie down.

I found him thumbing through a big stack of Korean-language magazines he dug up from God knows where.

Well, just for fun I picked up one myself and started poking through it, but it was pretty dull stuff.

For the life of me I wish I knew why every magazine that Chosŏn people put out is like that one. No pictures, no comics. And they've all got those complicated Chinese characters stuck in there—who are they supposed to be for anyway? Plus, for guys like us, even when you wade through the Korean in there, it's god-awful difficult to understand.

So when they combine difficult Korean with complicated Chinese, you can't make out the meaning and so you don't read it. There are these stupid stories written in Korean; they're hard to read, and what's more, stories written by Chosŏn people put me to sleep. Me, I gave up on Chosŏn newspapers and magazines a long time ago.

As far as magazines are concerned, you can't beat *King* and *Shonen Club*. They're top-notch! Every time there's a Chinese character it has *kana* tacked on to it, and wherever you open it up you can cruise right through it and know clearly what's going on.

And wherever you read, there's something to learn from it or else an interesting story.

The stories sure are fun! Especially the ones by Kan Kikuchi . . . nice entertainment, and they've got feeling too! And those swashbuckling epics by Yoshikawa Eiji—I just can't sit still when I read them.

The stories are all fun like that, there's a lot of comics, lots of photos too, and considering all that, the price is on the cheap side. You can get last month's issue for 15 *chŏn*, and after you read it you can sell it back for 5 *chŏn*.

As long as you're going to make a magazine, that's how it ought to be, but for all their bullshit Chosŏn people haven't come up with one presentable magazine yet!

But heck, I wasn't going to find anything nifty to read in that crummy magazine, so I tried to find some comics or photos, and what do you know, I came across an article with my uncle's name on it! I was amazed, and I held it up to take a look. The title had something to do with economy and the characters it was written in were as big as cows' eyes. Next to it was a smaller line that included the word *society*.

I knew what was what just from seeing that much. Economy was what my uncle had studied in college, so he knew about that, and society, well, he was involved with scotchalism, so he knew about society too. So it was obvious he was writing about how economy and scotchalism were related, and which side he was on, and which side was right—stuff like that.

I didn't have to read that article to figure it out. I mean, this fine gentleman went to college and studied economy and wasn't interested in making money so he got mixed up with scotchalism, and so he probably swears up and down the whole article through that economy is wrong and scotchalism is right.

Anyway, I was impressed to see he'd actually written something, so I figured I'd give it a try. But when I glanced through it—no way did I have the brains for it.

I could have gotten a rough idea if the words weren't so hard, but when I pieced together what I could, not for the life of me could I figure out what he was trying to say.

I was kind of irritated so I said to myself, *ah, the hell with this*, and instead I decided to corner him and give him a hard time, and I spread out the article in front of him.

"Uncle?"

"What is it?"

"You're writing something here about economy and society—are you telling people to do economy, or are you telling them to do scotchalism?"

"What?"

He didn't understand. My question threw him off. This article must have been something he wrote a long time ago and forgot about, or else I was being too direct and he didn't know how to handle that. So I tried to be a little more precise.

"Uncle—doesn't *economy* mean making money and getting rich? And doesn't *scotchalism* mean taking money that rich folks have saved up and spending it yourself?"

"What are you trying to say, boy!"

"Hold on and please listen to me."

"Where did you come up with the notion that economics and socialism are like that?"

"It's common sense: doesn't *economy* mean making a lot of money, spending just a little, and saving the rest?"

"That's usually what people mean by *economizing*, and that's different from the study of economics and the word *economic*."

"Difference? I don't get it. If economy is all about making money, then economics must be the study of how to make money."

"No. There's something called finance, and I guess you could think of it as the study of making money, but that's not what economics is about."

"Well, if that's the case, then you made a mistake going to college. You spent five or six years studying economics that didn't teach you how to economize—what's the use? I always wondered how come you went to college and studied economy but didn't make any money. Now I see it's because you didn't study economy the right way."

"I didn't? Well, well, maybe so. You're right, yes, you are!"

Doggone, I got him now! I said to myself. *So what if he went to college and knows all sorts of obscure stuff? See, didn't I tell you—doggone!*

"Uncle?"

"What is it now?"

"You mean you went to college and studied scotchalism, not economy? You studied how to take money from rich people and spend it, instead of making it yourself?"

"What do you know about socialism, talking like that?"

"Well, I know something about that stuff."

And I proceeded to give it to him straight.

He looks right into my face from where he's lying and gives me a little smirk. And then listen to what this fine gentleman had to say.

"So that's socialism, eh? Well, I'd call it thuggery."

"Well now, so you know scotchalism is thuggery too."

"I didn't say that."

"Did too! Just now."

"What *you're* talking about is thuggery, not socialism."

"There you go! Scotchalism is highway robbery—didn't you say so yourself?"

"Listen to you, boy—carrying on just for the sake of argument."

There! Got him again. Now he's showing his true colors.

"Uncle?"

"What now?"

"You should straighten out your thinking."

"What's that supposed to mean?"

"Aren't you worried?"

"Someone like me, what's there to worry about? *I* worry about *you*."

"But I've got a plan and I think it makes sense."

"How so?"

"You really want to hear it?"

And once again I gave it to him straight. That fine gentleman heard me out, and you should have heard what he had to say.

"You're pitiful."

"How come?"

But he didn't say anything.

"How do you mean, I'm pitiful?"

He still didn't say anything.

"Uncle?"

"What?"

"You said I was pitiful?"

"No, I was only talking to myself."

"Still—"

"Listen, you!"

"Yes?"

"No matter who you are, nothing's so disgusting as kissing up to someone."

"Kissing up to someone?"

"Well . . . in this world there's a structure. The emperors are at the top and the beggars are at the bottom and everybody lives according to his means. There's nothing so disgusting as kissing up to someone for your livelihood, and going so far as to lose your individuality in the process. There's nobody as pathetic as such a person. Why does a person need a second bowl of rice if the first one fills him up?"

"What's that supposed to mean?"

"You want to marry a Japanese, you even want a Japanese name, you want your whole lifestyle to be Japanese."

"What's wrong with that?"

"That's just the point. It would be one thing if what you say comes from profound cultivation and sound judgment. But it would seem from what you say that you have something else in mind."

"Like what?"

"You want to cozy up to your boss, and your neighbors too—"

"You bet I do! My boss has to trust me, and I have to be on good terms with the neighbors from the home country."

My uncle didn't have any answer for that.

"Uncle, you still don't know the way of the world. You're older than I am and you went to college, but I got out there at an early age and took some hard knocks, and you don't know as much about the world as me. Do you have any idea what's going on out there?"

"Boy!"

"Yes?

"Just now you mentioned the ways of the world."

"Yes."

"And you have a bright, shining future."

"Yes."

"And you're going to make a hundred thousand *wŏn* by the time you're sixty."

"Yes."

"The ways of the world as you would describe it and the ways of the world as I would describe it are different, but the fact is, they're quite complicated."

"I don't get it."

"No matter how a person tries, he ends up being controlled by powerful forces he isn't even aware of—the ways of the world, as you put it—and there's nothing he can do about it."

"What do you mean?"

"To put it simply, we can manufacture all the plans and opportunities we want, but things don't work out that way."

"Aw hell, Uncle, don't tell me . . . You know, there's an article on Napoleon in a recent issue of *King*. According to him, a man makes his own opportunities and *impossibility* is a word that's found in a fool's dictionary. If you keep planning and finding opportunities, there's nothing in this world you can't do as long as you fight for it. If you fail at something, then you pick yourself up and have at it again with twice as much courage. Haven't you ever heard the saying 'Seven times defeated, eighth time victory'?"

"Napoleon was successful as long as he adapted to the ways of the world. When he opposed them he failed. You talk about 'Seven times defeated, eighth time victory,' but you've only seen a few people who succeeded that way. Don't you realize how many people there are who succeed the eighth time, then fail the ninth time and can't get up anymore?"

"Well, you just wait. I'm going to succeed and nothing'll stop me. . . . You're even worse than I thought. You lose heart even before you try something because you're convinced you're going to fail."

"That's like saying a person has to go up in the sky before he can tell for sure it's high."

Brother, when the stakes are down he doesn't have anything to say, so he tries to get by with a completely irrelevant comparison. Is there anyone on earth who's dumb enough not to know that the sky is high? Where did he come up with that one?

I felt like dropping it right there. But then what? Well, I just had to start in again.

"Uncle?"

"Yes?"

"What are you going to do once you're all better again?"

"What do you mean?"

"I mean your future . . ."

"My future?"

"Don't you have any plans?"

"At this point, what's the use of making plans?"

"So, no plans? Just live from day to day?"

"I didn't say I didn't have plans."

"You do, then?"

"Sure I do."

"What are they?"

"Continue on like I've been doing . . ."

"You mean you're going back to that whatchamacallit?"

"Probably."

"Uncle?"

He didn't answer.

"Uncle?"

"What?"

"Why don't you give it up?"

"Just give it up?"

"Yes."

"You think I've just been killing time all along?"

"Well, haven't you?"

No response.

"Uncle?"

He still didn't answer.

"Uncle?"

"Yes?"

"How old are you?"

"Thirty-three."

"Aren't you old enough to turn over a new leaf and start taking care of family matters?"

"Take care of family matters, and then what?"

"If you're going to put it that way, then let's assume you take care of that whatchamacallit business—then what?"

"It's not a matter of 'then what.'"

"You mean you don't have any hopes or objectives when you do that other business?"

"Hopes? Objectives?"

"Yes."

"That's a different matter. One person's hopes and objectives—that's not the issue."

"That's a new one on me!"

"Really?"

"Yes, really!"

"Well, I'll be . . ."

"Uncle?"

"Yes?"

"Aren't you grateful to have Aunt?"

"Yes, I am."

"Isn't she pitiful?"

"Pitiful? If you put it like that, then, yes, she is indeed."

"So, you know that."

"Yes, I do."

"And still you act like you do."

"There are people who keep tasting bitterness and eventually they find some sweetness there—the joy you get from hardship. We're not born that way, but that's what happens when you put your heart and soul into something. And at that point hardship becomes joy. Now in your aunt's case, sure, hardship is hardship, but at the same time she finds joy in it."

"And you consider that a blessing?"

"No, I don't."

"Then, shouldn't you try to make it up to her?"

"Well, I'm not unaware of what she's done for me . . ."

"So, once you're all better, you'll—"

"Right, along with everything else."

Heck, can you believe that! There he is lying down, talking about "everything else" he has to do. What a bald-faced crock!

There's no hope for him. Look at him anyway you want, he's about as useful as a fingernail, he's a nuisance to others, a canker on the world. He'd be better off dead, and the sooner the better. He deserves to die, he has it coming.

But heck, he doesn't die, he just keeps twitching. It vexes me to no end. . . .

Translated by Bruce and Ju-Chan Fulton

9. CH'OE CHŎNGHŬI

Ch'oe Chŏnghŭi was born in 1912 in Tanch'ŏn, South Hamgyŏng Province, and was educated in Seoul. After a brief sojourn in Japan, and while still in her teens, she went to work for the journal *Samch'ŏlli*, where she made her literary debut in 1931. In a career that spanned fifty years she published essays, criticism, and twelve volumes of fiction. She died in 1990. Her daughters, Kim Chiwŏn and Kim Ch'aewŏn, are award-winning fiction writers.

Ch'oe, along with Pak Hwasŏng, was probably the most successful of the early-modern women writers. Her story "Sanje" (1938, trans. 1958 "The Memorial Service on the Mountain"), like Hyŏn Chingŏn's "Pul," can be read as a rebellion against sexual tyranny. "Chŏmnye" (1947, trans. 2004 "Chŏmnye") is an engaging sketch of a country girl of that name. "Hyungga" (1937, trans. 1998 "The Haunted House") is an unusual story for its time in its portrayal of a single mother (her son apparently born out of wedlock) who supports an extended family on her salary as a newspaper writer. The story translated here, "Umul ch'inŭn p'unggyŏng," first appeared in the journal *Shin sedae* in 1948.

THE RITUAL AT THE WELL

This was the day of the annual ceremony for the cleansing of the well. Since early morning the village head had rushed around reminding everyone to come out for the ceremony. I quickly put away the breakfast things and went out to the well.

The ceremony went like this. First, the well was cleaned until the water ran clear. Water was ladled into a brass bowl that was then placed on a small table, in the belief that a prayer asking for a plentiful supply of water said before this table would be answered. Besides, those who drank the water would receive the five blessings: long life, wealth, health, peace, and many sons.

In the villages where this ceremony was observed, every household, whether it had a well or not, felt obligated to attend. We had our own well, and a year might pass without my having used one drop from the village well. I participated because this was a community affair and not because I had some special wish like the others.

By the time I arrived a considerable number of villagers had gathered under the large shade tree and were busily binding together two tin kerosene cans. These were tied to a thick straw rope the size of a swing rope, and would become the bucket to be used to draw the water from the well.

This well was located in the center of the village next to the rice paddies and the fields that marked the boundary line of the road that passed in front of the village. No one knew when or by whose hand it had been dug. Year after year, season upon season, this village continued to drink the water from this well that never ran dry. Although most of the forty households in the village rarely missed a day of going to the well, there was always enough water.

Forty families. What is significant about the amount of water that a village this size might drink? Think of it, forty families with forty different kinds of daily chores. The amount of water used by one of these families each day is no small matter. Of course, well water flows continually, but this is not my concern. If water wasn't that plentiful how would one house manage, with its forty different daily uses for water? Let's not take just one year or even one month, but only ten days and calculate the amount that is needed. How many earthenware jars would it take? Quite a number. A large jar would have to be filled at least ten times.

Let's not think only of the beginnings of this village but of the future when the descendants increase with their offspring multiplying like the endless gushing forth of the water. The constant use of this water could be symbolic of an eternal year. The word *eternity* has little meaning when it is said without any special thought, but if you close your eyes it becomes a heavy, endless word, weighing on the consciousness.

Although like the others I felt an obligation to take part in the ceremony, more than that, I believed in honoring the flowing of water from eternity to eternity. By contrast, I was repulsed by the observance of the special ceremonies to the rocks, the earth, and the trees. The well ceremony, however, was different.

At a short distance from the well stood the shade tree. It was so large that it took three men to encircle it with their arms. Heavy branches spread out from its huge trunk. The tree was unusually broad and tall since its many branches had produced more than the original number of boughs. Not knowing the name of the tree, like the villagers, I called it the big shade tree. Tangled together, those spreading branches and the great quantity of leaves that grew out of them nearly shut out the sky. I didn't find it oppressive for the sky to be covered like that since the lovely shade tree was a sight to see more beautiful than the sky itself. No one talked about whether the seed was planted by hand or had quite naturally fallen and sprouted by itself. It had never been fertilized or pruned and yet had grown into a magnificent shade tree with only the help of the sun, the rain, and the wind. The bark on the trunk was not only ugly, but hard like a rock. Neither an ax nor a saw would make a dent in it. Compared with the other trees it had an impressive abundance of leaves.

Before anyone was aware of the coming of spring, and when the fierce winter wind was still dragging its tail across the sky, a wind blew in from a far corner of the earth. It was more like a fragrance than a breeze, and like pollen from a flower it blew so gently. The shade tree seemed to be the first to feel that stirring within that announced the coming of spring. Spreading out from that stonelike body its branches were the very first of all the trees to be covered with delicate green buds. It was the first to give shade. The local villagers were not the only ones to rest beneath it. Other villagers, who happened to be returning from their fields at sundown by way of this tree, sat down to rest after first filling a bucket of water to the brim and drinking it as the water dripped down the sides. Some led an ox by the rope while others had only a hoe in their hand. Those with an ox tied the nose ring to a stone at some distance from the tree. A constant stream of young men and women walked back and forth from the well carrying water or washing barley and vegetables. No doubt those from other villages came not only to rest in the shade but also because this was a good place to take a look at the young people who came to the well.

The tree served other purposes as well. During the summer months the merchant who sold household wares and the one who repaired cooking pots set up shop under this tree. The tree was used in other ways as well. At the Tano Festival in the spring a swing was tied to the tangled boughs. Swinging back and forth, the young women, their bosoms swelling like cotton candy, felt free and light.

The children easily climbed up into its branches, where they pretended to be riding a horse. Looking down on the houses of their friends, they called for them to come out and play. Some yelled at those they disliked, while others caught cicadas. There were boys who urinated from the branches. Others called out to the girls they fancied. None of the young men, who circled around underneath watching the comings and goings at the well, could recall when it was that they had stopped climbing the tree.

With the coming of spring the young men went to the far-off mountains to gather wood. On their return they picked an armful of cloudlike azaleas to throw down at the feet of one special girl under the tree. Here the berries from the mulberry tree were shared and eaten, dying the lips a deep wine red. Some sang any song that happened to come to mind, in an attempt to squelch the passions that were welling up inside.

The rice paddies and the fields spread out from the well and the shade tree. At the place where these ended a narrow river flowed, holding the blue sky in its bosom. Mountains were beyond, to the east and to the west, with a portion to the south also closed off by mountains. The presence of so many mountains seemed overwhelming. Besides this smaller river there was also a larger one. These two branches of the Han River surrounded this dreamy, idyllic village on the sand and then flowed on as far as the sky could see.

Here was nature at its best, with the sky, the flowers, and the shade trees. To all those who came here, this village gave the impression of having an intimate relationship with nature. The man who repaired the cooking pots and the merchant who sold housewares talked about how peaceful and blessed this village was. If this were true then there could be no hunger, illness, or ragged clothes, but only love and singing.

"Come on now, let's get going," ordered Mr. Yun of the pockmarked face. He lowered the cans into the well and struck the gong again and again. This striking of the gong set the rhythm and the pace. His job was to sound the signal while Haksu and Wŏnbae dumped the buckets. The young women held on to the end of the rope while the young men grabbed on in front of them. At one strike of the gong the cans were dropped into the well. Two strikes of the gong gave the signal for filling the buckets and pulling them up. Then upon three strikes Haksu and Wŏnbae were to empty the buckets. At the signal to lower the buckets into the well those who held the rope had only to walk forward. When the buckets were full they had only to walk backward, pulling up the buckets. Everyone must stop dead in their tracks at the signal for dumping the buckets. Over and over again, the same thing; it was that simple. If just one person from each house had been ordered to participate that would have been enough.

All were in a happy mood, as it was more like play than work. Some sang snatches of songs in a soft voice. The deaf man from Changwŏn, a vacant stare on his face, kept muttering meaningless words over and over. Now and then he stumbled on the stonelike roots of the tree as he looked around at the women to the rear. Among these were Mongbun, Yŏnsun, Sugi, Hongsun, and Kabi. Hongshik, Pongsu, Kkomaeng, Tŏkkyun, Sŏgyun, Pokkil, and the other young men, too, glanced behind. The number of young people was rather unusual for a village of this size. If I were to reveal the reason at this time, would it be properly appreciated?

Chattering among themselves, Yŏnsun, Mongbun, and the other young women appeared not to be bothered by the backward glances of the young men until their eyes happened to meet. Then their faces turned many shades of red.

"Hey, you rascals, you. Careful! Your eyes are about to be stuck there in the back of your heads," teased Mr. Yun. The deaf man joined in the laughter although he had no idea why they were laughing. "You too, deaf guy. Get a hold of yourself. Say, Hongshik and you other guys, take hold of that rope now. Don't let go of it! Watch it now!" Everyone was laughing, and in the excitement Mr. Yun began to sing.

"Say, Uncle Pockmark, you're getting excited again," said Pokkil.

"Excited, who's excited? I'm just mad from having been doused, that's all. I really feel great." Mr. Yun straightened his shoulders and started to move his hips in a dance. Sure enough, at a closer look, his clothes were soaking wet, as now and then the bucket got tipped the wrong way or the young men didn't follow the beat of the gong.

"You rascals, you. Why, you can only take part because you're pure, that's why. Who said it was all right to come out here looking for bride material? Whoopee! I feel so good I could fly. Whoopee!" he said, beginning to sing a familiar tune. His voice wasn't particularly good but they all felt good because of him. He stopped beating the gong and then, raising it high in the air, began to pound it repeatedly. "Say, you guys, sure enough, you can only take part 'cause you're clean and then you go and sneak glances at the young gals."

There is a phrase in the shaman's chant that refers to this being clean. The very reason they felt good was because of being clean, meaning they were bachelors. This is an important part of the story that needs an explanation. Women who were pregnant, or menstruating, or who had slept with their husband the previous night were not allowed to participate. Except for a few restrictions the men were exempt. Men or women who had been present in a home where there had been a death or who were in mourning clothes in observance of the death of a parent, or widows who were in mourning for a husband: none were allowed to take part in the ceremony as they were considered unclean. It was believed that a terrible misfortune might occur if they should participate. Naturally, a large number of women would be missing. With the exception of some adults, all who remained would be the children and young people. As the little ones weren't strong enough to clean the well it was up to the young men and women. Don't you wonder why there were so many bachelors and unmarried young women in such a small village? Wonder some more, as I'm not ready to tell you why just now.

The sky was high with the breeze announcing the coming of fall as the cicadas cried from the shade tree. Whenever a gentle breeze blew over the fields and the rice paddies down below the well and the shade tree, the green shoots, along with the soybeans, the sorghum, the red beans, and the cotton plants, mingled together swelling like waves on the sea. How can it be said that these are the same when the sea is dark blue and the plants are a dark green? That is an appropriate question. I'm not talking about color, however, but about the feeling that comes over one while walking back and forth holding onto the rope. It is that aimless feeling not unlike the wanderlust stirring in the breast, that helpless feeling one gets looking at the sea.

"You rascals, get gone, you. Ha, ha, ha!" shrieked Mr. Yun, looking like a drowned rat, having been drenched with water from the overflowing bucket.

"Yah, just look at you. God, but you won't feel the heat now. Great, isn't it, Uncle?" teased one of them as all again broke out in laughter.

"Well, so what if I got doused. If you get a good laugh out of it, well, so what? Whoopee! For God's sake, let's whoop it up. Whoopee!"

His wornout hemp knee pants clung fast to his bottom as he moved back and forth. He began to sing again as he continued beating the gong. What a sight! The young people were of an age when they laughed to see horse droppings so it was quite natural that they all burst into laughter. There was nothing to do but stop temporarily. Mr. Yun, too, seemed to have forgotten his assigned task.

"Look here, Ch'anggŭn, stop your laughing. We'll be back where we started. Come on now," the village head said, putting a damper on Mr. Yun's comedy routine.

Evidently he respected the village head, since without further delay he stopped shaking his hips and began to sound the gong. Hordes of dragonflies were flying everywhere while the noisy droning of the cicadas could be heard from the big tree. It was about noontime as the sun was overhead. The tree gave shade as usual, but still the shirts stuck to the sweaty backs.

"What happened to the *makkŏlli* they went to get?" asked the grandfather from Koryŏng. Standing there behind the others, he was feeling rather hungry.

"If it was anything like last year, why, we would at least be getting barley rice to eat," retorted Ch'ŏlgŭn, making loud gulping noises as he swallowed.

"Well, you ate good the year of liberation didn't you? What was it now? Rice cakes, meat, *sul*."

"That wasn't because of the well, that was just a party."

"Anyway, that's how we ate!"

"Isn't anyone going to treat?"

Even though they had eaten a huge breakfast of meat, rice, and many side dishes, it was noontime and they were famished. Only one person had to mention food and immediately the talk was of nothing but food. Loud swallowing sounds could be heard from the front to the back of the line.

As recently as last year Landlord Ch'oe had given rice mixed with barley. Even the year before, the year of liberation, with the well ritual for an excuse, rice and money had been collected from each house so that all ate well on meat, rice cakes, and a large assortment of vegetables, along with *makkŏlli*. This year was different.

The people in this village had lived by cultivating and harvesting the land of one man, this Ch'oe. I had no idea when this all began as it was that way when we moved here. I guessed that they had been living like that for a very long time. With the coming of liberation Mr. Ch'oe had hurriedly moved his family to Seoul. He left the disposal of his house and land in the hands of his steward, a Mr. Yi. When the villagers learned of this they were crushed and wondered how he could do this to them. Everyone cried as if some terrible calamity had struck. After some time they went to Mr. Yi and talked the matter over. He was upset by what they told him. He rubbed his chin as he sympathized with them, saying that he understood how they felt. Their difficult circumstances and the gaunt faces he saw daily pained him greatly. He went to Seoul to report on the plight of the villagers to Mr. Ch'oe.

"I told each one of them to buy the land that they had worked and they didn't. So what am I supposed to do?" responded Mr. Ch'oe, refusing to listen.

The steward asked, "Was there any way that they could have gotten the money together to buy the land?"

"Well then, there is nothing that can be done about it now, is there?"

The steward had nothing more to say. All he got out of the trip was a firm order to sell the land as quickly as possible. When he began selling off the land he was met with loud cries of anguish and the clasping of hands. The clamor neither rose up to the heavens nor fell back upon the earth, only turning in on those who had uttered the sounds.

Most of Ch'oe's property was bought by farmers from other villages who already owned their own land. Only some thirty percent of the land remained in the hands of these villagers, with none of them having more than two or three rice paddies. Each year in the past they had returned a certain amount of their rice harvest to the landlord. What remained now was far from enough for one year, or six months, or even two months. Since it was barely enough for one month, where would they find the money to buy the land? With liberation would money fall from the sky? Life became a living hell for the seventy percent or so who were unable to buy land. The only alternative was to do day labor or fell trees and sell the wood. Was this type of work available all year? What kind of day labor was possible in a village as poor and small as this one?

Many villagers went elsewhere to work during the spring planting, the summer weeding, or the fall harvesting. Some went as far away as Manchuria and China. Upon their return, they always found that their earnings failed to last for even three short months. What was to be done for the remainder of the year? There was nothing left to do but go to the mountains, cut trees, and sell the wood. The larger trees like pine and elm could be felled with a saw, but the smaller ones had to be cut with a sickle. Before the wood was ready to sell it had to be cut into firewood and chips. Day after day, month after month, for twelve months in a year, the whole village, to the very last person, lived like this.

The mountains became bare. Fearing that the hills would be stripped clean, the ranger from the county office, his eyes fairly blazing with anger, chased off the villagers. Even if someone of a higher rank than this ranger were to try to chase them off, there was no alternative but to continue. Their lives depended on cutting down the trees even though they faced imprisonment if they were caught. Hadn't Kappok been in prison three months before he was released? And Pokkil had suffered for twenty days in police custody. They were well aware of the consequences, but what was there to do in such a desperate situation? In order to keep the mountains from being stripped bare the cutting must stop. Some other way had to be found to keep the villagers from starving.

After Mr. Ch'oe sold his land and moved to Seoul various rumors circulated about his activities. Some said he was backing a certain politician, others said he was setting up an office, and some others said he was now the manager of a factory.

Sŏgyun arrived with three casks of *makkŏlli* from the brewery and set them under the shade tree. All turned their heads in his direction. Swallowing noises were clearly audible, sounding much like the gulping of water.

"Uncle Pockmark, let's eat," said Haksu and Wŏnbae, standing dead still, clasping the bucket to their chests.

"That won't do, not at all. If we quit now, all we've done is just gone down the drain. The water is still seeping out even though we keep on drawing it up. Why this year with such a long rainy season we'll just have to work harder and longer."

"So what's the use? There's still water even though we keep on dumping it. When will it be all cleaned out so we can eat?"

"I can't wait any longer," Wŏnbae said, throwing down the bucket and coming forward. Immediately Haksu also stepped aside.

"Who'll take their places?" Everyone pretended not to hear Mr. Yun. "Hongshik and Pokkil, come on, both of you."

"I can't, let's eat and then finish," said one, and then the other, also shaking his head, added, "I can't either."

"Well, even if you're hungry the right way is to clean the well first and then eat. Is this your first time? You rascals, you!"

An old man standing nearby swallowed and in a dignified tone of voice reproached them, siding with Mr. Yun. "That's right! What do you mean by eating before the ceremony is finished?"

"They're hungry, so just let them have a little something to eat," said the widow who had moved from Seoul in the spring. Upon hearing the complaints of hunger she went into her house and came out carrying a huge round wooden bowl filled with steamed bread made from white flour. As this was her first time participating, she didn't know that the ceremony was supposed to be finished before lunch was eaten. All she wanted was to ease the villagers' hunger pangs.

Her words "Come and get it" were the only signal needed. Like a bolt out of the blue they surrounded the bowl, the little ones included. Like a swarm of flies they pounced on the wooden bowl and each took a piece of bread. The old man who had cautioned them about the propriety of eating before the ceremony was over likewise helped himself to a piece. It was one thing to insist that eating was not allowed before finishing the ritual. But once the bread appeared there was no room for stubbornness; all that mattered was getting a piece of it. They all wanted to eat. Mr. Yun took a piece, as did the deaf man with the sunken eyes. Hongshik and the other young lads ate, too. It wouldn't have made a particle of difference if the bread had been dirty; they would have eaten it anyway.

Do we eat to live or do we live to eat? When I was in elementary school I took part in a debate on the side of "People eat to live." All the others seemed to be on the side of "People live to eat." This argument began to seem more reasonable to me so by the time I got up to speak I said that "People live to eat" was more accurate. Our side lost because of this hastily made stupid statement. My fellow students sent disapproving glances in my direction and reprimanded me, while the teachers only laughed.

The people in this village neither lived to eat nor ate to live. Life itself was the enemy. Since they could not stop living they ate because there was life. When someone died the only comment made by those who watched the funeral procession was, "Now you won't have to starve, and that's good." Do you think this is an untruth? No, to these people starvation was truly a curse. Since there was never enough food they were always hungry.

Plant roots and greens were the daily staples. As soon as the spring winds melted the snow on the mountains and the fields and the green sprouts began to appear, aunts, mothers, grandmothers, daughters, new brides, and young girls went out to dig up the roots. Each day until the fall harvest, a basket in hand and a cloth tied around the waist, they went to gather roots. After the harvest came, the amount of the yield determined the number of months there would be rice to eat. Usually the length of time was extremely short. They went out to strip the bark from the trees until winter set in and the distant mountains were covered with a blanket of snow. The bark, the dried greens, the rice germ, and the draff from the brewing of rice spirits saw them through the winter. More than the spring or the summer, the winter was a virtual hell, as all nature was dead.

Can you imagine how they awaited the coming of spring? Because of the hunger in the winter, it was impossible to tell whether one was dead or alive. "Spring, spring, hurry up and come" was the prayer of children and adults alike, obsessed as they were with this one thought.

"Awaiting the Coming of Spring" sounds like the theme of a poem or a novel, the waiting for the spring breezes that raise goose pimples. Or the undulating dark blue waves of mist that hover in the valleys before dissipating. Or the singing of various birds or the many colors of the blooming flowers. These are not the same as waiting for one thing—the grass. Green grass. The thing that could be used for food.

These young men, more than eleven pairs of eyes sitting around that wooden bowl staring at that steamed bread, lived on the mountain greens that the women of the family gathered. How do I know? Consider the evidence. You would know if you saw their bowel movements. Unlike myself and the many others who need an enema, warm water, or medicine for constipation, these people here have chronic diarrhea due to their daily diet of nothing but cooked greens.

The day was beautiful with the sky an unusual deep shade of azure-blue. Poksŏn's father was there, his face yellow from hookworm. So was Hongsu, who had been slapped by the woman in the house next door when he stole the dregs from the brewing of the rice spirits. Pokkil was there. Someone stole two measures of his barley, and in order to find the culprit he had gouged out the eyes of a frog. Hŭngnyŏl was there. That morning he had eaten a breakfast of salted zucchini leaves. Their mouths were moving as they slurped and smacked their lips in anticipation. Yellowish eyes, eyes that glanced sideways, black eyes, sleepy eyes, sullen eyes, all as big as the eyes of an ox, stared intently at that wooden bowl filled with bread.

It was like watching a play on a stage. What a shame to watch that scene alone by myself. I wanted to show that very scene to Landlord Ch'oe, who had gone to Seoul and was now reported to be backing some important political figure. Not only to him, but also to those he supported. The very ones who with the help of the rich rode around in nice cars, lived in big houses, ate well, and dressed in the latest styles, and for whom living was easy. These were the ones to whom I wanted to show this scene.

How do you see it? Have you ever seen people who lose their heads like this over the sight of white bread? How is it that people who can grow rice should be hungry? What is the reason they can't eat their fill of rice? It would be no problem if they could eat barley or some other grains instead of rye, which is slimy and causes diarrhea.

A few of them were able to wear traditional dress, but most looked like beggars. Some wore the uniforms that had been left over upon liberation, patching them over and over, patch upon patch. No one knew the source of the judo practice uniforms worn by some, winter and summer, night and day. Some wore the traditional unlined short jacket of summer with worn-out sleeves. Those young people who formerly had dressed as extravagantly as possible now wore hemp or cotton clothes covered with patches like all the rest. Others, unable to buy cloth, were stripped to the waist. No one knew the cost of a pair of silk stockings or the price of the material to make a skirt out of brocade.

Seoul was some thirteen miles from this village, a little over forty minutes by train. How could such a short distance seem so far? Not one of them knew about the machines for making silk and cotton thread quickly if you just sat down in front of them. Following the practice of years and years, they spun their thread on the spinning wheel. It took a day's work at the loom to weave three yards of fabric for a piece of clothing. At night the work was done by the light of an oil lamp. The materialism of the city was far removed from this village. These were farmers who had only a few hours of rest out of the daily twenty-four. There is nothing wrong with farming as long as there is some leisure and enough to eat. These farmers, however, starved and were poorly clothed.

I'm sure you would agree with me that the world would be a more pleasant place to live if ten people ate exactly the same amount rather than one person eating well and the rest going hungry. And wouldn't the world be a happier place if ten people were neither too hot nor too cold rather than only one person?

"As long as we're at it, let's just live it up, even if it's only *makkŏlli*," Mr. Yun said, smacking his lips upon finishing the bread, and then going over to the casks of rice brew. Everyone agreed. No manners or formality was necessary as far as eating was concerned. The elders became quiet also, no disagreement there.

"Oh my goodness, the bread! Why, we didn't give any to the gals." Mr. Yun suddenly remembered the young women who were sitting together in a group. Those hungry faces, gathered in front of the cask, turned in their direction. "Now that will never do." All agreed but none appeared to be particularly concerned.

"Come on now, this time let's give them some first," one of the older ones ordered in a loud voice to the younger ones. This time they were generous, as the bread was all gone. Haksu filled a bowl to the brim with *makkŏlli* from the cask and brought it to me. He also brought sour pickles. In the confusion of the moment I gulped down the whole bowl. The pickles were unusually sour.

My legs felt tired after drinking the *makkŏlli*, perhaps since it was before lunch. I was weary through and through and an angry feeling began to come over me when the bowl appeared. Seeing them in front of the bread I sensed the tragedy of their lives. Strange as it may seem, though, as soon as I had a drink of the *makkŏlli* my feelings underwent a complete change. I now found them disgusting and I wanted to pick a quarrel with them. This had nothing to do with not getting any of the bread.

"Haksu, come here for a minute. Do you suppose you could give me just one more bowl of *makkŏlli*?" I yelled loudly in the direction of the cask. The young women and the young men, their faces red, laughed at me with mouths wide open. No doubt they thought it odd for a woman to continue drinking like this. Whether their laughter had anything to do with it or not, after taking the overflowing bowl from Haksu, I gulped it down as before in one swallow. I munched on the pickles but this time I was unaware of the sourness.

My legs were shaking like a leaf. Standing there I could do nothing but quietly watch those chattering red faces. I looked neither at the sky nor at those rice fields that resembled the sea, nor did I hear the crying of the cicadas. I just stared. I felt tense. It was like watching a play. As I gazed at them I saw that their eyes had become sleepy, sullen, and dull, unlike the wide-eyed look when the bread first appeared. Now the faces were relaxed. In front of the bowl of bread those faces had been tight, but now the wrinkles on those faces were like gently rolling waves.

"Hey, you over there, don't you ever do anything day and night but beg?" I muttered to myself in my hometown dialect. Whenever I was happy or excited this happened. Not one of them had any idea what I said, nor would they have understood if they had known. They kept on laughing and making a racket. Hongshik and the other young men sent ardent glances in the direction of Mongbun and the other young women.

"Now look here, Hongshik. Didn't you get a piece of bread and give it to Mongbun?" I yelled.

No matter how drunk I was I knew I shouldn't have said that. Wide-eyed, Hongshik looked all around and the others, red-faced and chattering, stood dead still and stared at me. I had singled out Mongbun only because for some time I had liked her name, thinking it sweet and cute like the blooming four o'clock. She hung her head as her eyes reddened. I should have kept my mouth shut. What was I to do about it now? Bewildered, all I could do was to say in a composed voice, "Come on now, let's clean out the well."

Dusting off the seats of their pants, they promptly got up. From the look on their faces I could tell that they would like to have taken the time to smoke a cigarette made from zucchini leaves or one of the stale rationed ones. Yet they were anxious to get on with the ceremony, for it seemed they were uneasy about eating and drinking before the ritual was completed. I felt I had been granted a reprieve. I wasn't worried about Hongshik or the others, but what about Mongbun? How long would her face stay red? How long would she hang her head?

Mr. Yun raised the gong, sounding the signal, while Hongshik and Pokkil, the replacements, took the bucket and dumped it. They were lined up as before, the young men in front and the young women in the rear. As if to make up for having eaten before the ceremony was finished they acted as if they were able to scoop all the water from the well in one bucketful. I didn't try to take hold of the rope.

How was I to make any sense of the abominable plight of these people as they performed this ceremony in the belief that good would happen? I said earlier that although I found the ceremonies performed before the stones, the trees, and the earth repulsive, I did not feel that way about the ceremony to the unceasing flowing water. After two bowls of *makkŏlli* I was beginning to wonder what it was that made life so difficult. Why were they always hungry even though they prayed for blessings night and day? At that moment I felt an indescribable dislike for all of them.

The cicadas crying overhead were as noisy as a bunch of howling cats. Ordinarily I liked the cry of the cicadas, so how could their crying resemble the sound of a bunch of detestable cats? It didn't matter one bit that they cried. What did it matter that the shade was pleasant and the sky blue or the fields and the rice paddies in front of the village were like the gently rolling sea? All was nonsense, devoid of meaning. What if nature was good? What if the merchant and the man who repaired the pots said that this was a peaceful place filled with blessings? Who wouldn't want to write a poem or paint a picture of the scene at the well with the buckets made from two kerosene cans tied to a thick rope and then filled with water? Or the sight of the young women standing to the back with the young men up in front holding the rope and pulling up the bucket at the ringing of the gong? Or Mongbun and the others in their patched dresses looking like blooming peonies though they were starving? Or up in the front, Hongshik and Pokkil with the other young men?

The beautiful sky spread out above the cicadas singing in that big shade tree. Down in the front the fields and the rice paddies gave a feeling of being at sea. Where these ended the meandering stream reflected the blue in the sky. Here the very best things in creation enjoyed an intimate relationship. Yet how could this village be called blessed and peaceful when its poverty resulted in crying, disease, and fighting? Like clever snakes each waited for a chance to cheat the other.

Earlier I said that I would tell you why so many of the young men and women in this small village remained unmarried. The time has come. Poverty is the reason. I wanted first to describe the idyllic picture of the well ritual in this village. I changed my mind upon seeing that scene at the bowl of bread and after drinking the two bowls of *makkŏlli*. I must confess that I now feel different from before. Right before my very eyes this beautiful picture took on an ugly look. How was it that poverty prevented them from becoming brides and grooms? If you don't believe me, just come to our village and I will show you.

Weddings have always been an extravagant affair, so those with money plan ostentatious celebrations. The wedding clothes and the lavish feast are the first things to be considered. For these young people not even the simplest ceremony was in the realm of possibility. Marrying off daughters would be reasonable, since that would reduce the numbers in a family. In the case of sons, however, with food already scarce, there was fear about adding one more to the household. This, then, was the reason, and this alone, why so many of the young folk were unmarried. This wasn't living, this was only existing so as not to die. What good were the beauties of nature? What if this village resembled a poem or picture? A piece of bread, rather than a poem or a picture, that was art.

Now take a look at this. Here I was, standing under the shade tree in that tipsy state, the bucket line right in front of me. Suddenly the young men turned around and saw a partially eaten piece of bread that had fallen to the ground. The younger ones, already having spied it, swarmed around. Haksu saw one of them pick up the bread. As the child took to his heels, Haksu pulled him back by the scruff of the neck, taking the bread. All eyes focused on that scene.

Kkomaeng began to peck at him: "Haksu, you rascal. Who is that bread for, the piece that you hid? Come on now, tell us. If you don't I'll spill the beans."

"Well, if you've got something to tell, go right ahead. Why, I took it to give to my mom, so what!" Of course, that was only an excuse. It wasn't because of the *makkŏlli* that his face was flushed.

"Haksu, Haksu. He's the model son," Hongshik called out as he turned around, forgetting that his job was to dump the bucket.

"Yah, a devoted son, why, if that's all it takes, I'll do it, too," chimed in Sŏgyun.

"Hey, listen to this. That guy told me something. It was when we went to cut wood on the high mountain. Why, didn't he say he couldn't carry his mom on his back but he could carry a certain someone up that steep mountain one hundred times or more. I wonder who he meant?" As Kkomaeng was talking the young men looked back at the women.

"Hey, you there, Kkomaeng, you don't have to broadcast it. We all know," Pokkil joined in.

"Can't you guys keep your mouths shut?" Hongshik said, frowning and shaking his head.

"Come on now, someone's face is already fiery red," said Tŏkkyun, indicating those in back with his chin. They all grinned and turned to look behind. This time Mongbun's face was redder than earlier, when from under the shade tree, upon drinking the two bowls of *makkŏlli*, I had abruptly pointed her out and Hongshik and the others began to tease her. Sure enough, Tŏkkyun was right. Among all the girls, hers was the only red face.

Whether or not he knew what was going on, the deaf man scowled as he looked in turn from Haksu to Mongbun, moaning and groaning as if he were carrying a heavy load.

"So, Uncle Yun, you think that Haksu did that for his parents? You don't really know, so how can you say that?" Kkomaeng interrupted.

"You good-for-nothing. Kkomaeng, why do you keep on like that? Why I'm just going to wring your neck!" said Haksu.

"Well, what are you going to wring my neck for anyway? Why get mad at me just because you couldn't feed your girlfriend?" Kkomaeng continued, unwilling to give up.

"You young ones, these days you don't have any respect for your elders, carrying on like that in front of us." Seizing a chance to speak, the old man spoke in an authoritative tone.

"Yah, here you guys aren't much more then ten and already you're starting to chase the gals," Poksŏn's father chimed in.

"What about the twenty-year-olds? Are they just going to stay quiet when the ones barely dry behind the ears start going after the girls?" Mr. Yun said in defense of the young men.

"Come now, let's cool down. Look at you, Yun, here you're over forty and yet you're just like the young guys," said the old man who lived in the mud hut, clicking his tongue in disapproval.

In the same tone of voice as that of the old man, Mr. Yun said, "Yes, so you think you've reached an age when you know all there is to know, so what? Is that what it means to be an adult? To act with great authority in front of the others, just like you know everything?"

The old people pursed their lips and glared at Mr. Yun as he joined the argument.

"Come now, let's stop this talk and clean out the well. It's all because of a rascal like Haksu that this all started in the first place," continued Kkomaeng, not willing to leave Haksu alone.

"What's that guy saying? That it's all my fault? Let's kill him and throw him out." Haksu's face flushed with anger. He hated Kkomaeng, who like the quarrelling adults wanted to pin the blame on him.

"Well, if you hadn't hidden the bread in the first place there wouldn't be any fuss now, would there?" Kkomaeng was angry, too.

"Hey, what business is it of yours that I hid the bread? I didn't eat it, I just hid it, so what's the big deal anyway?"

Unable to stand the situation any longer the old man from Koryŏng stepped forward. His veins stood out on his neck as he said, "You guys, why fight on this special day."

But Kkomaeng continued, "Sure, you hid it to give to Mongbun." The mention of her name only made matters worse.

"You son-of-a-bitch, what business is it of yours."

"Stop it! Look what's happened. Now the teasing has turned into a fight," said Mr. Yun. But neither young man showed any signs of quitting.

Hearing the quarreling, Haksu's mother appeared out of the blue with a rag in her hand that dripped with water blacker than rat droppings. Swinging the rag at her son she yelled, "Why, that son-of-a-bitch! It would've been better if he'd never been born."

The bucket brigade stopped. The quarreling ceased. All were wide-eyed, their eyes glued on Haksu and his mother. The rag, blacker than ink, was wet with old urine and not with water as I had thought. The smell made my eyes smart. The deaf man, a look of great contentment on his face, seemed in good spirits as he patted Haksu's mother on the back and muttered, "Aba, aba." Standing there in front of his mother, Haksu screwed up his mouth as he brushed off his hair and his clothes. His mother looked at him with daggers in her eyes.

"This good-for-nothing son. Why in the hell was he ever born? That's about all you ever do, night and day. So you can't carry your old mother up the mountain and yet you can carry a young gal up one hundred times. Isn't that right? Well then, let's see you do it ten times that! She's turned your head. You said you'd hid the bread to give to your mother. What a liar! Only yesterday you hid a sweet potato in your load of wood and took it to her house! You're so worried about me? You're no son of mine. And, of all people, why that slut? The daughter of our worst enemy, why that wench of all people?!"

In her anger she struck at Haksu over and over with her fists. It couldn't have been more embarrassing for Mongbun. Her face changed from red to purple as she stood there helpless with the rope in her hands.

"Mongbun, why don't you rest a bit. Just go to your house and rest awhile." I couldn't help but identify with her difficult situation. In the meantime the anger that had welled up within me vanished and my trembling legs and shaking fists were now back to normal. The anger that I had felt against the landlord dissipated as I sympathized with Mongbun. Having been granted a reprieve, she withdrew without a word.

"The world's falling apart. It's just going to pieces! The children don't respect their parents. What's this world coming to anyway?" said the old man from Koryŏng, siding with Haksu's mother.

His words only excited her more. "Let me see, what's left at our house? Some touch-me-nots and four-o'clocks that his sister worked so hard to plant, and then didn't he take them and give them to that slut?" The reason she became this angry was probably because there was nothing left for her to do. Screaming at the top of her voice, she continued, "Look at that bitch's yard, will you! It's covered with four-o'clocks and touch-me-nots!"

Everyone, old and young alike, stopped and turned to look in the direction of Mongbun's yard, since it was visible from the shade tree. Just at that moment Mongbun's mother appeared. Either Mongbun had told her what was going on or she had heard Haksu's mother yelling. In any case she came out and walked up to Haksu's mother. She was about to speak when Haksu's mother, with no warning, took the pin from her bun and grabbed the hair of Mongbun's mother. There was no escaping. And then with the speed of lightning the deaf man took hold of Haksu's mother. As he lifted her up to move her aside she fell down.

From the moment that Haksu's mother swung the urine-soaked rag at her son, the deaf man had been on her side. When the mothers came to blows, however, it became apparent that he sided with Mongbun. The look on the faces of all the young men showed whose side they were on. Haksu, too, felt the same. Perhaps it was because she was Mongbun's mother or that his mother was the aggressor. Haksu's mother simply rose and began again. What a frightening spectacle!

"Now, look at this mess. Something awful is going to happen. Come on, let's dip out the water, the water," said the old man, a worried look on his face, as he saw how engrossed they all were in the fighting.

Then old man Sunbo chimed in, "When the hen crows, bad luck strikes the house, so when women fight like this something terrible is going to happen." The quarrel had begun over the flowers and the sweet potato. Had the flowers been taken or not? Was the sweet potato eaten or not? Then it went on to other things.

Haksu's mother cried, "You slut, God will punish you. That land that I worked and ate off, that two plots of land, why, when that bitch's family bought it didn't I cry my eyes out?" The sweet potato and the flowers had been forgotten and now the fight was centered on the land.

"For goodness' sake! Who told you to sell it? When you said you weren't going to buy it, then the landlord sold it to us. Didn't we sell our iron pot, our soy sauce and kimchi pots, and even the pig that we had fattened? We sold everything and bought the land. If you felt that way why didn't you sell everything and hold on to it no matter what? Why blame me?"

"Auntie, let's just forget it. My mother's wrong. If you hadn't bought the land he would've just sold it to someone outside of the village," chimed in Haksu, taking his chance to talk.

Then Haksu's mother started to pound on him. "This rascal, this is the way he treats his mother and father in front of that slut. And if we go hungry, as long as it's for her sake, that's just fine! All of that land out there to be sold, so why in the world did you have to take what we had worked? Oh, that slut—I'm really disappointed in that rascal—they took our land and still you take their side. You son-of-a-bitch, why did I ever have you! You dirty woman, you! So what? You sold your pots and your pig, too, all of that and bought the land that someone else couldn't? So what? Is that what you have to do in order to feel good? You just wait! I'll raise a pig, sell the piglets, and buy all of your land. You wait and see, *aigu, aigu*!"

After this tirade she stood there striking her hands together in frustration and looking up toward the heavens.

"Mother, why don't you stop and go inside? Why be bitter against them. All they did was to get together a little money and buy the land we had farmed. They didn't do it so we'd go hungry. Why, that was just a small piece of land! We didn't have the money so we couldn't hold on to it. What use is it to say such awful things? Please go inside."

But she appeared not to hear him and continued her lament.

From the moment that the dispute over the land started, all of them, as one, had serious looks on their faces. Those who held the rope, the ones who dumped the bucket, Mr. Yun who beat the gong. There was no talk of favoring one or the other, no assessing of blame, no fear over the main cause of this unfortunate affair. Nothing but a drooping of the shoulders and a slowing of the step, that was all.

Was it because of that broad, expansive sky that Haksu's mother's aggrieved clapping echoed like the beating of sticks by the night watchman?

Once again a different kind of feeling came over me, like when I sensed that Mongbun was embarrassed. My heart beat faster, skipping a beat. I was unable to feel hatred for Haksu's mother, who was much more spirited, ruthless, and mean than Mongbun's. I only wanted to take her mother, along with those with drooping shoulders, into my arms. While holding them I wanted to tell them the thoughts that were mounting, seething and surging within me.

There is no good reason for you mothers to fight. You're not starving because of Mongbun's family. Landlord Ch'oe is the one responsible. For decades you worked like slaves on the land that gave you your food. Your situation improved with liberation, but the landlords felt threatened by their former servants and sold the land. Then Ch'oe with all the others moved to Seoul, where they back politicians, who want to start a new government. Right now, those people are using the money that you earned by your sweat and blood in any way they wish, foolishly and recklessly. How is it used? For themselves, of course, in support of those who will set up a new government that will in turn take good care of them. Everything is being turned upside down. These kinds of people, these very people just like greedy Landlord Ch'oe, think only of themselves. It doesn't matter what happens to you. Not if you plead, or if you shake your fists, or if you starve, or if your young folk can't marry because you are too poor. They have no idea whatsoever how to care for others. They don't cry or shed blood. Those who will someday govern are supported with this kind of money. These are the ones who must rule to bring back the good old days. You have absolutely nothing to fight about. If you tore Landlord Ch'oe to pieces it would be no more than he deserved. He's the one responsible for your starving. He's the one responsible for your pleading, for your fist clenching, and for your children not being able to marry. He's one of those with money and land who is the reason for your hunger. This is a world that looks after the people with money and land.

As I rehearsed this speech in my head the rope continued to go back and forth. Before I had a chance to say anything, a small child yelled, "Look! A pig!"

"Oh, my goodness, if it didn't go and get out again." Haksu's mother stopped striking her hands together and hurriedly picked up a stick. "Here piggy, here piggy."

Letting go of the rope, Haksu started to chase after the pig. Hit on the rear by the stick, the pig ran like a streak of lightning in the direction of the well. As it circled the small table the brass bowl overturned. Without another word Mongbun's mother went into her house.

"Yah, that pig is only four months old and already she's looking for a mate. She's been acting like that since yesterday. Here piggy, piggy," said Haksu's mother.

No sooner had these words fallen from her lips than the old people, with serious looks on their faces, echoed together as if in chorus, "See here! This isn't right. Why, from this morning things haven't been just like they should be. Didn't we tell you that you shouldn't eat before the ceremony was finished? It wasn't only the eating, there were a lot of things that were said. Then the fighting got out of hand, and then that pig comes in heat like that. Something bad is bound to happen." These white-haired elders who had watched the ceremony year after year knew what they were talking about. They had a right to be concerned since they were well aware of the rules about who was allowed to attend and who was not.

Several times the pig circled the well as it ran around the trunk of the shade tree with Haksu and his mother in close pursuit. They looked like children playing a game of tag as they chased the pig round and round.

"Say you good-for-nothing-son, go and chase her over to that side. Piggy, piggy."

"What good will it do to just chase her? We'd better catch her once and for all. What if she escapes around the well?"

"You're right. Let's catch her. Well, we might as well mate her while we're at it. They say the pig at the drinking house is a good one."

"Just look at them. Stop that dirty talk and strike the gong and let's get on with it right now. What's this coming to anyway?" said the old man from Koryŏng, a miserable look on his face.

"Yes, hit the gong. What do you know? So a four-month-old pig already has a taste for sex, why, that's faster than a person," responded Mr. Yun, wanting to have the last word.

Not one person objected, nor did anyone laugh. Haksu and his mother were left to chase after the pig while the young men in the front and the young women in the back moved backward and forward to the ringing of the gong. The cicadas sang from the shade tree and the full blue sky made the fields and rice paddies look like a sea of water. Down at the far end the river flowed, bluer than the sky.

"Look at that pig! Why is she running in there? She's gone crazy! Piggy, piggy, piggy."

As the pig ran into Mongbun's yard her mother picked up a stone, hitting the pig hard. She was getting her revenge.

Seeing this, Haksu's mother again became angry and said, "That bitch isn't afraid of God! That's why she can do that. You keep on like that and I'll knock your house over. Heaven sent that dumb pig to punish you!" Taking the stick that she had been chasing the pig with, she shook it angrily in the face of Mongbun's mother.

Mongbun's mother picked up another stone, and calling "Piggy, piggy!"

chased after the pig. Then she grabbed Haksu's mother by the throat. In the confusion of the moment Haksu's mother threw away her stick and gripping Mongbun's mother by the throat, beat her with her fists and butted her with her head.

With blood gushing from her nose, Mongbun's mother cried out, "*Aigu!* This bitch is out for blood!"

The young people put down the rope and ran into the yard of her house. The deaf man followed.

"Hey, bring some cold water to douse them," Mr. Yun ordered Hongshik. He took the overflowing bucket and with the rope dragging behind ran toward the house.

"What in the world is this, that ends up in blood?" Looking as if he were about to burst into tears, the old man from Koryŏng followed the rope.

"Bring some cotton, some cotton!" yelled Haksu as he tried to separate the two, who were at each other's throats. As Yŏnsun was on her way into the house Mongbun appeared with cotton in her hand. Her face was pale.

"Hey, you guys, hurry over here. Come now, how in the world are we ever going to get the well cleaned?" At the shrill voice of the old man from the drinking house they gathered around as if they had completely forgotten, then suddenly remembered.

By this time the pig had gone into the buckwheat field and was making a big mess. Mongbun was angry. As she led her mother into the house she turned around several times and sent dark looks in the direction of Haksu's mother.

As Haksu's mother glanced at the blood on her hands and her sleeve she once again picked up the stick and yelled in a shriller voice than before, "You dirty bitch! You've made our life miserable! Now what more do you want? If I were to take out your liver, eat it, and spit it out I would still be mad. That rascal! Piggy, piggy! You rascal, surround her and chase her this way. Piggy, piggy."

Following his mother's orders, Haksu went behind the wall of Mongbun's house to chase out the pig. As Mr. Yun struck the gong once again, the villagers moved their feet in time. I, too, moved back and forth but my heart was not in it. I was frustrated because I was unable to say what I was thinking.

The young men turned their attention to chasing after the pig, but that didn't keep them from watching the young women. Their eager glances were more furtive than before. I felt utterly helpless. If the entire world could have become an erupting volcano, only then would I have felt a sense of relief.

Translated by Genell Y. Poitras

10. HWANG SUNWŎN

Hwang Sunwŏn was born in 1915 near Pyongyang and educated there and at Waseda University in Tokyo. He was barely in his twenties when he published two volumes of poetry, and in 1940 his first volume of stories was published. He subsequently concentrated on fiction, producing seven novels and more than one hundred stories.

In 1946 Hwang and his family moved from the Soviet-occupied northern sector of Korea to the American-occupied south. He began teaching at Seoul High School in September of that year. Like millions of other Koreans, the Hwang family was displaced by the civil war of 1950–1953. From 1957 to 1993 Hwang taught Korean literature at Kyung Hee University in Seoul.

Hwang is the author of some of the best-known stories of modern Korea: "Pyŏl" (1940, trans. 1980 "The Stars"), "Hwang noin" (1942, trans. 1980 "An Old Man's Birthday"), "Tok chinnŭn nŭlgŭni" (1944, trans. 1980 "The Old Potter"), "Hak" (1953, trans. 1980 "Cranes"), and "Sonagi" (1956, trans. 1990 "The Cloudburst"), among others. In a creative burst in the mid-1950s Hwang produced the story collection *Irŏbŏrin saram tŭl* (trans. 2006 *Lost Souls*). This volume, a series of variations on the theme of the outcast in a highly structured society, is unique among Hwang's story collections for its thematic unity.

Hwang began publishing novels in the 1950s. During the next two decades he produced his most important work in this genre. *Namu tŭl pit'al e sŏda* (1960, trans. 2005 *Trees on a Slope*), perhaps his most successful novel, deals with the effects of the civil war on three young soldiers. *Irwŏl* (1962–1965, The sun and the moon) is a portrait of a *paekchŏng* (outcast) in urban Seoul. *Umjiginŭn sŏng* (1968–1972, trans. 1985 *The Moving Castle*) is an ambitious effort to synthesize Western influence and native tradition in modern Korea.

Also in the 1960s and 1970s Hwang's short fiction became more experimental. Some of his most memorable and challenging stories date from this period: "Ŏmŏni ka innŭn yuwŏl ŭi taehwa" (1965, trans. 1989 "Conversations in June About Mothers"), "Mak ŭn naeryŏnnŭnde" (1968, trans. 1989 "The Curtain Fell, But Then . . ."), "Sutcha p'uri" (1974, trans. 1980 "A Numerical Enigma"). Hwang's creative powers were undiminished as late as the 1980s, as the highly original "Kŭrimja p'uri" (1984, trans. 1990 "A Shadow Solution") demonstrates.

Indeed, the length of Hwang's literary career, spanning seven decades, is virtually unparalleled in Korean letters. But it is his craftsmanship that sets Hwang apart from his peers. It is safe to say that Hwang is *the* consummate short-story writer of twentieth-century Korea. His command of dialect, his facility with both rural and urban settings, his variety of narrative techniques, his vivid artistic imagination, his spectacularly diverse constellation of characters, and his insights into human personality make Hwang at once a complete writer and one who is almost impossible to categorize. If there is one constant in Hwang's fiction, it is a humanism that is affirmative without being naive, compassionate without being sentimental, and spiritual without being otherworldly.

"Wang morae," translated here, was written in 1953 (in his collected works, with the exception of his first story collection, Hwang cites the month and year of composition for each of his stories) and was first published in his 1956 collection *Hak* (Cranes). It is one of a number of Hwang's stories that concern mother-son relationships.

COARSE SAND

It was the day that year when the apricot blossoms began to drop from the trees and scatter on the wind.

His mother always returned home by daybreak, but today it was nearing sundown and she still had not come back. Tori held back his tears and lay quietly looking and looking at the chamber pot by his head on the floor.

When his mother came back each day at dawn, the first thing she would do was reach for the chamber pot and use it. Tori always woke up to that sound. All too early in life Tori had learned to awaken at the slightest noise. When his mother pulled the bedclothes up over her head, Tori would reach out to touch his mother's breast. She would always push his hand away roughly, saying, "Did you come into this world just to pester me?" The strong smell of liquor would then roll over him like a wave. His mother's body would be hot and feverish, and lying there behind his mother's back, trying to hold in his breath, Tori would wonder whether she could be sick or if she hurt somewhere. And his mother would spend the whole day in bed exactly like a person who was sick.

Tori would wait for the sunlight to shine brightly through the papered door, and then slip carefully out of the bed so as not to wake his mother. He would slide the door open quietly and go outside. He would pick up his mother's rubber shoes and hold them. He would look inside them. As always, there would be mud and coarse sand in them. It was dirt from the tailings at the gold placer mine by the stream nearby.

When his father was still living and worked as a day laborer at the gold mine, he always came home with dirt and coarse sand on his shoes, too. Tori could not understand why his mother brought that same dirt on her rubber shoes every morning, when his father had worked during the daytime carrying earth at the mine.

It would be nearly evening when his mother finally got up and cooked something for supper and the next morning's breakfast. At these times the only part of his mother that barely suggested a sick person was her heavy-lidded eyes, and they seemed to get brighter every day. After she had fixed their supper, his mother would return to bed and lie down. Each day Tori would make up his mind to stay awake until his mother went out that night. This always turned out to be a useless exercise, for without realizing it, he would drift off to sleep anyway.

During the night he might wake up needing to go to the bathroom and open his eyes. Of course his mother would not be there. In the early morning he would open his eyes at the chamber pot sounds, and then he would know his mother had come back. As always his mother would turn her back and go to sleep, behaving like a sick person.

This day it was the usual time for his mother to prepare supper and breakfast, but still she had not returned. Tori was sleepy. He slumped forward, dozing where he sat waiting. Startled, he sat up in surprise at the sound of the door sliding open, and saw the landlady standing outside.

The landlady closed the door, saying, "So that bitch didn't even come back last night," and continued to mutter something to herself. Then she opened the door again and came into the room. She went straight to the wooden box they kept in a corner of the room, opened the lid, and looked inside. Quickly she picked it up and put it outside. After that she rolled up the grimy bedding that was lying open on the floor where it had been used, and said, "The cheap whore hasn't paid her rent for two months." Then she spun around, looked at Tori, and said, "Your mommy won't be coming back now. She's gone away, far away."

Tori could not take in what the landlady had said. Did she say mommy wasn't coming back? Why would that be? But when he saw the landlady take out the chamber pot, too, it really seemed as though his mother would not come back. Tori then burst into tears. He was eight years old at the time.

It was warmer than being in bed at home. At the same time it was colder than it had been in his own bed. Tori spent the night on the warm corner of the floor by the chimney at the restaurant that sold beef soup and rice.

"Hey, I've been looking high and low for you!" It was the pockmarked lady. He was glad to see her. She would probably know where his mother had gone.

One day not long after his father had died, Tori's mother had asked him to go and bring the pockmarked lady to her. That day his mother had even given Tori money to go and buy himself some candy. Tori had sucked the hard candy drops until they were all gone and then had returned home. He could hear his mother speaking inside.

"I can't stand this suffering any longer! I suppose I'll have to do what you say and try to improve my lot." Tori had no idea what she was talking about.

He did think, though, that his mother's eyes had a strange look in them that day.

The next day the pockmarked lady had come again. This time she brought a man with her. The man had a handlebar moustache and was wearing a suit with puttees on his legs. Immediately Tori had noticed that there was coarse sand from the gold mine on his shoes. Even to the little boy, though, this man gave the impression that he was not a person who carried hods of earth as his father had. That day, too, Tori had received money to go and buy candy. And this was the first time he had seen his mother put powder on her face. From that night his mother began her habit of coming home each day at dawn.

This time the pockmarked lady quickly started to wipe Tori's running nose with the inside of the hem of her skirt, and she was telling him, "Your mommy told me I should take care of you, so you need to do what I say." At first Tori couldn't grasp what she was trying to tell him. He simply thought that if he followed her he would be able to see his mother. "Sure," he thought, "Mommy is probably waiting for me over at the pockmarked lady's house."

The pockmarked lady's house was in a new neighborhood that had been built close by the mine fields. Now, however, she was taking him in the opposite direction, toward the foot of the mountains.

When they had arrived in front of a house with a big gate, the pockmarked lady put her mouth down close to Tori's ear and whispered, "From now on you're going to be the young master in this house. If you do what your new mommy and daddy say, the world is yours. All right?" But Tori could not figure out what this was all about.

They cut his unkempt hair and made it look neat. They scrubbed away every bit of the accumulated dirt from his whole body. They dressed him in new clothes. They even changed his name to Sŏbi. And he had to say Father and Mother to people he had never seen before in his life.

The next day he entered school. He didn't have any friends. During recess time he stood off by himself at one side of the playground. He would look down and see the road. Far down at the end he could see the piles of tailings at the gold mine. He tried to figure out the location of the house where they used to live.

The apricot tree there was just losing the last of the petals from its blossoms. Suddenly he thought about that day last winter when it had begun to sleet so quickly, when his father had come home and said he had passed blood in his stool. After that his father began to look paler every day, but he refused to give up a single day of work in the gold mine. His condition had become so weak that he died before he had been in bed ten days.

On his way home from school Tori went and looked at the house where he and his mother used to live. It seemed as though other people had already moved in, because he could hear the crying of a tiny baby coming from the room where they used to be.

Every so often the pockmarked lady would come to the gate of the house where Tori was living. She would go inside and talk with his new mother in her room. When the pockmarked lady left, she would be carrying a bundle in her hand. On these visits the pockmarked lady hardly ever said anything to Tori. But he was glad to see her, thinking that someday she was planning to give him a chance to see his mother again.

One day when his new father had been out all night, he said he had been involved in a game of mahjong with some of his friends. On nights like that his new mother did not sleep at all, and she would go without food the next day.

One day his new mother told Tori to follow his father and see where he was going. As he watched, Tori saw his father go into a house down a secluded alley. A young girl picked up his shoes and took them in.

When his mother heard this, she changed her skirt, and he could see that her hands were shaking violently. She then followed Tori out. His father came running out of that house looking completely flustered, grabbing his suit coat in his hand. Then his new mother came chasing out after him with her hair all in a tangle. Nothing happened in the street on the way back. When they were inside the house, though, his new mother began to claw and tear wildly at his father's chest and gave him a thorough tongue-lashing. "All right, you just kill me and go and live with that bitch! Kill me! Right now! Kill me!"

It was a long while before his new father could get in a word. "Look here! Do you think for one moment I was there because I care about that broad? I only wanted to find a way to have a son, and that's all."

After that his father did not stay out all night anymore. Then one evening Tori's new mother told him to follow his father, who was going out carrying the toilet kit he used for taking a bath. But his father went right past the bathhouse, turned down an alley, and went into a house. A young woman took care of his shoes when he went in. Tori was taken completely by surprise. It was the same girl he had seen the last time. She was now in an entirely different house. He turned around, but before he could leave the alley someone grabbed him by the back of the neck. How she had gotten there he didn't know, but it was the girl he had just seen at the door. "You little good-for-nothing! What's the big idea, making other people miserable like this!" Her fingernails made marks on his neck that smarted for days afterward.

The following year before the fruit was ripe on the trees, Tori noticed that for some reason his new mother kept buying green fruit, storing it, and eating it. Then at the time of the first hard frost, his new mother's stomach began to swell.

The pockmarked lady came. She asked the ages of Tori's new mother and father, and then after spending a long time counting by bending and straightening her fingers, she said it was a boy for certain. This time when she left she was carrying a bigger bundle than ever before.

During the first month of the next year his new mother had a baby. It was a boy. One day soon after they had celebrated the baby's twenty-first day, the pockmarked lady came, for the first time in a long while. This time she had not come on her own, but they had sent the maid to get her. And this time she didn't go inside and talk with his new mother in her room; she stood outside and talked with his father. When they were through, Tori's new father handed her a bundle of money.

On the spot Tori went with the pockmarked lady and left the house with the big gate. She was muttering something to herself. "When I figured it out, it was for sure going to be a girl, but then she had to go and have a boy." Then looking around at Tori, she said, "Well, all your luck seems to be bad, and there isn't a damned thing I can do about it!"

Tori did not know why the pockmarked lady was in such a bad mood that day.

Tori became the errand boy at the fabric shop. It looked as though the pockmarked lady had already talked to the people there, because when they left the house with the big gate, she had taken him straight to the shop. The work was not all that hard. The owner and his wife were really very kind. The pockmarked lady would stop in there every once in a while, too. The owner would always slip her a few pieces of material that was in season when she came.

Two years passed. He came to know the names of all the kinds of fabric. Then the owner of the shop decided to move to Seoul. He had plans to expand and open a larger store there.

He asked Tori to go along with them. Tori thought about whether he would go or stay. The pockmarked lady came rushing over and said that they would have to leave the boy behind. Now that she had said that, Tori thought so, too. Yes, he'd better stay where the pockmarked lady was, then he would be able to meet his mother when she came back.

The next day Tori moved over to the farm implements store. There was already an older boy working at this store. This boy seemed to have been doing his work for a long time, and would even take the place of the owner in buying and selling things. Unlike Tori, he slept at his own house and came to work every day.

From the day he arrived there, Tori had to sweep the courtyard and draw the water. When the owner was off in the country selling implements, Tori also had to take care of the shutters and open the shop.

There was an eight-year-old boy in the owner's family. In spare moments Tori also had the job of taking care of this child. Tori made things for him. He made eyeglasses out of wire, and whittled a top from wood. He made him a shuttlecock to kick and a kite to fly. Tori was happiest when he was taking care of this boy.

Once during the night Tori got out of bed and was on his way to the toilet. As he was passing by the door of the family's room, for some reason he paused and stood before the door. Through the small pane of glass in the center of the door he could see the boy lying asleep with his arms around his mother's breast. And the mother had one arm around the boy's neck.

In the darkness Tori, too, reached out instinctively for his mother's breast. His mother responded by holding him as well. But in the next instant his mother turned away and lay with her back toward him. Tori had to get away from that door as fast as he could. He made up his mind then that he would never again look in through the glass in that door.

The very next night, however, Tori found himself stopping again in front of that same door. This time the boy was sleeping facing the other way. All the same the boy's mother had one arm curled around his neck.

One night when the owner had come back from a trip in the country, he was sitting in the store working on the account books and figuring on the abacus. Tori took the chance to slip out as if he had to go to the bathroom, and went in the house to look through the door again. That night the boy had his arms tightly clasped around his mother's neck. In the darkness he also put his arms out and hugged his mother's neck. As he did this, someone's hand grasped him by the back of the neck. It was much stronger than the grip of the young woman who once had caught him in the alley next to the bath house.

"So, now that you've gotten your hands on someone else's gold ring, you're looking for something else to steal, I suppose!" It was the owner's voice. Next the palm of his strong hand caught Tori on the side of the face and made stars flash before his eyes. "Come on, now! Give me the ring!"

He said that a gold ring that had been on the dressing table had disappeared the day before while his wife was out doing the washing. Tori held his hand over his red, stinging cheek. He didn't know what the owner was talking about.

The older boy who worked in the store opened the back door a crack, stuck his head in, and then pulled it back quickly. At once Tori remembered. Yesterday when he thought the older boy had probably gone out to the toilet, Tori had caught his eye as he slipped out of the door of the owner's family's room, still wearing his shoes. Tori was about to tell the owner about that, but he couldn't bring himself to do it. He had heard some time ago that the older boy's father had suffered a stroke and was an invalid. The image of the boy's father appeared before his eyes, even though he had never actually met him. What he saw was the image of his own father before his death.

The owner of the store sent the older boy to bring the pockmarked lady. That night Tori was put out of the place and had to go with her. When they had gone a short way, the older boy came running after them in the darkness. He put something into Tori's hand. It was money. Tori shoved it back, and noticed that the older boy's hand was damp with sweat.

After they had gone a little farther, the pockmarked lady stopped walking and said, "I was planning to buy a spade and a hoe, maybe tomorrow, but now I guess I can't because of you. They said you took it, so let me see the ring."

Tori didn't know how to answer. Then the pockmarked lady became less direct and asked, "Did you sell the ring? Since you've already sold it, why don't you just let me have a look at the money?" Tori was still completely silent, so the pockmarked lady went on muttering to herself. "Your old man, too, he was hypnotized by anything gold. Kept swallowing bits of gold and coarse sand right along with it until it ground through his guts and killed him."

Tori thought there must be something terribly important for him to understand in what the pockmarked lady was saying that night.

The pockmarked lady's house was at one end of a row of houses a short distance from the gold mine. These houses had been in the mining area, but during the previous year when the mine was played out, the houses were picked up and moved away to their present location.

It was a small one-room house. Inside a young man and woman were drinking, passing the wine cup back and forth. They appeared to be quite drunk.

"Say, come over a little closer." The man grasped the woman under her arm and pulled her toward him, at the same time sliding his other hand into the front of her blouse. The woman twisted the top part of her body as if this tickled and said, "Are you sure you've had enough to drink?" Then she pushed the small serving table across the floor out of the way and turned out the light. She spoke and acted as though other people were not even there at the other end of the room.

The pockmarked woman lay down in the place where she had been sitting. She then reached out in the dark and with her hand signaled Tori to lie down, too.

The next thing he knew the pockmarked woman was already snoring. At the upper end of the room the young woman was giggling and then gave out a series of cries as if she was hurting. They acted as if no one else was in the room. Tori put his hands over his hears to stop the sound.

After a while the pockmarked woman's hand came and rested upon him. He thought she must have moved it in her sleep. The hand began to move, though, groping to find his jacket pocket. He thought about pushing it away, but left it alone. He recalled how she had asked him to give her the ring a while before on their way over. Her hand even went burrowing into his pants pockets. She was giving him a thorough going-over.

When daybreak arrived the young man had already left. The young woman was by herself, fast asleep with her limbs sticking out in all directions. The alcohol-induced animation had gone out of her, and compared with last night under the light bulb, her face now looked far more swollen and had a blotchy, yellowish cast. She looked older, too.

Tori went outside. He walked over toward the mine fields. This was the place where there had once been such a clamor about gold pouring out of the ground. Now there was nothing left but these endless huge piles of tailings that looked like enormous grave mounds.

Tori went over and sat on top of one of the piles of tailings. He picked up a handful of the worked-over earth and coarse sand. He tried putting some in his mouth. He could perhaps understand after all. How his father, not long after beginning to work as a laborer in the mine, had always checked the chamber pot after he used it. And what he was doing when he emptied it into a washbasin full of water and inspected the contents so carefully. Then also why blood had begun to appear from that day when the sleet storm came. Tori was suddenly overcome with fright. Now he could guess why his mother's shoes had coarse sand from this place in them, beginning shortly after his father's death. He remembered last night and how the young woman and the man had acted. Soon after his father had passed away, his mother had called the pockmarked woman. She had brought the man with the handlebar moustache. At that time the pockmarked woman's house had been here in the mine precincts. Even so, within Tori's heart there was a voice crying out, "No, no!" Wasn't the young woman still sleeping now at the pockmarked woman's house, even though it was broad daylight? His mother had always come back to him before the break of day.

"I've been looking all over for you. I didn't think you'd be here." It was the pockmarked woman. Now it wasn't like the last time she had come to find him, when he had slept in the corner by the chimney at the soup restaurant. This time he didn't feel glad to see her. He didn't feel anything.

"You've been crying. Why, do you hurt someplace? This time I found a job for you at the inn. But watch out. No more lifting things like the last time! Come on, let's go."

Suddenly Tori felt an impulse to ask the pockmarked woman what had happened to his mother, but he did not. He was afraid she would answer that she didn't know. At the same time, he thought how lucky it was that at least he didn't have to sleep again that night at the pockmarked woman's house.

One day at dawn, the third time that the apricot tree standing in the inner courtyard of the inn had begun dropping its petals, Tori was sweeping the courtyard. The pockmarked woman bustled in, acting very important. She had been coming to see Tori every once in a while. She would come saying she needed money right away and would ask to borrow some from him. Tori had been giving her money out of his savings from the customers' tips. This was the first time, though, that she had come so early, at daybreak.

"Well, your mother's back." It had been a long time since he had heard her speak in such a gentle voice. When he heard this, Tori was stunned and silent. The broom dropped out of his hands. He picked it up and stood it against the apricot tree. The broom would not stay straight and fell over. His hands trembled.

"Why are you hesitating so, child? Your mother's here, right outside." And sure enough, there was an older middle-aged woman standing just inside the gate. Her dull hair was completely disheveled. Her face was deathly pale.

"Well, what do you think? He's all grown up now, isn't he? Sixteen this year. Oh, how I've worked to try and take good care of him during all this time." Tori's mother made no response. His mother's puffy eyes, sunken deep in their sockets, with matter not even wiped from the corners, looked so dull that she didn't seem to be looking directly at Tori.

"Look, your mother's sick. Hurry up and take her inside so she can lie down."

She did walk like a person who was really very ill. He spread out bedding in a room in a quiet corner of the inn, and she lay down. As soon as his mother put her head on the pillow she closed her eyes.

As though she had been waiting for the chance, the pockmarked woman whispered in Tori's ear. "Last night your mother bought some medicine with money I gave her. No one else could have gotten it for her, but because of me she was able to take it." As she said this she put out her open palm before Tori. As always the pockmarked woman's hand was soft and smooth.

Tori said they should hurry and call the doctor. Without opening her eyes his mother then said there was no need for a doctor, and just to leave her lying quietly the way she was. Her voice was terribly hoarse. Tori's mother ate hardly anything for breakfast. At lunch time it was the same. For supper she drank only two or three swallows of broth from the seaweed soup.

All that day, whenever he had spare moments, Tori went into the room and looked down at his mother, who seemed to be sleeping and remained perfectly still. She didn't look anything like the mother he used to know. Well, perhaps you could say that the heavy-lidded eyes were still there from before, even though right now they were sunken so deep and messy with matter in them. Tori thought that all of this, though, was due to her being sick. He would get a house ready for his mother, even if it could be only a little shack, and he would nurse her until she recovered.

At dusk, when he had taken the bags down to the station for some of the guests at the inn, he came back to find everything in an uproar because a guest in one of the rooms had lost his wallet. He said he had stepped out to go to the toilet and that it had been taken out of the pocket of his coat hanging on a hook on the wall.

Tori's mother came inside the gate with tottering steps. It was the staggering walk of a very sick person. She said she had been outside looking for the toilet. Tori suddenly realized something he should have done. He hadn't brought a chamber pot for her to use.

Tori felt happy as he returned from the china shop with the best chamber pot he could find. His heart pounded as he thought how he had once been so afraid his mother wouldn't return when the landlady took away their old chamber pot, but now with this new one he would really make his mother his very own for good.

As soon as he returned, Tori's mother held out an injection vial and told him to go and get one like it for her. Tori ran to the drugstore he knew down at the corner. When the clerk at the drugstore saw the vial, he said that you couldn't buy that kind of injection without a certificate from a doctor. He said he had gotten into trouble with the owner the night before when he sold one of those to the pockmarked woman; she had kept after him until he gave in. Then a little while ago, too, an older woman had come and tried everything to get him to sell her one, but he hadn't done so. "Do you have any idea what kind of medicine this is?" he asked Tori. Then he told him that the injection was made from opium.

Tori's heart was cut to the quick. The pockmarked woman had talked about buying some medicine that was hard to get for his mother the night before. Then there was his mother's staggering walk a while ago when she said she had been looking for the toilet. One of the guests at the inn had lost his wallet. Still, Tori shook his head: no, it couldn't be so.

When Tori's mother saw him return empty-handed, she found the strength from somewhere to sit bolt upright. "You stupid little fool! Can't you even get one of these for me? It was a mistake to give birth to a thing like you to begin with! If I just hadn't had you, I wouldn't be in this mess today. Look here at my stomach. This all comes from giving birth to such a fine character as you! You know why that nice supervisor at the mine wouldn't have me? Because of this stomach! Next a crew chief on the railroad didn't want me because of it. Then a little while ago I met a kind old shoe repair man. I thought even he would reject me, so I did what he said and started to shoot this stuff. A few days ago he was taken in for stealing someone's shoes. There wasn't anything else to do, so I came to see if you could take care of me, and is this the way it's going to be?"

Immediately his mother's voice changed to pleading, though, and she said, "No, everything is my fault. Whenever I look at this snakelike scar on my stomach I always remember that you came into this world covered with my blood. All the males in this world are heartless. Child, have pity on your poor mother. You have to save me. Just get me one shot. If you don't, your mother's going to die!"

Tori couldn't stand to hear any more. He ran straight to the hospital. But they told him at the hospital that they always had to report patients like his mother to the police.

He ran back to the drugstore. He met the proprietor. "I'll pay whatever you ask if you'll sell me only one vial!" The owner looked skeptically at Tori's face with the tears welling up in his eyes, and then said, "All right, I'll let you have one if you promise you won't buy this medicine anywhere else."

Tori's mother fairly tore the vial out of his hands and hurriedly put its contents into a syringe she had prepared. Her hands trembled as she thrust it into her breast, which had become nothing more than an empty bag of skin. "Oh, I knew you were my very own son!"

Tori's face looked sad, but showed that he had made up his mind. He went to the owner of the inn and said that he would make up whatever money the guest had lost from his room that evening.

When he went back, he found that his mother's breathing was even and she had gone to sleep. He turned out the light and lay down beside her. He then slowly put his arm around his mother's neck. She did not push his hand away now. Tori gradually increased the pressure with his arm. His mother's emaciated body gave a shudder like a dragonfly when its neck has been twisted. She was having trouble breathing. But Tori did not let up on his arm as he pressed harder upon her throat.

October 1953

Translated by Edward W. Poitras in 1975, and revised in 2003

11. YI HOCH'ŎL

Yi Hoch'ŏl was born in the port city of Wŏnsan, South Hamgyŏng Province, in present-day North Korea in 1932. Serving in the North Korean People's Army after the outbreak of the Korean War, he defected to South Korea in 1950. "Far from Home" (T'arhyang) was his first published story, appearing in the journal *Munhak yesul* in 1955. "Tarajinŭn sal tŭl" (1962, trans. 2005 "Wasting Away") was honored with the seventh Tongin Literature Prize. Structured like a chamber play, it is reminiscent both of Becket's *Waiting for Godot*, in its ritual of aimless waiting, and of Chekhov's *The Cherry Orchard*, in its portrayal of a family facing imminent upheaval as it comes to realize that a family member long separated by the territorial division of Korea will never be seen again. But more than these works it was *Soshimin* (1964–1965, Petit bourgeois) that drew the attention of the Korean literary establishment with its depiction of refugee life in the port city of Pusan. *Sŏul ŭn manwŏn ida* (1966, Seoul is packed to capacity) is a wry portrait of a growing metropolis. More recently, in works such as *Namnyŏk saram pungnyŏk saram* (1996, trans. 2005 *Southerners, Northerners*), Yi has returned to the theme of the territorial division of Korea.

Yi is a prolific writer who has published essays and criticism as well as short fiction and novels; already by 1989 an edition of his complete works had been published. More important, as a native of North Korea, an activist who was jailed several times in the 1970s for protesting the dictatorship of Park Chung Hee, and a voice for reconciliation between the two Koreas, he is the conscience of the Korean literary world.

FAR FROM HOME

Any empty freight car we came across would be our home for the night. The car we'd slept in one night would never be there the next. Occasionally we had to switch cars several times. Whichever way it worked out, we were grateful for a place to sleep. The young ones, Hawŏn and I, would lie down in the middle, with Tuch'an and Kwangsŏk on either end.

Every now and then we would wake up to a strange noise in the middle of the night: our freight car would be moving along down the tracks coupled to a train.

"Hey, get up, get up, quick. . . ."

We'd rouse ourselves and jump out fast. Kwangsŏk always got it wrong, jumping in the direction opposite from where the train was heading. We usually found ourselves at pier 4 in Ch'oryang or in front of Pusan Fort Station. We then had to starting poking around again to find another empty car.

"This is too much to take. . . . Son of a bitch."

Kwangsŏk would get irritated and take it out on no one in particular.

No matter what befell us in the night, however, the four of us never failed to set out together for pier 3 in the morning. We would all sit down together at a roadside stand and eat our breakfast, watched over by its proprietor, a middle-aged woman.

"Have some more."

"Okay."

"Have some more."

"You have some more."

Each of us would offer the others the best side dish, even if it was just a slice of mackerel.

We used to make quite a stir in the dark freight car after we had downed a few bowls of *makkŏlli*. Hawŏn, the youngest among us, was always blurting things out.

"Hey, you know, it doesn't even snow in Pusan. Hey, hey, are you sleeping already? Are you asleep? Huh? You remember the well at Kwangsŏk's house?

When it's snowing? And the juniper that looks like a white parasol when the snow covers it? I was there early in the morning one time. Remember the girl from Changjagol who had married into our village? She was just about to pull up her first bucket of water when a clump of snow fell on the back of her head. I started laughing, but she didn't even bother to shake the snow off. She just laughed too, like this—ha ha ha. She was always laughing, wasn't she?"

Kwangsŏk grinned. "The local guys on the work crew asked if we were cousins. I said yeah and they said something like 'Oh really, that's something.' Hey, are you drunk already?" He paused for a moment. "Do you think we'll ever make it back?"

"Won't happen anytime soon," Tuch'an replied, slurring his words slightly.

"But this is all a good experience."

"Sure, of course."

"When we head back home, it'll be together. Understand?"

"Of course—wouldn't be any other way. The four of us splitting up here? Couldn't happen. Unthinkable. Ha ha ha. Feels good. How about some more? Another bowl for each of us, just one."

Kwangsŏk would start singing in a ringing voice while Tuch'an kept time knocking on the wall of the freight car. Hawŏn, the designated errand boy, would go get more *makkŏlli* and cigarettes. I used to collapse dead drunk and fall asleep.

One evening Kwangsŏk brought the foreman back with him. Tuch'an just lay there on his back without acknowledging his presence. Hawŏn was impressed, as if a VIP had arrived. Kwangsŏk put up the cash for several bowls of *makkŏlli*. Hawŏn immediately left to get it. He came back with the rice brew and a candle as well. Only then did Tuch'an deign to sit up.

"How do you manage to live like this?" asked the foreman, a worried look on his face.

"It's all an experience," answered Kwangsŏk politely.

"No need to concern yourself with it," said Tuch'an, his voice rising angrily.

"You've got to do something, don't you think? You simply can't keep on living like this day in and day out."

"I said, no need to concern yourself with it. What's there to be concerned about? It's none of your business."

The foreman said nothing and left a short while later. Kwangsŏk saw him off and came back.

"Why are you so stubborn, Tuch'an?"

"What do you mean, stubborn?"

"How pathetic."

When Tuch'an said nothing, Kwangsŏk muttered to himself, "When you're away from home the most important thing is to be sociable. You've got to be able to fit in, adapt yourself to what's going on around you."

Tuch'an and Kwangsŏk were both twenty-three. But Tuch'an looked four or five years older. He was on the taller side, with the appropriate amount of meat on his bones; he had a dark complexion, protruding eyes, and thick lips. A few bowls of *makkŏlli* and he would go on talking forever. Otherwise he wouldn't utter a word. Kwangsŏk was similarly tall but somewhat slender. He was always mincing around, small eyes peering out of a shadowy face brought to a peak in a sharp, pointed nose, tongue continually darting in and out of exceedingly thin lips. You could spend as much time as you wanted looking him over—you wouldn't be able to find an ounce of dignity in the man. Hawŏn was seventeen, a year my junior. His mouth dropped wide open in wonderment at everything he saw.

The Chinese Communist army had advanced down the peninsula like lightning, and before I knew it I found myself on board a ship headed south. The sense of loneliness and desolation was almost unbearable. When the four of us met out at sea we practically went out of our minds with joy.

"Hey, you got on board too!"

"You too!"

"You too!"

Early the next morning we were unloaded onto the streets of Pusan. We stood looking at one another in complete bewilderment—it was the first time away from home for any of us. Back in the village we were distant cousins, removed to something like the twentieth degree. But here, beneath the Pusan sky, we suddenly thought of ourselves as close relatives.

"The day the four of us split up now is the day we die, the day we die." In no time at all this had become Kwangsŏk's favorite refrain.

A month or so managed to go by without any particular trouble. But as time passed, the day we would be able to go back home seemed to recede further and further into the distance. Tuch'an and Kwangsŏk couldn't exactly be faulted for starting to secretly mull over their own individual plans—if you could go so far as to call them plans. Given that getting back home was not going to happen very easily, you couldn't just keep going on like this forever—you had to come up with some other way of making some cash.

Tuch'an and Kwangsŏk each began to think of himself as being needlessly held back by the others. The four of us naturally grew more and more distant; we began casting furtive glances at one another, each trying to guess the others' intentions.

It was hard to know whether to think of Kwangsŏk as overly gregarious or highly adaptable—he began to blend right in with the local workers, gulping down the *makkŏlli* they offered him, not hesitating for an instant to go on about what it was like up north. After only a few days the workers were singling him out from the rest of us, grabbing him by the hand as if he were an old friend.

"How's it going?"

"Your older brother is doing fine as usual."

"Hey, where are your manners? Calling yourself Older Brother."

"Since when do you worry about manners, the way things are going these days?"

Kwangsŏk would exchange everyday pleasantries with the workers in joking tones while the three of us just stood there staring at him. He grew more and more self-assured as the days went by. He seemed to enjoy being with them more than us.

It was truly a sorry sight. But what was more, it looked like gruff, uncompromising Tuch'an was getting ideas of his own as well. Even if he was able to filch a few things from the pier, he wouldn't so much as buy a meal for anyone. As soon as work was over he would shuffle off listlessly by himself into the narrow alleys in front of the pier, stumbling back to the freight car later in the evening completely drunk.

Hawŏn was always blubbering like a child. "Oooo, you never even get to see any snow here in Pusan, oooo."

Tuch'an's drunken, out-of-tune singing of what in all likelihood was supposed to be a ballad grew louder and louder, carried in on the wind. The three of us in the freight car were suddenly quiet.

"Open the door."

The cold, bluish lights of the pier poured into the freight car when we rolled open the door. There stood Tuch'an, tottering and laughing. Hawŏn, crouched in the corner, started sobbing. Tuch'an was breathing hard as he crawled up into the car. The first thing he did was look around for Kwangsŏk.

"Hey, Kwangsŏk, you bastard, where are you? You bastard."

"What? What do you want?" Kwangsŏk called out in an irritated voice. He didn't get up.

"Had a little bit to drink today. And ripped off some stuff. Two wool suits, that's something, got 'em myself. Had a drink by myself, too. Something wrong with that? I didn't think so. Huh, you bastard."

Kwangsŏk jumped to his feet. "If you're drunk, just lie down and go to sleep. Why make such a fuss? Going off and getting plastered all by yourself."

"You've sure got a way of putting things. That's right, I got liquored up all by myself. I pay for my own drinks, but you have a good time drinking with these guys from Pusan and you've got a lot of guys buying for you. Because you're such a good, kind-hearted guy. Not me—a contemptible guy, I'll admit it. But I've got nothing to be afraid of, nothing, not a thing. Wait and see, just you wait and see."

Hawŏn sat up and started whimpering loudly.

Kwangsŏk suddenly broke into song, his voice trembling in anger: "*I see Mother's face in the Southern Cross . . .*"

Not to be outdone, Tuch'an belted out another line from the popular song: "*Oh Shilla nights, O Shilla nights, ten years away from home* . . . Shit, let's see how it all turns out. Who knows what'll happen, you bastard, you damned bastard." His voice boomed through the entire freight car. He gave the wall a resounding kick.

Hawŏn's eyes were filling with tears again.

Raindrops spattered on the roof of the freight car. Early evening deepened to night, but still no sign of Tuch'an. Kwangsŏk had lain down and was lecturing Hawŏn again like an exacting old grump.

"Mind yourself when you walk around on the streets. Why peer into restaurants the way you do? When you buy sweet potatoes, just eat the potato. What kind of manners is it to lick your fingers too? You've got to behave properly at work—you don't want the local guys making fun of you. Why do you stuff your hands so deep in your pockets and pull your cap way down over your head and walk around without saying a word like you've got a muzzle over your mouth? If Pusan is that cold for you, how did you ever stand it up north? It wouldn't matter if you were alone, but you're embarrassing all of us. The local workers look at the four of us like we're cousins, you know."

Hawŏn didn't utter a single word in response. I drifted off to sleep.

"Hey, get up, get up, quick. . . ."

The lights of the pier, shining brightly over the low roofs of the storage sheds, were moving diagonally when I rolled open the door. We were already in front of pier 4. I leaped out in the direction the train was moving. And then, as I struggled to pick myself up off the cold, damp gravel, someone up ahead jumped out. He was back on his feet before I was. Further ahead someone else leaped out. By this time, the train had begun rounding a bend. I distinctly heard one more body thud to the ground. Actually, it was more of a crunching sound. A cold shiver shot down my spine.

I heard a scream. It was Kwangsŏk. And then the scraping, scratching sound of his body being dragged.

A flaming red fireball shot upward, lighting up the front of the engine against the dark sky, and then buried itself in the darkness.

I heard another scream. Someone grabbed me around the waist. It was Tuch'an. And then in the darkness I made out Hawŏn stumbling through the gloom toward us as fast as he could, his oversized coat flapping in the wind. He stopped in front of me and stood there dumbly as always. I started running toward Kwangsŏk.

"Hey!"

I jerked my head around. Tuch'an, hands thrust in his overcoat pockets, hadn't budged.

"Where are you going?" When I didn't answer, he called again: "I said, where are you going? What's the use?"

"What do you mean?"

"Just leave him. We can go back by ourselves, the three of us. What's the use? There's nothing you can do about it." Tuch'an shot a glance at me. "Do whatever you want. If you come, you come. If you don't, you don't."

And off he stomped. I stood there a moment digesting the crunch, one after the other, of Tuch'an's footsteps on the gravel.

Hawŏn was sobbing hard. He grabbed my sleeve, pulling me toward Kwangsŏk.

The freight train had already disappeared in the direction of Pusan Fort. Kwangsŏk's increasingly feeble cries were all that was left.

The night sky had cleared. The wind started to pick up.

Outside the freight car the wind had begun to blow fiercely. Hawŏn was whimpering again in the corner.

I wasn't mean-spirited like Tuch'an, a smooth talker like Kwangsŏk, or afraid of everything like Hawŏn. I didn't care anymore what happened among the four of us. But that didn't mean I had formed any clear plans of my own yet.

I used to feel a cold shudder when I looked into Hawŏn's childlike, pleading face. But I turned away each time. It was something I myself didn't understand. I came to feel apologetic toward Hawŏn, to feel a kind of vague responsibility toward him. And the more I felt this way, the more I could sense a burning irritation welling up inside me.

It seemed that Kwangsŏk and Tuch'an felt the same on this point, but that they weren't regarding me, at least, as much of a burden. There was no doubt, though, that the relations among us had worsened considerably while we had been living in the freight cars. This was to be expected, given that two months had already passed.

Actually, I couldn't help asking myself just what it was I thought I was doing by going to Kwangsŏk's side. But there was also a certain feeling of pride. In all likelihood what I was doing would make no difference whatsoever. But at least I could watch over him until his death. And when I went home, if I could ever go home, at least I would feel that I had done the right thing, that there was no reason for me to feel any shame.

Hawŏn, hands in his pockets, had been gulping down sobs again. I hefted Kwangsŏk onto my back—his left arm had been sliced off midway like a radish. Swallowing his tears, Hawŏn followed behind, holding Kwangsŏk up by the buttocks.

And so we made our way back to this empty freight car.

After a while, Kwangsŏk looked as if he was coming to.

"Where am I? Where's Tuch'an?" he asked in a startlingly calm, collected manner.

"He went to the hospital," I answered without hesitation.

"To the hospital? What am I going to do?" he moaned. "How can I get by with one arm? Is Tuch'an coming right back?" Kwangsŏk shifted position as if he was going to get up, then started gasping for breath. "The four of us will all be together when we head back home, that's for sure. Tuch'an didn't understand me, he didn't. I've got something to tell Tuch'an." Again he moaned. "What kind of person do you guys think I am? What did I do? Hey, are you guys going to take care of me? Are you really going to take care of me?"

In the morning Kwangsŏk was dead.

His left cheek was pressed against the floor of the freight car; his work cap was crooked. His normally gaunt face looked even hollower, and his lips were pure white. The tears below his eyes had not yet dried. His clothes were flecked with congealed blood.

Hawŏn took out his handkerchief and carefully wiped Kwangsŏk's chin. The two of us left for work.

Tuch'an was squatting, eating his breakfast. He finished his meal, wiped his lips roughly with his hand, and stuck a cigarette in his mouth. He puffed away furiously, scrunching his eyes up, resting his chin on his hand. Now and then he gazed up at some point high in the sky, his protruding eyes almost falling out of their sockets.

At the work site an older worker from Pusan said to Tuch'an, "Hey, where's the fourth guy, the chatterbox?"

"He went to a good place."

"A good place? You mean he got a job?" The worker took our silence to mean yes.

"Where? U.S. Army base? Well, good for him. What about you guys?"

Tuch'an jerked his head away. His eyes met mine, and he hastily turned aside, looking out across the ocean at a lighthouse far in the distance.

"So where'd he go? Did he land one of those jobs over at the ammo depot?" asked the worker, sucking on his pipe.

Tuch'an still didn't respond. The worker looked up at him, knocked the bowl of his pipe against the cement underfoot, and got up.

When I finished work and went out onto the pier, Tuch'an was again nowhere to be seen. Hawŏn came up to me and gave me a poke in the thigh. Startled, I turned to see Tuch'an stomping his way into a narrow alley, wrapped in the cold glow of the sunset. Hawŏn's eyes met mine. He was on the verge of tears again. I turned away.

I opened the door of the freight car but couldn't bear to step inside. Hawŏn went in first.

"Looks like he's sleeping." Hawŏn's frame loomed eerily large inside the murky freight car. His hands were thrust in his overcoat pockets as usual. He still didn't understand that Kwangsŏk was dead.

Tears finally began to flow down my cheeks. Flustered, I moved to wipe them away; Hawŏn was looking right at me. Only then did he break out crying. My tears were no match for his.

"Why are you crying? If you . . . don't cry, I won't cry. . . ." Hawŏn could barely be heard between his sobs. "Don't . . . don't cry. . . ."

Hawŏn was trying as hard as he could to choke back his tears. I sank down on the floor of the freight car, overcome with grief. Not so much for Kwangsŏk, but for Hawŏn and me. For having to face this.

A heavy winter fog set in that night. We managed to borrow a shovel and hoe from some people living in a shack nearby. We wrapped Kwangsŏk up in some pieces of a straw mat. Hawŏn kept on crying.

Late at night we set out, carrying Kwangsŏk. We talked to each other as we worked our way among the freight cars.

"It's actually pretty warm, isn't it?"

"Yeah."

"Did that refrigerator boat at site 15 leave?"

"Yeah, yesterday. Those strawberries were really good."

"They sure were."

We fell silent.

"Let's take a break," said Hawŏn.

"Is it too much for you?"

"No."

"What's wrong, then?"

"Whew, I'm really sweating."

On our way back, Hawŏn blurted out, "I thought Tuch'an was a good person, but he's not. How could he be like that?" He looked at me through the dark and punctuated his remark by clearing his throat.

The sun set later and later now. It had almost disappeared when Tuch'an suddenly showed up at our freight car the next evening. None of us said anything.

I was glad he was there. It was reassuring just to have another person around. Better than not having him there at all. Hawŏn poked me in the thigh. I couldn't figure out what he wanted at first. But then I realized that he wanted the two of us to leave Tuch'an and go off by ourselves somewhere. I ignored him, but he kept jabbing me. The night deepened, but Tuch'an didn't seem inclined to sleep. He sat against the freight car wall, smoking one cigarette after another. With every draw his face seemed to grow extraordinarily large. His bulging eyes rolled slowly. Every once in a while he heaved a long sigh. Sometimes he would cough, roll open the freight car door, and spit. I couldn't sleep. Even breathing seemed difficult.

"Hey, you asleep?" Tuch'an asked gruffly, after a while.

I pretended I was asleep. Hawŏn was busy in the corner, trying to swallow his tears.

The ocean wind howled as it beat against the freight car wall.

The three of us began our lives together again. We used to find time to joke around a little when Kwangsŏk was with us, but there was never any occasion for laughter now. Sometimes I sang to myself, "The floating clouds beyond . . . ," my voice echoing throughout the car. It made me feel a little better. But Tuch'an, it seemed, couldn't stand it. He had a way of glaring at me with a scowl so fierce it silenced me at once.

Tuch'an woke us up every morning. "Get up. I said get up and get ready," he would say. We'd open our eyes to see him in his customary position, just sitting there, looking up at the ceiling of the freight car and smoking a cigarette.

The three of us would set out for work together. Hawŏn was always either sobbing or on the verge of tears. He kept poking me in the thigh, wanting the two of us to go off somewhere else by ourselves. I ignored him every time.

At work they still thought we were close relatives. "Are they cousins? Sure look the same." They still looked us over and carried on among themselves just as they had when the four of us first showed up on the pier. They were forever asking us to talk about what it was like up north. Tuch'an would offer a weak smile but then shake his head as if he didn't know what to say. He seemed utterly dispirited.

When work was over, we went back together, back to the dark freight car. I would lie in the middle, flanked by Tuch'an and Hawŏn. I once tried to get Hawŏn to switch places with me. He pinched my thigh so hard I almost screamed.

Spring arrived in no time at all. The mountain ridge behind Ch'oryang was draped, day and night, in a shimmering haze.

It was really quite late, but Tuch'an hadn't come back. Hawŏn seemed glad and was talking on and on. He was definitely in high spirits, completely unlike his usual self.

"Looks like Tuch'an won't be coming back this time."

I said nothing.

"Hey!"

Still I remained silent.

"How come you never say anything?"

He said nothing more for a long time.

The familiar sound of Tuch'an's drunken, out-of-tune singing drew near. Startled, Hawŏn poked me in the thigh yet again.

"Open the door."

We rolled open the door, and the cold, bluish lights of the pier poured in. Tuch'an had a bottle of *makkŏlli*. There he stood, tottering at the door and laughing.

"Here, have a drink. It's rice brew, good stuff! Need something to eat along with it? Right here, can't drink without snacks. Ho ho. Look at you bastards, lying there curled up like a couple of frogs."

I took the bottle without hesitation and had a few gulps, hurrying for no good reason.

"Hey, Ha . . . Hawŏn, don't you . . . don't you want any?"

"I can't drink."

"I've heard that before." Tuch'an grabbed the bottle out of my hand and lumbered toward him. "Here, drink up, now."

"I said I can't drink." Hawŏn started getting weepy. "Let go. I said let go. Don't grab my hand, don't."

"Hawŏn, just do it," I barked, not knowing what else to say.

"Okay . . . I'll have some," he whimpered.

We were silent for a while. And then, suddenly, Tuch'an broke into tears. Hawŏn's blubbering came to an abrupt stop.

"Hey."

Tuch'an sat up. The door to the freight car had been open the whole time. Fierce gusts of wind were blowing in. Tuch'an leaned toward me, his disheveled hair obscuring his face. Hawŏn was gulping down sobs again in the corner.

"Tonight I'm gonna kill you. You bastard, why'd you go over to him alone? Why didn't you call for me to come, why? And now, you bastard, you're treating me like shit. You didn't say anything at the time, but now look at you. You think you did the right thing? Do you? Heaven's looking down on us, you arrogant bastard."

Hawŏn's whimpering abruptly stopped again. Tuch'an grabbed my knees, but then he threw himself backward and lapsed into tears.

"Huh, you dirty bastard, you son of a bitch, you think I'm drunk? Why should I be drunk? You son of a bitch, my mind's crystal clear, clear as a bell. Say something, will you? Why don't you go for me, stab me or something? How am I gonna face everyone back home? O, Kwangsŏk . . . Kwangsŏk." Tuch'an fell back with a thud. His sobbing reverberated throughout the car.

The next morning Tuch'an was gone. He didn't show up at the pier either.

A few days passed.

"Hey, let's work two shifts, days and nights, and get our hands on some money. Then we'll build a house on top of that hill in Yŏmju-dong. It's okay to put up a house there. Funny, isn't it, Cousin? Very funny. Do you know how scared I was that you were going to turn out like Tuch'an? Kwangsŏk didn't turn out to be so good either. Let's make sure we go back home together. Let's make some money. And then the first thing we do is buy some watches. If we work both shifts, it's no problem buying stuff like that. Let's not say that we ever saw Tuch'an or Kwangsŏk—nobody'll know if we don't say anything. Let's just say we never saw either of them. I'm going to start working both shifts tomorrow. I mean it. It's funny, Cousin, isn't it? I can't sleep. Let's just stay up all night tonight. And maybe we ought to have a drink? How about it?" Hawŏn rambled on and on in the dark freight car.

"Snowflake fluttering though the winds are still, O snowflake," I was muttering to myself.

I longed madly for something—something I missed unbearably. But who would understand? A whirlwind rising up from the bottom of my heart . . . *O Mother!* Deep down, I had already abandoned Hawŏn. I bit my lips suddenly. I pressed my arms tightly around Hawŏn. Tears streamed down my cheeks. Hawŏn was laughing. He kept on jabbering.

"Look at this guy, acting like he's drunk when he hasn't had a sip. It doesn't even snow in Pusan, no snow. You know how it snows up north. Remember the well at Kwangsŏk's house? It's really something. Those magpies screeching at dawn. And that juniper tree. That girl from Changjagol was always laughing, remember? Like this—ha ha ha. She was a hard worker. The first one to get her water at the well at dawn, always. Oh, I miss the snow, the snow."

Translated by Theodore Hughes

12. KIM SŬNGOK

Kim Sŭngok was born in Osaka, Japan, in December 1941 but returned with his family to Sunch'ŏn, South Chŏlla Province, upon Liberation in 1945. In 1960 he entered the Seoul National University Department of French Literature, then a hotbed of young intellectuals who were soon to shake up a staid literary establishment. During his student years Kim was a cartoonist for the *Sŏul kyŏngje shinmun* newspaper and published his first major story, "Saengmyŏng yŏnsŭp" (Practice for life), winner of the 1962 Newcomers Literary Award sponsored by the *Hanguk ilbo* newspaper. Soon after graduation Kim earned major recognition for "Mujin kihaeng" (1964, trans. 1980 "Record of a Journey to Mujin"), and his reputation was cemented when he received the tenth Tongin Literature Prize for the story translated here (Sŏul, 1964 nyŏn kyŏul), first published in *Sasanggye* magazine in 1965. In 1977 he was honored with the first Yi Sang Literature Prize, for "Sŏul ŭi talpit o-jang" (The moonlight of Seoul, chapter zero), thereby becoming the first author to capture both of these awards.

By accident of birth Kim and his contemporaries belong to a generation that has a unique place in modern Korean history—a generation that has, indeed, earned a name of its own. Some speak of them as the *Hangŭl* Generation, in view of their post-Liberation education. In contrast with their fathers, who were taught in Japanese, and their grandfathers, who had studied Chinese, they were instructed in Korean using *hangŭl*, the Korean script. Others call them the Liberation Generation, for the era of their birth, or the April 19 Generation, for their role in the student-led uprising that toppled the Syngman Rhee government on that day in 1960.

"Seoul: 1964, Winter" is a bellwether of a new generation. Kim Sŭngok's youthful, modern vocabulary of high-frequency words is notable for its explicitness and its concomitantly rare use of the sensory language that had been an essential attribute of creative writing since the colonial period. He has a generational worldview that is distinct from that of his predecessors, a worldview revealed through his slangy and sardonic characters, who brashly and egocentrically reject the reality of life around them. The language and thoughts of these characters are those of a generation that has tumbled from the heady sense of victory gained in the student revolution to a distrustful frustration engendered by the Park Chung Hee coup in 1961.

Marshall R. Pihl and Bruce Fulton

SEOUL: 1964, WINTER

Anyone who spent the winter of 1964 in Seoul would probably remember those stalls that appeared on the streets once it got dark—selling hotchpotch, roasted sparrows, and three kinds of liquor, made so that to step inside you had to lift a curtain being whipped by a bitter wind that swept the frozen streets; where the long flame of a carbide lamp inside fluttered with the gusts; and where a middle-aged man in a dyed army jacket poured drinks and roasted snacks for you. Well, it was in one of those stalls that the three of us happened to meet that night. By the three of us I mean myself, a graduate student named An who wore thick glasses, and a man in his midthirties of whom I knew nothing except that he was obviously poor—a man whose particulars, actually, I hadn't the least desire to know.

The chitchat started off between me and the graduate student, and when the small talk and self-introductions were over I knew he was a twenty-five-year-old flower of Korean youth, a graduate student with a major that I (who hadn't even gotten close to a college) had never even dreamed of, and the oldest son of a rich family; and he probably knew that I was a twenty-five-year-old country boy, that I had volunteered for the Military Academy when I got out of high school only to fail and then enter the army, where I caught the clap once, and that I was now working in the military affairs section of a ward office.

We had introduced ourselves and now there was nothing to talk about. For a while we just drank quietly and then, when I picked up a charred sparrow, something occurred to me to say and so, after thanking the sparrow, I began to talk.

"An, do you love flies?"

"No, until now, I . . . do you, Kim?"

"Yes," I replied. "Because they can fly. No, because even while they can fly, they can be caught in my hand. Have you ever caught something in your hand that can fly?"

"Just a moment, now. Let me see." He looked at me blankly from behind his glasses as he screwed up his face. Then he said, "No, I haven't. Except for flies, of course."

The weather that day had been unusually warm, and the ice had melted and filled the streets with mud, but as the temperature dropped again by evening, the mud had begun to freeze once more beneath our feet. My leather shoes were not solid enough to block the chill that crept up from the freezing ground. Actually, a liquor stall like this was meant just for people who thought they might stop for a glass on the way home; it wasn't the place to be drinking and chatting with the man standing next to you. This thought had just occurred to me when Four-Eyes asked me quite a question. *This guy's all right*, I thought. So I made my cold and numb feet hold on a little longer.

"Kim, do you love things that wiggle?" is what he asked me. "Sure do," I answered abruptly, with an air of triumph. Recollection can give you this sense of satisfaction, whether you're thinking of something sad or pleasant. When the recollection is sad, your feelings of satisfaction are quiet and lonely, but when the recollection is pleasant, you feel a sense of triumph. "After I flunked the Military Academy exams, I stayed on at a rooming house in Miari with a friend who had also failed his college entrance exams. That was the first time in Seoul for me, you know. My dreams of becoming an officer were shattered, and I was really depressed. I felt as if I would never get over my disappointment. You probably know, but the bigger the dream, the more powerful is the sense of despair that failure gives you. The thing I took interest in at that time was the inside of a full bus in the morning. My friend and I would get through breakfast as quickly as possible and then trot up to the bus stop at the top of the Miari ridge. I mean, panting like dogs. Do you know what are the most enviable and the most marvelous things in the eyes of a young man from the country who's in Seoul for the first time? The most enviable thing is the lights that come on in the windows of the buildings at night—no, rather, the people who are moving back and forth in that light. And the most marvelous thing is a pretty girl standing beside you in a bus, not one inch away. Sometimes it's possible to stand so that you're not only touching the flesh of her wrist but even rubbing against her thigh. For this, I once spent a whole day riding around town, transferring from one city bus to another. Of course, I was so exhausted that night I puked, but—"

"Just a moment. What are you leading up to?"

"I was getting ready to tell you a story about loving things that wiggle. Listen for a moment. My friend and I would work our way deep inside a full morning rush-hour bus like a couple of pickpockets. Then we'd stand in front of a pretty young girl who had found herself a seat. I would take hold of a strap and lean my head against my raised arm, a little dazed from running for the bus. Then I would slowly ease my eyes down toward the girl's tummy. I wouldn't be able to see it right off, but after a while when my vision had cleared, I could make out the girl's tummy quietly moving up and down."

"That up and down movement . . . that'd be her breathing, right?"

"Yes, of course. The tummy of a corpse doesn't move, does it? At any rate, I have no idea why it soothed and lifted my spirits so very much to watch that quiet movement inside a full morning bus. Really, I love that movement with a passion."

"That's quite a lewd story," said An in a strange voice.

That made me mad. I had remembered that story on purpose, just in case I got on some kind of quiz program on the radio and was asked, "What is the freshest thing in the world?" The others might say lettuce or daybreak in May or an angel's forehead, but I would say that that movement was the freshest thing.

"No, it isn't a lewd story, at all." I spoke with an unyielding tone. "It's a true story."

"Why should there be a connection between being true and not being lewd?"

"I don't know. I don't know anything about connections. Actually, though . . ."

"But still, that motion—a 'movement up and down,' wasn't it? That certainly isn't wiggling. It seems you still don't love things that wiggle!"

We fell into another silence and were just fingering our drinks. *Sonofabitch. If he doesn't think that's wiggling, it's okay by me*, I was thinking. But then, a moment later, he spoke.

"I've just been thinking it over, Kim, and I've come to the conclusion that your movement up and down is, after all, one kind of wiggling."

"It is, isn't it?" I was pleased. "No question about it, that's wiggling. What I love more than anything is a girl's tummy. What kind of wiggling do you love, An?"

"It's not a kind of wiggling. Just wiggling, itself. All alone. For instance . . . a demonstration . . ."

"Demonstration? A demonstration? Then . . ."

"Seoul is a concentration of every sort of desire. Do you understand?"

"No, I don't," I replied in my clearest possible voice.

Then our conversation broke off again. This time, though, the silence lasted a long time. I lifted my glass to my mouth. When I had emptied it, I could see him holding his to his mouth and drinking with his eyes closed. I thought to myself, with some regret, that the time had come for me to get up and go. So that was that. I was thinking that all of this just confirmed what I had expected to begin with, and I was considering whether to say, "Until next time, then . . ." or "It's been enjoyable," when An, who had emptied his bowl, caught me by the hand.

"Don't you think we've been telling lies?"

"No." I was a little annoyed. "I don't know whether you've been lying or not, An, but everything I've said is the truth."

"Well, I have the feeling that we have been lying to each other." He spoke after blinking his reddened eyes once or twice behind his glasses. "Whenever I meet a new friend about our age, I always want to tell a story about wiggling. So I tell the story but it doesn't take even five minutes."

For a moment I'd thought I might understand what he was talking about, but now I wasn't sure.

"Now let's talk about something else," he began again.

But I thought it might be fun to give this lover of serious stories a hard time, and, what's more, I wanted to enjoy the drunk's privilege of listening to the sound of his own voice. So I started talking before he could.

"Of the street lights that are lined up in front of P'yŏnghwa Market, the eighth one from the east end is not lit. . . ." As soon as I saw him getting confused, I continued with renewed inspiration. "And of the windows on the sixth floor of the Hwashin Department Store, light was visible only in the three middle ones."

But now, it was I who was thrown into confusion.

Reason was, a startled look of delight began to light up An's face.

He started to speak rapidly. "There were thirty-two people at the West Gate bus stop; seventeen were women, five were children, twenty-one were youths, and six were elders."

"When was that?"

"That's as of seven-fifteen this evening."

"Ah," I said and began to feel discouraged for a moment. But then I bounced back in great humor and really began to lay it on.

"There are two chocolate wrappers in the first trash can in the alley next to the Tansŏngsa Theater."

"When was this?"

"As of nine P.M. on the fourteenth."

"One of the branches is broken on the walnut tree in front of the main entrance to the Red Cross Hospital."

"At a bar in the third block of Ŭlchiro that has no sign there are five girls named Mija, and they are known in the order they came to work there: Big Mija, Second Mija, Third Mija, Fourth Mija, and Last Mija."

"But that's something other people would know, too. I don't think you're the only one who has visited that place, Kim."

"Ah, you're right! I never thought of that. Well, one night I slept with Big Mija, and the next morning she bought me a pair of shorts from a woman who came around selling things on a daily installment plan. Now, there was one hundred and ten *wŏn* in the empty liquor bottle she used for keeping her money."

"That's more like it. That fact is entirely your property alone, Kim *hyŏng*."

He called me "older brother" as our speech conveyed our growing familiarity with each other.

"I—" We both began to speak at the same time. And then each yielded to the other.

"I, ah . . ." This time it was his turn. "I saw the trolley on a streetcar bound from West Gate to Seoul Station kick out bright blue sparks exactly five times while within my field of vision. The streetcar was passing by there at seven-twenty-five this evening."

"You were staying in the West Gate area this evening, weren't you, An *hyŏng*?"

"Yes, only in the West Gate area."

"I'm a couple of blocks up Chongno. There's a fingernail scratch about two centimeters long a little below the handle of the door to the toilet in the Yŏngbo Building."

He laughed loudly. "You left that scratch yourself, didn't you, Kim *hyŏng*?"

I was embarrassed, but I had to nod. It was true.

"How did you know?" I asked him.

"Well, I've had that experience, too," he answered. "But it's not a particularly pleasant memory. It'd be better, after all, for us to stick to things that we happen to have discovered and kept as our own secrets. That other sort of thing leaves a bad taste with you."

"But I've done that sort of thing lots of times and I must say I rather enj—" I was about to say I enjoyed it, but I suddenly felt a sense of disgust for the whole thing and broke off with a nod of agreement with his opinion.

But about that time something struck me as strange. If this fellow in the shiny glasses sitting next to me really was the son of a rich family and was highly educated to boot, why did he seem so undignified?

"An *hyŏng*. It's true that you're from a rich family, isn't it? And that you're a graduate student, too?" I asked.

"With about thirty million *wŏn* in real estate alone. That would be rich, wouldn't it? But, of course, that's my father's. As for being a graduate student, I've got a student ID card right here. . . ." As he spoke, he rummaged through his pockets and pulled out a wallet.

"An ID isn't necessary. It's just that there's something a bit odd. It just struck me as strange that a person like you would be sitting in a cheap liquor stall talking with a guy like me about things worth keeping to yourself."

"Well, that, all . . . that's . . . ," he began in a voice tinged with excitement. "That's . . . but first, there's something I'd like to ask you, Kim *hyŏng*. Why are you roaming the streets on such a cold night?"

"It's not my practice. I've got to have some money in my pocket before I can come out at night, you know."

"Well, yes. But why do you come out?"

"It's better than sitting in a boarding house and staring at the wall."

"When you come out at night, don't you feel something—a kind of fullness and abundance?"

"A what?"

"A something. I suppose we could call it 'life.' I do think I understand why you asked me your question, Kim *hyŏng*. My answer would be something like this. It's night. I come out into the streets from my house. I feel that I've been liberated, untied from any place in particular. It may not be so, but that's what I feel. Don't you feel that, Kim *hyŏng*?"

"Well . . ."

"I'm no longer caught up, involved with all sorts of things—they're left at a distance for me to survey. Isn't that it?"

"Well, that's a little . . ."

"No, don't say it's difficult. In other words, all the things that just went grazing by me during the day stand stripped bare, frozen and helpless, before my gaze at night. Now, wouldn't that have some significance—looking at things and enjoying them like that, I mean."

"Significance? What significance does that have? I don't count the bricks in buildings in the second block of Chongno because there's some significance in it. I just . . ."

"Right. It's meaningless. No, there may be significance there, but I don't understand it yet. You probably don't either, Kim *hyŏng*. Why don't we just go find out together sometime? And not fake it, either."

"I'm a little confused. Is that your answer, An *hyŏng*? I'm lost. All of a sudden this 'significance' and all . . ."

"Oh, I'm sorry! Well, this would be my answer. That I come out on the streets at night simply because I feel a sense of fullness and closeness." Then he lowered his voice.

"Kim *hyŏng*, it seems you and I came by different ways to get to the same point. Even supposing this might be the wrong point, the fault isn't ours." Now he spoke in a bright and cheery voice. "Say, this isn't the place for us.

Let's go somewhere warm, have a proper drink, and call it a night. I'm going to take a walk around and then go to an inn. When I happen to go roaming the streets at night, I always stay over at an inn and then go home. It's my favorite plan of action."

Each of us reached into his pocket, about to pay the bill. At that point, a man addressed us. It was a man beside us who had set down his glass and was warming his hands over the coal fire. He hadn't come in so much to drink as to warm himself at the fire, it seemed. He had on a fairly clean coat and his hair, slicked down in modest fashion, glistened here and there with highlights whenever the flame of the carbide lamp fluttered. Though his background wasn't clear, he was a man of about thirty-five who had the look of poverty about him. Maybe it was his weak chin, or maybe it was because the edges of his eyelids were unusually red. He just spoke in our direction, not addressing himself to me or to An in particular.

"Excuse me. But would it be all right if I joined you? I've got some money on me," he said in a listless voice.

From the sound of that listless voice it seemed that, while he wasn't necessarily pleading to go along, he dearly wanted to. An and I looked at each other for a moment, and then I said, "Well, friend, if you've got money for the booze. . . ."

"Let's all go together," An added.

"Thank you," the man said in the same listless voice, and followed after us.

An's expression indicated that this wasn't what he'd planned on, and I, too, didn't have pleasant premonitions. There had been a number of occasions when I had enjoyed myself in the company of people I'd met over a drink, but they usually didn't ask to join the group in a listless voice like that. To make a go of it, you've got to come on lustily, wearing a face that bubbles over with good cheer.

We poked along the street, looking here and peering there, like people who had suddenly forgotten their destination. From a medicine ad pasted on a telephone pole a pretty girl looked down at us with a desolate smile that seemed to say, *It's cold up here, but what can I do about it?* A neon sign advertising *soju* on the roof of a building flashed enthusiastically; beside it, a neon sign for medicine would go on for long stretches and then, as if it had nearly forgotten, would hurriedly flash off and back on again; beggars crouched here and there like hunks of rock on the now hard-frozen sidewalks; and people, hunched over intently, quickly passed them by. A wind-whipped piece of paper skittered over from the other side of the street and landed at my feet. I picked it up and saw it was a handbill pushing some beer hall's "Service by Beauties—Special Low Prices."

"What time has it gotten to be?" the listless man asked An.

"It's ten before nine," An answered after a moment.

"Have you two eaten supper? I haven't eaten yet, so why don't I treat?" the listless man said as he looked at each of us in turn.

"I've eaten," An and I replied simultaneously.

"You can eat by yourself," I suggested.

"I guess I'll skip it," the listless man answered.

"Please. We'll go along with you," said An.

"Thank you. Then . . ."

We went into a nearby Chinese restaurant. After we'd sat down in a room, he kindly asked us again to have something. And again we refused. But he offered once more.

"Is it all right even if I order something very expensive?" I asked in an effort to make him withdraw the offer.

"Yes, anything you want," he said in a voice that was now strong for the first time. "I've decided to spend all this money, you see."

I felt sure the man had some scheme in mind, but still I asked for a whole chicken and some liquor. He gave the waiter my order along with his own. An stared at me in disbelief.

It was just about then that I heard the low moans of a woman coming from the next room.

"Won't you have something, too?" the man said to An.

"No." An refused curtly in a voice that seemed sobered.

We turned our ears to the moans in the next room, which were quiet but growing more frequent. From a distance came the faint click-clack of streetcars and the sound, like flooding water, of rushing automobiles. And from somewhere nearby we could hear the occasional ringing of a buzzer. But we in our room were wrapped in an awkward silence.

"There is something I would like to explain to you," the good-hearted man began. "I would be grateful if you would listen awhile. . . . During the day today, my wife died. She had been admitted to Severance Hospital." He looked searchingly at us but without sadness in his face as he spoke.

"Oh, that's too bad." "I'm sorry to hear that." An and I offered condolences.

"We were very happy together, my wife and I. Since my wife couldn't have children, we had all our time to ourselves. We didn't have a lot of money, but whenever we came by a little, we'd enjoy traveling around together. We'd visit Suwŏn when the strawberries were in season and take in Anyang for the grapes. In the summer, we'd go to Taech'ŏn and then visit

Kyŏngju in the fall. We'd see movies and shows in the evenings whenever we could."

"What illness did she have?" An asked cautiously.

"The doctor said it was acute meningitis. Though she had had acute appendicitis once and also acute pneumonia, she got over them all right. But this acute attack killed her . . . now she's dead."

The man dropped his head and mumbled to himself for a while. An poked my knee with his finger and gave me a look that said, What do you think? Shouldn't we get out? I felt the same way, but just then the man raised his head and resumed his story. So we had to stay put.

"My wife and I were married the year before last. I had met her by accident. She once said her family lived somewhere in the Taegu area, but we never had any contact with them. I don't even know where her family home is. So I had no choice in the matter." He lowered his head and mumbled again.

"You had no choice in what?" I asked.

It looked as if he hadn't heard me. But after a moment he looked up again and continued with eyes that seemed to beg our pardon.

"I sold my wife's body to the hospital. I had no choice. I'm only a salesman, selling books on time payment. I had no idea what to do. They gave me four thousand *wŏn*. I was standing by the fence in front of Severance Hospital until just before I met you two gentlemen. I had been trying to figure out which building had the morgue with my wife's body in it, but I couldn't. So I just stood there and watched the dirty white smoke coming out of the chimneys. What will become of her? Is it true that the students will practice their dissection on her, splitting her head apart with a saw and cutting her stomach open with a knife?"

We could only keep our mouths shut. The waiter brought dishes of sliced pickled radishes and onions.

"I'm sorry to have told you such an unpleasant story. It's just that I couldn't keep it inside me. There's one thing, though, I'd like to discuss—what should I do with this money? I'd like to get rid of it tonight."

"Spend it, then," An quickly replied.

"Will you two stay with me until it's all gone?" he asked.

We didn't answer right away.

"Please stay with me," he said.

We agreed.

"Let's blow it in good style," he said, smiling for the first time. But his voice was as lifeless as before.

By the time we left the Chinese restaurant we were all drunk, one thousand *wŏn* of the money was gone, and he looked as if he were crying with one eye while laughing with the other. An was telling me that he was tired of figuring out a way to escape, and I was mumbling *I got the accents all wrong, damn accents!* The street was cold and empty, like a ghost town you might see in a movie, but the sign was still flashing diligently and the medicine sign had shaken off its lethargy. The girl on the telephone pole was smiling, telling us, *Same old me*.

"Where shall we go now?" the man said.

"Where shall we go?" An said.

"Where shall we go?" I echoed.

But we hadn't any place to go. Beside the Chinese restaurant we had just left was the show window of a men's clothing store. The man pointed toward it and then dragged us inside the shop.

"Let's see some neckties. My wife is buying them for us," he bellowed.

Each of us picked out a mottled-looking one, and six hundred *wŏn* was eliminated. We left the store.

"Where shall we go?" the man said.

We still had nowhere to go. There was an orange peddler outside the shop.

"My wife liked oranges," the man cried and bounded over to the peddler's cart, where the oranges were laid out for sale. Another three hundred *wŏn* was gone. While we were peeling the skins off the oranges with our teeth, we paced restlessly up and down.

"Taxi!" the man shouted.

A taxi stopped in front of us. As soon as we had gotten in, the man said, "Severance Hospital!"

"No. That's useless," An quickly exclaimed.

"Useless?" the man muttered. "Where, then?"

There was no answer.

"Where are you going?" asked the driver in a sullen voice. "If you haven't any place to go, then get out."

We got out of the taxi. We still hadn't gone more than twenty paces from the Chinese restaurant. The scream of a siren rose from the far end of the street and came closer and closer. Two fire engines roared by us.

"Taxi!" the man screamed.

Another taxi stopped in front of us. No sooner had we gotten in than the man said, "Follow those fire engines!"

I was peeling my third orange.

"Are we on our way to see a fire now?" An asked the man. "We can't. There isn't enough time before curfew. It's already ten-thirty. We should find something more amusing. How much money is left now?"

The man rummaged through his pockets and pulled out all the money. Then he handed it over to An. An and I counted it together. There was nineteen hundred *wŏn* in large bills, a few coins, and several ten-*wŏn* notes.

"Good," said An as he handed back the money.

"Fortunately, there are women in this world who concentrate on showing off what it is in particular that makes them women."

"Are you speaking of my wife?" the man asked in sad tones. "My wife's characteristic was that she laughed too much."

"Oh, no. I was suggesting that we go see the girls in the third block of Chongno," An said.

The man gave a smile that seemed to show contempt for An and turned his head away. By then we had arrived at the scene of the fire. Thirty *wŏn* more was gone. The fire had broken out in a ground-floor paint shop, and the flames were now billowing out the windows of a hairdressing school on the second floor. We heard police whistles, fire sirens, the crackling of flames, and streams of water crashing against the walls of the building, but there was no sound of people. The people stood as if in a still-life painting, reflecting the blaze with faces as red as if overcome by shame.

Each of us took one of the paint cans rolling around at our feet, set it up, and squatted on it to watch the fire. I was hoping it would burn a little longer. The *School of Hairdressing* sign had caught fire, and flames began to lick at the *dressing*.

"Kim *hyŏng*, let's go on with our conversation," An said.

"Fires and such are nothing at all, not worth the bother. Only thing is that tonight we have seen ahead of time what we would have seen in tomorrow morning's newspapers. That fire isn't yours, Kim *hyŏng*, it's not mine, and it's not this man's. It's just our common property now. But a fire doesn't go on forever. Therefore, I find no interest in fires. What do you think, Kim *hyŏng*?"

"I feel the same way." I gave him the first answer that came to mind. I was watching the *Hair* catch fire.

"No. I was in error just now. The fire is not ours, the fire belongs wholly to the fire itself. We are nothing at all to the fire. Therefore I find no interest in fires. What do you think, Kim *hyŏng*?"

"I feel the same way."

A stream of water struck the burning *Hair*. Gray smoke billowed out where the water landed. Our listless friend suddenly leaped to his feet.

"It's my wife!" he shrieked, eyes bulging, as he gestured toward the glowing flames. "She's tossing her head back and forth. She's tossing her head, crying that it'll crack with the pain. Darling!"

"The pain was caused by meningitis. Those are just flames carried in the wind. Sit down. How could your wife possibly be in the fire?" An said as he pulled the man back down. Then he turned to me and whispered quietly, "This guy's giving us quite a show."

I noticed the *Hair* flickering where I thought the fire had gone out. The stream of water splashed it again. But their aim was off, and the stream wavered back and forth. The flames licked nimbly at *of*. I was hoping they would catch on to *School* as well and that I would be the only one among all the spectators to have seen the sign burn all the way through. But then, just as the fire was becoming a living thing to me, I suddenly withdrew my wish to be the only one.

From where we were squatting, I had seen something white flying toward the burning building. A pigeon that fell into the flames.

"Didn't something just fly into the fire?" I turned and asked An.

"Yes, something did," An answered and then turned to the man. "Did you see it?" he asked.

The man said nothing.

Just then a policeman sprinted up to us.

"You're the one!" the policeman said, grabbing the man. "Did you just throw something into the fire?"

"I didn't throw anything."

"How's that?" the policeman shouted, making as if to strike the man. "I saw you throw something. What did you throw into the fire?"

"Money."

"Money?"

"I wrapped some money and a rock in a handkerchief and threw it into the fire."

"Is that the truth?" the policeman asked us.

"Yes, it was money. This man has the strange belief that he'll be lucky in business if he comes to a fire and throws some money in it. Perhaps you could say he's a little odd, but he's just a small-time businessman who wouldn't do any harm," An answered.

"How much money was it?"

"A one-*wŏn* coin," An answered again.

After the policeman had left, An asked the man, "Did you really throw money into the fire?"

"Yes."

"All of it?"

"Yes."

For quite a while we just sat there listening to the crackling of the leaping flames. After a time, An spoke to the man.

"It looks as if we finally used the money up, after all. Well, I guess we've carried out our promise to you, so we'll be going now."

"Good night, sir," I added in parting.

An and I turned and started to walk away. The man came after us and grabbed each of us by an arm.

"I'm afraid to be left alone," he said, trembling.

"It's almost curfew. I'm going to go find an inn," An said.

"I'm headed home," I said.

"Can't we all go together? Just stay with me for tonight. I beg of you. Please come along with me," the man said, grabbing and tugging at my arm as if it were a fan. He was probably doing the same to An.

"Where do you want to go?" I asked him.

"I'm going to get some money at a place near here, and then I was hoping we would all go to an inn together."

"To an inn?" I said as I counted the money in my pocket with my fingers.

"If it's the cost of the room you're worried about, I'll pay for all three. Shall we go together, then?" An said, addressing himself to the man and me.

"No, no. I don't want to cause you any trouble. Just follow me a moment."

"Are you going to go borrow money?"

"No, this money is due me."

"Somewhere nearby?"

"Yes, if this is the Namyŏng-dong area.

"It certainly looks like Namyŏng-dong to me," I said.

With the man in the lead and the two of us following, we walked away from the fire.

"It's much too late to go collecting payments," An said to him.

"Yes, but I've got to collect it."

We entered a dark back alley. After turning several comers, the man stopped in front of a house where the front gate light was lit. An and I stopped some ten paces behind him. He rang the bell. After a while the gate opened, and we could hear the man talking with someone standing inside.

"I'd like to see the man of the house."

"He's sleeping."

"The lady, then?"

"She's sleeping, too."

"I really must see someone."

"Wait a moment, please."

The gate closed again. An hurried over to the man and pulled at his arm.

"Forget about it. Let's go."

"That's all right. I've got to collect this money."

An walked back again to where he had stood before. The gate opened.

The man bowed and said, "Sorry to trouble you so late at night."

"Who are you, sir?" came a woman's sleep-filled voice from the gate.

"I'm sorry to have come so late, but it's just that . . ."

"Who are you, please? You seem to have been drinking, sir."

"I've come to collect an installment on a book you've bought." Suddenly he broke into a near scream, "I've come for a book payment." He rested his hands against the gatepost, buried his face in his arms, and burst into sobs. "I've come for a book payment. I've come for . . . ," he continued in tears.

"Come back tomorrow, please." The gate slammed shut.

The man continued to cry for quite a while, mumbling, "Darling" now and then. We waited, still about ten paces away, for the crying to end. After some time, he came stumbling over toward us.

The three of us, heads lowered, walked through the dark alleys and back out onto the main street. A strong, cold wind was blowing through the deserted streets.

"It's terribly cold," the man said, sounding concerned for us.

"It is, rather. Let's go find an inn right off," An said.

"Shall we get one room for each of us?" An asked, as we went into the inn. "That'd be a good idea, wouldn't it?"

"I think it'd be better for us to share the same room," I said, thinking of the man.

The man stood vacantly, looking as if he wanted only for us to arrange things. He also looked as if he had no idea where he was.

Once inside the inn, we felt the same awkward confusion of not knowing what to do next that strikes you when you leave a theater after the show. The streets seemed narrower and closer than the interior of the inn. All those rooms, one after the other, that's where we had to go.

"How would it be for us all to take the same room?" I repeated.

"I'm exhausted," said An. "Let's each take a single room and get some sleep."

"I don't want to be alone," the man muttered.

"It'd be more comfortable for you to sleep by yourself," An said.

Each of us headed for one of the three adjoining rooms indicated by the houseboy. Before we separated, I said, "Let's buy a pack of cards and play a hand."

But An said, "I'm completely exhausted. If you want, why don't you two play?" and went into his room.

"I'm dead tired too. Good night," I said to the man and went into my room. After filling in a false name, address, age, and occupation in the register, I drank the water the bellboy had left and pulled the quilt up over my head. I slept a sound, dreamless sleep.

The next morning An woke me early.

"That man is dead," An whispered in my ear.

"Huh?" I was wide awake.

"I just took a look into his room, and he was dead, sure enough."

"Sure enough?" I said. "Does anyone else know?"

"It doesn't look as if anyone else knows about it yet. I think we'd better get out of here right away—no noisy complications."

"Suicide?"

"No doubt about it."

I dressed quickly. An ant was crawling along the floor toward my feet. I had a feeling the ant was going to climb my foot, so I quickly stepped aside.

Outside, hail was falling in the early dawn. We moved away from the inn, walking as quickly as possible.

"I knew he was going to die," An said.

"I hadn't the least suspicion," I said, telling the truth.

"I was expecting it," An said, turning up the collar of his coat. "But what could we do?"

"Nothing. We had no choice. I had no idea," I said.

"If we had expected it, what should we have done?" An asked me.

"Fuck! What could we do? How were we to know what he wanted us to do?"

"That's it. I thought he wouldn't die if we just left him alone. I thought that was the best way to handle it."

"I had no idea that man was going to die. Fuck! He must have been carrying poison around in his pocket all night!"

An stopped beneath a scrawny roadside tree that was gathering snow. I stopped with him. With an odd look on his face, he asked me, "You and I are definitely twenty-five, aren't we, Kim *hyŏng*?"

"I definitely am!"

"I definitely am, too." He nodded once. "It frightens me."

"What does?" I asked.

"That 'something.' That . . ." His voice was like a sigh. "Doesn't it seem we've become old?"

"We're barely twenty-five," I said.

"At any rate," he said, putting out his hand, "let's say good-bye here. Enjoy yourself," he said as I took his hand.

We separated. I dashed across the street where a bus was just stopping for passengers. When I got on and looked out the window, I could see, through the branches of the scrawny tree, An standing in the falling snow pondering something or other.

Translated by Marshall R. Pihl

13. CH'OE INHO

Ch'oe Inho was born in 1945 in Seoul and graduated in English literature from Yonsei University. He first came to public notice in the 1960s when three of his stories were selected in competitions sponsored by the *Hanguk ilbo* and *Chosŏn ilbo* newspapers and *Sasanggye* magazine (in 1963, 1966, and 1968, respectively). But he was not fully launched in his writing career until 1970, when, fresh out of the air force, he published "Sulkkun" (trans. 1993 "The Boozer"), a story he had written some years earlier. In 1982 he received the sixth Yi Sang Literature Prize for "Kipko p'urŭn pam" (trans. 2002 "Deep Blue Night"), an autobiographical story about a road trip in California.

He has continued to be a prolific and extremely popular writer whose work encompasses the morbidly fantastic "The Boozer"; a 1973 collection of sardonic anecdotes chronicling the adventures of a college boy and girl, *Pabo tŭl ŭi haengjin* (Parade of fools); and a historical novel set against the backdrop of Buddhism in Korea, *Kil ŏmnŭn kil* (1989–1991, The way without a way). He is a witty man whose penetrating sense of humor and visual, almost cinematic approach to his fiction sometime tempt him to write more for the audience than for the art, but whichever way he inclines, he is a master of his craft.

The story translated here, "T'ain ŭi pang," was first published in *Munhak kwa chisŏng* in 1971. While it shares some of the fantastical elements of "The Boozer," its focus is more on the alienation resulting from life in a rapidly industrializing urban society.

Marshall R. Pihl and Bruce Fulton

ANOTHER MAN'S ROOM

He had just come in from the street, so tired that it seemed as if he would collapse. He climbed slowly up the stairs of the apartment building and went to his own room. Fortunately, he met no one on the way; there was no one in the corridor either. From somewhere or other there was a smell of boiling spinach. He fumbled at the door and pressed lightly on the bell a couple of times. The letter-box had *press* written across it, and the bell was inside. He threw his cigarette butt on the clean, polished floor; it tasted acrid on his already burned tongue. He waited very patiently, waited for his wife to open the door. To open the door and greet him with a show of wide-eyed excitement. He listened, lit the last cigarette he had left, but still there was no sound from inside. Again he reached his hand through the tiny metal box, felt the spring of the bell beneath his finger, and began to press in a way that showed that the delay was getting on his nerves. There was a slight tremor in his fingers. Again he waited. At first he had misgivings about the bell: it might be out of order. But every time he pressed the bell, he heard a faint sound echoing far away on the other side. He concluded that his wife had been drinking alone and by now had fallen stark naked into a drunken sleep.

"A ghost could grab me when I'm asleep, and I wouldn't know it," his wife always boasted, as if this were one of her strong points. So, he stuck his finger indignantly on the bell button, holding it there for about five minutes, impatiently conscious of the dull, continuous ringing on the other side. Of course there were two keys; one which his wife kept and one which he kept himself on his key ring. If he wanted to, he could open the door with his own key. But he was the type of man who is very old-fashioned about some things, like it being his wife's job to open the door for him; the type of man who insists it is a husband's right to at least have his wife open the door for him before he goes in.

He began to beat the door with his fist. He beat gently at first, but in the end he pounded the door, almost as if to smash it to pieces. The corridor reverberated with the sound. Somewhere the crying of a child, as if awakened from sleep, could be heard. A door opened far away at the other side of the hall and a man clad in pajamas craned his neck to see; he wasn't the only one. The man pounding the door continued his pounding, unaware of the eyes of others. As a result, not only the man in pajamas but also the people in the other apartments began to open their doors and glare in his direction—cautiously but with faces that were exceedingly threatening, like whetstones.

"Hello!"

Finally a woman who had been watching him carefully spoke out testily.

"Have you some business in there?"

"No."

Although he was tired, he laughed amicably as he spoke, all the time continuing to pound on the door.

"There doesn't seem to be anyone at home. Have you come to collect money?"

"No."

He lifted the bag, which had given these people the impression he was a debt collector, and he laughed suitably.

"I haven't come about anything like that."

"I say!"

The man in pajamas came up close, cracking his fingers as he came, his slippers flapping.

"You have been pounding that door for the longest time and there doesn't seem to be anyone at home. Please leave now. Thanks to you the child in our house has woken up."

"I'm sorry."

He apologized politely. But inwardly he was disgusted, so disgusted with everything he felt like spitting it all out.

"Really, I mean."

He rummaged through his pockets and produced his key ring, awkward and embarrassed like a man caught breaking wind. His sense of touch was sufficient for him to search out expertly the key of his apartment from the five or six jingling keys on the ring.

"This is where I live."

"What did you say?"

The woman spoke in a high-pitched, doubting voice, glaring at him as she spoke.

"You say you are the owner?"

"Yes, that's right," he replied, and immediately the woman tilted her head.

"Is there something wrong?"

"Look here!"

The man in pajamas came up to him, as much as to say ownership would have to be proved before he would have an easy mind. The man in pajamas was a real giant, so that the other man had to look up at him.

"We've been living in this apartment for nearly three years and we've never seen anyone who looked like you."

"Ah, what are you saying?"

He let loose a cry of pain, a cry that came from an anger that seemed as if it would boil over.

"You say you've never seen me before. Does that mean you can take it on yourself to treat the owner of the house as a thief or a robber? We've been living here for three years too, but I'm looking at your face for the first time today. So, shouldn't you be an object of suspicion too?"

The man in pajamas was stubborn to the last.

"I admit that doubting you isn't so good, but you have to think of our position too."

"It's just the same for me."

He continued to grumble angrily as he pushed the key into the lock. The door opened without a sound.

"If you really can't believe me, come on in with me. I'll give you proof."

He went into the room. It was dark inside.

"Hello? Anyone home?"

He took off his shoes and groped along the wall for the light switch, angry as he called out. But it was dark inside and no one answered. Damn! He was so tired he dragged his puffed-up legs leadenly behind him, and it was only with great difficulty that he managed to find the light switch. He banged it on. The connection in the fluorescent light was bad, so that it fluttered three or four times like an insect in a collector's jar before it finally came on. He felt as if the light had come too abruptly. He stood there, not knowing what to do, like a man who has gone into a strange place. Just then he noticed the other man still outside the door, still staring at him suspiciously. It was too much for him. He slammed the door shut. Then he discovered a piece of paper lying beneath the mirror of the dressing table. With an effort he went over to the dressing table and casually picked up the paper.

Darling,
I got a telegram this morning saying that Father is critically ill. I won't be gone long. You will probably be tired, so I'll tell them you went on a business trip. Rest yourself. The table is all laid in the kitchen.

Your wife.

He heaved a sigh that was filled with resentment, dragged his feet, and, conscious of an illimitable tiredness sinking further and further in, he began to take his clothes off—coat, tie, shirt, everything extremely slowly and deliberately; and then, bending his stiff, almost inflexible knees like a penknife, he took off his trousers and hung them in a temper in the closet. In the mirror he saw an aging, heavily wrinkled man. He faced himself in the mirror and began to spit out violent, pointless curses.

Damn! Only barely made it back. Damn! And no one at home!

He felt an intense loneliness. Naked as he was, he stalked around the living room, which was oppressively hot due to the lack of an outlet for the steam-heated air, and he moaned like an animal just caught in a cage. The furniture seemed the same as a few days before; it was as if nothing had changed. There was a whirring from the transistor radio—his wife had left it on when she was going out. He turned it off. His wife's clothes were thrown in disarray all over the bedroom; holed stockings lying on the table, a container of rouge opened and left as it was.

He was hungry. He went into the kitchen first, but instead of a meal there was just some hard, stale bread, dry as paper, on the table. He swallowed the cold, soggy food: the feeling was like chewing rubber.

This was a bit too much.

He grumbled ceaselessly. He deserved to be treated to a hot meal. Was that all? He should be pulling on his pipe in a tidied room, listening to music. But he was on his own tonight; bad luck.

He surveyed the room on all sides, looking for the newspaper to read, but there was no newspaper anywhere. He gave up the idea of reading the newspaper. He looked at the clock; it had stopped at the date of a week before. It was a clock his wife had bought, actually a table clock, and a good one for the money. The nuisance of it was that it was designed to show date and day, and frequently it would go ridiculously fast for no apparent reason; the date dial would click past its proper position and the dial showing the day of the week would go a day wrong. Moreover, when the dials went wrong, there was nothing for it but to twist the hands thousands of times and laboriously get it right. He began to twist the hands in a fit of bad temper. What really got to him was that he had just cut his nails, so that he felt keenly the powerlessness in his fingertips, rather like a man with no teeth trying to crack a walnut with his bare gums. Barely controlling the urge to slam the damn clock on the floor, he kept on and on at this meaningless revolution of time.

He was at this for a long time, so that he became even more fatigued. Dragging his sore feet slowly behind him, he went into the bathroom. He put on the light, but the light was so bright the bathroom looked like a sanitized butcher's shop. The bath was still filled with dirty water where his wife had had a bath. There were a few strands of his wife's hair stuck on the rim of the tub, curled like live worms. He reached in and took out the stopper, which looked like the back of a crayfish hiding in dirty water. Whereupon a shiver ran through the tiny bath, the water ran out at a furious pace, and in a little while, with a sound like smacking lips, the bath was empty except for the dirt sediment that remained here and there.

He put the stopper in the washbasin; next he turned on hot and cold water together. The hot was too cold. He rubbed soapsuds all over his face, so that he looked rather foolish, like a comic's sidekick in makeup. He found his safety razor with the blade still in it, just as he had left it a week ago before setting out on the business trip. There were still bits of soap on the blade of the razor, beard stubble still stuck to its sides. He began to shave, angrily upbraiding his wife's laziness with curses that a streetwalker could not match. His beard was tough, the roots deep; it was no easy thing to shave with the already blunted, rusting blade. Because of this, he nicked himself in several places, and one of them that was especially deep began to ooze blood, so that he had to stick the first bit of tissue paper his eye fell on to the cut. The paper stuck to his face like a stamp wet with spit. The slimy gum sticks a stamp; this paper was stuck on his face with blood.

He gave vent to his anger. Standing there gloomily, he was aware of a frightening helplessness attacking him from the soles of his feet. He saw his clouded face appear in the bathroom mirror; it was like a parcel for the mail with a stamp stuck on it. Then he discovered there was something stuck on the mirror. He reached out and knew right away what it was.

It was gum. His wife was always chewing gum; it was one of her habits. When she was going to eat or take a bath, she would always stick her gum on the table or on the mirror, but only after calculatedly saturating it with sufficient saliva to ensure that she would be able to pull off every last bit of it. He giggled momentarily. He tossed the gum into his mouth. It was hard and shriveled like a dried raisin. The flavor was gone; it was an odd, slightly nauseous feeling, but after a while the gum became soft. His wife's gum comforted him in a way nothing else did. Gradually he got into better humor; he began to sing:

> Bird singing in the tree,
> I don't know why it is so.
> What am I going to do about him?
> If he doesn't like me I must go.

His voice sounded majestic in the bathroom. The whole room reverberated. The sound had nowhere to get out; it kept echoing round and round like gunfire.

The land of gum is indeed a happy, cozy place, he murmured to himself. Although he had murmured without much awareness, he suddenly felt as if the voice belonged to someone else. Startled, he looked behind. He felt the presence of someone or other. But he decided to pay no attention to it.

He discovered a magnifying glass in front of the mirror. Of course he was well aware of its use. His wife used it, together with tweezers, to pluck the hairs from beneath her arms and the down from beneath her nose. He lifted it and examined his face with it. His face, which had no really distinctive feature, was strangely puffed-up and magnified. He began to move the glass around, trying to catch in one place all the light of the fluorescent lamp in the bathroom. A magnifying glass manipulated in sunlight can burn up a fly whose wings have been cut off. He could feel the chill cold of the damp and sticky bathroom, and at the same time he was sweating, trying to concentrate all his energies in catching all the light in one place. He could actually feel again last year's long summer solstice.

Last summer he was happy. He began to think. Immediately he felt an urge to express himself vocally. So he spoke aloud.

So, I was happy. You can say it, I was happy.

He looked behind, startled as before by his own voice, but there was no one near him. He was a little ashamed, a little embarrassed, and he burst out in exaggerated laughter.

He stood there forlornly like a tall cockscomb and then went over to the shower, which was glaring at him. Every time he went toward the shower, he felt an urge to measure his height. The shower-head was broken, like the neck of a prisoner who had been executed, and it was staring at him very soberly. He caught hold of the faucet that controlled the supply of rushing hot and cold water. He turned on the hot water tap carefully, very carefully. Immediately a hot rain began to pour down. It struck the tiles on the floor of the bathroom, became steam in that moment, and rose up again. He thinks this is marvelous. This isn't yesterday's hot water, he realizes. He feels the marvel of it like a man who suddenly opens his eyes after being in darkness for a long time. This time he puts on the same amount of cold water. This isn't just any cold water, he is aware. The water felt so hot and so cold on the palm of his hand that he hesitated for a moment, and finally, still chewing his gum, he rushed into the raging, racing sea. He feels hot water lick his tired face; he gives himself up to the pleasant sensation of water flowing down his body, water gliding across his body like a young girl in dancing shoes.

He worked up a lather all over his body. The suds came up, and when his whole body was like the white fur of a pet pup, he saw his penis become as rigid as a stick, strong and erect. Desire boiled in him; he leaped into the water, and, with a little scream, he felt the violent rush of water on his chest and penis till it hurt. The hot water drenched his pink, blooded, meat-smelling flesh. In the end, even after all the soap had been washed away, he remained for some time in the grip of the water, chewing his gum, purposelessly playing with himself. When some of the tiredness had left him, he turned off the water and concentrated on drying himself. He felt an intense thirst.

He came out of the bathroom and took some fruit juice powder from the cool living-room sideboard. Careful not to spill any on the floor, he puts in some powder and three spoons of sugar. He keeps adding sugar till in the end he feels he must have added an extra ten spoons. He mixes cold water with this. He stirs it all patiently with a long-handled spoon. He lifts the cup, one hand still holding the spoon, and goes over to the record player. There are a lot of records; he takes one at random. He doesn't know the title of the music. He turns on the power; all at once the motor begins to whir and the inside light grows bright. The record table begins to revolve. He tosses the slender record onto the record table, like an athlete gently throwing the discus. The record player with its bad needle gives off static, but eventually it begins to spit out the music. He stretches out on the sofa and listens to the music. There are still a few things that haven't been straightened out yet, but he feels more settled. The subdued light of the shaded standard lamp fills the whole room gloomily. Seen from above, from the ceiling, he doesn't even look human. He is lying motionless. For this reason he appears lifeless, like a piece of furniture. While he is like this, his wife's letter on the dressing table catches his eye. He thinks of the contents of his wife's note and laughs cynically. He realizes that his wife has lied to him. Originally it was tomorrow evening he was supposed to arrive. The day he left on the business trip, too, he had informed his wife he would get back tomorrow evening. And still his wife writes she has received a telegram that her father is critically ill, that she is going to see him, and that she will be right back. He laughs. He is really pleased with himself and at the same time conscious of a creepy detestation. I know, he thinks. Since the day I went on the business trip, since that day she has been off somewhere. She figures I will come back tomorrow evening, and she won't be back till the following morning, at the earliest. She will be a little concerned, a little embarrassed, and she will apologize to me humbly and in a low voice.

I am well aware that my wife has sex organs different from other women's. It is as if she had a strong, high-quality zipper attached to them. In front of me and naked, she likes trying to run the zipper up and down, opening and closing. It makes one think of good-quality winter cloth; and it indicates a tremendous power of sexual embrace.

He laughed and stirred the spoon. It was then that he heard the noise. It was a footstep, moving lightly, churning the air. He listened. He had the feeling there was some noise or other coming from the direction of the bathroom. He got up abruptly and walked toward the bathroom. He saw water pouring down in the shower, and he was certain he had shut off the water. Damn! Grumbling, he shuts off the water. He comes back again to the sofa. As soon as he does, he begins to hear sounds coming from the direction of the kitchen. Clenching his teeth in an effort not to complain, he goes toward the kitchen. The kitchen kerosene stove is lit. He grumbles and turns it off. When he has come slowly back to the sofa, he discovers a lit cigarette, still burning in the ashtray. He looks around in automatic reaction. He feels a terrible solitude.

Who is it? he calls out cautiously. The vibrations of his voice are cut short. He is conscious of being trapped. He is conscious of eyes within the walls. He lies down fiercely on the sofa and begins to glare at the pieces of furniture his eyes fall on. All the furniture becomes a noticeably brighter color and begins to give off light like leaves after rain. He stirs the spoon stubbornly. The sugar water is already sweet and hot, but there is still undissolved sugar because the liquid is past the saturation point. Still he continues to stir the spoon. Suddenly he feels that this long-handled spoon gripped in his hand is no ordinary spoon. Immediately the spoon seemed to strip the skin off his consciousness and he saw it leap into the air; it was something beyond the range of visual experience, like the knowledge that a fish, scales flashing, is racing to the surface. He grasps the spoon with all his strength. Immediately the spoon begins to jump every which way, full of life, fighting to escape, like a live fish when you touch it. And the spoon, which he had gripped in his hand, slipped out agilely between his fingers. Dumbfounded for the moment, his mouth open, he watched the spoon float up and sail through the air, outside the force of gravity. Having assured himself that he was going to examine everything in the room closely, he opened his eyes wide. Everything of which he was aware began to shake all at once, to make merry. He rises shakily and walks over to turn on the living-room light. He presses the switch. The tiny starting bulb in the fluorescent light flickered on and off a few times. Then suddenly the room becomes bright.

He discovers that the spoon is gripped in the palm of his hand, quiet, like a freshwater fish. He begins to run his eyes carefully over all the objects in the room, one by one, over all the objects that up to a moment ago had been pitching and tossing and rattling.

Surprisingly, everything was back in its place, looking at him cheekily. He feels a terrible sadness. Everything deep in rest, quiet but mocking. He grumbles as he turns off the switch. Then, sitting on the sofa, he begins to drink the sugar water. In every dark corner within the room there is an audible whispering sound. Darkness and darkness conspiring together, discussing some treacherous plot. Friend, talk with us! In the right angle of every corner of the room one of them speaks out fearlessly. Sounds of the footsteps of millipedes crawling on the wall. Sounds of dressing-table mirror and clothes-closet mirror in transparent copulation. He opens his eyes wide in the darkness. The walls are rolling. He moves his body slowly. Sounds from between the two eyes of the wall socket for the electric iron. His ear makes contact at the narrow eyes of the socket, like an electrical accessory; his whole body begins to boil, like a high-class electric stove. Sparks spring to his body; his whole body feels replete with light. Listen well! the socket whispers. It was as if the voice were coming from a transistor earphone; it whispers in his ear alone. Tonight there will be a coup d'etat. Don't be afraid. He takes his ear from the socket. He bangs the light switch on again. The light comes on and everything that had been in commotion is stuck like paint to the wall, pretending to a disgraceful innocence. Leaving the light on, he goes toward the dressing table. Grumbling, he opens all the cosmetic containers, big and small, and examines them. He opens the pantry cupboard—even rows of empty dishes, matches, a candlestick; he opens the clothes closet—clothes hanging there like sea fish drying. He examines the pockets too. The clothes found it rather offensive, but they shook out their pockets quietly. He determines to examine everything individually. He ransacks the drawers and examines everything left there. In the process he found a few old leaves, already dry; they seemed as if they would disintegrate if he touched them. They conjured up thoughts of last fall. His mood grew gloomy for a moment. He looked intently at a framed, discolored photograph. He examined the book covers stuck in the bookshelf. He went to the kitchen, examined the wick in the kerosene stove, and looked at the inside of an old pair of shoes. He opened the attic door and examined all kinds of articles there, one by one, and in detail. He examined the bathtub right to the very bottom. Whatever was covered, he inspected beneath the cover; he even lifted the bedding and shook it out. Finally he looked at the chamber pot and examined the gaps in the windows. All the articles responded to his demands like patient, quiet, tax-paying citizens.

But the articles he was peering into were not, properly speaking, ordinary articles. They were not already yesterday's articles.

Aware of a fatigue now a further stage advanced, he returned to the living room, filled a brimming glass of liquor from the bottle, and drank it in a gulp. He felt an utterly desolate, unbelievable loneliness. He filled another glass and gulped it straight down too. The liquor tasted salty and insipid, sweet-sour.

He felt there must be a cigarette butt around somewhere, and he discovered one while rummaging in the drawers; it was thin and shriveled. He lit it. The liquor warmed him, cheering him up. He began to sing in a loud voice like a child.

> Bird singing in the tree,
> I don't know why it is so.
> What am I going to do about him?
> If he doesn't like me I must go.

Naked as he was, he began to pace back and forth all over. He walked and ran, as if it were the most normal thing in the world. He would survey the kitchen, and then the bathroom area would seem suspicious. When he was examining the bathroom area, the living room area was suspicious. He ran and ran again like a pulley, but he could not find anything, nor the hint of anything.

Getting upset about something inanimate is enough to make you blush, he thought. Whereupon, for the first time, his mind was at rest. Chest out, he walked across and put the switch down. He sat on the sofa and began to drink off the rest of the sugar water sip by sip. As soon as he put the switch down, rolling waves of darkness enveloped the room, covering everything like paint stuck to the walls, whispering carefully at first, but finally giggling and laughing to their hearts' content. Dry pieces of tissue paper like stretched hemp float into the air. In a closed drawer underclothes are flapping and leaping around. The four legs of the table begin to shake. In the pantry cupboard, dishes piled on top of each other start a clattering, clamoring revolt.

All this began very cautiously. But as soon as the conspirators realized that the man they were dealing with was defenseless, all at once and all together, crying with loud, high-pitched voices they began to run amuck. Crayons float into the air. The clothes in the closet flutter and dance. A belt wriggles like a water snake. The bolder among them came up brazenly close and tried to graze his face. Be careful, be careful! the matches in the match box grumble. Dried-up leaves stuck in a vase lift their stalks and begin to dance. Their underclothes are just visible. The walls would approach steadily, blink their eyes a couple of times, and then withdraw slowly again. The transistor puts up its aerial and balances itself on top of it. The ashtray begins to applaud. A song flows forth from the area around the wall socket. Just like when as a child he used to be entranced by the wonder of water running off the eaves and used to catch it in his shoes, so now he spread his tiny umbrella and leaped into his own enchanting garland universe. He felt the desire to become an accomplice.

That was when it happened. He felt his legs becoming rigid. Actually it was only by accident that he became aware of the fact. It was just when he was about to move off slowly after deciding that he would escape from this room, and he wanted to move as soundlessly and stealthily as possible. But he couldn't move his legs. This was strange. He reached down his hand and rubbed his legs, but they were already rigid, stiff as plaster and without feeling, so that he decided he would have to crawl over on his hands to the switch. He stretched out his hands and mustered all his strength in order to drag his heavy and increasingly rigid legs to the switch. But he found now that his whole body was becoming rigid and he was powerless to control it. He gave up the effort. Very strange, he thought, and he gathered his legs together and stood up straight. He looked as if he were rising from the dead.

Two days later, sometime in the afternoon, a woman came into the room. She saw signs that someone had been there. Very alarmed, she even considered telephoning the police. She controlled her beating heart and examined the entire room carefully. It was certain that someone had been there, but after examining every corner she realized there was nothing missing. This set her mind at ease.

Instead of something being missing, the woman actually discovered something that had been left lying there. It was something she had once been very fond of, so much so that she had dusted it for several days, even kissed it—though this was going a bit far. In the end she discovered she really did not have much use for it: she tired of it and threw it up in the attic with the bric-a-brac.

Now she decided to leave the room. She tore a page out of a memo pad, wrote off the following note with a flourish and left it on top of the dressing table:

Darling,
I got a telegram this morning saying Father is critically ill. I won't be gone long. You will probably be tired, so I'll tell them you have gone on a business trip and there won't be any need for you to come. I've left your dinner out in the kitchen.

Your wife.

Translated by Kevin O'Rourke

14. KIM PUKHYANG

Kim Pukhyang was in the words of Marshall R. Pihl a "prolific and consistently published author" in the Democratic People's Republic of Korea (North Korea), at least between 1959 and 1973. The story that follows was first published in June 1971 in *Chosŏn munhak*, a literary journal issued by the Central Committee of the Chosŏn chakka tongmaeng (Korean writers' alliance). For more information on North Korean fiction see Pihl's landmark essay "Engineers of the Human Soul: North Korean Literature Today," published in *Korean Studies* 1 (1977): 63–92, to which this translation was appended.

THE SON

Chun'gi came home after nearly a month away on special assignment. The snowy winter's night was already deep, but his wife had not yet put aside the piecework she did at home.

"Back at last? Have you been well?"

His wife greeted him with pleasure and took the coat that Chun'gi was removing. But he did not look at his wife. As was his habit when coming home, he first looked down at the little ones, an expression of loving satisfaction on his face. They were lying side by side at the warm end of the room with their quilts kicked aside and arms spread wide.

"How've our little friends been?" He did not wait for the answer. "Ippuni and Koptani seem the same as ever. They may take after their mother with those funny little noses but one's as sweet and gentle as the other. Chaeho takes after his father with his chubby cheeks and stubborn temper. But, look at him! He's all boy, isn't he?"

He gave a big laugh. Then he settled in the warm end of the room with his daughters and covered them with their quilts.

His wife, Kim-shi, ignored his explosive laughter while she hung up the overcoat. But then she turned to her barely graying husband and spoke as if chiding him.

"The children will hear you! Have you eaten dinner?"

"Oh, do I roar all the time? It's just because I'm thinking of you. Anyway, I ate dinner in the dining car on the train. Where has Chaeshik gone?"

Chun'gi finally looked at his loyal wife. Her face was lit with a smile of satisfaction.

"He's gone to his study group but he should be back soon."

"Anything happen while I was away? Not even a meeting of the school Parents Association?"

"Nothing. The children have all been studying well, there has been no trouble, and the boys' attitude has been so very good! They tell me our family should be envied! You must be tired—do sleep now."

As Kim-shi was making up the bed, Chaeshik came in, a book-bag slung over his shoulder. The new Youth Corps leadership patch on the left sleeve of his jacket was quite eye-catching. He was in charge of the local Corps bulletin board. Chaeshik saw his father and smiled wide as he removed his fur cap.

"Father, you're back!" he said with a bow.

Chun'gi looked at his son with satisfaction.

"Yes. Did you study hard while I was away?" As though the thought suddenly struck him, he pulled his vinyl travel bag forward and opened it. He took out a student's notebook and a bag of cookies and candy, which he gave to his son.

"Share these with your brother and sisters."

Chaeshik, his face wide with generous cheeks, smiled and chuckled as he drew a sheet of white paper from under his desk. On it he set out some cookies and candy from the bag and placed them in front of Chun'gi.

"Mother, please eat some too."

"No, it's just for you children to eat," said Chun'gi, impressed by the boy. He pushed it toward his wife.

"Here. Have a taste."

His wife, who had been watching her son with affection-filled eyes, responded. "I'd feel full without even eating," she said, picking up one piece of the candy and putting it in her mouth. She then placed the paper dish of candy and cookies back in front of her son.

Quite satisfied that everything had gone as usual during his absence, just as he had wished, Chun'gi could set aside his anxieties at last and stretch out for a good night's sleep.

The children, awaking the next morning, clung to their father and relished the candy and cookies that Chaeshik shared with them.

Then Chaeho, who was to enter school in the new year, came in from outside.

"Chaeshik! There's been lots of snow! Let's go out and play and clear the snow in the yard! Huh?" he said, dragging at Chaeshik's arm. Chaeshik screwed up his face.

"I've got things to do. You go out by yourself." He tried to free his arm, but the more he pulled, the tighter his younger brother held.

Mother had folded up the bedding.

"Let your brother be. He must do his studying," she said, taking Chaeshik's part. Chaeshik freed his arm from his brother's grasp and hurried to his desk and opened up a book.

Chun'gi glanced with satisfaction at his eldest son and took Chaeho outside to clear the snow.

When he went to work that day, Chun'gi reported on his special assignment and was praised for his efforts. With a sense of satisfaction, he threw himself into clearing away the work that had piled up. Then a phone call came from the teacher in charge of Chaeshik's class. Chun'gi usually paid a visit to the school when he returned from a lengthy special assignment. He picked up the receiver.

". . . In any event, I plan to see you today or tomorrow. You must have been quite busy at school—has anything happened while I've been gone?"

Thus he greeted the teacher. At heart he quite expected to hear some praise for his son.

"Well, no. Nothing new. But there is something I'd like to discuss."

"What is it about?"

"It has to do with Chaeshik, but it's no great cause for concern. I'd like to visit you this evening."

"No. I'll come to the school. Please wait for me."

It was the first time a phone call with Chaeshik's teacher had ended so unsatisfactorily.

What could it be? If it were good news, it oughtn't to be so difficult to express.

For him, a short winter's day had never seemed so tediously long.

The teacher in charge of Chaeshik's class was a young man just over thirty who had a very composed and introspective nature that Chun'gi found pleasing. Moreover, he felt trust and respect for the man.

The teacher received Chun'gi as warmly as ever.

"I should have called on you. I'm sorry you had to come here." After Chun'gi sat down, the teacher, with an apologetic look, spoke in a low voice as if taking care lest someone hear.

"Not at all. I haven't been able to do my duty as a parent, having to go on trips and leaving my child in his teacher's care. So, what is this about?"

Sorry for having asked so abruptly, Chun'gi rephrased the question: "Could it be, perhaps, that my boy Chaeshik has done something improper?" he asked. He studied the teacher's face intently lest he miss any change in expression.

"Oh, no. Nothing like that. How could Chaeshik do anything of the kind?" The teacher was rather taken aback. His eyes, which usually seemed lost in deep thought, opened wide; he was at a loss, sorry for having troubled Chun'gi.

Observing this reaction, Chun'gi let his breath escape as he relaxed somewhat.

"Is something weighing on your mind? Let's talk openly. Ours is a good world where the teachers show more concern for the children than do the parents. If we were back in the time of the Japs. . . ."

Chun'gi's rancor deepened as he thought anew of the harsh treatment he had received from the Jap teachers during those years when he was not able to pay his monthly fees.

"But conditions are so good today that parents like me can simply entrust their children to the school and know they have few concerns. So, does that boy Chaeshik keep up in his studies?"

"By all means. As far as that goes, well . . . The thing that concerns me about Chaeshik . . ." The teacher broke off and looked across at Chun'gi.

Unconsciously, Chun'gi drew in his breath.

"It's in the area of group activities."

"What? Group activities?"

"Yes. Several days ago there was a severe blizzard. We had organized a forced march for several of the classes, and our class was one of them. We were to cross Liberation Hill and return. . . ."

"Liberation Hill? That hill is so steep they used to call it 'Panting Hill' in the old days. But now it's paved for cars."

"Of course, you've lived in this district all along—so you should know it well!"

"I know it indeed. Many memorable events have taken place there," said Chun'gi, sighing a bit.

"It's about fifteen *li* to the mine on the other side of the hill, isn't it?"

"Easily fifteen *li*."

"So it was a thirty-*li* march both ways. Because of various other school activities, only one teacher took charge and left with them. I myself did not go. No stragglers were left and the march was evaluated as having been very productive. But a few days ago at a Youth Corps evaluation meeting I was surprised to learn that Chaeshik had not joined in the march. He was criticized for it, especially since he is a Corps leader; whether he could have set the pace is beside the point."

The local Youth Corps group had made plans to put together a bulletin board newspaper for that day. Chaeshik had dropped out of the forced march to work alone until late that night to finish the newspaper and, getting to school before the others early the next morning, he posted it on the bulletin board.

"Since it all seemed reasonable, I didn't look into it. But when the meeting ended, I sat puzzled for a long time. I couldn't get up, as if a great weight rested on my shoulders. Chaeshik had known there was going to be a forced march—why would he choose to make up the newspaper on that particular day? Even if it took him all night, couldn't he have done it earlier?

"Shouldn't we also consider the fact that he missed the tree-planting last fall and wasn't present at the Youth Corps conference? I can't dismiss the inference. But, then, perhaps I am going too far with my impressions."

The teacher looked worried. But then Chun'gi, who was deeply affected by the teacher's cautious remarks, spoke up.

"Not at all. What you say is for the sake of our children. Parents should understand and learn from the commitment of such an educator. You shouldn't hesitate to speak up."

He took out a pack of cigarettes and, offering one to the teacher, lit one for himself. The teacher accepted the cigarette readily. After one or two puffs he stubbed it out in an ashtray and continued speaking.

"At any rate, in this case I tried analyzing Chaeshik's life, as far as I know it. This also meant an investigation of myself as a teacher. As the Premier has taught us, unless you are a revolutionary you cannot be a teacher. I realized once again how heavy a teacher's responsibility is. Speaking frankly, I had the self-conceit to think I was doing everything a teacher should do. But when I examined myself, I felt as if I had been standing on top of a steep precipice. Until recently I assumed that Chaeshik studied well and, as a Corps leader, faithfully carried out the editorial duties assigned him by the group. And so, at every evaluation, I praised him as a model, a standard for judging other students. But Chaeshik's nonconformity forced me to realize a hard truth that, particularly with a student like him, the slightest mistake must be closely examined and strict control applied."

The teacher lit a match for Chun'gi, who had been trying to draw on his cigarette, unaware that it had gone out.

Chun'gi only then noticed the white ash sitting on his cigarette and, giving an embarrassed laugh, took the proffered light and puffed.

He wished the teacher would go on with what he was saying. Chun'gi had many times sat with the teacher like this but never before seen him so cautious. And these things he was saying in a low voice, like a whisper, were touching Chun'gi. The teacher went on.

"As a teacher, I thought it quite proper to excuse Chaeshik openly from most extracurricular activities since editing the bulletin board newspaper takes time. I didn't even pay much attention to his absences from meetings. And all the while, the students and I, the Youth Corps leadership, and even

Chaeshik thought everything was quite all right. So what need had Chaeshik to say anything further? But, as a Youth Corps leader, Chaeshik ought to be an activist; he must work harder than anyone else and take the lead in difficult tasks. That is, he must stand out from among the others in class, not only working with them but also doing better than them. All the while, he is expected to produce, as scheduled, the bulletin board newspaper, which is his responsibility. Where he ought to be exemplary in all his duties, Chaeshik has concentrated his efforts on his newspaper duties—for which he has been praised—and let it go at that. So it appears that Chaeshik doesn't show the correct recognition for and attitude toward the many duties of the group. The responsibility is mine for not giving him his proper guidance. As in the case of the forced march, it was the teachers who should have been in the forefront, setting an example. On this score I plan to examine myself mercilessly. And I am also thinking of ways to awaken Chaeshik to his errors and set him on the right path to improvement."

The teacher, his body slightly bent as if immobilized by a heavy burden, gazed intently at Chun'gi.

But Chun'gi only sat—silent, head down, a long-dead cigarette still in his fingers—like someone who had been scolded and didn't know how to answer. An awkward silence settled between the two.

At that moment another instructor came by to say something to Chaeshik's teacher, and the embarrassing situation was averted.

But when the teacher finished talking and had left, Chun'gi quickly rose and picked up his fur cap from the desk.

"I'm sorry you have been given this worry. I'll see you again," he said and offered his hand to the teacher.

Chun'gi and the teacher separated. The teacher's handshake had been firmer than usual.

It was dark outside. In the gloom, the snowflakes fluttered heavily like scattered moths. Though usually happy and satisfied when he left the school gates after a visit, Chun'gi this time stepped out into the street with a heavy tread, his heart sad and stinging like a wound. He could not come to grips with this state of things. He wondered, mightn't the teacher have carried his concern a little too far?

But Chun'gi knew this was a time for careful action, standing firmly on principle. As he grew older, he saw how the slightest mistake in thought or action could affect human destinies; he himself, indeed, had experienced it. Should he not, as a father, reconsider his own attitude toward his son? As he walked the unpeopled snowy streets where the night was now deep, the voice of the teacher still seemed to be ringing whisperlike in Chun'gi's ears. He reflected intently on how he had trained his son and how Chaeshik was developing at home.

Suddenly, Chun'gi was startled to realize that he and his wife, as parents, had been raising their son in much the same way that the teacher had handled Chaeshik's leadership in the Youth Corps.

Chun'gi thought with deep regret of his own early years, when he had struggled with hunger, trembled in rags, and not been able to study, in spite of his desire to do so. He wanted all the more to feed and clothe his son without worry and, further, let him study to his heart's content in this good, socialist world where he was growing up. For his son's studies, he would spare nothing to give him all he asked.

His sincerity of purpose and expectations of his son were not lost in vain dreams. Chaeshik was enthusiastic in his studies and proper in decorum, and always carried his work through with highest grades. The days when he would come home with a perfect report card were, indeed, quite like festival days. Chun'gi would buy his son a congratulatory gift, and his wife would set a table as if for a birthday feast.

But in thinking back he could see a huge mistake in this behavior. While a student should do well at his studies, he also has, though young, certain social, family, and moral duties as a member of society, as a son to his parents, and as an older or younger brother. When there is work to be done, even though not his own, he must roll up his sleeves and stand forth, helping when his neighbor's work is arduous and doing his part when his parents are busy. . . . But Chun'gi and his wife were intent only upon having Chaeshik study; from the start they had never let him lift a finger to work around the house or neighborhood. If Chaeshik got up early to sweep the yard, they would take away the broom and, telling him to study, push him back into his room. Lest he notice ashes in the firebox, they would clean them out as soon as they collected. And when Chun'gi was to leave on a long-term special assignment, he would chop up enough kindling ahead of time and stack it away in the shed. For fear their son would lay hand to such tasks, the parents would rest easily only if they kept work away from him. As a result, Chaeshik had only to study without touching a broom, working with a hatchet, or carrying out the ash-bucket; he didn't have to care for his younger brother and sisters or calm them when they bickered. In time, Chaeshik came to believe that hard study alone was a kind of be-all and end-all for him. Had not Chaeshik forgotten the moral and civic duties of the new generation, which is expected to move forward, shouldering the future of the country, the socialist fatherland?

When he realized that Chaeshik's dropping out of the forced work march was by no means coincidental, Chun'gi became aware that he had been remiss. Chun'gi was even more deeply concerned when his thoughts turned to Chaeshik's failure to cross over Liberation Hill. He recognized that the problem did not involve Chaeshik alone but was also a question of his duties as a father responsible for his son's training.

When his wife noticed that he returned home distracted, as though he had been arguing, she guessed right off that something unpleasant had happened and thought better of asking any questions.

Kim-shi went silently out to the kitchen and, as silently, came in with the supper table, which she placed in front of her husband.

Chun'gi normally ate like a youth, with a hearty appetite—always cleaning his rice bowl. But this evening he just nibbled at a few spoonfuls of rice, and, pushing the table away, went straight to bed.

It was the next morning.

The snow was still falling as before.

Chun'gi shook Chaeshik awake.

"That's enough. Let's get up and clear the snow. Come along, now."

"What? I've got to study," mumbled Chaeshik carelessly, stretching and pulling the quilt over himself.

"Study is study but you must also breathe the fresh morning air and get some exercise."

Chun'gi got Chaeshik up, saw that his bedding was folded away, and led him outside. Chaeshik, his cheeks puffed up, grumbled unintelligibly as he put on his shoes.

"Why are you getting the boy out to clear that little yard? It's no bigger than the palm of your hand! Not leaving him to study," scolded his wife from the kitchen, where she had been making breakfast.

"What do you have in mind, acting like that this morning?"

Chun'gi, not heeding his wife, made no response and gave the shovel to his son.

"Don't just stand there. Take the snow-shovel and try pushing it," said Chun'gi as he took a broom and began sweeping snow.

Chaeshik picked up the shovel but just scraped at the ground where he stood. Chun'gi took the shovel from Chaeshik and, grasping the handle, pushed through the snow to the far side of the yard and came back.

"Now you try pushing straight through like that. When you work, whatever the job, you should do it willingly. Only then will the work be well done and productive. From now on, you must help with tasks at home. And, at school, work hard in group activities," he said, giving the shovel back to his son.

Chaeshik had no choice. He braced the handle against his stomach and set out at a normal pace, pushing the snow ahead.

As Chun'gi sat up late that night, studying his daily readings from works of the beloved Leader, he felt greatly inspired. In the light of the Leader's teaching that the school, the family, and society must all share responsibility for the education and training of youth, Chun'gi seriously criticized himself as a father and as the parent of a schoolchild.

From that day on, Chun'gi kept in closer contact with the teacher and took a more active role in Chaeshik's life, trying to correct him at each step so that he would commit himself to group and organizational activities. While upholding his standards of study, he assigned more household tasks to his son.

Though Kim-shi was not satisfied at first, Chun'gi helped her understand; and, when Chaeshik's teacher visited and she heard him out, Kim-shi seemed to have been awakened, for she did not take her son's side.

At school, Chaeshik was assigned a new edition of the bulletin board newspaper to get him more involved with the young people's movement. Efforts were also made to have him participate actively in meetings and group affairs.

For this reason, perhaps, Chaeshik was a different person, even when he was at home. He would get out and clear the snow whenever his father asked him to, and when his mother was busy in the kitchen he would go in and carry out the ash-bucket for her. But for all this, his heart was not really in the work. Though he seemed eagerly devoted to his studies and to editing the bulletin board newspaper, he was doing his other tasks rather sluggishly and unwillingly—as if he were helping someone else out.

Then one day, when Chaeshik was given his first new assignment since that of editing the bulletin board newspaper, Chun'gi was asked by the teacher what he thought of it. Chaeshik had been told to gather samples of new ore at the mines beyond Liberation Hill as an extracurricular task for geography studies; he was also to produce a special edition on minerals for the bulletin board to point out to students the mineral nature of our country. The teacher set a deadline for the work, based on Chaeshik's ability to take on the extra task while editing the bulletin board newspaper.

Chun'gi understood the teacher's intentions.

"That'll be fine," he agreed quickly.

The intent of this special assignment, while asking Chaeshik to participate actively in the usual organizational affairs, was to train him to carry out any task given him by the organization, without question and unconditionally. This would train him not to think, as he did, that his duty was done once he had finished the bulletin board work the Youth Corps assigned him. Merely having Chaeshik climb Liberation Hill, which he had previously avoided doing by missing the group forced march, was not a pointless exercise.

Chun'gi, as concerned about this assignment as though he himself were charged with it, was at a loss for what to do.

When Chaeshik came home he sat mumbling at his desk until late at night writing copy for the new edition of the bulletin board newspaper and seemed to have forgotten all about going to the mines.

Chun'gi found himself watching his son's behavior closely while vainly fretting. When Chaeshik was at home he would worry that he wasn't thinking of going; and when he wasn't there, he would ask his wife, "Hasn't Chaeshik gone over the hill to the mines yet?"

Although Chun'gi wanted to prod his son, he wanted to wait for the right moment. It seemed to him that the slightest mistake would give the clear impression that home and school were conspiring with each other, against Chaeshik.

When Chun'gi visited the school one day when the bulletin board newspaper was nearly done and close to the day Chaeshik had to go to the mines, he learned clearly from the teacher how the revolutionary tasks assigned by the Youth Corps organization were working out. He heard that they were stressing a study of the group and organizational life of the Children's Brigade at the time of the unarmed anti-Japanese struggle. He also learned that Chaeshik was to present research on the recollections of revolutionary activity by the youth Mok Unshik, who had been a member of the Children's Brigade.

He left the school after exchanging views with the teacher on Chaeshik's life guidance, still feeling that he was ineffectual as a parent.

On his way, Chun'gi dropped by the library to borrow factual materials on the struggle of the youth Mok Unshik and read them through, then and there. He had once before read these recollections. But, for some reason, he was overwhelmed this time by emotions more deeply felt than ever before. Before his eyes appeared first the indelible image of Mok Unshik climbing step by step up the steep path to the ridge—snow-covered even though it was spring—and then the miserable sight of his stoic courage as his right foot, the straw sandal still on, was thrust into a firebox, red with coals, when he would not turn over a communication.

What a bright lad he was! No matter what charge the organization gave him, however he had to live, fight, or die for the revolution, he sacrificed his only life. Thus he teaches us, appeals to us!

Chun'gi thought again of his own behavior—ashamed both as a fighter for the Leader and as a father who did not train his son to be one of the new generation that is to carry forward the revolution.

Chun'gi took the factual materials on Mok Unshik with him and gave them to his son.

"Study these well. Then let us discuss them."

Chun'gi worked even harder at leading and training his son. When Chaeshik had studied Mok Unshik's recollections of revolutionary activities, Chun'gi spoke to his son of his own study and thoughts about the indomitable young revolutionary fighter, awakening the boy to how important revolutionary, organizational activity is in our lives.

On a Saturday morning, two days before the deadline for bringing back the mineral samples, Chaeshik finally spoke to Chun'gi.

"Father! I must go over Liberation Hill to the mines and back. . . . Can you get me a ride tomorrow?" he asked.

"A ride?"

Chun'gi repeated the words as by rote, unable to add anything further right away. He thought for a while before replying.

"I'll try to find out. But why are you depending upon me for what you must do? You should have a self-reliant spirit. If, perhaps, you can't get a ride, won't you go where you must? You must go even though you walk!"

As Chun'gi thought of his feckless son who couldn't carry out an assignment given him by the organization, he felt sick at heart for having been blinded earlier by unquestioning love for his son.

Chaeshik did not protest his father's scolding but sullenly picked up his book bag and went to school.

All the same, Chun'gi did telephone several government offices and enterprises in town on his way to work to ask if there would be a car going to the mines. He found there would be.

But Chun'gi, telephone receiver in hand, suddenly realized he was asking that busy cars be stopped for his son's private business; he couldn't easily answer the question from the other end as to why he was asking and, equivocating, simply hung up.

Even so, he somehow did not feel regret. Not having spoken was, after all, the better course, he thought.

When Chun'gi got home that evening he spoke in such a way that Chaeshik knew he should not count on a ride.

"Since you must go anyway, you'll have to walk."

"Oh, this is really terrible," moaned Chaeshik to himself when he heard the disappointing news from his father.

It was Sunday. Chun'gi had gone to his office and was straightening his desk after clearing up some work he hadn't quite finished the day before when, suddenly, his wife came hurrying in.

"Is something the matter?"

His wife, panting heavily, said that Chaeshik had just left, saying that he was going to the mines. With the weather so bad, what is to be done? she was asking.

Chun'gi set down his work and listened quietly to his wife.

"He said that it was confirmed yesterday at the Youth Corps meeting that he is to bring the mineral samples. I couldn't get him to go another day—he wouldn't listen."

A look of concern filled his wife's eyes.

Making no reply at all to his wife's words, Chun'gi looked silently out the window.

A snowy wind shook the window roughly.

Chun'gi was himself quite concerned that his son had gone out into a blizzard as harsh as today.

But, the next moment, Chun'gi shook his head.

No. He must make Chaeshik bring back the ore samples, even though he pushed through a blizzard. He surely had to carry out the task assigned him by the Youth Corps organization and, through that process, renew his commitment toward the organization.

He had to make him a true son of the Leader, a prepared successor to the age of proper devotion and revolution.

"But, what can be done by just sitting? Even his teacher came to the house and spoke of his concern." His wife, in frustration, had spoken again.

Chun'gi turned to face his wife and scolded her.

"Let's be done with that useless talk! There's no need for such worry. A boy that age could catch a tiger and bring it back. What use is a child who has only been pampered while growing up? Now, you just go along home."

He continued to sit where he was even after his disconcerted wife had left.

Chun'gi was determined that his son would cross over the hill and return even if he himself had to spur the boy on. With this thought, he cleared away the papers on his desk and headed out toward Liberation Hill.

Heavy flakes of snow were already falling, evenly and thickly.

Out beyond the streets of the city, the blizzard was well under way. Through the fall of thick, fluttering snow, electric power poles, mountain foothills, and huge old trees in the distance seemed to come and go.

Chun'gi walked quickly.

Snow that drifted on the sloping road was blown and piled again by the wind. At some points Chun'gi sank in snow up to his ankles. The blizzard, which had seemed to be blowing in from the distant plains, now swept down from the mountain ridges to drift on the road and cover the valley deep in white.

Chun'gi quickened his pace. He rounded a bend and, halfway up the slope ahead, a black movement caught his eye. As Chun'gi rounded each bend it disappeared—seen and then not seen as if playing a game of hide-and-seek. When the black movement was nearer, it grew larger and took on human form.

It was Chaeshik.

"Right! It's Chaeshik crossing over the hill!"

At the sight of his son climbing through the blizzard, Chun'gi was greatly reassured.

As he gazed at his son, Chun'gi's face was wreathed in smiles.

Having come around another turn in the mountain road—his heart filling with great joy and pride for his precious son—Chun'gi stopped short. While he had guessed as he walked that Chaeshik should already have rounded one more bend, wasn't the boy just idling by an old tree that stood at the edge of the cliff?

Why's this? Is he resting? If not, is he looking around for something?

While Chun'gi watched with a troubled look in his eyes, Chaeshik started up the hill again, as if with somehow renewed determination. The blizzard, which had paused for a moment, now swept the trail again with drifts and moved on.

Chun'gi rounded the bend and quickly looked up toward the crest of the hill.

Chaeshik was moving slowly, engulfed by the blizzard that buffeted him.

Chun'gi ran up the slope and called, without being aware, "Chaeshik!"

Enveloped in the blizzard, Chaeshik appeared only as a shape bent against the wind. His back was turned, as if he had not heard his father's call.

"Chaeshik!"

When Chun'gi called a second time, Chaeshik lifted his face, red with the cold, inside a fur cap that was white with frost.

"Father!"

As soon as Chaeshik recognized his father standing square in front of him like a wall, he ran, nearly falling, to Chun'gi's embrace and burst into tears of joy.

Chun'gi hugged his son tightly and then spoke in a quiet voice.

"Chaeshik! Let's cross over the hill. How can you turn back on what you've started?"

With this he turned his son around and, taking the lead, kicked a path through the snow ahead.

Chaeshik seemed to gain courage and followed his father's lead.

"Father, I'm all right," he said, reassuring his father, who was making a path for him.

But they hadn't gone far when his exhaustion made it difficult for him to walk and he fell behind his father.

As Chun'gi kicked his way through the snow, he thought with deep feeling of the times when as a youth he had crossed over this hill on his way to school. In those days Chun'gi had fulfilled the heartfelt wish of his father, who barely eked out a living in the Jap mines, by attending an elementary school located where Chaeshik's school now stood. But today was the first time he had crossed over this hill for the sake of his own son's training, and he was swept by a wave of emotion. This road—once barely wide enough for a donkey trail—that he had crossed back and forth in snow or rain without missing a day; this hill, over which he had once flown on the endless wings of eager desire for learning; this hill he had gazed at through his tears both morning and night—like a distant, thousand-league pass—when going and coming from the mines after he was finally kicked out of school for failing to pay the monthly fees; this hill—which had been paved with a broad, new road after liberation—where he would now ride instead of walk, charged with various responsibilities.

Chun'gi was looking back, eyes brimming with tears, at his son trudging through the snow.

Chaeshik had covered his nose and mouth with his mittens, and, when the blizzard was too much to bear, he would turn and walk backward.

As he watched his son attentively, Chun'gi's face gradually grew hard and expressionless. After wavering between anger at himself and encouragement for his son, Chun'gi spoke out in a loud voice.

"Brace up! If your heart is firmly set, even the rocks make way for you!"

When Chun'gi spoke thus, Chaeshik would hurry and catch up with his father, only to fall behind again after a while.

As Chaeshik plodded up the steepening slope he would look back from time to time, his eyes showing concern as if he were waiting for something.

Sometimes he would flip open an earflap and listen intently. But then, disappointed, he would grumble to himself.

"Oh! Why today, of all days, must the weather be like this?"

For Chaeshik, winter was a happy season when they would study in a cozy classroom and then, at recess, go out to the playground to have fights in the snow that so delighted them. Or, on the way to school each day, he and his comrades would play noisily in the streets, singing songs or rolling over and over in the snow.

But this winter had been more lonely and difficult to bear than any he had known.

His head, brow, and cheeks were hot and flushed, soaked with sticky sweat; the unpleasantly slimy feel, like some queer insect, put him in a bad mood. His body was so bathed in sweat that each time the cold air slipped in through his collar goose pimples ran down his spine. He regretted being dressed in so many layers of clothing.

But there are usually so many cars—where have they gone today? Not a sign of one here! Oh!

Chaeshik, panting from the effort to catch up with his father way ahead, couldn't make even half the distance before he had to stop and catch his breath. He looked back again.

His eyes burned as if they were on fire.

But all he could see was just an expanse of white; all he could hear was the scream of the blizzard.

Chaeshik was getting angry. "Oh, this is wretched!" he grumbled to himself.

Not caring how far he had fallen behind, he did not try to catch up but plodded heavily as if on leaden feet.

Then, at the sound of a horn from somewhere in the distance, he stopped, startled, listening intently. With a heart fervently hoping it was coming up the hill, he turned and looked back. At a lower bend, where the blizzard had just swept past, a black object suddenly appeared.

The instant he recognized it, Chaeshik dashed up the hill like a champion sprinter, seized with unexpected strength.

"Father! It's a truck!" he cried.

But his father, not seeming to hear, did not look back. Just then, as if in understanding of Chaeshik's state of mind, the truck's loud horn sounded again. Perhaps startled by the metallic sound, the blizzard suddenly quieted; for Chaeshik, the cold and lonely hill filled instantly with the friendly vitality of a city street.

But still there was no reaction from his father. As Chaeshik was about to call out again in frustration, the truck drew abreast of him, sounding its horn. He moved to the side of the road and waved his right arm.

"Driver! Please give me a ride!"

The truck was loaded with freight and there was no one in the cab but the driver. The driver, who had a broad face and appeared friendly, looked toward Chaeshik with a pleasant smile, but drove on. Chaeshik chased after the truck.

"Driver, . . ." he called, pleading. But there was no need to dash after the truck. It pulled to a stop beside his father. *Well, that's it.* Chaeshik's mouth opened wide as he ran, kicking the snow ahead of him.

His father was saying something to the driver, who had opened the door of the cab. It seemed to Chaeshik that his kind father was asking the driver to give him a seat in the cab.

But that wouldn't do. Father should ride there. I should ride in the freight compartment. In such cold . . .

"Father, you ride up front!" he said, when he got to the truck, and started to crawl up into the freight compartment.

But what happened? Father would not get in the truck. The door slammed shut and the engine began to roar.

Father, who had waited gruffly until then, approached Chaeshik.

"Chaeshik, let's you and I walk!" he said, placing a hand on Chaeshik's shoulder. Chaeshik had not caught the low tone in his father's voice.

"Father, why do we have to do that?" he protested, about to burst into tears.

To Chun'gi, it felt as if the voice of his son were cutting like a knife into his heart.

But he ignored the pain.

He thought it would be best to send the truck on its way. If they rode over the hill they would reach the mines early but without trial. Could one somehow expect only favorable conditions for carrying out an assignment given by the organization? Must it not, finally, be carried out no matter how difficult and strenuous the conditions or hardships? He must awaken his son's whole-hearted understanding that such was the nature of organizational duty, which must be carried out! Even were another truck to come, they would have to let it pass by and cross over on foot!

To the father this seemed the first time that his son had ever protested to him. Even Chaeshik himself could not imagine how he could be so disrespectful to his father.

The father, quite surprised, looked him over closely; his face, which had just grown stern, seemed to furrow as if bearing severe pain. Even in his tone of voice, the father showed distress.

"Chaeshik, how could I not understand what you feel? All the same, the driver is in a hurry."

Chaeshik was covered in frost from ankle to brow, but it was as though he saw his father's affectionate eyes and loving face for the first time; and his father's voice was so warm it stirred his heart. Aware that he could not go against his father's wishes, Chaeshik let go of the edge of the truck's freight compartment, which he had stood on tiptoe to reach.

The truck departed, leaving the air filled with the smell of gasoline.

Chaeshik gazed at the disappearing truck with eyes more angry than sad.

"Chaeshik! Let's go!"

Wakened by his father's voice, Chaeshik turned around.

His father waited for Chaeshik to come near and then, putting a sheltering arm around his son's shoulders, walked slowly as he spoke to him.

"If we stop a busy mining truck for our personal business, think how much we interrupt the work of carrying ore to the furnaces . . . even though we are headed the same way. What would happen if lots of people all stopped trucks? Think it over."

His father's affectionate voice soothed Chaeshik's pent-up heart.

"You studied the youth Mok Unshik of the Children's Brigade, who grew up in the embrace of Marshal Kim Il Sung—how faithful he was in his group and organizational life? How they dedicated their lives to carrying out the revolutionary tasks assigned them by the organization? Chaeshik! I hope that you'll turn out like them! Of course you can get a ride over this hill; but, even without a ride, you still must go—as I hope you will. Like a member of the Children's Brigade, faithful to the Leader!"

Chaeshik's heart overflowed with love. For the first time in his life he felt the warm love flowing out from his father. He cried *Father!* within his heart, while hot tears gushed out from his eyes.

His heart swelled with an emotion he had not known before. This wave of feeling gave Chaeshik strength and helped quicken his pace. A new toughness possessed him as he energetically kicked a path through the drifts ahead of his father and on up the hill.

Chun'gi watched his son from behind, reassured.

At this moment the figure of a man appeared behind him.

"Chaeshik's father? I'm so glad to see you. Doesn't he look strong and dependable!"

It was Chaeshik's smiling teacher, who was standing in the spot where Chaeshik had stood. The teacher laughed softly, blinking his eyes, his brows covered with snow. It was the happy smile seen only on the face of a truly pleased teacher.

After learning that Chaeshik had left, the teacher had gone back to school before setting out. In so doing, he had fallen behind Chun'gi. He had come to help Chaeshik along. At the same time, he was aware that he, too, had missed the earlier forced march, and he wanted to make up for it.

Chun'gi grasped the teacher's hand tightly without a word.

Chun'gi and the teacher gazed with trust at Chaeshik up ahead, as they walked together, hands clasped firmly.

It was one month later.

Chun'gi was on his way back from a special assignment at the mines, when he stopped at the ridge of Liberation Hill. Suddenly, the column of a forced march from the middle school came into view.

At the head of the column marched the teacher, and Chaeshik.

Translated by Marshall R. Pihl

15. CHO SEHŬI

Cho Sehŭi was born in 1942 in Kap'yŏng, Kyŏnggi Province, and studied Korean literature at Kyung Hee University in Seoul. After making his literary debut in the *Kyŏnghyang shinmun*, a Seoul daily, in 1965, he published but a single story during the next ten years. But then in short order, from 1975 to 1978, he published the twelve stories that would form the work that, with the possible exception of Yi Kwangsu's *Mujŏng* (1917, Heartlessness), is the most important one-volume novel of twentieth-century Korea, *Nanjangi ka ssoaollin chagŭn kong* (1978, trans. 2006 *The Dwarf*). Two books and a serialized novel have appeared since: *Shigan yŏhaeng* (1983, Time travel), *Ch'immuk ŭi ppuri* (1985, The roots of silence), and *Hayan chŏgŏri* (1989–1991, White jacket).

Industrialization in South Korea during the Park Chung Hee era (1961–1979) was gained at the cost of civil, labor, and environmental abuses of the sort that had attracted the attention of American muckrakers early in the twentieth century. In the *Nanjangi* novel Cho set for himself the daunting task of describing the dark side of this industrialization without running afoul of dictator Park's strict National Security Law. His solution was to utilize subtle irony in his narratives and at the same time, in order to reach the widest possible audience, to write in syntax simple enough to be understood by any Korean with a rudimentary education. The result is a book whose basic message—the social costs of reckless industrialization—is evident but whose deeper meanings—the spiritual malaise of the newly rich and powerful and of a working class subject to forces beyond its control—await discovery by the careful reader. Cho succeeded admirably in his undertaking: in his native Korea the book has appeared in more than one hundred printings. Meanwhile, South Korea's economic troubles and spate of industrial accidents in the 1990s as well as the more desperate environmental degradation and food shortages in North Korea have served to reinforce the continuing importance of the novel.

Structurally the *Nanjangi* book is a linked-story novel whose setting alternates among a laboring family, a family of the newly emerging middle class (as in the story translated here), and a wealthy industrialist's family. The twelve stories are written in a lean, clipped style that features rapid shifts of scene and viewpoint. Long paragraphs alternate with stretches of terse dialogue. Reproductions of bureaucratic forms and an extract from a laboring family's budget book give us a taste of the realities of a dwarf's life—the dwarf epitomizing the "little people" on whose backs the Korean economic miracle took place. These particularities of life in South Korea in the 1970s are juxtaposed with snippets of information on science past and present and allusions to the workings of the universe. Two of the stories, "Moebiusŭ ŭi tti" (1976, trans. 1998 "The Möbius Strip") and "K'ŭllain-sshi ŭi pyŏng" (1978, The Klein bottle), are built upon the concept of spatial form, their titles referring to objects whose inner and outer surfaces are interchangeable. This notion of interchangeability and the references in the stories to the history of science and space exploration suggest to us that the dualities, contradictions, and anomalies of industrialization described in the *Nanjangi* novel are not unique to Korea but result in large part from global economic forces that have accumulated over the centuries.

Abuse of power is a vivid presence in the novel. Typically power is exercised through intimidation and violence, as in the story translated here. Violence begets violence, as when in the penultimate story in the book a captain of industry is assassinated. Here the author is obliquely critiquing the authoritarian leadership that has plagued much of modern Korean history, as well as questioning Korea's traditionally patriarchal social structure.

"Knifeblade" (K'allal) was first published in *Munhak sasang* in 1975.

KNIFEBLADE

There are three knives in Shinae's kitchen. Two are kitchen knives—one large and one small. Once a year Shinae calls a knife sharpener to put a new edge on the large one. A good sharpener knows knives. There are some who don't. Those who don't will start with the grindstone for the first sharpening. Shinae snatches the knife from such sharpeners and goes inside. When the ones who know knives take this one in hand their eyes open wide and they silently observe it. Knife sharpeners are struck by the sight of a good knife. They start by gently putting the blade to a fine whetstone. Sharpeners these days will say that a person could live and die a hundred times and never produce such a knife. To make this knife, they say, the blacksmith would have tempered the blade numerous times, hammered it countless times. His son would have worked the bellows. Who knows, the son might still be alive. If so, he would be a grandfather by now. And someday he will die. The smith will have long since passed on. Shinae's mother-in-law, who had this knife made for her own use when the smith was alive and hammering—she too has passed on. Shinae is forty-six. It won't do to have the large knife sharpened by an amateur. With the small one it's all right. It's a run-of-the-mill knife she bought several years ago. There's not much to say about a knife like that. She bought it for 180 *wŏn* from a knife peddler who was hawking his wares in the usual way by scraping the blades of two knives together. It's a run-of-the-mill knife you can buy for a similar price just about anywhere. The third knife in Shinae's kitchen is a fillet knife. It's a frightening knife. Taut blade, 3 millimeters at the back; pointed tip; 32 centimeters long.

It doesn't seem like a knife made for kitchen work. The thoughts that come to mind when she takes it by the handle are truly frightening. Hyŏnu, Shinae's husband, bought it the previous spring. Why did he buy such a knife?

She can't figure it out. Shinae likes to compare herself and her husband to dwarfs. *We're tiny dwarfs—dwarfs.*

"Well, aren't we?" she asked her husband, who was home from work. "Am I wrong?"

"Well . . ."

Her husband was reading the newspaper.

High officials call for social reforms; no party restructuring, declares opposition head; commentary on National Security Law; UN Secretary-General calls for ROK-DPRK talks; U.S.-USSR spacecraft stage dramatic docking high above Elbe River; violent crime up 800 percent over past decade; foundation head embezzles 100 million *wŏn* from school; South Vietnamese refugees in U.S. demonstrate against extravagant ways of former officials; employment outlook dim despite recovery; add-ons boost budget to 1.52 trillion *wŏn*; new Yŏŭido National Assembly Building rests on twenty-four pillars costing 10 million *wŏn* each; residents of condemned dwellings in redevelopment zone lack 300,000 *wŏn*, give up apartment rights, seek new housing; Kunsan tearooms cite defense tax, hike cost of phone calls; "dead" man revived at graveside; armed robbery; rape; forgery; timber thieves; red pepper cut with sawdust; fishmongers add dye, pump up fish; pop song "Too Much" found indecent, banned; winning number for housing lottery; actress bares all; "For Whose Sake Chastity?" reads ad; university professor calls maldistribution of profits an invitation to crime and consumption. Nothing different here from the previous day's newspaper. Nothing out of the ordinary in these stories. And yet people read the same newspaper day after day.

Her husband was reading that newspaper.

"Am I?"

"Hmm?"

"Will you *please* put down that paper?"

Such is life, Shinae tells herself once more. Last night her husband tossed and turned, unable to sleep, till the owl in the wall clock hooted two in the morning. He leaves early in the morning. Spends twelve or thirteen hours away from home. What he does at work, what happens to him there, the anxiety, doubt, fatigue that follow him around constantly—his hopes have evaporated. From the radio in her daughter's room across the way came the voice of a foreign singer whose face Shinae couldn't picture, singing in whatever language those people spoke. Someday that girl would be *thinking* in a different language. Shinae worried about her daughter. If only their situation were a bit different. Why so much anxiety about managing their small family? Her husband was reading the newspaper, as if by doing so he wished to add to the fatigue that had already accumulated. He was exasperated with himself and the life he led. He felt ill at ease in society and in the times in which he lived. He had studied history. He had read many books. The thoughts written down in those many books had once upon a time influenced young Hyŏnu.

He had wanted to talk about all he had learned from books. And then suddenly he became taciturn. He grew up. Likewise Shinae had once been a girl of many dreams. A bright and pretty girl. One who grew up using her mind. Hyŏnu had said, the first time she met him, that his greatest desire was to write a good book. The two of them fell deeply in love. And so they married. They knew each other's ideals and they held high hopes. But in the face of reality those ideals, those hopes, were of no help to them. The husband found it necessary to earn money. This was the thing he hated the most. To earn this despised money he found it necessary to work hard. For his mother had fallen ill. It was her stomach. She died of stomach cancer. The mother having passed on, the father became ill. It was an illness the doctors couldn't identify. The father suffered terrible pain. Not even morphine injections offered relief. The doctors said he would soon die from the mysterious disease. But he lived another two years, fighting the terrible pain. He died at the mental hospital where he spent his last months. The father had lived his entire life at odds with society and the times. Shinae was well aware that her husband was cut from the same cloth. The man whose greatest desire had been to write a good book couldn't compose a single line. He decided he was aphasic. Although he worked with deadly determination to earn his detested money, all he had to show for it was debt. The hospital, while offering no cure for his parents, was forever demanding utterly prohibitive sums from the proceeds of that determination. He was too drained to weep when his father finally passed on. As they consoled each other, husband and wife sold the Ch'ŏngjin-dong home in downtown Seoul that they had long occupied, and paid off the debts. With what remained they had bought a small house here in the outskirts of the city. The problem was the water. There wasn't any the previous night, or the night before that. Three nights before, only a little came out. Shinae had squatted in front of the faucet in the yard, waiting for the water. And at two-thirty in the morning it had finally come on. It had trickled out, the tiniest amount, from the faucet there by the front gate, the lowest area of their lot. She had filled a bucket using a small earthenware water jar and taken it into the washroom. Before she could half fill the bathtub, the faucet gurgled and the water stopped. At four-thirty the heavens began to brighten. Sleepless and thinking dark thoughts, she forced herself to prepare breakfast.

Her husband didn't put down the newspaper. He had told her that at work, in pedestrian underpasses, when viewed by indifferent passersby, when surrounded by exhaust from vehicle tailpipes, he felt pursued and at a loss. He had said that every day without fail when he commuted on the packed buses he saw city garbage trucks leaving on their rounds several at a time. Shinae understands what her husband is saying. She wonders how many souls a day are loaded into those garbage trucks and then disposed of. But no one in this world talks in that manner.

Fatigue has accumulated on her husband's eyelids like covers on a bed. He puts the newspaper aside. He looks like he's about to faint dead away.

"You haven't listened to a word I've said."

It seems to her now that even the members of her own family each speak a different language. What they say never gets through.

"What in the world are you talking about?" her husband asked.

"I'm saying we're dwarfs!" Shinae said, practically shouting.

"How come we're dwarfs?!" came her daughter's voice from the veranda.

Followed by the idiotic blaring of a television. The family in the house behind theirs had turned on their set. *What are they, deaf? It's so loud. Aren't there any normal people anymore?* At the same hour each night the woman of that house called her young children, and even the housekeeper before she had finished the dishes, and sat them down, and they all proceeded to sniffle. First the housekeeper weeps, then the woman weeps, and finally the children sniffle. When they aren't crying they're laughing. And if it's not crying or laughing then it's singing. "Why, Why Do You Call Me?" or else "Nothing Better" or else "Darling, You Don't Know."

The children who live in that house read weekly magazines in bed. Among the articles they read is this one: " 'Sexy Sounds' from a Car—Orgasmic Outcries and Heavy Breathing, Recorded Live."

The soap opera continues to blare from the TV. Two members of that family aren't home yet. The man of the house and the eldest daughter. The man is an inspector at the tax office. What's lacking in that family is one thing alone—a soul. There's always plenty of everything else. Well, perhaps the "always" part isn't quite accurate.

Misconduct, corruption, bureaucratic cleanup—there was a time when those words appeared almost daily in the newspaper. Only then did the family in back lower the volume on their TV. They stowed away their refrigerator, washer, piano, tape player, and other such possessions in the basement and brought out their old clothes to wear in public. The newspaper often quoted a high official as saying that any government official whose misconduct came to light would be dealt with in accordance with the law. But the misconduct of the man of the house in back must not have come to light, for he emerged unscathed. "If misconduct comes to light"—these words smacked of a very peculiar irony.

In any event, the family in back emerged unscathed, the television soap opera continued, and the man of the house and the eldest daughter still hadn't returned. Where could that man be at this hour, and what could he be doing? Where could the eldest daughter be, and what could *she* be doing?

The eldest daughter had taken a drug. Fortunately they had found her shortly thereafter and had managed to save her. A doctor arrived, put a rubber tube down her throat, and flushed out the poison. The tax inspector and his wife heaved a sigh of relief. The doctor, though, shook his head.

"Too early. If you let her stay here, she'll take it again."

"Then what should we do, Doctor?" asked the woman of the house in back. She trembled pathetically.

"With all due respect, you should take her to a clinic."

"Excuse me?"

"A clinic."

"Then, would you please have her admitted to your clinic, Doctor?"

"I'm afraid I can't help you," said the doctor. "You need to find an obstetrics clinic."

At the time, the eldest daughter was wearing a long skirt.

That morning Shinae had seen her leave the house in long, loose-fitting pants that swept back and forth as she walked down the alley.

If you go by the government pay scale, the salary of the man of the house in back is quite a bit less than that of Shinae's husband. Her small family lives humbly on a larger salary but their large family lives extravagantly on a smaller salary. How do you explain it? *We've heard about the good life till our ears ache, but the family in back seem to be the only ones enjoying it.* No poverty there. And so Shinae asks herself: *For goodness' sake, which side is that family on? And which side are we on? Which side is good, and which is bad? And for goodness' sake, can you even say there's a good side to this world?*

Feeling edgier by the minute, Shinae claps her hands over her ears trying to block out the sound of the TV from the house in back.

"Hyeyŏng," she says, raising her voice to her daughter in the room across the way. "How about turning off the radio?"

"Is that better?"

The sound grows softer but the English-language song from her daughter's radio is still audible among the actors' voices from the TV.

"Kill it."

"Mom, you're acting weird tonight."

Her daughter approaches.

She's in her pajamas.

She's holding her math notebook.

"If you're going to study, the radio has to be off."

"Mom, you're saying that because you don't know any better."

"I don't? Are you telling me I'm wrong?"

"You're wrong."

Shinae hears her heart drop.

"All right, then, how am I wrong?"

Again she considers her age and her daughter's. They live in the same world yet fail to understand each other. It's because they think differently. She grows morose.

In the meantime her husband has fallen asleep. His face wears a scowl. But he'll be better come morning. What sort of anxieties had kept him awake until late the previous night?

"It's too loud!" called out her son from the room between his parents' and sister's rooms.

Shinae, daughter in tow, went out.

"What's the fuss?"

"We've got to move, or else! Listen to that racket. We get it from the front and we get it from the back. Why should we put up with it?"

The TV from the house across the alley sounded louder in the middle room. Shinae hadn't been paying attention to the sound of that TV that evening.

"At least *we* can try to be quiet," said Shinae. "Father's sleeping."

"Are you kidding? How can he sleep through this?"

"You're not old enough to know what it means to be exhausted."

In her son's hand is a black notebook several times thicker than her daughter's math notebook. Her son's classes are more advanced than her daughter's. It's amazing, the variety of knowledge that's accumulating in such orderly fashion inside his head. At this rate, a few more years of study and he'll have the opportunity for more privileges and income than anyone else his age.

But Shinae felt stifled when she mulled over her son's future. She sensed that for some time now her son believed that nothing was right except what he learned at school. The schoolteachers taught that everything is good. This was the accepted way of thinking in society at large. But to Shinae's son it was an absurd lie, behind which much was hidden.

The son had absorbed too much influence from his father. He would probably suffer on account of the ideas passed on to him by his father. Wouldn't those ideas, so forthright, so righteous, prove to be yet another source of aggravation for her son? It was clear that he would meet with a frightful shock when he ventured out into the world.

"Your father couldn't get to sleep last night," said Shinae.

The TV from across the alley was as loud as ever.

She recalled the face of the man of that house.

This man works in the advertising department of a baking company. Shinae was among those who had received a box of cookies from him. The wife had distributed a box to each of the neighbors, saying her husband had been promoted to assistant director.

"Just a little something—see how you like them," the woman said. "Daddy's assistant director now."

She was volunteering information.

"Things are looking up now. People who know our situation are making a big fuss because we haven't done anything for them. And it's understandable, since the budget for the ad department is several billion *wŏn*. The people who handle TV, radio, and newspaper ads have started coming around. And people from the ad agencies too. It's not just cookies—his company produces ice cream and milk too, and that's why they have such an unbelievable budget for advertising."

"Billions? I'll say it's unbelievable. But why do these people come to your house?"

The woman stared at Shinae. And then she spoke quickly.

"They want him to buy ads. They want his business, and to get it they come loaded with money. People who know our situation know that in six months Daddie's going to make a bundle."

"A bundle of what?"

"Money, that's what."

"How much of a bundle?"

That was the start of it. The family across the alley grew noisy. And more than just noisy, the house was unusually well lit and produced new smells. From the vent window of the kitchen, which faced Shinae's yard, the smell of broiling meat rode the breeze to Shinae's house. When her family sits down to dinner around their humble meal table dominated by vegetable dishes, the aroma of broiled short ribs wafts across their yard.

The sound of voices comes in too.

"Children, eat your dinner."

"I don't want it."

"I cooked some ribs for you."

"I said I don't want any!"

"Well, later, then. Poksun, why don't you bring everybody a glass of orange juice."

Like the neighbors in back, those across the alley became a scourge to Shinae.

"Would you like to see our new TV?" the woman had said not long afterward.

This was the TV that was blaring now.

"If a problem is important then you need to sit yourself down till you solve it," Shinae told her son. "You can do anything you put your mind to. Don't let yourself be bothered by the sound of a TV in someone else's house; if you do, then it means your mind is drifting. Didn't you say you wanted a job where you could make a difference? The great people of the past, they didn't dedicate their lives to outmoded notions. I think I heard that from you. You say such things and yet you let little things get to you. If you can't study, then go outside and get some fresh air."

Her son said nothing.

He wore a pained expression.

Shinae had spoken and her heart ached.

She closed the door to her son's room.

Her daughter had stepped down to the yard.

Shinae saw her turn on the faucet at the front of the yard.

"Not a peep out of it," her daughter said.

"No reason why there should be."

Shinae approached and her daughter observed her.

"Please go to bed early tonight," her daughter said.

"Why?"

"I'll get the water."

"What's this all about?" Shinae demanded.

"I want to do it, that's all."

"It doesn't come on until two in the morning or so."

"Still, I can sleep afterward. Every night I go to bed early and it bothers me to think about you sitting in front of the faucet. You're out here in the middle of the night. When other moms are sound asleep. Other moms let their housekeeper get the water; *they* go to bed early. The people in front and back of us, they have their own water supply—they don't need much from the city. It upsets me to think that every night when I'm going to sleep my mom is out here like someone on a remote desert island. Please go to bed early tonight—I'll take care of the water for you."

"You'll be dozing off in class."

Shinae spoke like this, but her heart thrilled. *All of a sudden our Hyeyŏng is so mature! And before I know it she'll be old enough to say, "Mom, I'm tired of everything."*

"But I'm still wondering about what you said earlier. Why am I wrong?"

"Did I say that?"

"Yes—when I said you have to turn off the radio when you study, you told me I was wrong."

"Really, Mom."

Her daughter blushed.

On the TVs front and back a commercial jingle came to a climax.

"I'd already forgotten," said her daughter. "But Mom, please try to be a little more understanding."

"About what?"

"I feel like I can study better when I'm listening to a pop song."

"That's a new one."

"Honest, Mom, that's how I feel."

"All of a sudden the world you two live in seems so narrow."

"You mean it was different when you were young?"

"Yes, it was. When your dad and I were your age we took part in campaigns in the farm villages—we were all quite devoted. And they tell me your grandfather spent time in China, Manchuria, Siberia, even Hawaii. Now there's a man who had a hard time of it."

"But why?"

"Why?" Shinae looked into her daughter's face. "For the country—that's why."

"But I don't understand why Grandfather was unhappy till the end of his life."

"The way things worked out didn't appeal to him. Bring me that bucket," said Shinae. "For you kids, there isn't a country to save anymore."

"Mom, why don't you go inside now," her daughter said again. "I'll go to bed after I get the water."

"Well, we could both get it."

"Is it on already?"

Shinae squatted, almost kneeling, at the front of the yard and lifted the iron lid of the water meter housing. Then she bent over. "Goodness—now how did I forget that."

To her daughter she sounded uncommonly composed. From the housing she retrieved the fillet knife.

"I was using it this afternoon and I guess I left it there."

"Mom, that's blood, isn't it?"

"Nothing to be scared of," Shinae said. "I had a little accident this afternoon." Her voice was still composed.

The daughter looked into her mom's face.

Shinae thought of the dwarf.

Earlier that day the dwarf had been standing in front of the two neighbor women, toolbag draped over his shoulder.

"Trust me, ma'am," said the dwarf. "Please trust me and let me take care of it."

The woman of the house in back shook her head. "I don't trust you."

The dwarf said nothing.

The woman inspected the dwarf. "How old are you?"

"Fifty-two, ma'am."

"Good lord, is that right?!" She inspected him once again.

The dwarf spoke up: "All of a sudden there's no more work. And my children lost their jobs at the factory and they're out of work. Please let me do this—I'll give you an honest job."

But the two women, looming over him like giants, shook their heads. The dwarf did not even come up to their shoulders.

Shinae had been looking out the vent window of her kitchen. The dwarf stood silently, toolbag over his shoulder.

"Mister?" Shinae spoke impulsively. "Could you do something for us?" She had said this without knowing what the dwarf did or what she could give him to do in their house.

"He's lying," said the woman from across the alley before the dwarf could answer. "He says he can put in a new faucet so we can have water sooner. Have you ever heard of such a thing?"

"Why is it a lie?" said Shinae. Her voice sounded louder than she had anticipated.

"Well, if it isn't, then you have him do it and see what happens," said the woman from the house in back.

"Thank you, we will," Shinae said as she closed the vent window.

She emerged from the kitchen and stepped down to the yard. The faucet stood in the sunshine, bone dry. There wasn't a drop of moisture in the house.

Out she went. But it was the strangest thing. No one was there. The dwarf was nowhere to be seen. As Shinae walked up the alley she looked toward the side street that connected with the main street. The dwarf had left the alley and was turning right onto the main street, where the bus ran.

Shinae scurried toward the main street. The dwarf was out of sight. She was met with the earsplitting sound of a stereo from an appliance shop. She followed the main street until she arrived at a weathered sign. On it were painted a faucet and a pump.

"What can we do for you, ma'am?" said a man inside the shop. "Are you planning to dig a well?" he asked politely.

"No."

Shinae peered inside.

"Come on in."

"We're not getting any water from the city line."

Shinae entered the shop like someone being pushed from behind.

"Then you ought to have a well dug." The man was standing in front of a heap of metal pipe. "Once you have the well, you put in your own water service. We've put in practically every private service in the neighborhood. Where do you live, ma'am?"

"Down below the vineyard."

"We've done a lot of work there. Hooked up the gentleman who works at the tax office."

"The missus here lives just this side of them," said another man. Half a dozen men were playing flower cards at the foot of the pile of pipe.

"Well, then, you probably know all about us, ma'am. We hooked up the baking company gentleman too. Turn on the tap and the water gushes out, anytime you want. No different from using the city water line."

As the man spoke, a chipped front tooth came into view. His right arm sported a tattoo of a nude woman. Again he spoke, revealing the chipped tooth.

"Don't let the cost of it be your priority, or you'll end up worrying about water the rest of your life. Just try it and see how you like it. We had a gentleman ask us to come and look at his water line—well, you can look till the cows come home but what good will it do? While we're on the subject, I might add that we did a job up there where the president of the wig factory lives. They have a big swimming pool and they fill it with their own water. It sounds simple, but when I tell people that an automatic pump does the filling, they're always surprised."

"What if we put in a new faucet? Won't we get our water sooner that way?"

"Hell, no—doesn't make sense."

Shinae regretted having entered the shop. "Well, that's all I wanted to know." Best be gone quickly, she told herself.

"Hey!"

The man's shout made Shinae's heart drop.

"You—I'm talking to you!"

With a frightening scowl the man hefted a cast iron pump by the bottom. It was unimaginable. The dwarf had appeared outside and the man was about to run out after him. Steadying the heavy tool belt on his shoulder, the dwarf stepped backward hesitantly, then walked quickly out of sight. Shinae nudged the man aside and left. The man said something, revealing his chipped tooth, and followed Shinae. She couldn't understand what he was saying. The dwarf was taking the main street. Shinae ran along, not looking back. From the shopfront the man shouted something. Shinae pursued the dwarf while trying to calm her racing heart. Presently the man's voice could no longer be heard. The dwarf stepped clear of a cultivator emerging from an alley on the left. This was the last place you would expect to see a cultivator, a machine manufactured at a farm equipment factory, transporting a load of coal briquettes.

Shinae walked right up to the dwarf. "So here you are."

The dwarf scanned the surroundings, then stepped into the alley. Shinae, remaining where the dwarf had stood, saw the man in front of the pump shop glaring in her direction.

"Is he still there?" the dwarf asked, not stirring from the alley.

"He went back inside," Shinae said.

The dwarf set down his toolbag and mopped the sweat from his face.

"Why are you scared of him?" Shinae asked.

The dwarf blinked like a scared rabbit.

What could possibly have inspired such terror? Shinae wondered. Several people stood in front of a drugstore waiting to use a pay telephone. As she turned to look at them the dwarf moved his hand. He tore off a piece of pastry from his pocket and put it in his mouth.

"Could you help us out, mister?" said Shinae.

Tight-lipped, the dwarf observed her.

Shinae turned and walked off. Behind her she heard the steps of the still-silent dwarf.

"I'm sorry," he said by and by. "I was afraid you and the neighbor women would get into a fight on my account, so I left."

The dwarf's toolbag, which he carried over his shoulder, contained a variety of well-worn tools. That toolbag was much too heavy for him.

"Why don't you set it down," said Shinae.

The dwarf set to work.

He removed the iron lid of the water meter housing and examined the meter. Then he produced a measuring stick and measured its depth. He also measured the height of the faucet above the ground in front of the soy crock terrace.

"Ma'am, look," said the dwarf. "This spigot's six feet or so above your water line. And it's about five feet above where the line joins your meter. The other problem is, the city doesn't have enough water for everybody. And the pressure's low. So I'm going to put in a new spigot for you that's lower. That way you can get your water before those other families, because their spigots are high too. I'm not a liar, ma'am."

"I know," said Shinae, her heart pounding.

"We'll keep the new spigot behind the meter," said the dwarf. "Can't put it in front; that would be cheating—same as stealing. You'll have to get down on your stomach to fetch water, but that's better than staying up all night. I imagine you'll get your water three or four hours before the other families. That will get you by for the time being. One of these days we'll live in a world where everyone has enough water."

The dwarf produced his well-worn tools and set to work. Shinae's heart was still racing. The dwarf bent over so far he looked as if were planted upside down, and cut through the city water line. His tools had been used so long they were pretty much useless now. That seemed to make his work more difficult. He had one advantage, though: his small build enabled him to work bent over inside the cramped water meter housing.

Shinae squatted beside the meter and made conversation.

"Where do you live, mister?" she asked politely.

"Over there, below the brick factory," said the dwarf. "You can see the smokestack from here. There's a bunch of houses clustered below, all with a big number painted on them. Out front there's a sewer ditch. Come on down sometime. It's kind of a mess there, but we manage to have fun. The neighbor children don't grow right, so they look real small, but they're cute kids. The wife drives pigs down the bank of the sewer ditch to wash 'em."

"You raise pigs too?"

"People next door do. If our children hadn't been canned at the factory, I could have bought a few for us to raise ourselves."

"How many children do you have."

"Three." The dwarf came to a stop. "*They* aren't dwarves."

"Now why do you say that?"

"Well, look at me."

"Mister?" said Shinae. "I like a person like you. I was just thinking how nice it would be to have you next door to us."

Shinae felt a lump in her throat. The dwarf bent over and returned to work.

"Once the children catch on at another factory, the first thing we're thinking to do is buy a few pigs. Why don't you come around then?"

While the dwarf worked, Shinae passed her hands over the tools and the sections of cast iron from his bag. These consisted of a pipe cutter, monkey wrench, socket wrench, screwdriver, hammer, faucets, pump valves, a selection of screws, T joints, U joints, and hacksaw. Metal, and nothing else. All of it resembled the dwarf. These instruments that resemble the dwarf probably rest quietly in the shadow of the brick factory's smokestack while he sleeps. His family too, they'll all be sleeping quietly. On windy nights the rippling of water in the sewer ditch will carry over the wall to the yard of the dwarf's family, all of them quietly sleeping. On windy days they'll tremble uneasily, all of them. The brick factory smokestack looms too high for them to sleep peacefully. For the dwarf there lies yet another danger just one step outside his neighborhood. That danger takes several forms. This world is not a safe place for the dwarf. Could that be the reason for what happened next? The dwarf finished his work, and when he had gathered all of his tools into his toolbag, one by one, that man appeared. The man with the chipped tooth, whose arm sported the tattoo of the nude woman—the man from the pump shop. It was hard to believe, but he kicked open the gate and entered. Slap went his hand against the face of the dwarf, who had turned toward the man in surprise. The dwarf's face snapped backward. And then forward, from a slap to the opposite side of his face. The dwarf crumpled up, blood streaming from his nose. It was frightening. Shinae took the dwarf in her arms. She felt a choking sensation. "What are you doing!" she shouted. "Who do you think you are!" The man yanked Shinae by the arm. Helplessly she was dragged clear and thrown to the ground. With one hand the man picked up the dwarf. His fists drove into the dwarf's chest—*thunk! thunk!*—and then he lifted the dwarf with both hands and tossed him to the ground. The dwarf fell like a dead stump. He resembled a dead thing. But he wasn't dead; he was squirming. The man dealt with the dwarf as if he were an insect. He placed a foot on the dwarf's stomach. "What are you sniffing around here for? You got some kind of magic for making the water run? What do you think you're doing messing with houses that need wells? I think we need to fix you. How about it? Huh? How about it?" he said, stomping on the dwarf's stomach. The dwarf's face was a bloody mess. It had all taken place in the space of a few breaths. He was killing the dwarf, thought Shinae. And now he was kicking him in the ribs. The dwarf rolled over twice, then curled up like an inchworm. She had to save him, thought Shinae, and she ran. She sprang onto the veranda, then down to the kitchen. She picked up the big knife and the fillet knife. The big knife, tempered numerous times, hammered countless times by the smith while his little boy pumped the bellows, and the sharp fillet knife, 32 centimeters long and frightening to hold by the handle—Shinae took these knives. Her teeth were chattering together. She was going to kill the man. In one brief instant Shinae had sprung back onto the veranda, then down to the yard. "I'm going to kill you! I'm going to kill you!" She stabbed at the man's side with the fillet knife. The man screamed and fell back from the dwarf. The fillet knife could have pierced the man's flesh and dealt him a fatal wound to one of his internal organs. But luck was on the man's side. Because he had fallen away from the dwarf so quickly, the knife had missed. It had glanced off his side and merely traced a line of crimson down his arm. The man clasped his arm and backpedaled as blood began streaming from the wound. He was seized with fear. When Shinae had brandished the knife and shouted, "I'm going to kill you! I'm going to kill you!" he realized she had tasted blood. The man shook his fist at Shinae, but it was a last, feeble effort that couldn't have deterred her. He whirled about and ran off. Shinae latched the gate and the hands holding the knives dropped limply to her sides. The dwarf had risen partway and was watching. The two of them were silent. Shinae thought of chickens inside a manufactured coop. She had seen a photo of breeders using artificial lighting to increase the hens' production. The terrible ordeal those hens go through in their coop—the dwarf and I are undergoing the same sort of thing. But all she could think of was that she and the dwarf, unlike the egg-laying hens, were being used in an experiment to see how well they could adapt to a painful disruption of their biological rhythms and to what extent they developed pathological symptoms. Across the back wall the neighbor woman looked at the dwarf, a bloody mess, and at Shinae, her hands with the knives hanging limply at her sides. And the woman across the alley was looking at them through her window. As soon as their eyes met Shinae's the women flinched and went back inside.

"Mister?" said Shinae. "How are you? Are you all right? Tell me you're all right."

"Yes, I'm all right," said the dwarf

His bloody mess of a face had swollen suddenly. He forced his split lips into a smile. He had a strong grip on life. Shinae was startled—where in that weak body was hidden the strength to weather such a terrible ordeal? Thus far he and his family had been more than equal to their filthy neighborhood, filthy living quarters, meager diet, terrible diseases, and physical fatigue, as well as all the other ordeals that had oppressed them in various guises.

Again the dwarf gathered his tools together in the toolbag. If the two neighbor women hadn't been peeking out at Shinae, she would have burst into tears.

"Mister?" Shinae spoke quietly. "We're dwarfs too. Maybe we've never thought of each other that way, but we're on the same side."

She put her bloody fillet knife beneath the newly lowered faucet.

And now her daughter was startled to see the knife. She didn't know what had taken place that day. Shinae could try to explain, but her daughter was as yet unable to understand properly. It was a most complicated thing. More complicated than simultaneous equations and the symbols of the chemical elements—the two most difficult things for her daughter at school. It was on a different scale altogether.

Shinae took the fillet knife from her daughter and set it aside.

"Bring me that bucket, will you?"

"Mom, it's only eleven o'clock," said her daughter. "I said I'd fetch the water, so you go to bed."

"No, starting tonight we'll be getting our water early."

"Did someone come from the water department?"

"They don't come around except to get the water bill."

"Well, then what?"

"Just wait a bit."

Shinae took a deep breath.

She thought of the dwarf's face.

"Mom, what is it?"

"Actually, I had a new faucet put in. Don't need that stupid thing sticking way up out of the ground. We'll be using that one down there."

"So we'll get a good flow now?"

"What do you think?"

"I really don't know."

"The neighbors didn't believe him when he said they'd get their water sooner."

"Who's *he*?"

"Someone."

"Someone good?"

"Yes, someone good."

Again Shinae knelt and bent over. In that position she took the bucket from her daughter and placed it beneath the new spout. She was afraid she might tumble over. "Dear God, please . . ." With a trembling hand she turned on the tap.

A gurgling sound coursed up the pipe. She turned the tap all the way on.

She could hear it, the gurgle of water.

And then it was spilling from the pipe into the bucket.

"He was right! Here it is!"

The TVs in the two houses front and back were oblivious to the lengthening night. Her daughter bent down next to her and shouted something. But Shinae's ears heard only the sound of water.

Translated by Bruce and Ju-Chan Fulton

16. CH'OE ILLAM

Ch'oe Illam was born in Chŏnju, North Chŏlla Province, in 1932 and was educated at Chŏnju Teachers College and Seoul National University. In addition to his creative writing, he has held a variety of editorial positions with Seoul dailies. After publishing not quite two dozen stories throughout the 1950s and 1960s he became more prolific beginning in the 1970s, which featured his first book of fiction, *Sŏul saram tŭl* (1975, People of Seoul). He was the recipient in 1986 of the tenth Yi Sang Literature Prize. Apart from his fiction writing he has authored several volumes of essays and criticism.

"Ballad" (T'aryŏng) was first published in 1976 in *Hyŏndae munhak* and was the title work of his second volume of fiction, a story collection published the following year. This and his first book offer a good introduction to Ch'oe's fictional world, which is populated by common people undergoing a change from an agrarian to a commercial lifestyle as their society industrializes. Often appearing in his stories are people who have moved to Seoul from the countryside and experienced not only a physical but a spiritual dislocation as they come to grips with life in an urban consumer society. Ch'oe combines a proclivity for the novel of manners with a satirical touch, placing him in the company of such accomplished stylists as Ch'ae Manshik, Pak T'aewŏn, Yŏm Sangsŏp, and Yi Hoch'ŏl.

BALLAD

1. The Time to Live Is the Time to Die

The evening market was a free-for-all. Housewives and kitchen maids carried wrapping cloths and baskets that dwarfed the purses they clutched. Groups of women would materialize at one stall, hesitate briefly, and then disperse with equal suddenness, only to repeat the process elsewhere. Poking here, prodding there, the shoppers lurched to and fro. The sun still glared, but the awning darkened the market's interior. Somehow, despite a month-long dry spell, the pathways remained as sticky and sludgy with mud as porridge. A musty, slightly offensive odor slashed the nose; sickly sweet, stuffy air permeated the flesh.

Right in the center of the market stood Kisu, hawking his wares.

"Fresh mackerel from the East Sea—fresh mackerel! You'll never rest in peace if you die without trying 'em. Nope, you won't rest in peace."

His voice resonated.

He twirled the fish, their mouths impaled on a skewer, in circles. With every revolution the eyes of the plump, fleshy fish bulged, and the mackerel suddenly seemed to twitch with life, as if to confirm what Kisu had said. No one, however, paid any attention—idle talk, they thought, bluster about second-rate fish, just a noisy part of the scenery. What else would you expect in a market out here on the city outskirts? Nobody gave him more than a moment's glance.

"Over here, ma'am. Have a look over here, I said. What, you're going to ignore fish so fresh they're practically jumping and just stroll on by? Have a look. Tell you what: chop up some radish, scatter it over the fish, and then cook it all up in just a little broth so that it's all on the spicy side. You can't beat a side dish like that these days."

"How much?"

"Starting with the price, eh? Please come have a look. All you have to do is agree with me how good they are and I'll give you a fish for free."

"You're certainly quite the talker."

"One of my ancestors was a lawyer. I've got a silver tongue, you know. My only problem is that I don't have an education."

The woman he had been addressing as "ma'am" had no choice at this point. She approached Kisu's stall hesitantly.

"Have a look, ma'am." Kisu thumped the bellies of the mackerel with the skewer, and pried open the gills.

Suddenly a lad with a crew cut popped up at the customer's elbow.

"Dad, Dad, something's wrong! Mom is . . . Mom . . ."

"Oh, so it's you. Now what's this about Mom?"

"Something's wrong. All sorts of drool is coming from her mouth and . . ."

"What!?"

Kisu turned the stall over to a neighbor and darted off after his son. Colliding with people every few steps, shoving some of them aside, he ran panting all the way to his hillside neighborhood. Ominous thoughts kept surfacing along the way.

Here it is at last. The shadow of death flickered before his eyes. Inwardly he cried out, "You can't die now! You have to live just a little longer! Miserable woman, how can you die already!"

This morning his wife had complained in a weepy voice about how awful she felt. Clutching her hand, Kisu asked her what sort of nonsense she was spouting. "Didn't the doctor say it depends on how determined you are to get over your sickness?" Why, if she just faithfully took all the medicine she'd laid aside she'd get better in no time at all, Kisu admonished her. Nonetheless his wife persisted irrationally, shaking her head back and forth and repeating "no, no" just like a child. Tearfully, she said, "I know my own body. Anyway, I don't think I have much longer."

Like all people of his age and background, Kisu had simply been giving his wife medicine without really understanding her condition. She had worked with tremendous determination hand in hand with Kisu, but for quite a while had been suffering from a lingering illness. Finally she had to take to bed. Kisu, suddenly gripped by fear, went to the hospital, but the doctors were unable to provide satisfactory responses: one said the problem was that she hadn't received proper care after the birth of their second child; another doctor said her kidneys had severely deteriorated; yet another said he wouldn't be able to determine what was wrong without a comprehensive examination, and patients usually had to be hospitalized for that. As soon as Kisu's wife heard the word *hospitalize* she started and cried out in fright, "No, I'll get better if you just give me medicine for a few days." Never mind that their finances would not allow it, there simply would have been no way to get her to the hospital.

After that, his wife's condition became steadily worse. She showed absolutely no sign of recovery. An attentive listener would have noticed that as time wore on, Kisu's voice had started to flag when he was hawking his wares. Oh, he kept shouting that he had fresh mackerel from the East Sea—so fresh they were still flopping about—just like before, but his voice cracked, and it had lost its luster. And the fish were far from thrashing around; they simply dried out and their movements became feebler and feebler.

Kisu and his spouse had led a life of difficulty upon difficulty. Yet they had still managed to acquire a small stall in a market on the city outskirts and set up trade in fish. Kisu had had nothing to offer at the start but his own manhood. For a man in such a plight to marry a woman of equal poverty meant utter uncertainty about how to make ends meet. Their youth was their only capital, and the two flung themselves indiscriminately at all sorts of jobs. At last they were on the point of easing their money worries just a wee bit, but then Kisu's wife had become sick. Thud. The life had seeped out of them. It was inevitable. Isn't there a saying that people who are destined to suffer do nothing but suffer? Just when it seems they can breathe a bit easier, they suddenly give up the ghost. Now, such a conclusion was premature, but the condition of Kisu's wife inclined him to gloomy thoughts.

Kisu and his wife had met in the countryside. They had come to Seoul with barely a *wŏn* to their names and then worked with sheer desperation. Who could count all the different jobs they had had? They had experienced virtually every hardship people of their status went through. Eventually they acquired this stall in a suburban market and began to see light at the end of the tunnel. Kisu's wife suggested that they keep saving diligently for a few more years and then head to East Gate Market. Sometimes Kisu would grow annoyed with her—if they really did earn more, they should just quit this business altogether and take up something more respectable. If she was so shortsighted, how would they ever escape this way of life? But that wasn't it at all, she protested; it was just that ever since they had begun working as vendors, she had wanted to go to the biggest market and earn a decent living, as if to shout to the world, "Hey, look at me!" That was her wish, a wish that had become her only hope and goal in life. She worked morning, noon, and night solely for the day her wish would come true. Even though they lacked the resources to make such a move yet, she would go off to the East Gate Market to scout out a suitable spot whenever she had free time. She became as delighted as if it were a fait accompli.

Rushing into the house, Kisu found his wife hovering on the brink of death. Her eyes had rolled back and she recognized no one. The only sounds she made were shrill, incoherent moans.

"Darling, darling, it's me! It's me!" Kisu cried out, shaking his wife repeatedly, but she was now a lifeless, unresponsive weight.

"Hyŏngch'ŏl, call the doctor! Quick! Go next door and tell Auntie! Hurry!"

Hyŏngch'ŏl ran off.

But there was no point in calling the doctor. His wife's head slumped weakly to the side. And that was all. There was no use.

"Darling, we've got so much to live for. Why are you dying? We've been struggling to death—why are you leaving now? Just a few more years and we'll get to East Gate Market. Why are you dying? WHY?"

Kisu clasped his wife's face to his chest and sobbed. A silent, gut-wrenching sob.

When night fell, people came to pay their respects, bearing two or three hundred *wŏn* each, and grieved over the young wife's death.

"Things were just looking up and she passed away . . ."

"Yes, isn't it the truth?"

"Exactly. All that hardship and they were finally turning a corner . . ."

"Why is life like that?"

"Who knows? It's all fate."

"Heaven just doesn't care."

Three days after his wife's death Kisu was out again trumpeting his goods. "Fresh mackerel from the East Sea! Top quality!" Outwardly, at least, there had been no change. But he no longer added that anyone who died without tasting the fish wouldn't rest in peace. He used a shred of newspaper to wrap a customer's fish that day. On it was a picture of some women who had been swindled out of huge sums of money in a gambling scheme.

2. *The Time to Love Is the Time to Leave*

The savory aroma of sesame oil filled the shop. Sesame seeds were sizzling and hissing in a large cauldron at one end and being squeezed in a bulky press at the other. Outside, people buying the oil were busy pouring it into a motley selection of piled-up bottles. The store seemed the oiliest, shiniest one in the market. It wasn't simply that the interior was splattered with grease stains or that every piece of equipment was smeared with oil and slippery; no, it was because the people within were so noisy and lively. Maybe that explained all the gleaming faces. One would even suspect that, just as the children joked, "even their bumholes were greasy and slippery."

A healthy-looking young woman squeezed through the crowd. She popped her head in the shop, and her eyes darted around. Taech'ŏl, wrestling with the sesame press, immediately cast a furtive glance in her direction. He seemed to have been anticipating her arrival. As soon as their eyes met, the two smiled slyly at one another. Taech'ŏl stopped and hesitantly drew near the counter. He didn't say anything or wink, but merely stood there, looking like an idiot. Then he began to putter about, shaking the oil funnel back and forth and rearranging the already evenly stacked bottles of oil. The young woman was slow to say what she wanted. In contrast with her abrupt entry, she now hesitated shyly.

Broad shoulders, a stocky build, firm rump—you could tell at a glance that she did a lot of hard work. Nonetheless, she had a pleasant face and fine features. The layer of peach fuzz on her face looked as though it would blossom at the lightest touch. When the young woman saw Taech'ŏl, a slow blush spread over her cheeks.

"Sesame oil?" Taech'ŏl asked.

As the girl nodded, the woman who ran the shop suddenly muscled Taech'ŏl aside and stepped between the two of them. "What do you think you're doing, leaving the press like that? I've told you not to worry about being a salesman too."

"But you looked busy."

"I don't care how busy I am, we've got different jobs. It doesn't take much to figure out what you're up to."

"What do you know?" Taech'ŏl sneered. His oil-smeared face grew crimson.

"My god, don't you go trying to put me on." The woman's knowing expression seemed to ask what kind of fool he took her for. She smiled wryly and turned to the girl.

Taech'ŏl went back to the seed press and tried to attract the girl's attention from behind the owner. In the instant the girl looked up at Taech'ŏl, he held his hands far apart in the air, palms outward to make a silent sign that asked: "Got it?" The girl signaled that she understood. Two palms held far apart meant ten o'clock at night. One hand with three fingers raised was eight, and two fingers raised was the sign to meet at seven. Because the girl worked as a maid, the opportunity to meet at seven or eight o'clock came rarely. Usually, as today, their date began at two palms spread wide—ten o'clock.

Occasionally Taech'ŏl would call her on the phone to meet, but this was very nerve-wracking, sometimes desperately so. The woman who employed the girl seemed inevitably to answer the phone. A typical conversation ran like this:

"Hello, is this xxx-xxxx?"

"Yes, but . . ." Instantly the woman was on her guard.

"May I speak to Kŭmhŭi?"

"Who's calling?"

"Uh . . . this is a good friend of hers."

"Yes, a good friend, but you still have a name, don't you?"

"Please just tell her it's Taech'ŏl, okay?"

"Taech'ŏl? And what's your connection to Kŭmhŭi?"

"Look, just tell her it's me, she'll know who it is."

"Well, you say she'll know, but I'm the mistress of the house. How can I ask her to come when I don't know what your relationship is?"

"This is beginning to get on my nerves."

"How dare you speak to me like that?"

By then, Taech'ŏl would usually say, "The hell with this," and hang up. Kŭmhŭi fretted as she observed all this. Though the call was for her, she got to say nothing. Frantic pounding in her heart was the only result.

Kŭmhŭi had yet to arrive when Taech'ŏl went out about ten o'clock to the neighborhood playground, their regular meeting place. The children who swarmed over the playground all evening had gone home, and all was quiet but for a few young couples and elderly people, cooling off in the summer heat or chatting. Every so often a long chain swing swayed in the breeze. Taech'ŏl sat at one end of a seesaw and playfully raised his bottom up and down from the seat, enjoying the ticklish sensation.

Kŭmhŭi appeared about then. "Have you been waiting?"

"I always have to wait. . . ."

"How long?"

"I don't know—thirty minutes? An hour?"

"Don't lie."

Kŭmhŭi pinched Taech'ŏl's inner thigh.

"Ow, ow, ow . . ." He cried out a dozen times or so and then played dead. The moon was nowhere to be seen, but the mercury street lamps high above noticed and smiled.

"You won't get off so easy if you fib like that again."

"Okay, okay, I get the point. Let's eat." Taech'ŏl produced a bag of junk food from one pocket and a bottle of *soju* from another.

"*Soju* again? Don't you know what happens if you drink on an empty stomach?" As she scolded him, Kŭmhŭi took out a hunk of bread wrapped in plastic from her pants pocket. The two placed their snacks between them at their knees and began to eat.

"This is boring," said Kŭmhŭi after a while.

"What do you mean?"

"Why is it like this?"

"Why is what like this?"

"I don't know why our dates always wind up this way."

"What's wrong? I think it's nice. Nice spot, too. Besides, we have something to eat." Taech'ŏl finished off the rest of the bottle with one swig.

"Don't you want anything better? How about going somewhere nicer?"

"Now, don't go getting all stuck up. We should know our place."

"Stop being sarcastic."

"I'm not being sarcastic. It's a fact of life. We both have bosses. What else can we do besides meet and talk like this?

"Yes, but . . ."

"Well then, can you meet me when I have the day off? Can you? Can you?"

"Why are you always pushing me?"

"Now, calm down. There's no law that says we've got to live like this. I've got my plans too. It's like that tune by Song Taegwan, 'Pop! The rising sun is high in the sky . . .' "

"Don't make me laugh."

"No, just wait and see. There'll be a time when you look back and say 'Those were the days.' "

"When? A hundred years from now?"

"Hey, why are you making fun of me like this? Don't tell me you're looking down on me too?" Taech'ŏl put his arm around Kŭmhŭi's waist and drew her close, hoping to make her feel better.

If you have a long tail, they say, it's easy to get caught. And so their love affair soon drew the attention of the market folk. When Kŭmhŭi appeared on the street with a shopping basket, people snickered and watched to see if she would buy sesame oil. She hated being such an object of attention and purposely gave the sesame oil shop a wide berth as she wandered about. Even when she had to buy some oil, she pretended not to see Taech'ŏl but simply finished her purchases quickly and slipped out. But Taech'ŏl always sensed that she was there and would then watch her as she made her way about the market. Every time, however, the woman who owned the store caught him. "My god, would you stop staring already," she scolded. "Your eyes are going to wear down her back if you keep that up. I remember what those days were like."

Yes, they say that with a long tail it's easy to get caught. And so the rumors also came to the attention of Kŭmhŭi's employer. The woman, who was not unperceptive, had in fact formed her own suspicions even before hearing the rumors: after washing the dishes Kŭmhŭi would go out from time to time, saying she was visiting her sister, that her brother-in-law had summoned her, that a friend had come up to Seoul from the countryside, or some such thing. The woman claimed that although she was well aware that Kŭmhŭi was playing around, she had pretended at first not to notice and allowed it; as Kŭmhŭi's nocturnal outings became more frequent, however, she warned her sternly not to do it again. But Kŭmhŭi slipped away secretly. The following day the woman called Kŭmhŭi over, sat her down, and gave her her final notice. "This simply will not do. Once more, and I'll have to let you go. Your going out at night is, first of all, filthy, and I'm not going to condone it. Second, it's bad for the children's moral education. It may sound coldhearted, but what can I do? You are sullying the atmosphere in our home, and I for one am not going to stand for it."

Kŭmhŭi was tempted to turn the remark about loose morals and the children's education back on her: the woman's eldest daughter was seven months pregnant when she married; the second daughter, who still wasn't engaged, would often stay out all night simply on the basis of having promised to get engaged. Kŭmhŭi was on the point of asking how all that contributed to the children's moral upbringing. The retort rose in her throat, but she fought it back down. No one knows what happened to Kŭmhŭi and Taech'ŏl after Kŭmhŭi left the woman's house.

3. Getting Out the Smell of Shrimp

Lunchtime had passed, and the woman who sold salted shrimp now found herself on pins and needles: time for Hogŭn, her second son, to come home, but he still hadn't returned. It was still early and customers popped up only occasionally, like bean shoots in a drought. But she was a bundle of nerves; she stood up and sat down and stood up and sat down, craning her neck toward the market entrance. Still no sign of her son.

All sorts of horrible thoughts came to her. Maybe a car accident when he was on his way here? No, no—there aren't any big streets to cross on the way to school. That didn't make sense. Maybe he got hit by a bicycle? No. . . . Well, maybe he was lured away by some creep and kidnapped. But her son wasn't the child of a millionaire. What a ridiculous thought. But supposing it was true . . . let's see, there are one, two, three, four jars of salted shrimp. . . . If I sell them all and get the deposit for our room back, would I be able to raise enough money? She laughed. Why am I acting like this? Heavens, if someone kidnapped the son of a salted shrimp vendor, it would certainly appear in the papers. But still . . . who knows? He's such a terrifically handsome, cute kid—some rich man might take him away to adopt him. No, he's too bright for that. It wouldn't make sense. Maybe it's like that other time when he stopped to read comic books on the way home? He's a good kid, but he does have that one fault.

"Oh dear, why isn't he coming? I'm worried to death." She slapped her side in vexation and finally stood up. Mr. Yu from the dried fish stall next door gave a long yawn, then broke in, now that a good topic of conversation had come up.

"Why are you so worried? There's no reason to get so uptight. He'll be home when it's time. You're overdoing it."

"But wouldn't you worry if your kid didn't come when he was supposed to?"

"What, me worry? He'll be here when the time comes, right on the dot. Where would he go?"

"Nice for you to be so calm."

"If I weren't calm, I'd have a breakdown, y'know. Go ahead, drop an atom bomb; see if I bat an eyelash." Mr. Yu laughed scornfully. He had his reasons for saying the salted shrimp vendor was overreacting.

Her son's intelligence and good grades had given her something to boast about. This year Hogŭn, a third grader, was in the running for tops in his class, and his mother's pride knew no bounds. Her entire being was enmeshed in her son and his schooling, and she announced to the other vendors in the market virtually every little thing he did.

To Hŭishik's mother, she said, "Hey! Listen how Hogŭn did on the comprehensive test this time: 100 in math, 95 in science, 100 in Korean, and 98 in social studies."

"My, very nice," the vegetable seller agreed with an attitude that suggested utter apathy.

"But that's not all. Hogŭn was chosen for the choir. Next month they're going to sing at the radio station."

"You've done very well in your life. Our kid is always at the bottom of the class and he snacks too much. We failed with him."

So the other day the woman who sold salted shrimp brought a radio from home. As five o'clock rolled around, she began to gather people up here and there: her son's singing appearance at the station was being broadcast. Market people were hardly available at such a busy hour, but she still managed to collar the women nearby—the lady who sold American goods, the pickled radish vendor, and the fruit seller. She turned the radio up full blast. But although solos and duets by this child or that were being announced, Hogŭn wasn't called. What was happening? Hogŭn's mother became anxious. Eventually the announcer read the name of Hogŭn's school and said they would sing as a chorus. Hogŭn's mother pricked up her ears and tried to single out her son's voice amidst the harmonies. "There! There!" she kept shouting as if deranged. Those nearby stood dumbfounded, as she alone became all excited about the one voice that rose above the others. Was that really him?

The people in the market were sick and tired of her continual boasting about her son and grumbled from time to time. Whenever Hogŭn's mother would swagger over beaming, there were those who would harumph: what was it going to be today? They turned away to avoid her. It didn't matter what other people thought; Hogŭn's mother didn't feel satisfied until she reported what her son had done. It was ridiculous. Today Hogŭn this, today Hogŭn that. She was flatulent with hot air.

Hogŭn's mother boasted not only to the market people, but dropped hints with her regular customers as well. Usually these people would exclaim how wonderful he was, adding, "Well, you've struggled hard. That's how it should be." Even though it wasn't their business, they were stunned at such devotion to her child's education, and they offered unstinting praise for how she lived with such hope in her son's future even though she was much worse off than they. Pity seemed to have attracted many more customers to her than to the other salted shrimp vendors.

Hogŭn's mother was also diligent about visiting her son's school. She attended the occasional student-mother conferences without fail, and would butter up the teacher to ingratiate herself, acting coquettish and smiling uncharacteristically sweet smiles. Although she never took the lead in collecting money as a gift for the teacher, she enthusiastically followed others' example. Some parents, knowing she was a salted shrimp vendor, would roll their eyes. Some would shrink from her, saying she had a fishy odor. She would have her hair done and scrub for a few days in advance. When the time came she would put on her Sunday best and stride out. The people in the market would tell her she looked stunning and tease her: men might think she was some hot-to-trot widow and try to pick her up. But she didn't mind their jokes. On the contrary. The jokes made her proud. The teacher, too, perhaps in recognition of her enthusiasm (whether it was false praise or not), told her at every opportunity what a great job she was doing: with such zeal for education on his mother's part, no wonder Hogŭn was a good student. This pleased her immensely. When it was time to pay tuition or to send a thank-you envelope at the end of the semester, she would carefully pick out crisp bank notes. If the bills were wrinkled she even ironed them one by one before sending the money on.

How, then, could such devotion or virtue have been lacking?

She smiled brightly when she saw her child come home. Hogŭn said not a word in front of his mother.

"What's the matter, baby? Did something happen at school? Did something bad happen at school today, hmm?"

Hogŭn picked his nose, saying nothing.

"Tell me. Mommy won't get mad, no matter what. Okay? Tell me."

But Hogŭn just kicked at the ground. Then he blurted out very softly, "The kids say I smell like shrimp."

"What?!" His mother's heart began pounding immediately and her face turned purple. "No, you . . ." She washed his clothes almost every other day. How absurd. She flung her arms around her son and began to smell him. Sniff. Sniff. "Who told you that? Where do they say the smell comes from?"

Hogŭn yelped. "Don't you get it, Mom? It's not my clothes. It's 'cause you sell salted shrimp. That's why they tease me."

"Huh? . . ."

Hogŭn's mother couldn't sleep that night. Her thoughts roamed wildly. All sorts of ideas came to her. Suddenly she woke her child as he slumbered.

"Son, son, get up for a second."

"What do you want, Ma? I'm exhausted."

"How many kids are in your class?"

"Why are you asking? . . . About 60."

The next morning Hogŭn's mother bought six packs of gum for her son. She told him to give one stick of gum to each of his classmates. "Don't say much. Just tell them it's your birthday and divide it up. Got it, got it?"

Hogŭn, though completely bewildered, nodded.

The salted shrimp lady thought her idea was pretty good: with a little bribe they would never look down on her and her son again; just as gum killed the aftertaste of food, so it would block the smell of shrimp.

When Hogŭn came home from school, she grabbed him and drew him close as though in supplication. "The kids don't tease you anymore, do they? They don't say that now, right?"

"Yeah. The kids really liked it. But what do I do if they tease me again when the gum is gone?"

"Then we'll just buy them some more. We'll just buy some more." The salted shrimp lady roared and roared with laughter.

4. The Sixth Sense of an Idiot

"Get lost. I haven't even made my first sale; why the hell are you hanging around?" The vegetable seller squawked at Tongt'ae as he loitered in front of his stall.

Being yelled at did not deter Tongt'ae. "D'ya have anything for me to carry? Anything?"

"I just told you no. Are you deaf?"

"My hearing is real good."

"Stupid."

After this scolding Tongt'ae walked off to the fish stall, humming. He limped badly.

No one knows when he came to the marketplace. Because he limped, because he was stupid, and because one of his eyes bulged, he had acquired the sobriquet Tongt'ae, or "Fish Eyes." Still, the nickname never angered him. Every market has someone like Tongt'ae, and since every market needs someone like him, he had appeared here.

He ate, slept, and did all sorts of odd jobs in the market. He mainly carried loads because of his strength, but he also often took on useless tasks that earned him nothing. Instead of waiting for an invitation to work, he did whatever caught his eye, helping to hold sacks open while they were being filled at the rice stall or unloading apple crates when a fruit cart came by. But he actually got in people's way, and they would tell him to sit still and keep his hands to himself. Even so, he was relentless and stuck his nose into everything, despite playing servant to the market people.

Nonetheless, the market folk did not treat him too harshly. How can you scold someone who acts with good intentions? He wouldn't hurt a fly. Who could criticize him as he limped around? But the main reason they took pity on him and fed him may have been that everyone was ultimately in the same boat—life was hard, and Tongt'ae, cripple that he was, was in many ways even worse off than they. As long as people are in a similar situation, they're on their guard against others, aren't they? But if someone else has it worse, and there's no way he can compete, or even overcome his poverty, sympathy develops. They can deal with others contentedly and disguise their selfishness.

The market people looked down on Tongt'ae because he was a cripple whose existence meant nothing to them, but in their own way they treated him with compassion.

In any case, Tongt'ae was an institution at the market. If people didn't see him for a few days while they sold their goods, they even showed a drop or two of interest in his whereabouts, even if it was only as much as a chick would pee. Today he had slapped a young maid on her rear end, and she had then beaten him up; he gave them something to talk and to laugh about.

But he played around too much for someone in his condition. When housewives entered the market with their children, he would pinch the kids' cheeks and pull the ribbons out of girls' hair. If a youngster grew frightened and stepped back or burst into tears, he would giggle, finding it funny.

He could just as easily say, however, "I'll buy you a goody." He would then fish out the money crammed deep in his pockets and buy sweets for children he had never seen before. When he saw young maids struggling with their shopping bags, he would grab them and carry them quite a distance. In general, though, young women would be terrified and run away or even hurl abuse at him when he came close.

"You idiot. Who asked you to help?"

"It's 'cause you're pretty."

"Get the hell away from me, you horny old cripple."

"Aw, I'll carry them for ya."

"Beat it, you moron."

"Hee hee hee."

The merchants in the market would grin when they saw this pestering. The vegetable seller, the butcher, and the shellfish vendor laughed merrily. Tongt'ae wanted to show that he had balls too, these women joked—he was just trying to act like a man.

No one knew when Tongt'ae had come to the market, if he had parents, or how old he was, but if nothing else he provided an occasional source of laughter. Though an innocent bystander, he was a target for their frustrations. He was one of the market's products, just like one of the goods for sale.

One day the afternoon was getting late, and customers were beginning to trickle in to the market. The vendors, eager to sell their goods, were calling out ever more loudly to drum up business. Suddenly someone raised his head and pointed to the large utility pole in the center of the market. With a frightened look he called out, "Fire! Fire!"

Everyone looked where he was pointing. What was happening? A transformer perched on top of the pole sputtered and crackled with sparks. One wire was already aflame.

"Call the fire department. Quick!"

"Call one-one-two!"

"One-one-two? What do you mean? It's one-one-nine."

"Fire!"

"Someone had better go up there, fast."

The market was in a frenzy with people rushing back and forth in confusion. Some went off to call the firemen, while others busily locked up their cashboxes and goods.

Then: "Who's that?"

"Huh? Is that Tongt'ae?"

And so it was. Somehow Tongt'ae, bad leg and all, was inching his way up the pole.

"What the hell does he think he's doing?"

"Yeah."

In no time at all, Tongt'ae had climbed to the top. With gloved hands he fiddled here and there, banging away at the transformer. What was going on? Suddenly the shower of sparks ended, the smoldering wire spewed forth white smoke, and the fire sputtered out. Could this be? Right away all who had been holding their breath watching began to cheer. As soon as he had put out the fire, Tongt'ae shimmied effortlessly down the pole into a waiting mob.

Tongt'ae flexed his muscles as if to ask, "How was I?"

"Great job, Tongt'ae."

"When did you learn how to do that?"

Everyone praised him as a hero. Strangely, however, he said nothing. With a slightly embarrassed expression he just pulled back the flaps at the entrance to a sausage stall.

"That ain't an idiot's sex sense—that's an idiot's sixth sense."

The loud joke betrayed only a hint of sarcasm. Everyone burst into laughter, but within that laughter lurked respect for life's unexpected surprises.

5. *Poetry on a Rainy Day*

A rainy day. The market was damp and dank. Everything about it seemed to droop. Sole lay sprawled out, white bellies turned up, eyes slightly closed. Yellowing corvina dangled in silence from the eaves of the dried fish stall, awaiting purchase. You might even say the skinny one was the husband, the one whose belly bulged with eggs was his wife, and that the slightly smaller one was the eldest child. . . . From the salted fish stall came a vaguely foul smell that mingled with the stuffy air. The cabbage had wilted and the radish had puckered. Nothing showed signs of life except the blood red hunks of meat hanging in the butcher's shop.

The woman who sold wild greens was as scrawny as a bean sprout and smelled like bracken fern; the dried fish vendor looked like a pollack; the woman who sold poultry cackled all the time; and the face of the girl who sold peaches had the color of a ripe plum.

How could the market be so peaceful? Usually there was banging and screeching, pushing and shoving, crashing and clattering. The muddy path that was wont to bear porters calling "Look out! Look out! Load coming through!" was now quiet. The rain, neither heavy nor light, fell steadily. It was that sort of day in the market.

The women, who in an hour or two would be squabbling with one another over customers, were gossiping to while away their boredom. As the women who sold various items—vegetables, wild greens, soy sauce, deep-fried snacks—yawned and blew their noses from time to time, they spoke:

"So, did your sister-in-law get married?"

"Yeah."

"What does her husband do?"

"He's a technician."

"She did well! These days a technician is the best. We're going to send Kyŏngch'il to technical school too."

"Huh? You're not going to have him work as a vendor?"

"Look, we don't have the money to get him set up. All I do is sell a few cabbages, how can I get him started?"

"You're right. It's true. What's the point of going through all this every day if we don't get some joy out of raising our kids?"

"But aren't you glad you're still young and your husband is strong?"

"What good is it if he's strong?"

"Oh, you know what I mean. It's nice to have that soothing touch at night, ain't it?"

"Come on, don't say that. Do you mean to tell me your man doesn't snuggle with you because he's weak?"

"Don't even talk about it. Just when the going gets good, he fizzles out," she snorted.

"What are you talking about that's so funny?" interrupted the soy sauce vendor.

"Oh nothing . . . ha ha ha . . ."

"This rain makes me restless for some reason," the woman who sold fried snacks cut in. "On a day like today I feel like closing up shop. I wish I could just cook up some chicken soup at home and then have a nice long nap."

"That's the life."

"Hold on a second. Do we have it so bad we can't even do that?"

"Don't even talk about it. When I think about my lot in life, my innards knot up."

"Why is she being so sulky all of a sudden?"

"Think about it. She was widowed when she was young. Her only kid went off to the army and she got news that he broke his leg in an accident."

"Oh no. That handsome boy of hers?"

"Handsome or ugly, that's what happened."

"It's just like they say, if someone with bad luck slips, he'll fall flat on his face and break his nose."

"Yeah."

The women's conversation suddenly took a gloomy turn. The rain fell as before, making them look shabby and lifeless.

At this point a well-dressed woman carrying a shopping basket came by. Right away a vendor who had been bemoaning her fate got her energy back and piped up, "Over here. I just got these in this morning. This way."

Then the other women collected themselves, as though suddenly reminded of something, and everything returned to normal.

The market came back to life and people resumed their dizzying pace. Rain kept falling, but had there ever been a time without rain?

Translated by Jennifer M. Lee and Stephen J. Epstein

17. YI CH'ŎNGJUN

Yi Ch'ŏngjun was born in 1939 in Changhŭng, South Chŏlla Province, and majored in German literature at Seoul National University. He quickly established himself as a major writer, his sixth published story, "Pyŏngshin kwa mŏjŏri" (1966, trans. 1999 "The Wounded"), earning him the thirteenth Tongin Literature Prize in 1967. His output since has been profuse, some two dozen volumes of his fiction appearing in the 1980s alone. Yi is a conceptual writer who has tackled some of the weightiest issues of the times: the lingering trauma of the Korean War (the subject of "Pyŏngshin kwa mŏjŏri"); abuses of power during the Park Chung Hee era, allegorized in such works as his 1974 novel *Tangshin tŭl ŭi ch'ŏnguk* (trans. 1986 *This Paradise of Yours*) and the sinister "Yeŏnja" (1977, trans. 1999 "The Prophet"); the passing of traditional culture, exemplified in "Sŏp'yŏnje" (1976, The western style), which was made into a motion picture that has assumed iconic status in South Korea; and the dislocation of the intellectual from home (often the generations-old ancestral home) and family, as depicted in the story translated here.

"Footprints in the Snow" (Nunkil) is "a classic example of *kwihyang* ('returning home') fiction," notes translator Julie Pickering; it "depicts the plight of urban intellectuals who have abandoned their rural roots but have not escaped them." The story was first published in the journal *Munye chungang* in 1977.

FOOTPRINTS IN THE SNOW

I

"I'll have to go back tomorrow morning."

I leaned back from the lunch table and blurted out what had been on my mind all morning.

The old woman and my wife stopped eating and looked across at me quizzically.

"Tomorrow morning? Just like that? Again?" The old woman gave me a look of disbelief as she lay her spoon on the table.

There was no turning back now. I'd have to leave sooner or later, so I thought I might as well get it over with now that I'd brought up the subject.

"Yes, tomorrow morning. I'm not some schoolboy on vacation. How can I lounge around like this when everyone else is working? Besides, I have a couple of projects I really need to get back to."

"But can't you rest up a bit? I figured you'd stay a few days. I mean, you come down here in this heat and all. . . ."

"Since when can I choose my vacation time?"

"But it's such a long way—are you really going to go without resting a bit first? I know, you always used to leave at the crack of dawn, but you ain't alone this time, and besides. . . . Why not take it easy for a day or two?"

"I'm taking it easy today, aren't I? One day here and I miss three days at work. It still takes a day to get down here and a day to get back, even with the new roads."

My wife stared across at me with a disapproving look. "You should have taken care of your business before leaving."

Of course, she wasn't blaming me for my ineptitude at work. She knew I didn't have anything particularly important waiting for me in Seoul.

As we were leaving the city, I had told her I had taken care of all my immediate business. Besides, I was the one who had suggested combining a summer trip with a few days at the old woman's place. No, it was my impatience and change of heart that bothered my wife. She resented my cold-hearted decision to leave, but there was an inexplicable look of compassion and pleading in her eyes.

"Well, if you're that busy, I guess you better be on your way. Can't very well keep you here when you got work to do. . . ."

The old woman sat in silence for a moment, then continued in a resigned manner. "I know you're busy, but I am your mama. I feel bad not being able to give you a decent place to sleep after you come all this way."

She fell silent once more, a dejected look on her face, and began to fill the bowl of her long bamboo pipe. She resigned herself so easily.

I studied her face as she tamped the tobacco but could find none of the resentment I had seen in my wife. Nor could I detect anything resembling disappointment toward a heartless son, so impatient to leave his mother's side. There was only distance and dejection in the old woman's gaze as she tamped away at the tobacco without ever striking a match to it.

I, on the other hand, was simmering with irritation at her all-too-simple resignation.

I finally stood up and left, propelled, perhaps, by the blank look on her face.

In the yard outside the sliding papered door, a small gardenia bush stood in the scorching rays of the midday sun.

2

In the middle of the bean field out back was a graveyard lush with alders. I sat hidden in their shade, looking down over the field radiating the subterranean heat. My mother's house looked like a toadstool, the kind that grow in swamps during the summer.

I felt uneasy, as if a long-forgotten debt was about to pop out at me.

It was all because of that damp, dark, cramped little shack. That shack was the reason for my strange sense of obligation. It was also the reason for my sudden change of plans. But I didn't owe anyone anything. I was in the honorable position of never having owed the old woman a thing.

She understood that, of course.

Some years ago I had casually suggested she be fitted for dentures, inexpensive ones of course, since her teeth had worn down and she was having such difficulty chewing.

"I'm over seventy now. Ain't long for this world anyhow." She rejected the idea immediately, almost as if she didn't believe I would actually follow through on my suggestion. "I'll hold on, one way or another. No sense hoping things'll get better just 'cause I'm getting old. . . ."

On another occasion, when she was suffering from a bad case of hemorrhoids, I had suggested surgery. But her response was much the same.

"I may be old, but I'm still a woman. Ain't showing my private parts to no stranger! I'll just put up with it till I go."

She must have resigned herself to the fact that she didn't have much longer to live. More important, though, she probably sensed she was in no position to make demands on her son.

It had been that way ever since my elder brother's drinking wiped out the family fortune during my second year of high school. Ultimately he died, leaving me with the responsibilities of the eldest son, including the support of his three children and their widowed mother.

While I was completing high school and university and serving my three years in the military, the old woman was never able to play the conventional role of a parent. Nor could I hope to fulfill my obligations as a son, even when my university and military days were over. It wasn't that she hadn't been good to me. Rather, I simply had no choice but to decline the responsibilities of the eldest son left to me by my brother.

As a result, the old woman and I could expect nothing from each other. She knew that better than anyone and so could harbor neither hope nor resentment toward me.

That was the way it was between us, and yet there was something strange about the way she was acting now. Could this old woman who had refused the dentures and hemorrhoid surgery suddenly be dreaming of a better life now, just two years short of eighty?

She seemed to be dreaming an outrageous dream, a truly preposterous dream.

It all started with the roof improvement program.

"Everyone in the village's putting on a new roof."

At first, she had made it sound as if it had nothing to do with her.

Last night at nightfall my sister-in-law took her children to a neighbor's house to sleep, and the three of us spread our bedding on the floor of the cramped one-room shack. Heave ho! Heave ho! A chorus of men's voices echoed through the night. I listened awhile, then asked where the sound was coming from. The old woman answered offhandedly, as if only just remembering.

"Everyone's in a fuss, up all night fixing their houses."

It was all part of the rural roof improvement program, she said. Ever since the introduction of the Unification rice strain, the villagers had been hard put to find thatch for their roofs. And so the roof improvement campaign, launched early that spring, had been most timely. She said the villagers received a fifty-thousand-*wŏn* grant to convert from thatch to tin or tile. Nearly every household in the village had completed the improvements, either before the spring planting or since early summer after planting had finished.

My heart sank when I heard this. It was then that the notion of a debt to the old woman first entered my mind. What if she gets some wild idea? I thought, but immediately recovered my composure. I didn't owe her anything. She couldn't have forgotten that. She couldn't make any needless demands on a son like me. That was one aspect of her personality I could be sure of. And even if she were entertaining some misplaced wish, that miserable excuse for a house was out of the question. You couldn't put a new roof, tin or tile, on that hovel. Even she must have recognized that, and from her tone of voice, she obviously felt it all had nothing to do with her.

Or so I thought. In fact that wasn't how she felt at all.

"Well, if the government's in on it, I'll bet they've asked you to fix this house more than once."

Overly confident, I made the mistake of trying to console her with an idle comment.

She sat up in bed, took the pipe from beside her pillow, and began packing another pinch of tobacco into the bowl.

"Why should our house be any different?" she countered in a placid tone, again as if it had nothing to do with her. "The village headman came by, dropping hints, then someone from the sub-county office got on me about it. . . . If that had been all . . . Later they came right out and pleaded with me."

"And what did you say?"

I still didn't know how she really felt.

"Say? What could I say? They got eyes, don't they? They pleaded with me and I came right back and told them my side of the story. I may be old, I says, but I'm human, ain't I? Why wouldn't I want to live in a nice house? If it was up to me, I said, I'd put in a tile roof and new posts a hundred times over, but look at this miserable little shack. How you going to put a tile roof on a grass hut like this?"

"And then what happened?"

"They stopped by a couple more times, but I ain't heard a squeak from them since. It's not like they're blind or something. After all, they seen the house."

With the callused tip of her thumb she pressed down on the tobacco glowing in the bowl of her pipe.

"They're probably hoping for a one hundred percent conversion rate so the government will designate this a model village."

I felt a bitter sensation and tried to steer her off the subject. That turned out to be a crucial mistake.

"To tell the truth, that's exactly what they said. After they finish the house they're working on tonight, there's just two houses left: our place and Sunshim's down in the lower village."

"But they can hardly force you to put a new roof on a house like this just because they want to be a 'model' village!"

"Well . . . if it was simply a matter of a few tiles or some tin, who knows, I might do it. But with this place, you'd have to start from scratch, from the foundation up. . . ."

The talk of a model village had sent our conversation off in a preposterous direction. My heart sank again. But it was already too late.

"To tell the truth, it may be called 'roof improvement,' but they had to lay new foundations for a lot of them houses."

The old woman proceeded to describe village affairs in minute detail.

It turns out the "roof improvement program" was a remarkably flexible enterprise. In principle, it simply involved replacing thatched roofs with tile or tin. But many houses required new posts to bear the weight of the new roofs. Most people used that as a pretext for rebuilding their houses from the foundation up. This, of course, had been suggested to the old woman on a number of occasions. All her talk of posts too weak to hold up a tile roof was just an excuse. Three households had held out on the pretext that their posts were too old, and the villagers were putting in a new foundation for one of them that very night. It wasn't the weakness of the posts that had made the old woman give up on the idea of a tile roof. She had given up because she was afraid she would have to put in a whole new foundation.

I couldn't count on those old posts to save me.

It was still too soon for optimism. Suddenly all I could think about was that old debt.

Mother seemed completely absorbed in the bamboo pipe flickering out in her hand. She choked back a sigh.

"Would have liked an extra room or two, and a tin roof would be nice," she added, almost as an afterthought, "but . . ."

She was finally coming out with it.

"No telling when it'll happen, but everyone's got to go some day. When you've lived as long as me, you get all sorts of wild ideas. I've been shoved around from here to there without so much as a spot to keep that old clothes chest, and sometimes I'm tempted to just go right ahead and do it. . . ."

She was finally making her wish clear. She may have given up already, but it was clear she had once cherished such a wish.

What could I say? I lay there listening with my eyes closed, vowing over and over to myself that I owed the old woman nothing.

"The people from the sub-county office let it go this time, but I doubt they'll take no for an answer next year. To tell the truth, I don't care what they think. I just hate pretending I don't know what it's like for your sister-in-law and them kids. There's room for them here but every night they go from house to house trying to find a place to sleep. . . . Can't stand the smell of an old lady, I guess. . . ."

She was grumbling to herself now that I had stopped answering. She clearly had an elaborate plan worked out in her head.

"They give you a fifty-thousand-*wŏn* grant. And once you get started, it don't cost all that much. . . . Of course, wouldn't have been easy for us, with no man around the house and all, but Yongsŏk's dad next door would have helped if your sister-in-law offered to work in his fields all summer. . . ."

She could have asked Yongsŏk's dad to dig the foundation, she went on, and the village headman to give her a good price on timber for stud posts.

On she droned in that dejected voice, drawing on her pipe even after it had gone out. She seemed reluctant to give up on the project, if only because it was a shame to waste the fifty thousand *wŏn* and her neighbors' assistance.

Yet she never demanded anything of me, nor did she show the slightest sign of resentment. She spoke as if it was all in the past, as if it was simply something she had considered and almost gone through with. It was as if she was trying to avoid making me feel a sense of direct obligation, in any way. And her voice never lost that special composure of hers, so thick with resignation.

"Ain't no point to it now, though. If everything always went the way we wanted it, why'd anyone worry about getting old? They say people start acting like children again in their old age. Guess I'm just getting senile."

Imagine—blaming that secret wish on senility.

I could see what she was getting at, though. Even my wife, who lay there eyes closed without a word, had clearly figured out what the old woman was saying.

"Couldn't you come up with a better response for your mother last night?" she had whispered earlier that morning in the front yard as she brought me a basin of water to wash with. I glowered at her as if to say, "Stop your worthless meddling."

"You know, you can be so cruel sometimes," she chided in a scornful tone. "Don't you feel sorry for your poor old mother? Couldn't you have at least tried to comfort her with a warm word or two?"

She clearly understood what the old woman was saying. She was more concerned about her than I was. Of course, it was only natural that she should know exactly how I felt about the old woman. In fact, she was angry at my sudden decision to return to Seoul because she understood why I felt I had to go. *But what can she do about it?* I thought.

It was obvious the old woman wanted to rebuild the house, even now. I simply couldn't understand it. Who knows? Maybe people really do turn back into children when they get old. Had she forgotten that I didn't owe her anything? It was obviously a case of senile behavior, just as she had said. She had gotten so old she had lost all sense of shame. Still, there was no need for me to resent her senility. The problem was that sense of debt I felt. All that mattered to me was the fact that I owed her nothing. Who cared if she had lost all sense of shame? Who cared if she had gone senile? In the end, the only thing that mattered was that I owed her nothing.

Not a thing! Not on your life! And she knows it! That's why she can't come straight out and say what she wants.

The lazy buzz of a cicada drifted through the muggy heat.

I jumped up from my spot in the shade of the alders, as if I had finally confirmed something to myself. The village stretching out below the bean field unfolded before me. It was true. Only two thatched roofs were left: the one on the old woman's little mushroom shack and another in the lower village.

Damn it! Why does everyone have to make such a big deal about those stupid roofs? And why now?

I cursed the roof improvement program out of petty spite. Something just didn't feel right.

3

The sun had dropped much lower in the sky by the time I crossed the bean field and entered the old woman's yard. There I found my wife had brought up a most unwelcome subject.

"Why'd anyone want to add on a new room and tile roof at my age? I ain't no fool. It ain't for me. I just can't stand to think what it'll be like after I'm gone. . . ."

As I rounded the corner of the house, I could hear the old woman's voice drifting quietly from the half-opened door.

"I wouldn't worry so much if it happened in spring or fall when the weather's cool, or even in summer since we could always put up an awning in the front yard, but what if I take my last breath in the middle of winter? My body will take up one end of the room, and then what will you do?"

There they were, talking about the house again. Was my wife trying to make her feel better, or did she simply want to bring it all out in the open so I couldn't possibly ignore the old woman's wish any longer?

My wife resented my tentativeness, but was her resentment really as deep and wise as all that? She was obviously trying to coax out her mother-in-law's story, and the old woman was finally confessing her wish about the house clearly and frankly.

She was also explaining the circumstances behind her wish. That wish, which she had struggled so long to overcome, wielding her resignation and sense of honor as a shield, was finally revealing its true face. I had already guessed what she was feeling, but I had never expected to be confronted with it in such explicitness. I felt as if my last hope had crumbled. Her explanation did, however, clarify something for me finally: the story behind her preposterous wish for that house. She still didn't desire anything for herself; she was simply concerned about what might happen after her death.

"I know I just drifted into this village, but I ain't never hurt anyone here. I spent my old age poor—no decent food to eat, no decent clothes to wear, not even a decent place to sleep—but I ain't never heard anyone say a word against me. What I'm saying is, when I die my neighbors are going to come to my funeral. And they're going to want to shovel some dirt on my coffin and lay a piece of sod over my grave. Young and old, they're going to come, and what are we going to do with them? Ain't nothing worse than being miserable after you die. Is it a sin for a poor old lady to want to offer a little drink of *soju* to the guests at her funeral? So I been thinking. If I don't get buried the day I die, the living will be stuck with the dead in this tiny little room. You two'll be here, you know, after coming all that way. . . . So I figured we could add on another room—you know, something to block the wind and give people a place to sit. . . . But things never turn out the way you want. Guess it's all just the senile raving of a silly old lady . . ."

I should have guessed as much. The wish was tied up with her concern about what was to be done upon her death. After losing her home and leaving her village, the old woman had never neglected the preparations for her death. She had already arranged with an old gentleman in the neighborhood for her "plot" (that's how she always referred to her grave site) on a sunny spot at the foot of the mountain behind the village, and when the weather was fine, even in the middle of winter, she would go there to soak up the sun. Now she was rushing to make her final preparations for death. I couldn't bear eavesdropping any longer. I wanted to steal away.

But that's when it happened. Apparently my wife, who tends to get emotional over the slightest thing anyway, couldn't restrain herself any longer.

Abruptly she changed the subject. "I hear your old house had a big yard and lots of rooms."

Lacking a better way of comforting her mother-in-law, she must have settled for trying to revive the older woman's memories of days gone by and life in a large house. Reminding the old woman of her days managing a fine household would boost her spirits and would have the added benefit of restoring to a small degree the old woman's self-esteem in the face of a daughter-in-law who had known only the poverty of her husband's family. There was no need for me to leave just then, I decided.

"It sure did. It was big all right—five rooms on each side, and the front and back yards were big as playfields. But what's the use now? Someone else has owned it for the last twenty years. . . ."

"At least you have the memories. That's more than most people have, isn't it? Whenever you feel fed up and frustrated with this house, try to remember the old days."

"'Remember the old days!' What for? I feel bad enough already! Who needs to think about the old days?"

"I guess you're right. Thinking about life in the big house must make it even more frustrating for you now. I mean, living in this tiny little room and all . . ."

For a moment it was difficult to tell whether the two women were trying to console each other or were simply complaining. After listening for a while, I began to suspect my wife's motives again. It didn't sound like she was trying to cheer up the old woman. In fact, she was making her more upset. By reminding her of the old house, she was making the present seem even more miserable, instead of easing the old woman's mind. She was digging away at the old woman's secret wish to fix up her house. She wanted to hear her mother-in-law's story—that's what she was after.

"Mother, this room is so cramped. Why not move the clothes chest outside? It makes the room seem even smaller."

My wife didn't stray far from my interpretation. She was finally focusing the conversation on the one place I had been struggling so awkwardly to ignore.

The clothes chest . . . Back I went, seventeen or eighteen years—it was winter vacation, my sophomore year of high school in Kwangju. My elder brother's drinking had been getting worse and worse. I'd heard rumors that he had sold off the family dry fields and paddy, then the ancestral burial grounds, and finally the house where we had lived since our father's time. I wanted to find out what had happened, so I returned home. The house had indeed been sold. I didn't expect to find anyone there, but I had nowhere else to go for information. I waited for dusk, and when I turned down the lane to our house, it became clear that the rumors I'd heard in Kwangju were true. The house was completely empty, everyone was gone. A distant cousin lived across the way, and much to my surprise, she told me my mother was waiting for me still.

The old woman scolded me when she found me lingering in front of our place. "What are you doing out here? Why should you have to stand around waiting in front of your own house?"

She had come running the moment my cousin told her of my return. I followed her through the gate on the off-chance that things had not changed, but when I stepped into the courtyard, it was obvious that the house had been sold.

She made supper as she always had, and we spent the night together in our old house. The following morning she sent me back to Kwangju at the crack of dawn. Only later did I learn the new owner had allowed her to wait for me there. She wanted to cook me a meal and spend that final night together. Perhaps she had wanted me to relive, for one last time, life as it had been in that old house. The moment I stepped inside, however, I could tell she had moved out.

She returned to that empty house every day to dust and scrub the floor. A set of bedding and the clothes chest had been left in the corner of the main room as always, evidence that she was still caring for the house.

As I set out on the road to Kwangju that next morning at dawn she finally told me that the house had been sold. Clearly she had wanted to ease me through that troubled night by re-creating the atmosphere of our old home, with only that clothes chest to help her.

Such was the story behind the chest.

It was the only piece of furniture she had been able to keep the last twenty years.

Which was why I had always felt so uncomfortable about it. Again and again I assured myself that I owed her nothing, and yet whenever I saw that chest I felt uneasy—there was that long-forgotten, intangible debt again.

So it was this time as well. The chest was the first thing I saw when I entered the room. In fact, now that I think about it, the chest was a major factor in my sudden decision to return to Seoul the following day.

Of course, my wife had heard me tell the story of the chest many times. And if she understood what it meant, she had to realize how I felt. Perhaps she had brought up the subject on purpose, knowing I was eavesdropping.

I was getting so nervous I almost fell into an old habit—picking my nose. Was that old debt going to reappear? Maybe the old woman was trying to get back at me.

Just try it! I don't care what you say—I don't owe anyone anything! You can't create a debt where none exists!

I waited, eyes closed, hoping, almost praying.

Fortunately, however, the old woman seemed oblivious to her daughter-in-law's prodding.

"But if the chest goes outside, what about my clothes? Ain't no place to put it anyway, but say there was—where would I put my clothes and things?"

The old woman didn't seem concerned about the chest, though I wasn't sure if this was intentional or not.

"All you need is a couple of nails in the wall to hang your clothes. It's more important to have a little leg room, isn't it? You'd think this house was meant for that chest, not for people!"

My wife was practically insistent now. It was obvious to me she was testing her mother-in-law's attachment to the chest, but the old woman remained calm.

"You just don't understand. Weren't for that chest, no one would know anyone lived here at all. I got to keep it inside, just to show someone lives here."

"There's a story behind that chest, isn't there? Was it part of your dowry?"

Given the difference in their ages, my wife sometimes acted like a spoiled granddaughter around the old woman, but now she was teasing.

"Story? No. . . ."

The old woman clamped her mouth shut.

My wife wasn't the type to be put off so easily, though. After falling silent for a moment, she took the offensive once more.

"Well, I can understand how you feel. When all's said and done, it would have been nice to keep the old house. How did you end up selling it, anyway?"

Back to that house again! She wasn't asking out of ignorance, of course. She knew all about the chest and the circumstances behind the sale of the house, but still she tried to raise the issue in the old woman's mind once more. It was her way of tempting the wish out.

The old woman was, in many ways, as tough as my wife.

"'How'd we end up selling it?' Well, no one would sell a perfectly good house for fun. It just wasn't in the stars for me to own that house, that's all. . . ."

The old woman knew her daughter-in-law wasn't asking out of ignorance and did her best to avoid answering.

"But there must have been a reason. My husband told me that his late father worked so hard to build that house."

"Of course we worked hard for that house. Couldn't build it all at once, the way most people do. Took years, one room at a time. We'd add a room here and a room there whenever we had the money, but in the end it just wasn't ours to keep. What's the point of talking about it now? That house just wasn't meant for us, and harping on it ain't going to bring it back. . . ."

"All the more painful to lose a house you worked so hard to build. And now you have to live like this. Please tell me what happened."

"Let it rest! What's the point of talking about it now? Besides, it's been so long, I hardly remember. . . ."

As the old woman struggled to avoid the subject, my wife prepared to play her final card.

"All right, Mother. You're probably afraid I'll be upset if I find out. But I won't. In fact, I've heard most of the story already."

"You have? Who from?"

For the first time, the old woman seemed a bit surprised.

"From him, of course," my wife answered. I couldn't see, but from her voice it was obvious she was referring to me. She must have known I'd been eavesdropping all along.

"I know how the house was sold, and I know how you made it possible for him to spend one last night there afterward. I pretended not to know, but actually I've heard all about that chest too. How you kept it in the house after it was sold so he'd think you were still living there."

Her voice was trembling.

"Mother, why don't you let it all out? Don't keep it inside any longer. You'll feel better if you talk about it. We're your children, aren't we? Do you have to hide your feelings from us too?"

She sounded close to tears.

The old woman was silent a moment longer. Perhaps she didn't know how to respond.

The lining of my mouth was completely dry. I held my breath—what would the old woman say?

She refused to give in, however, despite the anxiety my wife and I felt.

"You mean that boy hasn't forgotten what happened that night?"

"Of course not! He said that when you found him standing out in front of the house, you took him inside and cooked him dinner, as if the house had never been sold."

"So you know! Then why make me tell it all over again?"

"Because he's starting to forget. And I can't get the real story from him. He's so stubborn, he forgets on purpose. That's why I want to hear the real story from you this time. Not his version. Tell me about your feelings that night."

"My feelings? Why would they be any different from his? We didn't have no choice. We had to sell the house, but I kept going over there, and then I saw that boy standing out front . . ."

She finally gave in to her daughter-in-law's meddling. Still, there wasn't a trace of that night's feelings as she began her reluctant account.

"So I scolded him and took him inside. I cooked him a hot meal and put him to bed, and the next morning before daybreak, I sent him back on the road again. . . ."

"How did that make you feel?"

"How would you feel? We'd sold the house, but I wanted him to sleep there one more night. I hated going back to that neighborhood, but I snuck over and swept the courtyard and scrubbed the floor. And you know, after feeding him a hot meal and having him sleep there that night, I felt like at least one of my wishes came true."

"Do you mean you felt good when you sent him on his way? But did you really? After all, he was going back to school, but you didn't have a place to live."

"What do you want me to say?"

"I want to hear how you felt after you sent him back. I mean, your feelings after you sent your son back to study in a strange city and you were left alone with no place to live."

"Oh, bother! What's the use of talking about it now? You wouldn't understand how I felt, even if I did tell you."

The old woman refused to go on, but in that voice, laden with resignation, there seemed to be yet another story, a story she had kept to herself all those years.

I couldn't bear it any longer. My wife may have figured out that I was listening, but not the old woman. I had to keep her from telling her story. No matter what my wife said, I knew the old woman wouldn't want me to know. Her story couldn't go on with me standing there.

I waited a moment, then cleared my throat and stepped out in front of the door where the old woman could see me.

4

One way or another, the worst was passing.

That evening, the old woman had my wife put a bottle of rice brew on the dinner table. Our household may have been ruined by my older brother's drinking, but the old woman never seemed particularly concerned about mine. Whenever I came to visit, she always had a bottle or two ready for me.

"Have a drink before you go to sleep." That was her way of sending me off to bed.

It was no different that night either.

"Are you really leaving tomorrow morning?" she ventured when the dinner table was brought in.

"I told you I have to go back, didn't I?" I snapped. "I have work to do!"

"All right, all right. Then have a drink with your dinner and go to bed early." She knew we had a long journey ahead of us.

I complied in silence, finishing off the bottle with my dinner. Then, early as it was, I spread out my bedding and lay down as if overcome by drink.

My sister-in-law had taken her children to the neighbors', so it was just the three of us again that night.

The worst was almost over. I closed my eyes. It would all be over when I woke. I wouldn't have anything to worry about. No roof, no chest. Did the old woman really have an IOU hidden somewhere? It didn't matter now. All I had to do was get through the night and the debt would be nothing more than wastepaper.

Just sleep. Sleep and that'll be the end of it. What could I possibly owe her, anyway?

I felt surprisingly good as I closed my eyes and drifted off to sleep. A tingling drowsiness settled over my eyelids. Perhaps it was the drink.

I wonder how long I wandered inside that cozy slumber, for suddenly my sleep thinned and through that dim veil of drowsiness came the old woman's cautious whisper.

"There was a terrible snowstorm that night. I couldn't have slept much, but I must have dropped off for a while and when I went outside the next morning the whole world was white. Of course, there wasn't nothing we could do about that. I fixed some rice to warm him up, then we set out through the snow. . . ."

Suddenly I was wide awake again. She was telling my wife the story of that night, piece by piece.

"If I hadn't felt so ashamed, maybe we could have waited till daylight. . . . But how could we show our faces? So we set out before dawn. . . . It seemed so far. . . . Three or four miles over that mountain road. . . . All the way to the bus station by the market."

As the old woman sifted methodically through her memories, the distant sound of her voice felt comfortable and warm. She sounded like a grandmother telling a fairy tale to her small grandchild.

My wife had finally coaxed the story out.

"You wouldn't understand, even if I did tell you." After that hint earlier in the day, there was no way my wife was going to let the story go untold.

That night—no, it was early the next morning by then—the old woman relived that lonely journey and her recollections of that walk through the snow that I too had wished would someday fade beyond the distant shores of my memory. Her voice was devoid of hope, as if she really was revealing a long forgotten IOU that she now had no hope of collecting on.

"It was dark still, and the road across those mountains was awful. We kept slipping, but somehow we managed to make it to the bus station on time. . . ."

The scene rose so vividly before my eyes I felt I could reach out and touch the snow. Had she felt sorry for her young son? Or was it because she had no choice under the circumstances? At first, she was just going to walk me to the entrance of the village. But when we got there, she insisted on taking me up the road over the mountain behind the village. When we reached the pass at the top, she changed her mind again and said she'd walk me down to the new highway. We'd argue back and forth each time. Soon we had nothing more to say to each other. It would have been nice to wait until daybreak, but neither of us even considered it. We both felt more comfortable leaving under cover of darkness. As she said, we slipped on the snow over and over again. Each time I fell down, she would help me up. I did the same for her. And so we made it to the highway, without another word. It was still a long way to the bus station in town, and she ended up walking the entire distance.

The day had yet to break.

But what happened then?

I boarded the bus and left, and she turned back through the snow and darkness.

That's all I knew.

I hadn't heard the story of her return. From the moment I left her standing alone by the roadside, I hated the very thought of her, and to this day, she had never told me what happened after I left on the bus. But for some reason she had chosen tonight to reflect on her memories of that day.

"We finally made it to the market street, and as we turned the corner, we could see the bus off in the distance. It'd just turned on its lights and was pulling out of the station. I flagged it down, and . . . well, you know how bus drivers can be. So mean and always in such a hurry. . . . So the driver sort of slows the bus down, without really stopping, and then the boy was gone, just like that."

"And what did you do, Mother?" my wife asked, breaking her silence.

Suddenly, the old woman's story frightened me. I wanted to sit up and prevent her from going on. But I couldn't. My arms and legs wouldn't move. My body felt like cotton soaked with water. I couldn't budge. A sweet, indescribable sadness, a luscious fatigue wrapped itself around me.

"What could I do? I just stood there in a daze, staring down the road in the dark. I felt so empty."

She sifted through her memories in that distant fairy-tale voice.

"I stood there in the cold wind for a while, then I came to my senses. The road back seemed even emptier. At least there'd been two of us before. Now it was just me, an old lady all by herself. . . . And it was still dark. . . . Couldn't stand the idea of walking back like that, so I went into the bus station and curled up on a bench. Wasn't long before the sky began to light up and I set off again. I'll never forget it."

"Never forget what?"

"As I headed back, I realized we were the only ones who'd passed along there that morning. It had stopped snowing by then, and our footprints in the snow—the boy's and mine—they were the only thing on that highway."

"Must have made you miss him all the more."

"Miss him? Why, the whole way back I kept thinking I heard him whispering to me from those footprints. I could feel his warmth in them still. And when a turtledove took flight, I jumped, thinking it was that boy's spirit flying back to me. And when I saw them trees covered with snow, I expected him to come jumping right out at me! I followed his footprints the whole way back. 'My boy, my little boy,' I cried, 'Your miserable old mother is all alone now!'"

"Did you cry?"

"You bet I cried! Why, the tears melted holes in every one of them footprints! 'My boy, my little boy, you take care of yourself! Good fortune and a long, rich life!' Yep, I cried so hard, I couldn't see a thing. I just prayed and cried, prayed and cried the whole way back. . . ."

Her story seemed near its end. My wife was quiet. Perhaps she didn't know what to say.

"Yep, just kept trudging along in a daze. Wasn't long before I reached the mountain behind the village. But I couldn't stand the idea of going straight back, so I cleared a spot at the top of the mountain, set myself down, and waited."

"You had no place to go."

My wife broke her silence to urge the old woman on. Her voice was trembling. She was on the verge of tears. It was as if she couldn't take it any longer.

I couldn't take it any longer either. I wanted to stop the old woman. I was afraid of how she might respond to my wife's prompting. I couldn't bear to hear her answer. And yet there was nothing I could do.

I still couldn't open my eyes. I couldn't open my eyes and stand up with the light on. It wasn't simply my arms and legs, heavy and paralyzed. And it wasn't because I still felt drowsy. I couldn't let them see what was pooling beneath my eyelids. I was too ashamed. My wife seemed to understand.

"Darling, couldn't you get up? Why don't you sit up and say something?"

She was practically crying. She began shaking me. But I couldn't get up. I feigned sleep, squeezing my eyelids shut in order to hide the hot liquid gathering beneath them.

Only the old woman remained calm.

"Let him be. Bad enough he has to leave so early in the morning. Why wake him when he's so worn out?"

She then went on to finish her story in that distant, calm fairy-tale voice.

"You know, I think you got something mixed up. I mean about me sitting up there on the mountain like that. It wasn't like I didn't have no place to go. After all, I was alive, wasn't I? I could always find a place to stay, a rented room if nothing else. No, it wasn't that I didn't have no place to go. It was because my eyes were stinging from that morning sun. I couldn't see a thing! The sun had spread over the whole village by then, and it was so bright I couldn't even see the roof of our house. Besides, I could tell from the smoke coming out of them chimneys that everyone was up cooking breakfast, and I was just too ashamed to go down there with my eyes stinging and all. I couldn't face that bright morning sunshine. So I just sat up there. You know, to give my eyes a chance to stop their stinging. . . ."

Translated by Julie Pickering

18. YI MUNYŎL

Yi Munyŏl was born in 1948 in Seoul. After the outbreak of the Korean War he and his family resettled in their ancestral home of Yŏngyang, North Kyŏngsang Province. He was schooled in Andong and at Seoul National University. Much has been made of Yi's father's defection to North Korea early in the Korean War, and of the shadow that this event has cast over his life and oeuvre. History, though, will probably remember him more as the modern Korean fiction writer who best embodied the premodern Korean literatus-statesman as an intellectual with an obligation to enlighten the masses through his command of the written word.

His debut novel, *Saram ŭi adŭl* (1979, Son of man), is a rare Korean novel dealing with issues of spirituality and religiosity. His second and perhaps best-realized novel, *Kŭdae tashi nŭn kohyang e kaji mot'ari* (1980, You can't go home again), comprising sixteen linked stories, is a panorama of a traditional way of life replete with an intricate code of extended-family protocol; this way of life is quickly passing, and the reader is left with no doubt that the author deplores its absence. "Kŭmshijo" (1981, trans. 1998 "The Golden Phoenix") compares Eastern and Western aesthetics; it gained its author the 1982 Tongin Literature Prize. *Yŏngung shidae* (1982–1984, Age of heroes) is perhaps the work most directly inspired by the defection of Yi's father: the narrative weaves together the stories of a convert to socialism in North Korea and the wife and mother he left behind in the south. The novella "Uri tŭr ŭi ilgŭrŏjin yŏngung" (1987, trans. 2001 *Our Twisted Hero*), an allegory of the abuse of power, was honored with the 1987 Yi Sang Literature Prize and became the first contemporary Korean work of fiction to appear in book form from a major American commercial press. *Shiin* (1991, trans. 1995 *The Poet*) is a fictionalized account of Kim Pyŏngyŏn, the "Rainhat Poet" of Later Chosŏn times. In recent years Yi's didactic propensities have been realized in editorial writing and in a mid-1990s stint as a Korean literature professor, as well as in fiction. Never one to back down from the issues that drive much of contemporary Korean literature, Yi offered his views on gender-role expectations in *Sŏnt'aek* (1997, Choice), an exhortatory account of a virtuous Chosŏn woman. Whatever one's response to Yi's sometimes tendentious approach to his material, his reputation as one of the most important novelists of twentieth-century Korea is secure.

"The Old Hatter" (Sarajin kŏt tŭr ŭl wihayŏ) first appeared in *Hanguk munhak* in 1979 and was published the following year as part of *Kŭdae tashi nŭn kohyang e kaji mot'ari.*

THE OLD HATTER

I

The first encounter between our clan's urchins and the horsehair-hat maker, Top'yŏng, took place one summer on a market day toward the end of my childhood. To be sure, his modest hat shop had stood there for as long as we could remember, but we had no more noticed it than the pebbles on the shores of our creek or the grass in the shade of our valley. However, we had happened to discover that horsehair, being strong and nearly transparent, made excellent string for hanging bait in a squirrel trap or making cicada nets. After making this momentous discovery, we would go to his shop almost every market day to get horsehair. For children without money like us—this was before parents gave their children regular allowances—the only way to get what we needed was to steal. In the childish parlance of the day, we "snatched" it.

Of course, old man Top'yŏng didn't just put himself at our mercy. But we were indefatigable, and we needed horsehair badly, having neither toys nor recreational facilities. Old man Top'yŏng was bound to be defeated by our brilliant tactics. On days when the old man tried to drive us away, believing he had safely hidden his horsehair, we took more of it than was necessary. Our strategy was to start a conversation with him on a topic like "the day Venerable Hahoe[1] came back without his topknot."[2] He was sure to get ex-

1. Hahoe is not the man's surname, but either his given name or sobriquet, probably the latter. The translator has used "Venerable" as an approximation of *ŏrŭn*, which denotes a respected elder. Venerable Hahoe obviously went on to become a respected elder, in spite of the disgrace he met in his youth for doing away with his topknot.

2. During the Yi Dynasty, *yangban* men grew their hair long, gathered it up into a tight knot on top on their heads, and wore a headband. Then they wore horsehair hats or crowns over the headband. A *yangban* wore his hat on all formal occasions, even in his study, as he might receive visitors there at any time. A *yangban* never undid his topknot even when he went to bed because his head and hair were not to be touched lightly and casually for any reason. In folklore, the topknot was also a phallic symbol.

cited and hotly denounce the impious act of the late clan elder, failing to notice what was going on around him. Meanwhile, our commandos circled around to the back of the shop and snatched some horsehair. It took us a decade to understand why the anecdote so excited and infuriated the old man, but we were clever enough to use the circumstance to our advantage.

Even on days when the old man generously handed each of us horsehair not good enough for him but quite usable for us, he would still lose good horsehair, though in somewhat smaller quantities. On such days we would express our gratitude effusively and insist on helping him, by blowing on the glue stove until the shop floor was covered with white ash or by embellishing with our crayons his small and humble signboard, which said "horsehair hats and headbands for sale—repairs also done," to make it still more ridiculous. The hatter would then scowl at us and click his tongue in disapproval, but always ended up handing out superior-grade hair.

Sometimes we distracted him. For example, some of us would throw sand or fiercely knock on the door of his bedroom, which adjoined the shop. That was sure to send him rushing to his apartment. Then those of us who lay in wait would dash into the shop and carry off as much horsehair as we could grab. We used this tactic only when we were desperate, however, because not only did we take as much as we wanted, but the remaining horsehair often got so messed up that it was rendered useless, creating a heavy loss for the old man.

But the Goddess of Fortune didn't always favor us. The practical jokes we played on each other even into adulthood derive from her frequent neglect of us. The joke we called "hatband" consisted of drawing a line across someone's forehead with the hard knuckle of a tightly clenched fist. It sometimes hurt so much that it brought tears to our eyes; but none of us could get angry, because it was the punishment we used to get from the old hatmaker if he caught us. Grinning to himself, he would repeatedly draw hatbands on our foreheads. We, his helpless captives, could only smile with tearful eyes in a feigned display of good sportsmanship. Those of our gang who eluded the old man's grasp were sure to observe the punishment from a distance, taunting and provoking the old hatter:

> Old man, old man, foolish old man,
> Old man, old man, fallen into a piss jar,
> Old man, old man, fished up with a tobacco pipe,
> Old man, old man, washed with dishwater,
> Old man, old man, dried on a stove rack,

Old man, old man, how much does horsehair cost?
Old man, old man, you'll never be rich however much you
grudge us.

To tell the truth, not one of us escaped getting a hatband at old man Top'yŏng's hands. Huni—one of our gang in those days and now a respectable municipal office clerk in the provincial capital—received such a harsh one that he couldn't wash his face for a whole week.

But the "hatband" notwithstanding, we raided the old hatmaker's shop for three summers and caused constant trouble in our own houses with the horsehair. When a family member had a sudden stomachache or if one of our cows got bloated, it was always attributed to having inadvertently swallowed horsehair. So our mothers wouldn't allow us within ten feet of the kitchen, and the house servants wouldn't let us near the cowshed. In addition, dead cicadas tied to strings dangled from pillars and door handles, and squirrels sprang out of empty jars, frightening the wits out of the women who opened the lids. Such troubles would have gone on for at least a couple more years had it not been for the incident we call "the hat disaster."

This catastrophic event occurred in the third year of our gang's warfare with the old man. It started when a member of our commando team snatched a hatbox from the old man's shop instead of a handful of horsehair. At first we were all shocked by his audacity. But when the boy removed a smooth, shiny new horsehair hat from the box, we were overcome by curiosity and the desire to imitate adults. A horsehair hat was an emblem of adulthood and authority.[3] The boy who had dared to steal the hatbox became our hero, and we spent one of the most pleasant afternoons of our childhood trying on the hat under the flattering illusion that we were fearless adventurers.

But what made the afternoon unforgettable for decades afterward took place that night. Having reduced the delicate new hat to a rag by wresting it out of each other's hands and trying it on, we hid it between two big rocks on a distant hill and parted, agreeing to meet for another adventure on the next day. But we were to meet again that night, as criminals awaiting justice. When we returned home, our houses were already lit, and a summons awaited us from Venerable Yean, who was then the most revered clansman. Our parents dragged us to this living law of the clan, who thundered at us:

3. In olden days, horsehair hats were worn only by married men of the *yangban* class. Unmarried men, commoners, and slaves were treated as minors regardless of their age. Thus hats came to symbolize manhood and authority. A *yangban* took much greater care of his hat than the rest of his apparel.

"A gentleman's hat and robes are more important than his body. Zi-lu[4] gave up his life pausing to straighten his hat while fleeing from his pursuers. You little devils, how dare you steal the august hat that has covered scholars' heads since the time of the Three Han States!"[5]

The elder was so furious he could not continue. On his face there was no trace of the benevolent and gratified approval he would bestow on us when we brought him the biggest fish we had caught by spreading pounded poison weeds in the pool or the most succulent fruit of the year as a token of our families' respect and solicitude. Sitting behind him was a row of elders who also regarded us with grave disapproval. In the next room a young uncle was whittling a bunch of bush clover switches.

To us it was totally incomprehensible fury and an unjustly severe punishment. Only his lament as he regarded us wailing and writhing in pain—"Alas, are these the future heirs of our noble ancestors?"—and his sad eyes made any impression on us.

That night, back in our homes, we heard how with his complaints and his search the old hatter had turned the town upside down, and what a colossal recompense he'd demanded for the stolen hat. That washed away any sense of guilt we may have felt and made us regard the old man as the cause of all our undeserved sufferings. When he could find neither the hat nor any of us till nightfall, he'd demanded a payment from each of our parents equivalent to half a bag of rice, insisting that the missing hat was his father's masterpiece.

That night, as they spread ointment on our calves, our mothers told us for the first time that from the very beginning the old man had collected payment each autumn for the horsehair we'd stolen from him. Although land reform and then the war had drastically reduced our clan's wealth, at that time most families still harvested more than two hundred bags of rice each year; our parents therefore paid him liberally for the horsehair because they didn't want to break our spirits.[6] Thus we discovered that our frequent victories in

4. Confucius's disciple Zi-lu was a very headstrong man, and was absolutely loyal to his master and his ideals. While pursued by invaders he stopped to straighten out his hat, as befitting a gentleman, and was killed at that instant. This incident is often cited as an instance of exemplary dedication to the ideals of gentlemanly self-government.

5. The exact dates of the three Han tribal states (Mahan, Chinhan, Pyŏnhan) are hard to fix. They probably existed from several centuries before Christ to the first or second century A.D. Here, the reference is to the dawn of organized society, or civilization, on the Korean peninsula.

6. Most *yangban* of the Yi Dynasty lived in their own clan towns; therefore, the children of the same clan tended to be each other's playmates. Since, by custom, children received no spending money, parents readily compensated for any damage their children caused while at play.

the war with the old man were not entirely due to superior strategy, nor was the old man's relatively light punishment due to generosity. Not knowing that, we had spent many a summer's day exulting in our victory and lamenting our defeat! "Oh, the impudent old fox! You won't pull such tricks on us again!" we vowed.

Over a period of many months, we carried out our crude vengeance. If on market days the old man left his shop, even for a few minutes, some calamity was bound to occur. Sand would show up in his boiling black lacquer, the bamboo-splitting knife got chipped, or the smoothing iron was stuck in the stove, handle-first. Someone smashed his signboard, and on the plank door was a crude drawing of a ridiculous male figure with horrendously large private parts and the caption "Old Man Top'yŏng's *something something*." In addition, his carefully selected and stored best-quality bamboo, which was to be split thin and woven into hat frames, got sprayed with urine. Sometimes even his rice pot and soup bowl stank of the same. After we had satisfied our thirst for revenge in that way, we stopped even going near his shop.

2

Years have gone by since then, and my hometown has changed as much as we have. Just as the scampering urchins in black cotton outfits and straw or rubber shoes grew into pimply adolescents in neat school uniforms, so our village underwent drastic changes. From a rustic village dominated by an old clan, it was transformed into a new town trying to catch up with modern times. The cheap rent for newly cleared land and the fertile soil, so favorable for cultivation of tobacco, attracted many immigrants, while the rich forest and newly discovered deposits of copper lured greedy city folk and their capital.

Thus, many time-honored traditions disappeared and were supplanted by new things. On the empty grounds where ash battles and tug-of-war games took place stand a colossal tobacco warehouse and mushroom culture house; and by the clear pond where my ancestors held poetry competitions sits a lumber factory powered by a huge electric motor. The copper mine office appropriated the site of the Unhyŏndong Sŏwŏn, the Wise Hermits' Academy, and on the site of the old horse station, long-distance buses daily disgorge hundreds of passengers.

Changes were especially rapid in and around the marketplace, where the inhabitants were mostly descendants of our clan's bond servants and hired hands with little reason to cherish the old and every reason to welcome the new. The roads and alleys, which on rainy days had ended up as so many puddles, are now solidly paved, and the vendors who used to sell their wares displayed on low food tables have built neat shops with shiny showcase windows. On the fair grounds where unlicensed peddlers used to spread out their goods for sale on pieces of cloth now stands a row of booths run by tradesmen belonging to a cooperative. In one corner of the square, where roving clowns and itinerant actors used to set up their portable stage, a modern cinema house now attracts moviegoers. Other unheard-of amenities have sprung up: a coffeehouse, a billiard room, a shoe store, a dry cleaner's, an audio shop, and a clock and watch store.

The proprietors are no longer commoners, as they used to be, but petty bourgeois, sure to become the future lords of the town and far more powerful and prosperous than their erstwhile masters, the descendants of the former nobility.

Not only have the vendors changed, but the merchandise and the buyers are different, too. In the old days the women of my clan would cross the marketplace rapidly, their faces hidden behind headcloths.[7] As recently as my childhood, the customers of fairs were almost all women and servants, and the merchandise used to consist mostly of farm produce, fabric, and artisans' wares. But now, in this age of equality, the market teems with people of both sexes from all walks of life who loudly haggle over the price of a wide variety of mass-produced goods.

Once you've passed the marketplace, however, the rest of the town is totally different from what it used to be, especially the section inhabited by my clan, which is sinking deeper and deeper into the abyss of history and whose disintegration is almost palpable.

Oh, the glory of a past whose sun has sunk without even a magnificent final glow!

The power and wealth our clan had enjoyed for many centuries came to an end in my father's generation. We had failed to adapt ourselves to the new system, and in the whirlwind of social change could not even preserve our inherited wealth. With the single exception of a cabinet minister in the caretaker government after the fall of Syngman Rhee, our clan produced not a

7. Women of the *yangban* class of old were supposed to stay indoors and not be seen by any male except the men of their family. If a *yangban* woman had an insufficient number of servants and had to leave the house to fetch water from the well or make purchases in the market, she took utmost care to expose as little of herself as possible. She made trips to the well after dark, and wrapped herself with a capelike headcloth when going out to the streets during the day.

single high-ranking official, and the vast land estate once owned by its various families passed bit by bit into other hands.

The clan itself, which at one time comprised more than three hundred families, also dispersed. The many grandfathers, once so numerous that they filled the spacious head house study to overflowing; the many uncles and aunts who dotted the hillside on picnic days; the many cousins who constituted half the pupils of our elementary school—most of them have disappeared into senior citizens' halls, or dark cramped offices, or shabby, low-roofed houses in the back alleys of the city. Only those major families[8] that had an obligation to remain with the clan and those clansmen who returned to their hometown after failing to obtain footholds in the cities were permanent residents. But those who adhered to the old scholarly tradition, rejecting both the costly modern education and physical labor, were sinking into destitution. And the old mansions on the hills were decaying and crumbling, their gates warped by the storms of many decades, their plaster walls soot-stained, their roofs overgrown with grass, and their servants' quarters collapsing from long disuse and disrepair. Sometimes unfamiliar faces replaced those of the old occupants of these houses and made our homecomings even more gloomy.

The mountains and rivers, which over the centuries were the clan's unofficial domain, became depleted and disfigured once they fell into the hands of new inhabitants. The forest that used to be a quiet retreat for my ancestors and supplied us with many necessities of life; the fertile land that enabled my ancestors to live the life of true scholars, unhampered by the need to earn livelihoods, spending their days in philosophical speculation; the clear, deep pond that taught them the wisdom of the sages and provided a haven for many varieties of fish: all these have been depleted, and we are left with a mountain denuded by reckless logging, fields acidized by chemical fertilizers and ravaged by flood, and a polluted pond. But saddest of all is the complete disappearance of the spiritual heritage that for generations inspired and sustained my ancestors.

What declined first was the old learning that for centuries upon centuries had nurtured my ancestors' minds. It had given my ancestors everything but can give us nothing now. The books, which every house is said to have had at least five cartloads of, were scattered and discarded by their owners' descendants, and the fragrance of Chinese ink has long since departed from the

8. Each clan has one head family, descended in a line of first sons from the clan's founder. Besides the head family, there are several major families, descended from the first sons of other prominent ancestors.

men's quarters. The village *sŏdang*, which used to resound with the voice of children reciting passages from the elementary classics, is now piled high with dust. Its last teacher, a renowned master of both Confucian and Buddhist teachings and one who shone at scholarly gatherings with his superb wit and erudition, moved to the city with his son's family without so much as composing an ode of parting.

Our old morality went the way of the old learning. The pious man who cooked his son to feed his old father; the filial daughter-in-law who cut off her finger to bring her mother-in-law back to life by feeding her drops of blood; the faithful wife who took her own life after her husband's death—we have totally forgotten these virtuous people, whose memory once shone brighter than any monument of gold. The world now belongs to those sons who are deemed filial if they don't strike their aged fathers, daughters-in-law who earn praise just by not throwing out their old fathers-in-law, and wives whose fidelity simply means not having children by other men.

Concepts like loyalty to one's country or friend are trampled upon by colossal selfishness, and decorum between the sexes is nonexistent. Lovers carry on openly, not hesitating to hold hands in public or walk entwined in each other's arms. Girls no longer bind up their chests to avert male gazes and now expose their legs without any sense of shame. And none of them hesitates to laugh and giggle in public places.

Codes governing the relationship between clansmen are also forgotten. They are now divided into common-interest groups; loyalty to the clan and solidarity among its members, which used to be so precious to us, have crumbled before trifling self-interest. Reverence for ancestors has also disappeared, so that permanent tablets[9] are now discarded and even the neglect of commemorative ceremonies goes unreproved. What gods would protect and take care of us with so much tender concern and loving care as the spirits of our ancestors?

The legends and tales of our people, the creations of childlike imaginations and naive explanations of natural wonders, are now smothered by scientific theory. The ancient kings who were born from eggs; the hero who married the female dragon; the embittered ghost that punished her children's evil stepmother; the monk who could make icicles form on his beard in the summer; and the Chinese general who drove ceramic stakes into every auspicious spot of the country to prevent the land from producing great war-

9. Spirit tablets are wooden panels with names of dead persons, stored in the family shrine and brought out when commemorative services are offered to those persons. Permanent tablets are the spirit tablets of the clan's founder and those illustrious members of the clan who are commemorated perpetually, unlike the less eminent ancestors who are commemorated by their descendants over four generations only.

riors;[10] the goblin residing in the old pond; the dragon, which is the foremost of the four auspicious animals; the phoenix that only nests in paulownia trees, eats only bamboo fruits, and drinks solely from the divine fountain; the holy giraffe that neither treads on living grass nor consumes living creatures; the thousand-year-old snake; the cunning fox with nine tails and various other legendary animals; the spirits of the fields, the mountain, the kitchen, the pond. . . . All these myths and legends made us cling to our grandmothers' knees as children and made the scent of our grandmothers linger in our memory long into adulthood. At one time they prompted tingling fear, but now they are the stuff of delicious memory. And our grandmothers were the last transmitters of those wondrous tales.

The old religion has also disappeared. How profound and firm was our ancestors' religion! None of them thought that the will and the acts of Heaven could be explained in a few volumes of scripture. None of them sought to ascribe a name or a personality to the divine creator, and it never occurred to any of them that God could be partial or selective in his love and protective care. Instead, our ancestors saw wind as the breath of the mother goddess, and the net of heaven as vast and loose but tight enough to catch all human guilt. They believed Heaven was silent but responsive to the prayers of honest men. To them not a meteor fell, nor a mountain heaved, without the distinct will of Heaven, or without presaging some major cataclysmic event. Our ancestors, therefore, strove to obey the will of Heaven and to live in accordance with the laws of Nature. But this religion of our male ancestors has disappeared, together with the many guardian deities worshiped by our female ancestors.

The guardians of the land, of the pillars, the beams, the kitchen, the gate, and the toilet, together with the guardians of crops and property and the various figures represented on talismans, have all vanished. The blind fortuneteller, whose shop is just outside the town, has few customers, and the mortuary plank of the neighborhood geomancer[11] is coated with dust. Without fear people step on the charcoal dropped on the kitchen floor, and let rice

10. East Asian peoples believed in the power of the "flow of auspicious force" along invisible veins in the earth. (This belief is commonly known in the West as geomancy, or *feng shui*.) Therefore, one had to carefully choose "good" spots for building houses, shops, and graves. Not only the Chinese but later the Japanese drove ceramic or iron stakes into Korea's earth to "cut" the veins of auspicious force, in hopes of preventing the birth of formidable national heroes.

11. A mortuary plank has seven holes representing the Big Dipper and is used by geomancers to identify directions. Anyone who could afford it consulted a geomancer in selecting the burial site for his dead parents, since it was believed that not only the dead people's eternal rest but their descendants' well-being depended on the potency of the good or bad forces inhabiting the grave site.

grains fall into water jars. Children paint each other's sleeping faces for fun.[12] An imposing church was built in the center of my hometown. On Sunday evenings its vesper bells sound like a death knell to all the profound and subtle heritage that has passed away for good.

3

One thing in the marketplace remained unchanged despite the rapid transformations going on all around. It was old man Top'yŏng's hat shop. Already quite advanced in age, the old hatter opened his shop every market day to receive an ever-dwindling number of customers; his own appearance was as unchanging as his shop.

His constancy at first struck us as ridiculous, accustomed as we were to change. His shop was the only remaining thatched-roof store, and the only store without a show window. And there was something comic about an old man who clung to his old trade despite constant losses. But, as we approached adulthood, we began to have different thoughts about such stubbornness. In the course of our painful encounter with the new ways and mores, we had learned to see the old and the new from a different perspective. And in the shabby old hatter and his shabby hat shop we began to see the fate of our clan as it was sinking into the bottomless abyss of history.

The history of the old man himself, which we learned around the time we came of age, also made a strong impression on us. His grandfather had been a master hatter who had made no less than four hats for the kings; his father had also owned the most famous hat shop in T'ongyŏng, the foremost city for traditional headwear. But the 1895 ordinance prohibiting topknots[13] deprived his family of half their customers, and the subsequent loss of sovereignty to Japan and abolition of the hatmakers' association hastened the hat-

12. Until quite recently there was a strong taboo against painting the face of a sleeping person. This was based on the belief that a man's soul leaves him when he falls asleep and returns to him when he wakes up. Therefore, if someone painted a sleeping man's face, his soul could not return to him because it could not recognize its host. The man might then become demented or turn into an idiot.

13. In 1895 King Kojong decreed an ordinance prohibiting topknots, which led to desperate and horrified protests. His aim was to alter the heavily Confucian frame of people's minds by eliminating that Confucian symbol of masculine dignity. The ordinance was not a simple recommendation, and police enforced it by stopping passersby and cutting off their topknots. Few willingly complied, and a number of scholars even committed suicide, as "defacing one's body" was considered a cardinal impiety against the parents who gave one birth and raised one with loving care.

makers' ruin by creating reckless competition among them. Old man Top'yŏng's father moved to our hometown as a final haven. Once every three years my clan used to invite a master hatter to our town and have him make new hats and mend old ones for all its members. Old man Top'yŏng's father, who had been to our town previously on such an invitation, remembered our clan's munificence and moved here as a last resort.

The route the hatter's family traversed—one hundred and forty miles—was a bitterly painful one. When at last they arrived in our hometown two months after leaving T'ongyŏng, the nine-member family had been reduced to just three. At the outset the old man's grandmother died of heartbreak; his mother died of travel fatigue; and his two older brothers left the group with their wives. When they arrived in our hometown the family consisted of only old man Top'yŏng, who was then a child, his father, and his grandfather.

Our clan, an island of conservatism in the sea of rapid change, gave them a warm welcome. They were given an empty hut and the farmland normally given to grave keepers, as well as a year's sustenance. Thus began the nine-year-old Top'yŏng's bond with our clan. Though he moved later on to the market, in his heart he surely must have considered himself an inhabitant of our clan's hill.

So, at about the time we came of age, the bitterness occasioned by the "hat disaster" was forgotten, and reconciliation was effected between us and our old adversary. It became a custom for us to pay the old man a visit when we came home on vacations. Most of the time we brought him liquor and snacks, drank with him, and reminisced about the incidents of our younger days. On such occasions, the old man became for us a living monument to all that has disappeared. His utterances were like an epitaph in a dead language remaining on the ruins of a dead city.

It was during one such visit that we learned the real meaning of the story we had used, as children, to infuriate and distract the old man, the episode about "when Venerable Hahoe came back without his topknot." The incident had taken place the year after the old man's family came to live in our town. A young man of the clan who had gone to Seoul on some errand came back "enlightened"—i.e., without his topknot and in a Western suit. This was Venerable Hahoe, who later became the first in our clan to acquire a college education. In any event, the entire clan was beside itself with horror and fury. At the time our clan stuck so adamantly to the old ways that it hadn't even complied with the royal ordinance to free the bond servants; to cut off one's topknot, therefore, was an unthinkable sacrilege. Venerable Hahoe's tribulations began at the entrance of our town. Before he could proceed far, he was splashed with excrement. Then the clan installed a thornbush fence around the house of this irreverent rogue who had defied the teachings of all the holy sages, this renegade who had profaned the sacred hair inherited from his parents. Even after the thornbush was removed, clan members continued to avert their faces when they saw him on the street. To obtain his parents' forgiveness he had to undergo a week's penance, kneeling on a rush mat in the yard, and his wife wore robes of mourning and stopped grooming her hair or wearing makeup until they were granted a pardon.[14]

Each time this story was retold, Venerable Hahoe became more and more degraded and his tribulations increasingly severe, but none of us blamed the old man for that. His fury toward this traitor was a righteous one. Even supposing Venerable Hahoe was a pioneer, what could the Western civilization he and men like him had imported offer to our old friend but insult and indignity?

4

About a dozen years ago the shocking rumor that old Top'yŏng was a changed man created a stir in the marketplace. One autumn morning people stared in disbelief at the old man's shop, where renovations had begun on a grand scale. The onlookers acted as if they were witnessing a terrible outrage. An unknown carpenter was renovating the old man's shop, and a familiar cabinetmaker from a nearby town and his assistant were making a modern display case. In a matter of days the shop took on a refreshingly modern look.

Everybody assumed that with the refurbishing of the shop the merchandise would also change. In truth, people had long harbored many questions about the old man. For whom did he open his shop every market day, when no one wore horsehair hats any longer? And whose orders was he filling by working so hard so constantly? What did he live on? It had been a long time since he'd sold his last hat, and even the repair work he was given occasionally had altogether stopped coming in some time ago. People made guesses. But the best they could come up with was the supposition of a well-known gossip. Citing her nine-year-old grandson as an eyewitness, the woman said that the old man only pretended to make hats but never completed any, that he wove a crown or a brim on market days and unwove it in the intervals. As to what he lived on, she repeated, without conviction, that the old man was seen bringing rice husks from the grain mill and carrying away a piglet that had died from eating poison. Sometimes, getting excited, she said that he ate

14. The absence of grooming was a token of repentance and shame.

frogs and mice, but if anyone asked for further details, she would immediately back out, saying that it was just what she had heard from other people.

When her words reached his ears, the old man became furious. He rushed to her at once and gave her a violent tongue-lashing. Together with the famous incident of a henpecked husband knocking his wife out in a moment of reckless fury and a *kisaeng* biting a philandering town mayor's nose, their battle has become one of the "three major brawls" of the marketplace. Since the shop's renovation was undertaken shortly after the momentous incident with the town gossip, people expected a drastic change in the old man's way of life. The prevailing assumption was that he would switch to some other trade.

But that assumption soon proved wrong. What the old hatter placed in his new display cabinet were several horsehair hats and various headgear accessories. And on the varnished floor were laid out the same old iron stove and hat-making instruments. A few days later a large new signboard went up; on it was written the shop's name, Shinhŭng Ipchabang, or New Sensation Hat Shop, and in flourishing strokes such fashionable phrases as "most elegant" and "time-tested skill."

At first people were simply astonished. Gradually there were other reactions. Some people laughed themselves hoarse at the incongruity. However, a few gazed at the shop and the old man with mixed emotions and turned away, their eyes downcast. But most felt, in an indefinable way, snubbed and cheated, and were angry with the old man. They began to laugh at his impracticality and scoffed at his stupid stubbornness.

The old gossip he had bawled out was the most elated. Till then, she'd been intimidated by his fury and her own lack of hard evidence, but this time she thought he'd supplied visible proof of his madness. She rushed about, asserting that the old man was both senile and demented.

The old man repaid the hostility of others with his own. He had changed as drastically as his shop. From being a talkative and gregarious man, he was now uncommunicative and belligerent. He drank without restraint, and when drunk he quarreled with anyone who offended him in the least. Within a few months he had quarreled with just about everyone in and around the marketplace.

Once, more than half my childhood buddies and I happened to be visiting our hometown at the same time, after completing our military duty.[15] It was

15. Military duty is mandatory for every Korean able-bodied male. The term in the years following the Korean War was three years, but this has been gradually reduced, so that at present it is twenty-six months. A young man receives his draft notice at twenty years of age. He then must comply or request postponement if he has a valid reason, such as attending college.

shortly after the old man had created a stir with his harsh treatment of the barber and his younger brother. The barbershop stood facing the old man's shop. It seems that the barber's kid brother had stolen some horsehair from the old man's shop, just as we had years before. However, instead of letting the boy off with a "hatband" as he'd done with us, the old man gave him a heavy thrashing. When the boy's older brother, the barber, came to protest such excessive punishment, the old man warded him off with a bamboo-splitting knife.

My buddies and I did not blame the old man. Rather, we felt profound pity for what resembled the last defiant fury of a cornered beast. This sentiment led us to renew our acquaintance with the old man, which had been interrupted by our military service. We called on him several times while waiting to return to our jobs or for the new school term to begin. Even though our motive for visiting him had changed, we took the usual present of liquor and snacks. But his blind hostility extended to us, too. Sometimes he would stare at us petulantly, as if mocking our goodwill; at other times, he embarrassed us with a determined silence. On occasion, he would feel insulted by our trivial jokes and become infuriated. If it hadn't been for the deep impression his words made on us the last time we visited him, we might have parted from him with an unpleasant memory.

That visit took place the night before most of us were to depart. We went to say goodbye but also to make an important proposition. One of our clansmen, who had long had his eye on the prime location of the hat shop, had asked us to persuade the old man to sell or rent it to him. This kinsman, like most people in my hometown, knew our special friendship with the old man, so he called on us to be his emissary. But our mission was a failure. The old man not only refused the offer but became enraged when we gently recommended that he combine his hat trade with some other business.

After gazing at our dismayed faces for a long time, he said quietly, "Don't you understand? I'm not doing this for my livelihood any more. That's why I'm so hard on little boys who steal horsehair. I'm waging a war now, and horsehair is my weapon. The people who once splashed a young man with feces for abandoning his hat laugh at me now for sticking to this trade. To wage war against such thoughtless people and against these barbarous times I need more and more horsehair to make more and more hats. And this shabby shop is my fortress. If I give it up, from where can I fire my guns? And how can I face my father and my ancestors when a short while from now I encounter them in the next world?"

His gleaming, tearful eyes exuded maniacal fury. His hands shook with drunken infirmity. He went on.

"I know I'm at the end of a blind alley. In the old days we were able to move from T'ongyŏng to here, but there's no further retreat. Even if there were, I couldn't undertake such a journey a second time. Even now I dream of that long and bitter journey and awaken to find my pillow soaked with tears. I will keep up my battle here as long as I can, and when I can't endure any more I'll just die. That's why I sold off all but one last piece of land to improve the shop. My father had seen hard times, so he scrimped and bought land for security. I sold it off bit by bit, almost to the last. But I don't regret it. I sold my last major piece of land to keep this shop, and most of the money is still here, transformed into the showcase and the signboard and these hats. Hats enabled my father to buy the land. So how can I not sell the land when the hats need it? As long as there is one man in this country who still wears horsehair hats, I'll continue to make them."

5

"Wouldn't it be better to go back home and marry old man Top'yŏng's daughter?" That was the joke that circulated among us shortly after, a roundabout way of acknowledging we were depressed and our prospects dim. Then others would catch our meaning, recall our unfortunate old friend, and gloomily down their drinks.

Old man Top'yŏng had a daughter, left behind by his late wife after an otherwise long, childless marriage. The girl grew up to be a sultry beauty. To tell the truth, there was a time when she made our hearts beat wildly. But the joke was not just sexual, with its allusion to her seductive good looks. The girl embodied the old man's sad wish. Determined not only to preserve his craft until the end of his own life but to extend its life for one more generation, he had long been looking for a successor. But it was hard to find an apprentice, and even more difficult to keep one. All traditional Korean crafts are intricate and require a lengthy, arduous apprenticeship; making horsehair hats is perhaps the most intricate and complicated craft of all. Moreover, the old man was a master of not just one kind of traditional hat, as with most hatmakers, but of several, from the royal hat to hats worn by ministers and officials of various ranks down to ordinary scholars. He had also taught himself the skills for making numerous hat accessories when their supply became scarce. Each required several years of devoted study. Realizing he didn't have long to live, the old man was in a hurry to pass on his various skills. He consequently exhausted one apprentice after another. Moreover, traditional hatmaking had no future. So the apprentices ran away after just a few weeks.

Nor were their parents especially eager to have them master such a difficult and moribund craft.

Under these circumstances, the old man hit upon the idea of acquiring an apprentice son-in-law. After his fourth apprentice had run away, he dropped hints that horsehair hat-making had a bright future as a protected traditional craft and let it be known that if he saw promise in his next apprentice he would make him his son-in-law.

This new strategy brought in applicants. Although she was thought to have a roving eye, his daughter was a buxom beauty, and the hat shop was located in a very advantageous part of the market. But this time, too, in spite of the alluring prospect of marriage and heirship, successive apprentices still ran away. The intricacy of the craft and the discipline it required were simply too demanding.

At last the old man came by a patient and devoted apprentice, but was not able to make good on his promise. A widower brassware artisan, whose trade had been swallowed up by mass-produced stainless steel and plastic wares, became his next apprentice and devoted himself to acquiring the complicated skill. But one night the enticing lass eloped with the assistant manager of an insolvent cinema company. Despondent, the widower then also departed.

The old hatter returned to his lonely battle. We, most of whom were at the time living the life of college dropouts or were low-salaried clerks in industry or government offices, would jokingly mutter when we got together, "Oh, wouldn't it be better to marry old man Top'yŏng's daughter and be his heir?" Which was a way of saying that we were tired of the race for survival in the city and weary of being tiny cogs in the gigantic wheel of our industrialized society.

6

We next heard that the old man had sold off his last remaining bit of land and departed on some kind of quest. People now assumed that the old man had gone in search of someplace new to settle, but a friend of mine, who was staying in our hometown at the time, told us that in fact the old man had left in search of the "blue bamboo." Like the legendary bamboo that supposedly grew on the shores of Lake Xiaoxiang, the blue bamboo was a divine plant whose roots were said to penetrate boulders and whose new shoots could sprout through marble. It was a tree so rare that only one of its kind could be found in the country in any one decade.

"I've been living like a fool all this time. My grandfather told me that the king, the monk, and the butcher each has his own perfection. But instead of devoting myself to perfecting my skill and creating great masterpieces, I've let myself be distracted by anger and have waged a stupid war against the times. Now I'm returning to my true way. I don't care anymore about what other people might think or do. I'll concentrate only on producing a work worthy of the great master I hope to become, if only once, in the last days of my life."

He aimed to produce a hat woven with five hundred bamboo strands, which the blue bamboo was intended to supply. As he left on his journey early one drizzly winter day, the old hatter reportedly muttered that, like Ju Zhizi of old who boiled his wife to get the perfect liquid to smelt a pair of divine swords, his own devotion was sure to move Heaven, which would direct him to a blue bamboo. My friend said that he didn't dare try to dissuade the old man, who seemed to be setting out on a journey ordained by Fate.

It took a long time. During a blizzard toward the end of that winter, the old man returned. His clothes were ragged and he limped, but as he pulled a few stalks of bamboo from his backpack his eyes shone with a strange gleam. He told my friend, "I realize that there's no such thing as the blue bamboo. But I also realize that what makes a bamboo divine is not the plant itself but the artisan who uses it. Look at this. This is just an ordinary bamboo, but in my hands it's going to be as good as a blue bamboo."

Our old friend's last battle began about a fortnight after his return home. It took him about that long to work the bamboo until it became pliant. But even during that fortnight he was not idle. He washed and cleaned all his tools and whetted all the steel implements. And each morning at dawn he washed himself clean. My friend said that the process resembled an ancient priest's preparations for a solemn tribal ritual, and the people of the marketplace no longer denigrated or ridiculed him.

At last the real work began. After making a simple but solemn ritual offering to the guardian spirits, he commenced his work by skinning the bamboo. The thin skin was split into strands fine as hair. Throughout the process beads of perspiration stood on the old man's aged forehead. But as he examined the gossamerlike strands one by one, his eyes seemed to burn with a thousand flames.

He made another small offering to the spirits on the morning he wove the hat's crown. Once he began the delicate work, he kept at it without eating or sleeping. Once—probably on the day he was to complete the hat's ribbon hook—a neighbor, taking pity, made a fire in the stove to heat the cold floor on which the old man worked and slept.[16]

But the old man rebuffed him with, "Don't do me any unwanted favors. Warmth is no good for an artisan. Warmth just makes a man dull and lazy."

The old man was strict with himself. In the extremely intricate process of weaving the fine bamboo strands with the most delicate silk threads, he undid his work many times on account of a tiny mistake not perceptible to ordinary eyes.

The work showed steady progress. While weaving the hat's outer silk lining, the old man told my friend, "Today I've decided to make this hat a gift to any man who still wears horsehair hats. You can't set a price on it. Even if you could, no one could afford it. Now, after the ribbon hooks are wrapped with red silk thread and if I can give the brim the right curve,[17] it will be worthy to grace the head of a king. If only these were my grandfather's times. . . . But I won't begrudge it. Any man who has to this day loyally adhered to the ways of his forefathers has ample right to this priceless creation."

My friend said that, as he spoke, the old man sounded utterly forlorn.

There were four in my hometown who still wore horsehair hats until the early 1970s. There were even more if you included those who wore them without topknots, but the old man despised such boors. In his view, there were only four who wore them properly. But the previous year one of these had moved away to Kangwŏn Province with his children; and another, a clan elder and a revered patriot, had died the year before. And that very night, old man Kim Ch'ilbok, a commoner who had been wearing horsehair hats ever since commoners were allowed to wear them, passed away. He had been a most faithful customer and friend of the old hatter. That left only one candidate for the gift of the priceless hat—Venerable Kyoch'ŏn, an elder of my clan.

Hearing of his friend's death, the old hatter sank into thought, but before long he took up his work again with a stony face. Only, his hands seemed to shake a little. He sped up his work. When people asked him why he hurried, he explained that he had to finish the hat and give it to its rightful owner as

16. Rooms in traditional Korean houses have heating flues underneath the stone or cement floor that carry heat from the heating stove (located below ground) to the chimney at the opposite end of the room.

17. This refers not to the swirl of the hat's brim from left to right, but to the natural arc created by the tautness of the brim's edges, a curve that runs from its inner to outer edge. The curve has to be even throughout the brim.

soon as possible. But it was obvious that he was spurred on by some ominous premonition.

The hat was completed without further mishap or delay. The brim traced a beautiful curve, and the hat looked so light and elegant, you thought it might float up and dance in the air any minute. Its smooth silken surface gleamed with high-quality lacquer paint, and the amber buttons on its headband gave it ineffable dignity. Even to an ignorant layman it looked like a work of art, the creation of a great master craftsman. Our worthy old friend had at last made the incomparable, true silk hat, woven with five hundred bamboo strands. It was a glorious day.

7

When the old man hurried with his priceless hat to Venerable Kyoch'ŏn's house, the elder was not home. He had gone to Seoul to attend his grandson's wedding, and his return was delayed by bad weather. The old hatter became restive. For days on end he hovered around Venerable Kyoch'ŏn's house and kept asking his family when they expected him back.

Then one day the clan was surprised by a noisy quarrel from the direction of the village entrance. Venerable Kyoch'ŏn was walking toward the hill, supported by his grandchildren. The old hatter followed, shaking his fist at the clan elder, from whose head the accustomed horsehair hat was conspicuously missing.

"How could you do this? How could you cut off your topknot and expose your bare head to the sun? Aren't you ashamed before the spirits of your ancestors who protested to the king that they'd rather have their heads cut off than get rid of their topknots? Tell me, how could you do this? Tell me, if you're not utterly dumb!"

The elder tried hard to appease the infuriated hatter. He explained that a horsehair hat was too inconvenient in the busy metropolis and that he'd had his hair cut because he couldn't go around with a bare topknot. He kept repeating to the hatter, "Please understand."

But the old hatter's fury was unabated. He kept repeating the phrase "as a *yangban*," and "your hat that's more precious than your head," and went on to accuse Venerable Kyoch'ŏn of deceiving and betraying him.

Venerable Kyoch'ŏn was at last driven to anger. "Are you crazy? When did I deceive you and how did I betray you? If you made this hat for me, why don't you just give it to me? Did you make the hat to insult and harass me?"

The hatmaker followed Venerable Kyoch'ŏn to the gate of his house. "Pay me for all the hats I gave you for free over the last seven years. You accepted my gifts without any scruple and now you give up your hat because of a small inconvenience. Isn't that deception? Isn't that betrayal?"

The clan elder disappeared into his house in embarrassment and anger. His entire family came out and tried to appease the hatter, but it was no use. The other townspeople looked on with heavy hearts. Tears ran down the old hatter's cheeks. Nobody could think of anything to say. Then somebody said quietly, "Let's go back. The hat doesn't belong to Kyoch'ŏn."

What that person probably meant was that the old hatter should wear the hat himself. But, wildly sobbing, the old man said, "You're right. This hat belongs to Ch'ilbok. Yes. Ch'ilbok's the rightful owner. Let's go to Ch'ilbok, quickly." Then he led the way, keening loudly, and muttering, "This town's come to an end. It's a town without shame."

He walked the mile to Kim Ch'ilbok's grave weeping, and sobbed even more bitterly when he stood before the grave. He addressed the grave, "Are you having a good rest, Ch'ilbok? Why did you leave in such a hurry? I'm sure you're resting peacefully in Heaven. You never did anyone any harm and were always kind to everyone. You were the only true man in these evil times."

Then he gathered into a heap the fallen leaves and dry straw scattered about the grave and, putting the hat on it, lit the pile before anyone could stop him. The hat burned up with a loud crackling noise.

"Ch'ilbok, I send you this precious hat. It's yours. You won't be ashamed to wear it where you are. It's the last great work of my life. Do you hear me, Ch'ilbok? Please accept it and wear it in your eternal home!"

Long after the hat had turned completely to ashes and the ashes grown cold, the old man continued weeping. Only after nightfall did he come down the hill, his steps uncertain.

After that, he didn't open his shop on market days and never came out of his house. Even when his signboard dangled precariously over the shop's entrance from a broken wire he did nothing about it. Out of pity, his neighbors brought him food, but he just turned to the wall, lying on the floor under his quilt. He died one April day, before it was fully spring. Somehow the news must have reached his daughter, for one day she appeared in town, colorfully attired and accompanied by a new husband. She sold the shop to the first bidder, then went away, never to appear again.

Translated by Suh Ji-moon

19. PAK WANSŎ

Pak Wansŏ was born in Kaep'ung, Kyŏnggi Province, in 1931. Like millions of other Koreans she was bereaved by the loss of family members during the Korean War. For almost twenty years she endured these tragedies, raising five children in the process, before finally giving voice to her experiences in the novel *Namok* (1970, trans. 1995 *The Naked Tree*). Since then she has written profusely, focusing in turn on wartime trauma ("Puch'ŏnim kŭnch'ŏ" [1973, trans. 1996 "In the Realm of the Buddha"]), the ideological and territorial division of the Korean peninsula ("Kyŏul nadŭri" [1975, trans. 1993 "Winter Outing"]), the emerging middle-class lifestyle in Seoul ("Talmŭn pang tŭl" [1974, trans. 1997 "Identical Apartments"]), and changing women's roles and self-perceptions ("Chippogi nŭn kŭrŏke kŭnnatta" [1978, trans. 1999 "Thus Ended My Days of Watching Over the House"]).

Pak deserves credit for introducing a variety of women's voices to modern Korean fiction. With the possible exception of Pak Kyŏngni, author of the sixteen-volume novel *T'oji* (1969–1994, part 1 trans. 1996 *Land*), she is the first female author to have achieved widespread commercial and critical success in Korea, her engagement with contemporary Korean history and society finding approval in the conservative Korean literary establishment and her empathic, chatty, and often wry narratives winning her a mass readership. She is also one of a handful of Korean writers who are household names not only in Korea but in Korean communities abroad. Such is her stature as a public figure who has personally born witness to the upheavals of modern Korean history and who through her writing has performed a cathartic function not only for herself but for an entire generation.

The "Mother's Hitching Post" trilogy (Ŏmma ŭi malttuk, 1979, 1980, 1982) concerns several of the themes just enumerated and is centered in a mother-daughter relationship. The story translated here, the second of the three, was first published in *Munhak sasang* and was honored with the fifth Yi Sang Literature Prize in 1981.

MOTHER'S HITCHING POST

Every disaster that has ever befallen my family, no matter how large or small, happened while I was away from home. I know by experience that if I leave home, body and soul, and thoroughly indulge in the delights of the outside world, oblivious to my family, I can expect an accident to be waiting for me when I return.

It was so when I had just weaned my first child. Dizzy with the relief that comes from having made it through the most difficult part of child rearing, I had stayed on after a get-together with friends to play *hwat'u* as if I had all the time in the world. My experience with the card game was limited to occasionally watching friends play before I would hurriedly take my leave, giving the lame excuse of living with parents-in-law and having to take care of my baby. But this time, winning with the proverbial beginner's luck, I had become caught up in the freshly learned merriment and was unaware the afternoon was waning.

"Look at her. I wonder if it's all right for a girl with a mother-in-law at home to stay out late," I heard someone murmur behind me and sobered up at once. Although even in those days I wasn't so naive as to let fear of my mother-in-law keep me from staying out late with friends, whom I met only occasionally, a very strange sensation came over me as I realized I'd never once thought about my home the whole day. I was also flustered to realize that I had let the charms of *hwat'u* thoroughly distract me from the mother's role I'd been so anxiously performing for my firstborn. A chill ran up my spine as it suddenly dawned on me that my fascination with the card game was due to a malevolent trick of fate, not of gambling; I had played right into the hands of destiny.

I knew immediately it was a preposterous thought but the uncanny sensation remained as vivid as a living creature. To shake off the nasty feeling I fussed over my winnings. I tried to cheer myself up with a cunning accounting of them. I told myself that besides having fun enough to lose all track of time, I had earned a small bundle.

I was soon to realize that the uncanny sensation was a premonition. While I was away from home, my toddler turned a kettle of boiling water over on her leg and had to be treated for severe burns in the emergency room. As soon as she saw me, my mother-in-law, who had been crying by the side of my groaning child, jumped up, not to scold me for being away from home all day, but to apologize.

"It happened in the blink of an eye. I got a bit hungry toward evening, so I boiled us some eggs, one for her and one for me. I brought the kettle into the room and was just turning around to get the salt—" She couldn't finish her explanation because her lips puckered like a child's and she burst into tears.

"It's my fault," was all I could stammer.

"Babysitting sure is a thankless job. . . ."

"It's all my fault, I tell you."

"The doctor says the burn won't scar as long as it doesn't get infected. And it won't get infected because she's got my skin. I was just like her when I was little. I spilled a piping hot bowl of soup on my left foot. It was so bad that when they pulled my sock off, my skin came off with it. That was a long, long time ago when soy sauce was the only thing we had to treat burns with. All they did was brush the burn with soy sauce several times but I healed like new. My skin sure deserves taking after. And they have so many good medicines these days. Oh, by the way, they also gave her some shots."

She was trying to make me feel better but I could hardly stand her endless babbling. What good was such talk when my child was suffering? It made me crazy that I couldn't share with my little girl even a feather's worth of the horrible pain she was going through. For the first time in her life, my little girl, a mere child who had come into this world because of me, was experiencing pain. She was too small and too young to know that people are strangers to each other; we're all on our own. Perhaps that's why I kept trying to attach significance to the eeriness I felt after neglecting her the whole day. I thought that uncanny sensation must have been a warning message sent through a mysterious cord invisible but surely existing between my child and me. If only I'd realized it was a warning, she wouldn't have had to suffer. I hated myself for being so dense I hadn't recognized the warning and vowed I'd never be guilty of such stupidity again.

Whether it was because her skin took after my mother-in-law's or because she was given good medicine, my daughter's burn healed without scarring. I had four more children at intervals of two years. Raising five children, I had gone through not just burns but broken bones, bad falls, car accidents, drug poisoning, and countless other accidents that made my heart sink and the sky pale. And just like the first accident, they all happened when I was away from home. The strange feeling that always seemed to accompany my thorough neglect of my family was always the same as it was the first time but, as is true with everything, I became used to it and began to doubt its potency. If it was truly a premonition or a warning, the sensation should come before an accident, but I realized in retrospect that I felt it almost always *after* an accident happened. Although my children's accidents all occurred when I was away, what about the accidents that had nothing to do with my flesh and blood? Why did my mother-in-law's fall, a boiler explosion, a burglary, and the like have to happen when I was away? The answer was simple: it was the nature of an accident to occur in the absence of the person who was responsible for the safety of the family.

The eerie feeling was probably due more to my total negligence than to any mysterious ties of blood. The temporary neglect of my family and home was due only to my immersion in work or play. It was comforting to think that the eerie feeling was brought on by nothing more than the guilt and embarrassment any housewife who normally holds her family sacred would experience upon realizing she has been neglecting them. Once I had provided a rather sensible, if not reasonable, explanation for a work of supernatural energy assumed to exist between one's inner state of mind and the physical world, the magic of the eerie sensation dulled gradually.

In fact, the sensation was a false alarm more often than not. It was quite understandable, too. Now that all my children were grown up, my mother-in-law long dead, and we had moved into an apartment that seemed to have been built to be unlived in, it became quite natural for me to leave it locked up at every opportunity. There wasn't anyone or anything left at home to be involved in an accident. If an accident were to befall my family, it would occur outside our home rather than inside.

Strangely enough, I sometimes missed that unsettling sensation, and its uncanniness. It was not an ordinary feeling that would come over me every time I left home. I had to leave home in mind and body. After all, isn't it a housewife's lot to worry and wonder about her home even when she's away from it? My own superstition that the thorough neglect of family and home was the cause of accidents made me vigilant when I was away from home, and sometimes I would actually put the superstitious belief into play by telephoning home. Nevertheless, every now and then I would get carried away with the delights of the outside world and completely forget about my home, and each time I would be sobered up by that uncanny sensation. I came to love that feeling. For it cast a lightning flash on the dump of meaningless sediments of the routine that was my life and illuminated the ancient dust of my household vividly and beautifully. Thanks to the magic of such moments, I was able to return to my routine anew, fresh and breathless like an actress on her first stage. How could it not be exhilarating to have boredom shine like happiness and dust sparkle like gold even if it was only the illusion of an evanescent moment? It was an unexpected blessing of life.

How I loved that uncanny, ominous feeling. When I was young, it was hardly ever wrong. I guess that's why I feel the way I do about my family and home, that I'm their mainstay, their foundation.

What's going to happen to the household without me? I would grumble as I flailed a duster after returning from a trip of only a couple of days. Perhaps I grumbled out of a vain memory of the glory of those days. At such times, it was a big disappointment to find that the only bad things that had happened during my absence were that the shelves had become covered with dust and a couple of dirty socks had been thrown in the corner. That would only make me reiterate my routine threats of what dire things would happen without me. My children would giggle and roll their eyes in mock despair. Of course I also grumbled I couldn't wait until the day I would be free from the worries and boring chores that come with being a housewife. Perhaps I said that a bit more often than the what-will-become-of-the-household line. However, it was only a halfhearted exaggeration, my secret intention being a lifelong reign as mistress of the household.

On that day, I had more fun than I had had in a long time. The snow that began to fall lightly on my way to my friend's farm turned heavy in the afternoon. The big trees at the entrance to the village were a soft blur like in a painting, their limbs misty in minimal lines of nobleness. Every now and then a tree branch would break with a wail under the weight of the snow. The fresh-smelling pine branches burning in the fireplace warmed the room and our hearts as well. In the garden just outside the window a Nanking cherry bloomed with snow flowers. It was heavenly. I never imagined there was such a place so near Seoul, near enough that my friend's husband could easily drive to his office at the center of the city every day with no difficulty. I had been invited here last spring when the cherry trees were in full bloom. I had come with my friends. Our cars packed the lanes in the garden and the orchard and our children's laughter rang through the clouds of blossoms, making the place look like a suburban tourist farm. In my mind that farm and the one I was now visiting were two different places, each of which I liked for a different reason. Because they were different, the sense of distance was also different for me. I felt peaceful and sweetly weary like the faithful followers of the mystical Chonggamnok faith once they had found refuge at their promised haven on hallowed Kyeryong Mountain.

As I listened to the crackling of the unseasoned wood in the fireplace, I imagined the trees singing. It was still snowing outside and the window looked like a lace curtain swaying in the wind. It made the room seem like it was floating to some faraway place. If the room was moving, it was moving in time, not in space, and I was willing to move with it. The thickly falling snow was erasing not just the footprints of humans but their achievements and was returning the world to primordial times.

My friend poured a red liquid from a moonlike glass jar into a crystal glass. "Try it. It's Nanking cherry wine."

The wine was as beautiful and clear as a ruby.

"I've come to learn there's nothing better than farming. Take the cherries in the garden. I thought they were plain old garden plants, but I was grossly mistaken. They bore so much fruit we got three bushels from as many trees, and that was after our helper's children gorged themselves on them and I gave heaps of them to relatives, friends, and every visitor to show them off. The jar I used to use to make grape wine wouldn't hold them all, so I put them in a huge earthen pot and buried it. You can drink as much as you like."

"So, you think I'm a lush," I quipped.

I kept sipping the lovely, sweet wine without giving it a second thought. I could not stop marveling at the cherry trees, the days between spring and winter, between cherry blossoms and snow blossoms, when they were weighed down by three bushels, no, five bushels of fruit clustered on their short little limbs.

"This farming business, you see—" My friend was about to boast some more about farming.

Recalling the housewarming party she had had during the cherry blossom season, I couldn't help becoming sarcastic. "How can you talk as though you've been farming for years? You're making me green with envy. Wait until you've gone through some bad times. This city slicker who's been stuck in a concrete chicken coop her whole life wouldn't mind hearing some regrets coming from you."

"I've been farming less than a year, but why should the future be any different?"

She was right. Although she and her husband owned the orchard and surrounding farmland, they had other people do the farming, but not as tenant farmers because they did not expect any income from them. All they wanted from the farm was to be able to pick fruit to their heart's content and know that it was all theirs. They had more than enough income from their business in the city. They had bought the farm in the belief that a change of air would be good for my friend, who had been unexplainably sick for a number of years. So what she meant by farming was gathering the fruit from the few cherry trees in the garden.

I found the whole idea ridiculous. The farm was too extravagant for a simple change of air for a nervous condition or some other minor illness. But I didn't let the thought bother me for long. Drinking always made me different—elated, talkative, and much too ready to laugh. Thoughts stowed away tightly inside me, absurd anxieties, and heartaches would pour out like water from a crystal-clear spring. I didn't care if my audience found them crystal clear or murky, enraptured as I was with the verbal release of the things that had long been pent up inside me. It meant liberation from them. Perhaps that was the way I could experience freedom, which for me was a star hung at the tip of a tree branch. I would climb the tree in vain to pick it. The higher I climbed, the farther away the star became and the farther away became the ground to which I had to return, so that in the end I was left with only a sense of crisis.

Maybe that was why I tried to indulge myself in freedom in such a tasteless manner, like a drunkard. My friend's farming truly deserved endless boasting. The cherry wine was so sweet, clear, and beautiful and its fragrance so pure that it made me giddy and lighthearted the whole day.

My friend's husband came home. The snow had stopped, but his trip through the snow-covered fields, guided only by the headlights of his trusty car, was like the homing of a wild animal. My tipsiness made me shower him with praise. Fortunately, whenever I drank, I could never get beyond being tipsy.

Flustered at my flattery, he offered to drive me home because the road to Seoul was hazardous. My friend hugged him and jumped up and down saying happily, "Would you? I've been wondering how I could dare entrust my precious guest to that rattly old country bus and expect to have a good night's sleep."

"Rattly or not, there's no bus. The drivers all got scared and disappeared some time ago. If your friend isn't going to stay the night, my car is her only way home. So if . . ."

So if they were to get rid of me, their only choice was to drive me was what he wanted to say, I fathomed even in my drunken state, and I promptly stood up to leave.

"I don't want you to fall asleep driving," said my friend, and so she came along. She sat in the front seat beside her husband, and I gladly went to sleep in back.

I had no idea how long the drive took. I struggled awake as they helped me into the elevator. When I opened my purse for my compact, I found a pack of gum on top. "Here, chew this so you won't smell," I seemed to remember my friend saying as she shoved it into my purse. I couldn't remember at what point during our journey she did so, but it showed she was concerned about me returning to my husband and children smelling of alcohol. Then I realized that I'd not even thought about my family until my friend mentioned them. No, not even then. I had forgotten them completely. A familiar feeling crept down my back. It was the most uncanny I had ever experienced. It felt like some reptile was creeping down my spine. The pleasure the day had given me disappeared like a dream. I staggered. Not out of drunkenness. I had already sobered up completely. I counted my years. I thought I couldn't go through another disaster or misfortune. In the order of things, it was my turn to become the disaster for my family. Although in recent years these uncanny feelings had proven to be false alarms more times than not, I didn't have a moment's doubt that one of my family had had an accident; the uncanny feeling that came over me that day was so powerful and vivid. The elevator stopped and the door opened. All of my family were there, each one hale and hearty, but rigid like a statue.

Yes, they were like people immortalized in stone, motionless but looking at me. Their stiff expressions not changing. They seemed not to know me. How could it be like this. It was a disaster. A disaster of my own making. I can't go through with it, I thought.

How lovely the tedious life from which I had run away could suddenly become when I was to be denied re-entry to it. Oozing flattery from every pore, I tried to give them a big smile. But one would have thought I was trying to smile for the first time in my life because my whole face tensed up, making it impossible for me to smile naturally.

"Sorry I'm so late. What a snowstorm. It was really terrible. The buses stopped running. They wanted me to stay overnight but I begged and begged so they drove me home. Them, not their driver. I was so uncomfortable, making my friend's husband drive me. They risked their lives to bring me home. Oh, it's really a horrendous snow fall," I babbled, looking over their shoulders and down the hall of our apartment, which was a far cry from the snowy scene.

"Mom, don't be alarmed."

"Dear, don't be alarmed."

"Something happened while you were away."

"Don't be alarmed, Mom."

Is there anything more alarming than being warned not to be alarmed? But then, that was the only thing I could say to myself to calm my pounding heart. Don't be alarmed. All your family are right in front of you, all in one piece. As long as they were healthy and intact, nothing could scare me. No, never. Even if they were conspiring to deny my very existence, I was not going to be scared.

"Grandma got hurt, Mom."

"She fell in the snow."

"It looks serious."

"She hasn't regained consciousness."

"We've been waiting for you."

"We couldn't wait any longer so we were just leaving for the hospital. Will you come with us?"

Everyone had something to say. There was not even the faintest trace of disapproval, but I felt so ashamed I wanted to hide from them.

"Oh, no. Please go ahead. I'll be along soon. My heart is pounding. And my legs are wobbly," I whimpered, covering my burning face with both hands.

"See, I told you she'd be shocked. We shouldn't have dumped the news on her that way."

"Why not? We had to tell her."

"Okay, okay. I've heard of people hiding bad things that happened to a child from its parents but I've never heard of hiding a parent's accident from a child."

The children argued among themselves. Quietly my husband hustled them out of the apartment, leaving one behind to keep an eye on his traumatized wife. Declining her company, I locked myself in my room and collapsed in a heap on the floor. Not because of trauma but because of my shame and sleepiness. How relieved I was when I realized it wasn't one of my immediate family but my mother on whom the disaster had befallen in my absence. I was embarrassed and ashamed, but my sense of guilt was not enough to keep sleep away. Feigning sorrow to my child who was so eager to offer me moral support, I slipped into sleep, a sleep as sweet as a clandestine affair.

The first thing that surged into my mind like an icy stream after the short but deep sleep was that my mother was as much a family member as my children, that she was as much my flesh and blood as them. Still I was relieved to have shoved a disaster that could have happened to one of my children onto my mother as if she were a total stranger.

Moreover, I was the only first-of-kin my mother had left. I had five children but she only had me now. People say that though you have ten fingers, there is none that wouldn't hurt if you were to bite it, meaning that one's love for one's children cannot be halved and quartered into smaller pieces like a watermelon. Still, wouldn't a person cherish a finger all the more if it were that person's last one? This thought made me come to my senses.

I thought about my brother, who died during the Korean War. He was well known far and wide among our relatives and neighbors for being a model filial son. A vivid image of him as a young boy popped into my mind. When he, Mother, and I were in the pit of abject poverty, I used to pester Mother for candy money, although she only earned a pittance as a seamstress, and I finally caused her great financial difficulty by breaking the window of the candy shop. My brother took me to the old stone wall on Mount Inwang and beat me, crying all the time he was doing it. As if he were beating me awake now, my sleepiness disappeared completely and for the first time in a truly long time I felt him near me. His tears of that time made me cry even now. The nearer I felt him, the greater became my longing for him.

I could no longer avoid the reality that I was responsible for my mother. I pulled myself together and headed to the hospital.

To my surprise, Mother had regained consciousness; she even smiled faintly when she saw me. The two sons my brother had left in this world were now older than he ever was and had children of their own. With my big family and theirs, my mother's cubicle in the emergency room was impressively crowded. Because I had been thinking of my brother, I was saddened at the simple truth that the dead could not age.

As was appropriate for the first-of-kin, I hurriedly shoved them aside and grabbed Mother's hand. It was the proverbial arrival of the first-of-kin that is said to move even a corpse to tears. Tears welled up in Mother's eyes and streamed down her cheeks. The sorrow that I was the only child left to her crystallized into streams of tears for the two of us.

"How did this happen, Mom?"

"I was looking out the window at Sŏgi's dad clearing the snow and I thought I could help him, I'm not *that* old, but my first step out in the yard, I just . . ."

Sŏgi's dad was my brother's eldest son, my mother's grandson, and my nephew. Mother lived with him.

"Help him, my foot. You just wanted to meddle," muttered Sŏgi's mom.

"You mean all of you were there and let this happen?" I said, blaming my nephew and his wife automatically.

"You know how Grandma has to supervise everything. What could we do?" My nephew promptly sided with his wife.

My mother was long past eighty, and my nephew and his wife were both barely over thirty. It would be an understatement to say it wasn't easy for young people to live with a grandparent, when some people downright refused to live with their parents-in-law. Even so, never was my mother's unwanted presence so dramatically revealed.

I could hear the moaning and groaning of sick people and the agitation of their families coming from every corner of the emergency room.

"So where did you get hurt?"

My nephew's wife lifted the sheet and pointed. Mother's left leg was twisted to the outside and was so swollen it looked like someone else's leg was stitched to her body.

"They should be fixing it soon," Mother murmured as if to comfort us.

"Does it hurt?"

"It hurts so bad I wish I could faint again."

"Oh, Mother!"

A nurse called at that moment, and we all rushed over to the doctor who was with her. The resident in charge of the emergency room, he looked too young and too exhausted. The red hand on the clock on the wall was already past the twelve, and on the X-ray screen the bare bones of my mother's hip and thigh awaited judgment.

"We'll have to admit her and, depending on her progress, we'll operate."

"Excuse me?"

"What I mean is we have to determine if she can endure surgery. There's no possibility of natural healing."

"But she's eighty-six years old. Surgery would be too . . . Oh, my mother wants a cast. It doesn't matter how long it will take. Please put her leg in a cast."

"I'm mentioning surgery because she's too old for the fracture to mend in a cast. To put her leg in a cast at her age is to put her in a coffin. She would develop all kinds of complications and definitely end up dead," the young doctor said coldly.

"She believes she's getting a cast. Er, are you sure a cast won't do?" I implored.

"It's not a patient's job to diagnose or treat."

"So you're saying we don't have any choice."

"That's right. Surgery is the only way."

"Will she be able to walk?"

"If she makes good progress . . ."

"So you can't even guarantee the result of the surgery. This is pure nonsense!" I lifted my voice, hackles raised, but the young doctor was singularly unperturbed. His calm seemed to stem not so much from his medical knowledge as from fatigue.

"You can talk in detail with the doctor in charge tomorrow. In the meantime, you need to take care of her hospital admission."

"If you're not the doctor in charge, how can you be so positive she needs surgery?"

"Because that's practically the only thing today's medicine can do for her."

"Ha! You can't even guarantee the result!"

"I told you it was the only way. I didn't say it was the safe way. Sometimes the only way is risky," said the doctor, his temper finally roused.

"Come on, Auntie. This is a hospital. We've got to do as the doctor says." My two nephews, who had been watching in silence, stepped in.

"But you don't know anything. You don't know!" I shrieked in a blind outburst of emotion that was boiling up in me.

"What don't we know?"

"Your grandma is eighty-six. Do you think she can survive a big operation?"

"What else can we do? Let's get her admitted first. Then we can discuss it with the doctor tomorrow. This is an emergency room, Auntie."

My nephews manhandled me out to the hall as if I were a mobster. Little did we know that those few words we exchanged with the young doctor were to be the most comprehensive discussion we would ever have with Mother's doctors.

As is true of doctors' rounds at any big university hospital, the doctor in charge entered Mom's room with an entourage of residents, interns, and nurses the next morning and acted very dependable and authoritative. Perhaps it's their authoritative manner that makes people refrain from voicing what they want to say. I stood aside deferentially and waited for him to speak. He said several things to the residents that sounded like a foreign language and the next thing I knew he was gone. I hurried after him but all I could do was buttonhole the resident who'd been in the emergency room the previous night. Before I could utter a word, he told me the surgery would take place about three days later and disappeared into another room.

In the next three days, the only information I was able to glean from the doctor by chasing him here and there was that the prognosis was not very good for a person with a fracture in the place where Mom's was, that the broken bones would have to be hooked together with metal pins because the bones of someone her age would not fuse together on their own, and that the operation was not a simple procedure. The doctor hadn't told me this in so many words at one time, but that's what it added up to when I patched together the few words he reluctantly and sparingly dropped from time to time.

I don't know if it was because I was overwhelmed by his authoritativeness or whether reticence was contagious, but whenever I came face-to-face with the doctor, I could not properly voice what I had been determined to say. As much as the doctor frustrated our family, we were frustrating my mother.

"You know, we could have done better with the old bonesetter. A bonesetter can work wonders with broken bones. And here I am, lying up in this fancy hospital doing nothing but making you spend a fortune. Instead of getting busy fixing what's broken, these people just keep drawing blood out of this old bag of bones to do this test and that test. I can't understand it for the life of me. It hurts awfully. And it isn't as if they're doing it for free, is it? I guess they think there's not much money in fixing bones so they're just trying to bleed a fortune out of us. Go tell them we don't have any money. Aw, my leg. Is this my leg or a mortal enemy? If it's going to hurt this much after they fix it then I want to die. Let me die. It's shameful enough to have lived this long when my own son had to go before me. What other sin have I committed to have to go through this kind of pain?"

Despite saying such things, my mother was looking forward to having her leg in a cast, and never imagined anything else. All the family balked at the idea of informing her otherwise. Of course, the task naturally came to me as I was her daughter.

When a "Nothing By Mouth" sign was hung on her bed the night before the surgery, I had no choice but to tell her of the impending operation.

"Operation? Who wants an operation? No. Never. I'd go to the devil before I'd let them take a knife to me. Don't think it's from any fear of dying that I haven't ended my life of unjust burdens before now. I was afraid of what would happen if I took the life I was given. Let me be, even if they tell you I'll die if I don't get an operation. I'm soon going to be ninety. No one would blame you if you just let me be."

Mother was adamantly opposed. But her eldest grandson had already signed the surgery consent form and tomorrow morning she was scheduled to be hauled off to the operating room regardless of her wishes. But I did not want to heap insults on the shell of a body that was my mother. Except for the hideously swollen leg, Mother's body was so fragile it wouldn't be more than a handful if wadded up. As long as there was any pride left in it, I believed she had the right to know what was going to happen to it. My belief stemmed from the love and hate I harbored for my mother as her only remaining offspring.

Without mincing words, I explained in detail all I knew about the operation she was to undergo. I even had the presence of mind to compare the fracture of her thighbone to a broken stick.

"Just think about it. If you had a broken stick and wanted to fix it because you really needed it, would you glue the pieces together or would you join them together with nuts and bolts? Which would be stronger? And then, what if you didn't have any glue or not enough of it? There's nothing to worry about, Mom. The doctors are going to fix your bones good and strong with nuts and bolts. No matter how many more days you're going to live, you want to be able to use all your limbs, don't you? That's living, isn't it, Mom?"

A bright smile came over Mother's face. Her eyes, which had been dim a long time, suddenly shone like a dreamy girl's.

"You mean the mountain marrow is still the best remedy for broken bones?"

"Huh?"

I had no idea what she was talking about. Her sudden change of attitude was so weird I almost screamed.

"So, there's still nothing better than mountain marrow. Yes, indeed. Mountain marrow is the best. It sure is a godsend," Mother chanted sweetly in a dreamy voice as if remembering a long-forgotten nursery rhyme.

"Mother, what are you talking about? Straighten up, Mom." I shook her emaciated shoulders.

"If only it were a small bone, I could just swallow a little mountain marrow. But since it's a big bone that's broken, they'll have to open me up and put the mountain marrow in. Children, I'm not a bit afraid of surgery. Don't you worry. I know bones fixed with mountain marrow are stronger than ever. Just look at this wrist of mine."

Wielding her right arm proudly, Mother beamed a knowing smile. But anybody could see her wrist was deformed. It had a crook in it and looked larger than her left one.

I knew why it was like that. And then I realized what she meant by mountain marrow.

The next morning found Mother still smiling. She looked like a baby because her dentures had been removed in preparation for surgery. The secret that made her smile so broadly in the face of a serious trial at an age nearer to ninety than to eighty made me unbearably sad.

Our first winter in the house with the purse-sized yard at the top of Hyŏnjŏ-dong, which we managed to buy our first time in Seoul, was harsh. It was brutally cold and once snow began to fall, it kept falling for days like rain during the monsoon. Even our waterman, Mr. Kim, dared not trudge through the deep snow to deliver to us. No water was no big deal for us, however. All we had to do was shovel some of the snow that had accumulated in the yard, on the soy-crock terrace, on the roof, everywhere, and heat it in an iron pot. Water wasn't a serious problem, but fire was.

Every day we had to buy two bundles of thin pieces of firewood. Mother never bought firewood at the neighborhood store but went all the way down to the firewood market near the streetcar terminal, saying that even though they looked alike, the bundles from the market were heavier. The vendor would deliver them if she bought ten bundles at a time, but we must have been unable to afford even that, for every day my mother would bring one or two bundles herself. When the steep alleys of our neighborhood became dangerously slippery with the snow that fell night and day, my brother said he would fetch the wood, but my mother was not one to let her son do such a chore.

"I don't need such trivial shows of filial piety as fetching firewood. You're an only son so you should do far greater deeds. You must study hard so you can be successful and make lots of money. Then we'll be able to buy logs by the cartload at the Ch'ŏngnyangni market to cut and chop into enough firewood to fill the shed. Then we'll be warm all winter."

"That's then. We have to think about now. People will make fun of us if you keep doing it when you have a big, strapping son. It's not the way for a son, either."

"And sending him on good-for-nothing errands is no way for a mother to treat a son who's going to be a great person some day."

Because my mother was so stubborn, there was little my brother could do, even as deeply devoted as he was.

Then one viciously cold day, Mother returned home with cuts and bruises all over because she had slipped and fallen while carrying firewood bundles on her head. The injuries were not serious, although they looked frightful for some time. Her wrist, however, swelled up very large and caused her great pain.

My brother and I lay awake through the night listening to her stifled moans. We felt as if our very pillar of strength had been shaken. The next morning, my mother did the household chores as usual and was as bright and spirited as ever with no sign of pretending. But try though she might, she could not do her needlework. She asked the old woman who used to bring orders from *kisaeng* to come retrieve the unfinished dresses, apologizing over and over. On seeing my mother's swollen wrist, the woman immediately cited a string of excellent acupuncturists, each and every one known to be the best in the city, but it was obvious that my mother had no thought of listening to her.

"I'll be all right soon. It's already much easier to move today than it was yesterday."

The old woman came back later with a few pods of gardenia seeds and said, "Try a gardenia paste. It does wonders for swelling."

Then she muttered to herself, "But what good will it do if the swelling goes away. She's got to have her bones joined. Mountain marrow is wonderful for joining broken bones, but that woman won't listen to anything that costs money. She's just too stubborn for her own good. When will she realize she has to take care of herself first if she's to take care of those children."

Brother also heard her. He got me out of Mother's earshot and asked me if I knew where the old woman lived. Without telling Mother, we went to that woman's house and Brother asked her what mountain marrow was and where we could find some.

"Your mom didn't send you, did she? I should think not. You certainly are nice kids. You're acting the way good young'uns should. That's why people have children. What's the use of bundles of money if you don't have any kids. Money's just useless," the woman fussed. Then she told us stories about mountain marrow that were outlandish, to say the least, but as fascinating as ancient legends. We had already taken our first step into the world of myth. To us in the throes of despair, without even a needle's eye of hope, myth had swung open its door, beckoning us to become its heroes.

The woman told us that there was only one cave in the whole country that produced mountain marrow and that it was on the ridge of Muak Hill not far from our place in Hyŏnjŏ-dong. She said the grains of marrow were shaped like tiny dice, just a bit bigger than millet and shiny like metal, and that each side of one had to be perfectly square for it to have a medicinal effect. She warned us that even though the vendor always did his best to select good ones, we should double-check them. Mountain marrow was very powerful, she said. One time they were moving the grave of a man who had taken mountain marrow for a broken bone and found the bone rejoined with a cluster of sparkling metal pieces so hard they could not break them free from the body.

It was more than enough to convince us that once swallowed, the mountain marrow would go directly to Mom's broken bone and put it back together.

"Is it expensive?" asked my brother, blushing.

"No, not at all. There's no reason for it to be expensive. It's formed naturally, like earth or sand. The man who's in charge of the cave charges something in the way of a premium, but it's not much. The people who go there are mostly people who can't afford a single prick of acupuncture—though there are plenty who go there after doctors and acupuncturists have failed to cure them."

"Let's go."

My brother and I climbed up Muak Hill. The climb was quite difficult, as the day was extremely cold and deep crusted snow lay everywhere. Still, it was not far from our house and it wasn't as though we had to climb up and down twelve steep hills as in a legendary journey after a miracle drug. So it was a good thing that the road was rough; that way, we felt the catharsis of myth.

The mountain marrow cave that we finally found after asking people again and again for directions was a grotto closed with a door. Although it was daytime, there were candles burning. We could tell at once that the cave was different from others. The walls and the ceiling, covered with tiny metal granules, sparkled, undulating to the dance of the candle flames, creating a mysterious, dreamy world. The master of the cave was a young man clad in a long white cotton coat. If he had been an old man with a white beard, we might have thrown ourselves at his feet and begged him to give us the divine medicine for our mother.

Nonetheless, we deified him. Emaciated and otherworldly, he had a spiritual air about him. My brother was a strapping figure compared with him. Looking up at him, I clung to my brother.

My brother bowed politely and told the man the purpose of our visit. The man went to a small table lit by a pair of candles and began to select some mountain marrow. Confirming what the old woman had said, he told us that not all of the marrow in the cave was medicinal, only the perfectly square cubes that had no blemishes. However, he didn't go so far as to say they would cluster around broken bones to rejoin them.

He selected the marrow in a most peculiar way. He knelt down in front of a table on which marrow was piled and nodding his head slightly as if dozing, picked up a few grains at a time and wrapped them in white paper. Being so entranced in his work made his pale, emaciated face look even more spiritual. He seemed to be doing the selecting with his mind's eye rather than his eyes.

Seeing that my brother was stooped in a reverential bow with his hands clasped together, I quickly did the same.

"I'll give you enough for ten days to begin with," said the man, bundling up the white paper packs. His voice was dry and hollow. "Come over here. It will work better if you pray to the Mountain Spirit."

Beyond the table in a deep corner of the cave, two candles illuminated a painting of the Mountain Spirit enshrined on an altar of mountain marrow. A bowl of water was on the altar and ten-*chŏn* and twenty-*chŏn* coins were scattered around it.

"Here, bow to the spirit and offer payment if you brought any. Pray to him for healing, like this."

Brother did as he was told. He prostrated himself again and again. Although I loved him dearly, I couldn't help being somewhat reserved and well behaved in my manner toward him, not only because there was a ten-year age gap between us, but also because he had a certain air about him that others found sobering. Clear intelligence and dignity that would never be tainted by stupidity or blinded by cunning superstition were his most prominent characteristics. Those marks of character that set him apart from the lowly brood of our impoverished neighborhood were the mantle I wore with pride.

And that brother of mine was kowtowing again and again to a cheap painting of the Mountain Spirit that even I could tell was the work of an amateur. Oddly enough, that superstitious ritual seemed to make him more dignified rather than degrade him. Maybe when you do something with so much care and heart, contradictory ways do not contradict but harmonize of their own accord. Unbid, I stooped reverentially and watched my brother absorbed in his ritual.

I have no idea if the amount of money my brother dedicated to the Mountain Spirit was enough for the mountain marrow, but his devotion was obviously more than enough to please the marrow man.

"I told you to try ten days to begin with but I can see that she will be hale and hearty in no more than ten. I'm never mistaken. You wait and see. Mountain marrow is a mysterious thing that works spiritually more than physically, and what spirit on earth could remain unmoved by your devotion? Besides, the Mountain Spirit is truly a miracle worker."

Needless to say, my brother's mountain marrow moved Mother deeply. She was much happier than before she got injured and, after reporting the decrease in swelling and pain every day with hourglass precision, on exactly the tenth day she announced she was completely healed.

Still, her wrist didn't look normal. She said the bulging was due to the mountain marrow that had clustered there to join the bones. To prove she was healed, she resumed her needlework on the tenth day and her quality was as good as ever. She would lift heavy objects just to demonstrate how strong the mountain marrow had made her bone. And of course she resumed her routine of buying one or two bundles of firewood at the Yŏngch'ŏn market and adamantly refused my brother's offer to fetch the wood until the arrival of spring.

"Don't worry, son. If I slip again, I have this hand to break the fall. It's strong as iron," she boasted, flaunting her ugly, misshapen arm.

The meeting between a surgeon and the patient's family immediately before the patient goes into surgery is a heartwarming event in a TV show, a drama, or a movie. For a brief moment, the doctor sheds his armor of authority and shows warmth and compassion for the anxious family. The family is comforted by the feeling that, possibilities of failure notwithstanding, they have made the right choice to entrust their loved one to a fellow human being rather than a robot that doesn't make mistakes. That comfortable feeling makes them play the baby with the doctor and shamelessly beg and plead, and the doctor becomes generous enough to indulge their all-too-human weaknesses, though it is questionable if it is genuine generosity rather than condescension or sentimentalism.

I too hoped to have such a warm, if only brief, encounter with Dr. Hong outside the operating room. I couldn't bear the thought of entrusting him with my mother's ancient, frail, female body, made lifeless by anesthesia. I needed to be comforted by him.

But the operating room of the large medical center was more like an arena than a room. A multitude were operated on every day. Like products on an assembly line, patients were put through one process after another until they entered the operating room for a final processing and, after some time, were sent out. Many people did things to Mother before she entered the operating room, but I didn't feel that a single one of them was the type of person to whom I could pour out my heart.

The operating room was off limits to family, and we could not see anyone who was in charge, much less what was going on inside. Either the surgeons had a permanent residence in the operating room or they had their own private entrance somewhere, for I could not catch a glimpse of any doctor, including Dr. Hong, no matter how long I hung around outside.

I sorely missed the pre-operational ritual and rapport that was only natural to have when entrusting a human life to another person. I believed it was more important than signing the surgical consent form. In the midst of everything, my mother's cheerful innocence as she entered the operating room was a great comfort for me. It was a wonder she could be so relaxed and free of anxiety when her more than eighty-year-old body was going to undergo a major operation. She was comfortable because she identified the operation with the mountain marrow treatment. For my mother, my brother was still her religion.

The surgery was a large L-shaped area with an entrance at one end and an exit at the other. The exit was no better than the entrance for peeping inside. A great many people, relatives of people undergoing surgery, hovered around the exit. A young mother who had sent her child all alone into the operating room was crying on her husband's shoulder, and an elderly woman was chanting with prayer beads for her grown-up son. A nurse came out every now and then to write some numerals next to names on a roster of patients. The numerals indicated the time the surgery was over and the patient was moved to the recovery room. It took another hour for the patient to be wheeled out. Every time a patient was brought out, people flocked around the gurney to see if it was their loved one.

There were TV scenes in which the door of the operating room swishes open and a doctor emerges and, still swathed in his surgical gown, calmly removes a mask that covers all but his twinkling eyes to reveal a fatigued but content smile peculiar to a person who has successfully accomplished a difficult task, and finally announces "It's all right. The operation was a success," whereupon the patient's family all look up at him adoringly or kowtow, spilling tears of gratitude. Such scenes never took place this side of the exit. There was only the entrance swallowing up the patients and the exit spitting them out, the families looking on helplessly.

The list on the wall had the name, gender, and age of all the patients scheduled for surgery. At eighty-six, my mother was the oldest. The next oldest was fifty-seven, which made having an operation at eighty-six seem all the more risky. Although it was nine in the morning when Mother went into surgery, it was not until after one in the afternoon that her name was listed as having been moved to the recovery room. We heard nothing more for the longest time. Every time the door opened and a patient was carted out, I would rush to the gurney to see if it was her. My eyes dimmed because of all my misgivings, fatigue, and hunger, and I took longer and longer checking each patient.

"God, Auntie. Do you think Grandma had her wrinkles removed?"

I hated my nephews' ability to joke at such a time, but I found their presence comforting nonetheless.

At last my mother was brought out. She muttered something when she recognized us, but we couldn't make it out because she was so feeble and she didn't have her dentures in. The cotton sheet printed with the hospital's logo was not over her bare shoulders. Indignant about such mistreatment, I pulled up the sheet and tried to cover them, but the IV and drainage tubes made it difficult to cover her properly. Her naked body was shivering under the sheet.

"Cold?"

"No, I just can't keep from shivering."

Excited to hear her speaking lucidly, all the family flocked around and one after another tried to test her.

"Grandma, do you know who I am?"

"You're Sŏgi's dad, who else?"

"Grandma, Grandma, what about me?"

"Sŏgi's mom."

"And who am I?"

"Kyŏnga's dad."

Passing the tests with flying colors, Mother smiled at me proudly. The eerie sensation with which I was so familiar shot through me.

Two robust orderlies wheeled the gurney rapidly down the long corridor and stopped at the elevator. Believing them to be proof the operation was a success, we continued our ridiculous questions as we hurried alongside, but once inside the elevator we began to ignore her.

"God, am I worn out. Tonight I'm going to have a real good sleep for a change."

"My stomach's hurting because I didn't have lunch. How was the beef soup in the hospital restaurant, Brother?"

"Whose turn is it to stay tonight?"

"Don't worry. I'll stay with her. She seems all right now but I expect she'll have a rough time tonight when the anesthesia wears off. All of you go home and get some rest."

"Yeah, that's a good idea. You stay tonight, Auntie, and I'll send Sŏgi's mom first thing in the morning to relieve you."

"Grandma's really something, so wiry and tough. Can you imagine someone being so clearheaded after such a big operation, and almost ninety at that!"

"You naughty boys. Would you have been happier if she hadn't come around? She took forever in the recovery room. I was scared something bad had happened. After all, one can't cheat one's age. It took her more than three hours to regain consciousness when it took others less than an hour to come around."

"No, it didn't. I woke up soon enough," Mother butted in, having heard our whispered words. "I woke up and hollered for someone to take me back to my children, but nobody ever paid me any attention. And I was shivering all over. I told them I was dying of cold but it was no use. Although I was in my right mind, my voice just wouldn't come out. It was like something was pulling it back inside. Those folks in there were just heartless."

We winked at each other, our eyes conveying both our amazement and our disdain at the unbecoming toughness of the woman pushing ninety.

Back in her room, everyone became even more garrulous and Mother had to put in a word regardless of what we talked about. Even I became fed up with her toughness and began to ignore her now and then. It was tiresome to try to understand her speech, which was garbled because of the absence of her dentures, and worse still, it was embarrassing in front of my nephews and their wives. I wished she would pretend to be critically ill as was expected of someone who had gone through major surgery. Finally, I hustled them out even though visiting hours hadn't ended.

"Why don't you all go home. You look more worn out than your grandma does. Have a good meal and go to bed early. Besides, Grandma won't go to sleep with all of you around. She thinks she's all right, but who knows what will happen, her being so old. We should be extra careful so she can pull through without a hitch."

Even after they left, Mother kept babbling. She looked like a cow chewing its cud. I became increasingly irked at her inexhaustible strength.

In the evening, Dr. Hong appeared with residents and interns in tow. As it was not time for doctors to make their regular rounds, I assumed he was probably checking on the people on whom he had operated that day. However, it was no better than his regular visits, for he and his entourage left as soon as they arrived. The doctors I saw in the halls were no less hurried. They made rounds like a whirlwind. They swept by cold and fast like a wind that will not stay in one place.

I had prepared the highest words of appreciation to say to Dr. Hong but I couldn't. Such words should be said courteously, with a little hesitant stammer, but there was too little time for me to catch the right moment to do so. I hurried out into the hall after him and, after mumbling my thanks in the tritest, most desultory fashion, asked Mother's prognosis.

"The operation was a success. There's not much to worry about. But because of her age, she needs to be watched very carefully."

I dared not ask another question, overwhelmed as I was with his words, the most I had ever heard him utter, but I was far from satisfied.

Mother kept mumbling. Residents and nurses came and went frequently to check her and the many hoses and tubes that came out of her. They also instructed me how to care for her and to keep a log on her condition throughout the night. I was to encourage her to cough and spit out mucus every now and then, inform the nurses when the IV was running short and when the drainage bag for the incision was full, and keep a record of her urine output.

I tried to ask them all the things I had failed to ask Dr. Hong, but all I could get out of them was that Mother was progressing normally. And not a one of them failed to add that she was extremely old. Old age understandably was not a malady or health problem but an annotation.

Mother refused to cough, pleading a lack of energy, and gave me a fright every time she began to choke on mucus. It was useless to warn her that she would get pneumonia if she didn't cough up the mucus. She just kept mumbling, sounding like dry autumn leaves rustling in a breeze.

"Close your eyes and try to sleep, for god's sake," I blurted out when I could no longer put up with it.

Mother stared at me wide-eyed, her eyes pools of chilling resentment.

"Shall I turn off the light?" I asked shakily.

"No," Mother said, shaking her head.

"I'll cover your eyes. Relax and try to sleep."

I held her hand and, with my other hand, gently covered her eyes. She soon became impatient and brushed my hand away.

"The place that was cut hurts, doesn't it? It will tonight. But it'll be much better tomorrow. Tell me if it hurts too much and I'll ask them to give you something for the pain."

"No, it doesn't hurt a bit. I just can't sleep."

"Then I'll ask them to give you a sleeping pill."

I went to the nurses' station, asked them to give her something, and was told to wait in the room. Soon an intern brought a tiny pill and suggested I keep the room dark. After helping my mother take the pill, I turned off all the lights except for a dim lamp on the wall next to the guest cot. Mother didn't protest this time. Relieved by the knowledge that the pill would soon take effect, I became unbearably sleepy. After making sure there was more than half a bottle of IV to go and the urine bag and drainage bag were less than half full, I lay down on the cot with the intention of dozing for a few minutes.

I had no idea how long I'd been sleeping when I was awakened by a strange stirring. The room was astir with silent restlessness. My mother was beating the air with her hands. But not recklessly beating. She seemed to be working hard at something, beating the air regularly and purposefully. I jumped up and turned on the lights. Mother squinted for a moment but her hands never stopped.

"What are you doing, Mommy?" I asked, unconsciously speaking in the way I used to when I was a little girl.

"Can't you see? When you do laundry, you've got to put the blouses with the blouses, the panties with the panties, and the socks with the socks. It won't do to bundle everything up together," she said in a strong voice.

"Laundry? You should be sleeping. . . ."

"How can I go to sleep with these things scattered all over the place? You naughty kids."

Screeching in a metallic voice, Mother stared at me. The look in her eyes was so cold it gave me the shivers. I wanted to run for help. She kept her hands busy sorting and folding laundry only she could see. Where did she find such energy after all the fasting and enemas of the previous day and the anesthesia and surgery of today? I was more frightened than amazed. A nurse walked in at that moment.

"My mother is acting strangely. She keeps beating the air. It seems like she's hallucinating."

"Some patients become like that because of the anesthesia. She'll get over it," the nurse said perfunctorily and, after checking Mom's temperature and pulse, left. I followed her out into the hall and begged her to do something to make Mother sleep.

"But she was given a pill already. You asked us to."

"It didn't work. Come to think of it, she's become worse after taking that pill. That must be it. Before she took it, she wasn't hallucinating even though she couldn't sleep. What should we do?"

"I don't think it's because of the pill. But even if it is, it's nothing serious. She was given a tranquilizer clinically proven to have the least side-effects."

"What could be more serious than this? She's out of her mind."

"She'll get better."

"Why don't you forget the tranquilizer and give her a sleeping pill or a shot."

"I can't."

"Why not? It doesn't make sense that a patient can't be helped to sleep in this big medical center where all kinds of operations are done."

"We know much better than you how to take care of patients. Families should cooperate instead of making such unreasonable demands," the nurse said, turning away in a huff. Angry and humiliated, I returned to Mother's room, vowing never to plead with the likes of her again.

It seemed Mother had not finished her laundry. Her hands continued the folding action until she suddenly thrust them out in front of her, palms outward, as if to defend herself. Her eyes, which had been like icy pits, now popped out with fear.

"What's wrong, Mom?"

I ran over to her. She threw her arms around my neck and hung on so tightly I could hardly breathe. Her strength was unbelievable. As I tried to catch my breath, she whispered in my ear in a terror-stricken voice coming from hell, "He's back. My god, he's come again."

Mother stared at the door, a hand still held defensively. I turned around to see who had followed me but there was nobody. My hair stood on end.

"Mom!"

Fear gave me the strength to shake her off. Her face contorted and she stared at the door, her body shaking uncontrollably. She was confronting whomever she saw there with all her body and soul. It suddenly dawned on me that she might be seeing the messenger from the other world come to fetch her. Terror-stricken, I dared not take a step toward the door to go for help. It was only natural the messenger from the other world would lurk at the doorway of this eighty-six-year-old woman. In all likelihood she was probably not only the oldest person to undergo surgery that day but also the oldest patient in the whole medical center. It was useless to whine and fuss if the messenger was that discerning. I had already made up my mind to let him take her. No one would complain that she had not lived out her allotted time. Still it was certainly abominable of Death to drag her away when the blood from her wound had not yet dried. But then Death would not be Death if he did not cause the survivors pain.

We're ready but for god's sake don't you show your ghastly self to her, I begged the messenger. It is us mortals' nature not to welcome death even after we have lived a hundred years. The greatest act of mercy you could do is not revealing yourself until the very last minute. Go away, I beg you. Go away, I implored silently, unable to bear the terror that was gripping Mother. I was also afraid that he might decide to reveal himself to me as well. Instead of going away, he was obviously coming nearer. I could see it in Mother's blazing eyes. My god, I was facing her death alone.

"It's him again. What're you doing? We've got to hide your brother. Hurry!"

"Please, Mom. Don't do this. Where's there a brother for us to hide?"

"Have they already taken him away, then?"

"Please, Mom."

Mother groped all around with her hands and, coming upon her bandaged leg, whispered anxiously, "Ah, here you are, my poor boy. Sit tight. I'll protect you."

Mother tried to hug her leg with her shaky hands. From that moment on, her leg was her son. Shielding her leg with her body, Mother glared at her enemy. It wasn't the messenger from the other world after all.

"Comrade Officer, Comrade, sir. There are just us women here in the house."

The chill in her eyes wavered pitifully, and a groveling smile appeared on her face. I realized what she was seeing in her hallucination. Poor Mother. It would have been much better for her had it been the messenger from the other world.

Mother was trying desperately to hide her leg but of course she couldn't.

"Comrade Officer, there's no one but us women, I tell you. You don't need to search, Comrade Officer."

I watched helplessly as she became even more frantic. As she clung to a strand of hope, beads of sweat popped out on her face, which was distorted with fear and servility. Her hands and emaciated shoulders trembled like tree limbs in the wind.

Poor Mother. God can be so heartless. It would have been better to let her die than make her undergo this horror again.

"Mother, Mother. Don't do this. Please calm down," I cried, shaking her shoulders. With a strength I could not fathom, she thrashed violently and shook me off as easily as one would a dead leaf.

"No. No. You wretched creature. You brute! You brute!"

Backed up against the wall and shaking helplessly, I could only watch her becoming increasingly agitated by the minute. Except for her wounded leg, all of her body was heaving up like raging waves. That made the leg look even more bizarre and alien, anything but part of her body. The leg frightened me. Identifying her leg with her son was contagious.

In her violent writhing, which was punctuated with harsh cries of "No, you brute!" and sly flattery of "Mister Officer," "Comrade Officer," and "Officer, sir," the IV needle was dislodged and blood ran out onto her hospital gown and bed sheet. The sight of the blood upset her even more.

"Stop right there, you brute. You'll have to kill me before I'll let you go in there."

With tears streaming down her face, Mother ground her gums together. There can be nothing more gruesome than to see a toothless person trying to grind her teeth. If only I were dreaming. Mother emitted ghastly shrieks and pulled at her hair. She pulled out her catheter. I felt faint from the smell of blood. I tried to pull myself together and was just turning to go for help when a nurse ran into the room, obviously reacting to Mother's shrieks. The duty nurse followed her.

It took a lot of people to get all the things reattached to Mother. She was as strong as a wrestler. It took me and two nurses to pin her down so the duty nurse could replace all the tubes and gadgets she had pulled out. This time the nurse put the IV needle in her foot.

"How can things like this happen?" I addressed the head nurse bitterly.

"Don't be upset. This type of reaction is extraordinary but it is certainly not uncommon. She'll be better in no time," the nurse told me soothingly.

They thought my mother's nightmare was the result of her peculiar physical disposition. But then, who could really understand another person's nightmare?

My mother's writhing was desperate and hell-bent. The head nurse had Mother's arms and legs tied and the side rails of the bed put up on both sides.

"I know it's not easy to see one's mother like this, but you have to put up with it. This is the only way to deal with this kind of situation. Try to get some sleep. Otherwise, you'll end up sick, too. Don't worry about your mother, she'll soon be all right."

The nurses left me after making sure the restraints were tied securely. I was so tired I flopped down on the cot without even bothering to remove my shoes. But lo and behold, Mother, who had been growling like a rabid animal, let out a yell and the restraints broke with a crack. She was driven by an inhuman power. She was not uttering incoherent words but chilling shrieks and venomous curses. With a gut-ripping pain, the same inhuman power surged up inside me. I gritted my teeth and dashed to her. This time I wasn't about to ask for help. I would confront her head on. This was nobody's business but our own and we were the only ones who could deal with it.

I threw myself on Mother, practically straddling her. My body convulsed with hers. I knew I could not relent lest she should ride me instead. Still, I could not match her strength, and I had to slap her when she almost overpowered me.

"Calm down, Mom. Calm down."

I slapped her. Startled by the unprecedented immoral action committed by my hand, I slapped her even harder, and at the sight of the swelling hand mark on her face, I slapped her again. I was losing touch with reality. We were in either a nightmare or hell. Mother's strength was terrifying, but her face was even more terrifying. It was not my mother's face. Now I was not fighting with my mother but with the terror inside myself.

I loved my mother and I loved her face. My mother was one of those rare people who became more beautiful with age. Perhaps it had something to do with Buddhism, in which she had become steeped in her old age. Her trust in Buddha had helped her overcome the terrible rancor she harbored about her son's wretched death. As she aged, her face took on the gentle, complacent look of a Buddha. Although she lost her son, she still had his children and their wives and children to love. Loving them but never to the extent of obsession, she was aging happily. Watching my mother age more peacefully and beautifully than anybody I knew, so enchantingly beautifully, I thought she was a Boddhisatva.

The human heart is fathomless, but never did I imagine such violent emotion was hidden in my mother's heart. I was shattered to find that it was not goodness, peace, and love but resentment, curses, and hatred that were hidden deep inside her. Even if all other humans were hopeless bundles of sins, my mother could not be so.

She finally began to lose the violent and ruthless battle between two evils. Only then did I cry aloud, rubbing my cheek on the swollen finger marks on her cheek.

I don't know why at that time Mother thought that hilly slope in Hyŏnjŏ-dong would be a good hiding place. By then we had long risen above the poverty of that slummy neighborhood and had no reason to envy others, but we were in a predicament truly undeserved and unmanageable. We were helpless. I think it was this sense of helplessness that made my mother turn to the neighborhood that she had made her hitching post the first time she came to Seoul. It was also caused by the peculiar nature of our situation. Although it was only a tiny part in the great tragedy that gripped the nation during the Korean War, our predicament at that time was directly related to the hypocrisy and treacherous nature of that respectable middle-class neighborhood.

It had to do with my brother joining the North Korean Volunteer Army. He had participated in the leftist movement for a brief time soon after Korea was liberated from Japanese colonial rule. When we were unable to evacuate to the south and were trapped in Seoul under the Red army, he was extremely nervous lest his conversion from communism be revealed. He anxiously tried to learn what other converters in similar situations had done. The dubious information he managed to glean was that they had fled to the south at all costs and those who failed to do so had converted again. Unfortunately, that knowledge only increased his anxiety.

He cursed himself for gullibly trusting in the government that had proclaimed it would defend Seoul to the last, instead of heeding the ominous roaring of cannons, thus missing the chance to seek refuge elsewhere. He cursed the government leaders for irresponsibly misleading people and then fleeing themselves. Nevertheless, he was not clever enough even to think about converting to the left again. Even though he had courageously converted from the left when he realized his mistake, my brother was the type of person for whom the word *convert* caused moral indignation. If he had thought his choice of communism was a lesser mistake, he would have stuck to his original choice just to be consistent and faithful to himself rather than rectify the wrong by converting.

My brother was like the literati of old, who valued integrity as the highest ideal. His conflict was inevitable, as the literati spirit could not tolerate the true nature of communism, which justified means for its ends. The only reason I was unaffected by the leftist movement that attracted so many young people on the eve of the Korean War was my belief that there had to be something wrong with it to cause a man like my brother to convert from it.

As one who loathed even the thought of converting as a means to survive, he greatly resented the bureaucrats who sweet-talked people into staying in the city, only to sneak out themselves, abandoning those people to the Red army. Day by day his mind was increasingly wracked by resentment, suspicion, anxiety, and loneliness. He was already ill when, betrayed by a neighbor, he was hauled away. There was nothing we could do but watch helplessly. We expected to hear that he was executed on the spot at a people's court, tortured, or even worse, so we were shocked when word came that he had joined the army, the first to volunteer at a large people's rally, and had even encouraged a great many young people to join. We had no way to check if it was true or what kind of trick fate was dealing him.

But then fate was playing tricks on all of us. The neighbor who had harassed us and reported my brother to the authorities now wielded great power under the Red regime. He changed his attitude completely and became a self-appointed patron for us. Although the conscription of young people had not been so severe at the beginning of the Red army occupation, it was now being undertaken at such a pace that there was virtually no family who had not lost a son to the Volunteer Army. Thus my brother's joining the Volunteer Army was no reason for us to deserve special treatment, but we received special benefits in food rations and other things, all because of that neighbor's influence on the People's Committee of our district. We didn't have the presence of mind or the nerve to question whether we should take the benefits. Just trying to make it through a day made us stuporous, and food was unquestionably necessary.

We would stop with a start while greedily gobbling down boiled barley, not because we were eating when others did not even have thin porridge, but because we were eating at the cost of selling a member of our family.

"A sharp stomach makes short devotion, they say, but how can I eat this well and this easily when I got this in exchange for my son, my precious son's life," my mother would lament, dropping her spoon abruptly. But she had no forebodings.

Three months later, when the world changed back to what it had been, we were persecuted by our neighbors. We were reported as being Reds, and members of the young men's association came with clubs and guns and ransacked our house. They broke our furniture and pots and pans and with their clubs they poked my sister-in-law's stomach that was huge with a baby, while our neighbors looked on with the same enjoyment with which they would watch a shaman entertaining spirits. The target of their revenge for the ordeal they had gone through in the three months Seoul was in the hands of North Korea, we could do very little to defend ourselves against their wrath.

"Listen. Who was it that abandoned people in the pit of fire and took to his heels? I will gladly die if you want to kill me for the crime of surviving that fiery pit but just let me die after I look that person in the face and ask of his crime." Sometimes Mother would wail and rail like this, but all she got in return were scornful comments that she was a cold-blooded cheat and that Reds sure were glib talkers.

That was nothing compared with the charge that we were hiding the high-ranking Red who had used and protected us. My mother, my sister-in-law, and I were summoned and interrogated for days, each separately and at different times. The ill treatment my young nephew received at our relative's home during those days left an indelible scar on every member of the family. At that time, the whole world would shudder with revulsion at the mere mention of the word "red."

Then the war reversed again and the army began to retreat. The first thing Mother did was send my brother's wife and son to her parents because her baby was almost due. Needless to say, Mother wanted to remain in Seoul to the last minute in the hope that my brother might come back. It was a reasonable hope, because quite a number of young men ran away from the Volunteer Army and returned home. Mother trusted her son would return, even if it was with the Red army, were he unable to run away from it. She didn't care if he was a Red or not, her only worry being if he was dead or alive.

My brother did return. But his return was more like an omen than a miracle. Even my mother, who had been waiting for his return with so much trust and hope, dared not welcome him on the spot. His hideous appearance was understandable after a long period of starvation and ragged existence, but he was reduced to a complete wreck from deep inside. His eyes were glazed uneasily, never focusing on anything, and his body was emaciated due to acute insomnia. He became paranoiac and would suffer anxiety attacks countless times a day. He showed no affection for his family, nor did he miss or want to know the whereabouts of his wife and child. There was no way to know what harrowing experiences had wrecked him so completely. Like a timid child left alone at home, he locked himself inside his shell and denied the outside world.

To make matters worse, the war was turning from bad to worse and everyone was leaving Seoul, fleeing southward. This time the government didn't make the mistake it had made in the summer; it warned the people of Seoul of the impending crisis well in advance and helped them to evacuate. En masse the city's residents joined the ranks of refugees, preferring to risk freezing to death than go through another Red occupation.

His mind wracked as it was, my brother was more than eager to leave when it came to the matter of evacuation. He was desperate to leave. The only lucid thought left in his disheveled mind was that he should flee from the Reds. In his wretched condition, it would not have been possible in the first place without that obsession of his to break through the fierce battleground.

My brother did not have an identification card so he could not prove he was a resident of Seoul. Because of the possibility of spies or enemy soldiers hiding among the refugees, ID checks were getting stricter by the day. A young man would not dare step outside his home without proper identification, to say nothing of leaving the city. A person needed guarantees from two people in one's neighborhood to apply for an identification card, otherwise the person would have to go through a police screening. My mother begged and begged our neighbors to help, but no one would vouch for my brother. They would ask why someone should be afraid of being screened if he were not a Red, which was actually a quite reasonable question. When, before the return of my brother, the three grown-ups in our family applied for cards, we had to report to the police numerous times for investigation because none of the neighbors would vouch for us. We were the last in our neighborhood to get cards.

My brother's case was far more complicated, however, for he became petrified and trembled abjectly at the mere mention of the police. He begged us not to take him to the police even if it meant he would not be able to seek refuge or to go out of the house for the rest of his life. But then he would rave, "Let's go. We can't sit here and get stuck again. Let's seek refuge." He was so nervous he drove us nuts. When we proposed that we just set out, card or no card, our situation being risky whichever course we chose, he glared at us with those glazed eyes of his and accused us of wanting to get him shot.

We were driven up the wall. My brother wanted us to get him a card by whatever means necessary as long as we did not involve him.

"Mother, sell everything. Sell the house and the furniture and buy me that damned card. What do you want to keep these things for?" He nagged Mother like a child until she burst into heart-wrenching tears. He clamored after me with unspeakable demands. "How come you don't get out there and hook up with someone powerful to save your poor brother, huh? What's the good of having a sister?"

These fits of shameful petulance were in truth the last convulsions of his wrecked spirit. The day the government announced its last evacuation order, warning that it was abandoning Seoul and that those still remaining should evacuate in an orderly fashion, the three of us left our house carrying bundles on our heads and backs. We had to show the few neighbors who had wavered to the last minute with false hopes that we too were fleeing lest they accuse us later of being Reds. Besides, we were deathly afraid of being in that house when the Reds returned. Running away from the Reds' Volunteer Army was obviously a far more serious crime than converting and deserved the supreme punishment. In those days, all of our thoughts and deeds were controlled entirely by the question of whether someone was a Red.

We mingled in the throng of refugees surging toward the south like a tidal wave, but we did little more than circle the downtown area several times to keep away from the checkpoints. Having no mind or will of his own, my brother was good for nothing except sensing the whereabouts of the checkpoints and dodging them, which he did with an animal-like instinct. I was so sick of the burden he had become that I was looking for a chance to run away by myself, when Mother suddenly said, "Children, let's go to Hyŏnjŏ-dong."

The moment I heard those words, I became as humble and meek as a prodigal who decided to return home after prolonged straying. Something like joy flickered through my brother's glazed eyes.

"Those shabby, ragged folds of Hyŏnjŏ-dong will be the best place to hide," Mother said calmly, obviously relieved at the thought. Her description of the village as shabby, ragged folds was more nostalgic than derogatory.

"That village must be deserted too. We can hide in any of the empty houses there and go back home when the National Army returns. I've never been so scared of people. Either I'm evil or the world is. But I wouldn't mind coming across one or two people there, they're all so good-natured."

The remembrance of the classic poverty and good-natured neighborliness of the shabby village where we had weathered our first hard years in Seoul glimmered like a key to salvation for us after we had been sneered at and hurt by our pompous neighbors. We hoped that even my brother's wrecked spirit could be healed there. We climbed up the mountain slope to Hyŏnjŏ-dong, brimming with quiet happiness as if we were returning home, as if we were returning to the arms of the Buddha. Every little alley, familiar and friendly, seemed to welcome us. Being the evening of the last night of the evacuation, the village was completely deserted with no trace of any living thing. At our foot the city lay unlit and deserted in the dusk like an empty expanse of marsh.

Mother sighed softly and murmured, "The Reds are a hopeless lot. How can they say they will rule the Red way when they can't win even the support of the poverty-stricken people here?"

We went around to the houses of several people with whom Mother had kept in touch but of course they were all empty. We chose a house with a well and let ourselves in. Being a humbly built shack, it was easy to unlock. We could have chosen a better house, the whole neighborhood being empty and ready for us to break in, but Mother wanted to take one owned by people she knew so that later she could apologize and thank them.

For the next several days, we never came across anybody and had no way of knowing if the world had changed or not. We had brought staples that would last about a month and there were various grains, pots of kimchi, firewood, and water in the house. We were content. I wondered if it was a life like this that my brother had dreamed of as he ran away all that long distance. I became hopeful that not having the pressure of having to pretend in speech and behavior to impress others might help my brother. Already I could see tiny signs of healing. He indicated, though vaguely, worries about his wife and son, who had gone down south. He wondered if she had given birth at her parents' house. It was the first time he had shown any concern for them since his return, so we became excited at the possibility that he was beginning to open up to the people closest to him.

Overjoyed at finding a perfect shelter, we were blissfully unaware of its vulnerability. We were found one day by a party of soldiers of the People's Army who were wearing white bed sheets for overcoats. Stationed at the Sŏdaemun Penitentiary in the foothills, they had noticed smoke rising morning and evening from a few houses on the upper slopes. They had checked every house from which they had seen smoke rising, only to find invalids and old people who were half dead. But now their luck had changed, they said, greedily eyeing me as I opened the gate for them.

"Sure. Sure. There are just the two of us women here. You don't even need to check." Mother rushed out after me and rambled about things that would have been better left unsaid. They pushed her aside and went inside the house.

"You, too, are a woman, Comrade?" the officer at the head of the troop asked my brother with an icy sneer.

My brother became speechless at the sight of the soldiers and could utter only tortured moans and no coherent words.

"That's not a woman, but an idiot. He's worse than a woman 'cause he's a useless idiot. He's my curse, my deathly curse." Terror, humility, and flattery crossed each other on Mother's face. It was needless for her to emphasize this; my brother was not a whole person in anybody's eyes. He looked even more wretched because of the contrast with the rough, coarse soldiers. He was pale and emaciated, with vacant pits for eyes, and could utter only monosyllabic sounds no one could understand. If only Mother had not emphasized he was an idiot.

After that day, the soldiers took turns coming to our house. One of them was an intelligence officer who seemed to have a hunch about my brother. He would be talking to us good-naturedly about his home and family when out of the blue he would glare at my brother and in a piercing voice say things like "Did you run away from the People's Army, Comrade?" or "Didn't you straggle out of the National Army?" My liver would shrivel up to the size of a pea every time. My brother's pitiful trembling did not get worse or better no matter how often they showed up and the aphasic symptom he acquired the moment he first saw the soldiers did not go away. His idiot act was so flawless that we no longer thought it was an act. Sad and bitter as it was, we had to admit there seemed no chance of his returning to normal.

Nonetheless, the intelligence officer was exceptionally tenacious. He threatened, cajoled, and sometimes begged to learn the truth.

"I can't help being sorry for you, Mother. What happened to cause your only son to become such a mess? He wasn't born like that, was he? If he wasn't born an idiot, he can be cured. The medical advancements in North Korea are world famous. And the poor are given priority. I can send him to any number of good doctors. Just tell me the truth. Tell me when he became like that."

The man called Mom "Mother" and often talked to her like a pampered child, which made her more frightened than when he was icy and ruthless so that she would cringe and ramble helplessly. Her rambling made me nervous. When the man left, she would wink at me and say she was playacting. It was amazing.

There's nothing a person won't do to survive. Every day was a bloodcurdling, life-splitting acrobatic act like dancing with a viper.

The sound of cannons loomed near again and the soldiers' eyes became bloodshot. Mother prayed day in and day out that they would leave without causing any harm. "Please, let them not harm my boy. Please let them not harm my poor boy."

At last the intelligence officer came to say goodbye to us. But his way of saying goodbye was special.

"Comrades, did you think I could be deceived by such sly lots as you? It's not too late to tell the truth. Let's see if you really can't talk," he said, drawing his pistol and taking aim at my brother.

"No, you can't do this to us. No, you bastard!" Mother screamed and threw herself onto his arm. My brother only groaned like a stricken animal. The officer shook Mother off.

"Talk. Or I'll make you talk."

The gun went off. The bullet hit my brother's leg. Still, he merely groaned like an animal.

"All right. You asked for it."

The gun went off again. The same speech and the same sound were repeated over and over again. The officer aimed at the lower part of my brother so he wouldn't die on the spot.

My brother collapsed in a pool of blood and my mother, who had fallen down when the soldier shook her off his arm, let out a blood-curdling scream and fainted.

"I'm not going to kill you right away. I'm going to give you a chance to tell the truth before you die."

But the officer never returned, for in a few days the world changed again.

None of my brother's wounds was fatal, but he died in a few days from loss of blood and lack of proper medical treatment. He remained aphasic till the end. We could never forget all that blood and the unrequited grief of those few days that reached to Heaven. We could not forget those things, but we could hide them. I by meeting a man, falling in love with him, having children, and loving them, and my mother through raising and caring for her grandchildren and trusting in Buddha.

Mother was so exhausted from her exertions that she lay utterly spent for a long time. She was like a sheet of paper, thin, weightless, and breathless, ready to blow away at a whisper of wind. Relatives and friends who visited looked grim and shook their heads at the chance of her recovering. Some of them, thinking she was in a coma, would talk openly about funeral procedures, and some, as if they were already at her funeral, would say not to grieve because she had lived out her allotted life. We did not try to tell them otherwise nor did we resent their insensitivity. Mother showed only slight signs of consciousness, grimacing when the nurses gave her injections or when we fed her one or two spoons of liquid.

A friend came to visit me at the hospital. She took one look at Mother and said straight out, "Have you prepared her shroud?"

"No, why should I prepare such an awful thing in advance?"

"My, my! Then, how about her grave?"

"Grave? Do we have to get it in advance?"

"You haven't done that either, huh? You're really hopeless."

"What do you mean?"

"You're hopeless as a daughter, you dummy. What a pitiful thing to have no son, only a dummy for a daughter."

I didn't mind her calling me hopeless or a dummy, but it made my mother look rather bad and I thought I should do some explaining.

"We have our ancestral burial ground."

"Where is it?"

"You know. Kaep'ung County, near Kaesŏng."

"What's the use of having a burial ground in North Korea?"

"Still."

"Still? That's the most miserable excuse I've ever heard. Next, you'll be trying to get a loan on your land and home in North Korea," chided my sarcastic friend.

"I mean it's a kind of unspoken promise between us. Mother would want to be buried in her ancestral land even if she could never return there in her life. How could I get a burial plot elsewhere when I know only too well that she really pines to return even though she doesn't say it in so many words? Of course, it won't matter after she's dead. It won't be too late to buy some land for her grave when that happens. After all, a grave is just a house one needs only after death."

Mother opened her eyes. They were so clear and bright in her paper-pale face that my friend shrieked and grabbed hold of me.

"Come here," Mother called to me in a clear voice.

"Yes, Mother." I approached her nervously. She grabbed my hand. The warmth and strength of her hand surprised and saddened me.

"Don't bury me in a grave when I die," she said, her voice as calm and irrefutable as usual.

"Ah, you heard us."

"Yes, and I'm glad I did. I've been meaning to tell you. You think of this as my will and you do as I tell you. When I die, do for me as I did for your brother. Don't mind what others say, just do as I tell you. I'm asking you because only you can override what others say."

"Like you did for Brother?"

"Yes, exactly like that. You haven't forgotten, have you?"

"Forgotten? How could I ever forget?"

My mother's hand was as strong and commanding as when she was healthy, as when she pulled me over Nongbawi Hill when I was a little girl and we were moving from her hometown to Seoul the first time.

We buried my brother in a temporary grave at a corner of someone's field on the other side of Muak Hill. The burial was a shabby affair without formality, no better than a burial for a vagrant, but anything better was beyond the ability of us two women stranded in the deserted city.

As soon as Seoul was recovered and the crematorium resumed operations, Mother broached the idea of cremation. My sister-in-law, who had rejoined us by then, maintained that we should move his remains to the public cemetery because the least we could do for her fatherless children was to give them their father's grave. Mother had been meek with her daughter-in-law as if her young widowhood was her fault, but she would not give an inch in that matter. Although my sister-in-law was understandably hurt and disgusted by Mother's hardheartedness in emptying her husband's grave when she was still grieving for him, she eventually obeyed, overwhelmed by Mother's undefiable dignity and grief-stricken determination to carry on.

My brother's flesh became smoke and his bones a fistful of dust. Without a word, we followed Mother to the terminal for buses to Kanghwa Island. On the island, asking directions again and again, Mother found the seashore that overlooked Kaep'ung County in the north across the sea. There, toward the land that lay so near yet was so forbidding, she threw the dust to the wind. Granted, Kaep'ung County was the site of our family's ancestral burial ground, but I didn't think she was doing all this to appease my brother's spirit for not being buried there. There was no trace of a frail, pliant woman who meekly obeyed her destiny with sorrowful acceptance. She looked spirited and daring like a warrior heading into battle. With her fistful of dust cast on the wind, Mother was challenging something far too tremendous for her. The dust and wind were her only weapons to defy the monster called national division that trampled her life and destroyed everything she held precious.

Mother wanted me to repeat what she had done. This time she was going to become the dust on the wind and I had to do what she had done. Thirty years have passed. Is there no other way we can nullify that monster?

"I'm sorry. Please do as I ask. I beg you with all my heart."

Mother looked pathetic. She appeared truly apologetic that she had no other legacy to give me.

Ah, it seems I have to go through it again.

Mother is still fighting.

Translated by Kim Miza and Suzanne Crowder Han

20. O CHŎNGHŬI

O Chŏnghŭi was born in Seoul in 1947 and studied creative writing at Sŏrabŏl College of Arts. If Pak Wansŏ is the first woman writer to have gained widespread critical and commercial success in modern Korea, then O Chŏnghŭi is the author who has put Korean women's literature on the world map, her work drawing comparisons with such writers as Virginia Woolf, Alice Munro, and Joyce Carol Oates.

O was just out of her teens when she burst onto the literary scene with "Wangujŏm yŏin" (trans. 1989 "The Toyshop Woman"), the prize-winning story in a competition for aspiring writers sponsored by a Seoul daily, in 1968. That this highly original story was begun while the author was still in high school suggested the arrival of a gifted literary talent. O has since published some four dozen stories and novellas. A comparatively meager output for a writer whose career spans five decades, it is also an oeuvre of consistently high quality, consisting of provocative, densely textured stories, many of them infused with a restrained intensity that is often unsettling. Not until 1977 did O publish her first collection of fiction, *Pul ŭi kang* (River of fire), notable for the nameless first-person narrator in each of the stories. There followed an especially productive period in which many of her most memorable stories were composed—"Chŏnyŏk ŭi keim" (1979, trans. 1989 "Evening Game"), "Chunggugin kŏri" (1979, trans. 1989 "Chinatown"), "Pyŏlsa" (1981, trans. 1989 "Words of Farewell"), "Tonggyŏng" (1982, trans. 1993 "The Bronze Mirror"), and the story translated here. The first three stories appeared in her second volume of fiction, *Yunyŏn ŭi ttŭl* (1981, The garden of childhood), the latter two in her third collection, *Param ŭi nŏk* (1986, Spirit on the wind). O's production has since been more sporadic, but works such as "P'aroho" (1989, trans. 1998 "Lake P'aro"), "Yet umul" (1994, The old well), *Sae* (1996, Birds), and "Ŏlgul" (1999, Face) suggest that the author has maintained the high standards she set for herself at the very beginning of her career.

"Wayfarer" (Sullyeja ŭi norae) first appeared in *Munhak sasang* in 1983.

WAYFARER

The snow had started that morning. Hyeja opened the window, sat on the sill, and watched the carefree flakes turn the world giddy. The neighborhood was still, the snow muffling every tiny, squirming noise. There were no calls for the baseballs that came flying into her yard several times a day, no sound of children sneaking over the wall after them. When the young woman who rented the room near the front gate worked the day shift, the neighbor children had taken advantage of the house being left empty and climbed over the wall. Hyeja would have her hands full putting a stop to it. The day she had returned home, a boy nonchalantly climbed over the wall, glancing at her where she leaned against the door to the veranda watching him. When finally she shouted "Hey!" the boy protested: "We do this all the time, me and the other kids. When nobody's home, what are we supposed to do?" Strangely, the boy's grumbling had reassured her. It had helped her dismiss the notion that the house was haunted, that the cursed, unkempt garden was being kept by some wicked ogre.

Now and then a clump of snow weighing down the bare branches plummeted to the ground and the sparrows searching for food took wing. There were no footprints in the snow between the rented room and the gate; the young woman must not have left for work yet.

Hyeja went out to the yard and gathered a handful of snow. The white blanket came up to her ankles. If it kept coming down like this, it would easily be knee-deep by nightfall. She ought to sweep it away, she told herself, but she didn't move. The sound of a piano, an unadorned, inelegant melody, had caught her attention. Hyeja sang along in a soft voice:

Hills, fields, trees
Under white, white snow.
We grow up pure of heart, you know.

She had sung this ditty as a child, and so had her own children. Probably some young mom, alone at home with time on her hands after sending her children off to school, had been watching the snowflakes fall when the melody came to mind and she had tapped it out on the keyboard.

The music abruptly stopped, leaving Hyeja standing blankly, mouth open. In the profound silence, her dream of the night before came back to her.

She had first dreamed this dream as a child, but the last time had been long enough ago that she had almost forgotten it. In this dream she was on a street, always the same street, following an endless stone wall, a mossy, crumbling structure that resembled an ancient fortress wall suffering from neglect. "Where am I? I've been here before," she would murmur happily enough, taken with the familiar ambience of the place. She followed that wall seemingly forever, because she had a hunch, which became a conviction, that if she reached into one of the crevices where the wall was worn and crumbling, she would surely find a token of something that had been promised her—a small, pretty button, a secret mark, a tiny, folded piece of paper. But then she would awaken. She couldn't identify the street, not at the beginning of the dream, not at the end; all she did was wander it. Awakening from the dream meant yet again the loss of this street she had constantly followed, and the return of that helpless sensation of being deserted. She felt like a lost child. Where could that street be leading? And why did it all seem so familiar? Her old, wraithlike mother, who was still alive, would have answered right away in her lucid, precise manner: It was the road to the otherworld, or else a road traveled in a former life. That Hyeja was having this dream again after almost two years offered a hint, no, an assurance, that she was actually back home.

Her hands were growing numb. The snow she clutched was melting. Hyeja wiped her wet hands on her clothes, stamped the snow from her feet, and returned inside. Her room and the veranda were in utter chaos, and it seemed she was always stepping on a water glass, a rag, a transistor radio, her pajamas, and other such things. It was only natural. She had returned home a week earlier and hadn't tended to the house since. Of course she cooked to satisfy her malignant hunger, but the dirty dishes would be shoved aside. She would fill the bathtub and soak for hours, until the hot water cooled, chilling her, and then, without bothering to dress, she would pace the darkened veranda. Two days earlier she had spent much of the day gazing at her daughter's yellow, flower-shaped hairpin, which she had found in a crack in the concrete patio out back. The girl, now in her last year of middle school, was long past the age of using such hairpins.

Her mother-in-law had lived here until the month before, looking after Hyeja's husband and the two children. But now the house was empty except for Hyeja's belongings. What to do with Hyeja when she comes home from the hospital? There must have been a lot of discussion and thought. And finally her husband had made a clean break, removing her name from the family register and turning over the house to her—a rather unusual display of concern on his part. "I'll be moving out before too long," he had told her after the doctor said she was ready for discharge. "One option, if you don't want to go back to the house, is to sell it and get yourself a small apartment. Coming from me, maybe that idea doesn't appeal to you, but an apartment would have its advantages. And you could stay with your family till the house is sold. . . ." Hyeja hadn't seen him since. In any event, for an ex-husband, he had sounded considerate. Technically she had initiated the divorce, and he tended to agree it was unavoidable. But while she was in the hospital? That seemed to have pained him.

Hyeja had returned to this house, though, as soon as she was discharged. Humans are forgetful creatures, the doctor had said. She was completely healthy, mentally and physically. She could live a full life, like she had before. And she shouldn't be afraid; that was the most important thing. As if resting after a long journey, she felt extremely lazy. Now and then she was startled into a sense of reality by the sound of the telephone and the voices of people seeking her departed husband and children. "No, they're not here, they moved. . . . I don't know." Curt, blunt responses and the conversation was over, after which she would frantically rummage through the house for some trace of them. It was as if she wanted to obliterate all the time she had been away. The stickers on the wall, the long, black strands of glossy hair in the hairbrush, the handkerchief with the embroidered corner—she discovered these and other traces, but all they did was make her powerfully, vividly aware of the enormous gap that now separated her from them. They wouldn't be coming back, and she could never recover the hours she'd been away from them. Hadn't they been capable of the stronger ties that a deeper love offered? Even if they couldn't conceal from each other the shame and fear that lurked persistently in the depths of their hearts? After scouring the house one last time she had clasped her arms about her upraised knees and silently sobbed. After she had cried herself to exhaustion, she felt a gentle gnawing in her empty stomach. That familiar hunger was like an old friend who had come to comfort her.

The doorbell jarred Hyeja awake. Her late lunch of cold rice mixed with spicy pepper paste had been followed by a short nap. Who could it be? Confused and startled, she opened the door to the veranda just as the bell rang again. "Registered mail! Your seal, please!" The mailman's cap was visible above the iron gate. Flustered by the mailman's insistence, doubting that anyone could have sent her a registered letter, she opened the vanity drawers in succession from force of habit. Most were empty, and sure enough, her seal wasn't there. "I don't have it!" Hyeja shouted in agitation toward the gate. "For god's sake, then use your thumb!" came the response.

The letter was for Hyeja's tenant. There was no sign of life from across the yard, and the young woman's kitchen door, which gave access to her room, was padlocked. Hyeja pushed the kitchen window open, deposited the letter, and went back inside. As she steadied her pounding heart, her hand stopped in the act of closing the yawning drawers of the vanity. There it was, her little appointment book, long forgotten but certainly hers, smudged by her own hands. She fished it out and hastily turned the pages. "29th: Tŏksu Palace"; "dry-clean winter suit"; "16th: 3 P.M., Araya"; "Shinsegye, Bargain Sale, 15th–21st, woolen shirt & vest"—among these notes were items faintly remembered but many she couldn't recall. "3rd: Umi Florist, flower basket, mixed carnations X 60"—a gift for a teacher's sixtieth-birthday celebration? Sometimes smiling, sometimes frowning as she searched her memory, Hyeja read the entries one by one. And then in back, a column of telephone numbers, those of her college classmates. They were members of a circle, friends who met once a month, women she felt comparatively close to. Why hadn't she thought of them? Finally, something to do. She began quickly to dial. First the editorial offices at the women's magazine where Sukcha worked. But Sukcha had long since left, she was informed. Then Aegyŏng's house. "The number you have dialed is out of service; please check the number and try again." She examined the arabic numerals and redialed. Same result. It was strange. She felt bewitched. Myŏnghwa's telephone rang incessantly—no answer. Patiently she dialed Ch'unja at home. "Not at this number anymore," a voice answered curtly before disconnecting. Hyeja replaced the receiver and let her mind go blank, oppressed for the first time by the enormous reality of the two years she had lost. She felt bitter and betrayed.

This'll be the last one, she swore to herself, and like a gambler staking her destiny on her last card, she dialed the fifth number with grim determination. She heard ringing and then "Hello," and immediately Chŏngok's face rose before her. She forced herself to speak slowly: "Chŏngok? It's me, Hyeja." "Oh, my goodness! My goodness!" This ambiguous exclamation was followed by silence. Hyeja imagined a terrified look on Chŏngok's face, the look of someone who had received a call from the dead. "It's been a long time." "It really has. How is your health?" Chŏngok finally added, still flustered. "Where are you?" "I'm home now. How are the others doing? I haven't been able to reach anybody." "Well, that's understandable—a lot of us have moved."

Hyeja told her friend she would like to see her. There was a brief pause. "Well, as it turns out, we're throwing a farewell party for Pongsŏn. She's going overseas with her husband. Remember the Sky Lounge on the thirteenth floor of the Kolon Building, in Kwanggyo? We're meeting there at seven o'clock. Everyone'll be happy to see you."

Next, Hyeja telephoned the puppet center. Min, her teacher there, made puppets, but he also played an important role in puppet theater. He had produced puppet shows on television—*The Scarlet Hat* and *Master Sun and Mistress Moon*—using puppets Hyeja had made. Back then Min had praised the originality of her conceptions and the puppets' lifelike expressions. He had piqued her interest by suggesting she hold an exhibition. But now Hyeja discovered that in Min's case as well, the two years had made a difference. Though she gave her full name when he answered—Kim Hyeja—Min failed to make the connection. She had to explain she was the creator of the puppets in *The Scarlet Hat* and *Master Sun and Mistress Moon*, and finally Min uttered a faint exclamation. He then slipped immediately into his usual tone: "It's been a while, hasn't it. How have you been?" He must have known all about it, too. Among the people who knew "how she had been," she had no doubt been fodder for dozens of stale conversations. "How is your health?" he asked. "Couldn't be better. Are you still doing puppet shows?" She wished to talk at great length. He'd been kind to her; he'd liked her puppets. "Why don't you come around sometime when you're free," he suggested. She wanted to say she could see him right then, that she had three or four hours till her dinner appointment, but she reluctantly set down the receiver, tempering her regret with the realization that he was perpetually busy. He was so taken with his work that he was still single in his forties, writing books about puppet shows and rushing from little theaters to grade-school auditoriums to broadcasting stations. Even so, he wouldn't have forgotten his interest in displaying her puppets. He wouldn't have forgotten his suggestion that she hold an exhibition and do a puppet show in the exhibition hall itself. She had to see him, the following day if possible. She could resume making puppets. With her puppet shows she could tour schools on remote islands and other out-of-the-way places. And if she supplied each of the schools with a set of puppets from the show at a low price, then the children could set up little theaters at home and have their own puppet shows. Wouldn't that be fun. This was exactly the kind of meaningful work she wanted, and she could earn a bit of money doing it. It would be a wonderful thing to do, and it made perfect sense. If she could live on her own earnings, she would for the first time be independent, would have an existence genuinely her own. Determined to begin creating puppets again, she felt a sudden burst of vitality. And then she scolded herself relentlessly for the disgraceful life she had led, a life that had been parasitic, pure and simple. That evening she would tell her friends what she was doing now. She would tell them her rosy plans for the future. After all, did any of them know as much about puppets and puppet shows as she did? It wouldn't be stretching the truth to talk about the exhibit she'd do with Min, her teacher, and about the touring performances. True, they hadn't been arranged, but they would be sooner or later, she was sure of it. Hadn't Min always shown an interest in her puppets? Maybe it was all in her mind, that business about herself being the focus of repeated conversations among her friends. And Min's initial failure to recognize her on the phone, the electric shock of recognition, the evasiveness she had read into his vague invitation to visit—wasn't she acting out some sort of victimization complex? Other people don't have as much interest in us as we think they do, her doctor had said. And they don't remember us for as long as we think they should. To Min and her friends, the story about her was merely a single short column buried in the evening newspaper one summer day two years before. Had they spent the last two years making sure they remembered this unfortunate incident involving an acquaintance of theirs? Of course not. While they were raising children, accumulating property, and clutching greedily for some joy in their lives, she had been killing time with endlessly tedious games of cat's-cradle, sitting in the sun from one to three in the afternoon, enduring those stupid question-and-answer sessions with her doctor, and all the while cherishing a desire to put that incident out of her mind. Instead of following her husband's suggestion to change her surroundings she had returned home. And a very good thing it was. If not for the solitude of the empty house, if not for the despair of being alone, would she have thought of resuming her work with puppets? Would she have turned up that little address book?

Hyeja went up to the attic, to the corner where she had moved the huge trunk in which she had packed her work things. Her basement workshop had been filled with odds and ends and locked up.

Thick dust coated the trunk. The ornamental lock had rusted, but it was open. And there, under a single sheet of newspaper, were her things, just as she had left them. Sections of wire mesh of various thicknesses, tubes of hardened adhesive, dyed feathers, a handful of sparkle, the faces of the weaver and the herdsman, and the unfinished winged clothes of the fairy. Strangely, she felt pangs of sorrow as one by one she uncovered these things lying silently like ashes in the trunk she herself had closed and no one had opened. And when she had brought them all into view, the heads, arms, and legs, the remnants of fabric for the various costumes—all of it swept haphazardly into the trunk—another layer of newspaper appeared. She closed her eyes and took a deep breath. She knew all too well what lay hidden there at the bottom, entrenched like a rock in the depths of her bosom. It was her last creation, the lovely princess, sunk deep in a century-long slumber from which she couldn't awaken. Hyeja had dressed her, was ironing her gorgeous dress one last time—and then it had happened. With trembling hands she removed the newspaper, and there was the face of the princess, lush hair streaming proudly through her coronet. There was her body. And there in her gorgeous costume, like so many severed links of a chain, were the glittering, golden remains of moths.

The snow had dwindled to flurries and the distant skies were clearing in spite of the approaching dusk. It was four o'clock. Plenty of time until Hyeja's meeting with her friends, but she began to prepare. She couldn't deny the joy and excitement she felt at the prospect of leaving this house where loneliness settled along with the night. She washed her face, then took her time with makeup. At night there was no problem if it was a bit thick. Besides, wasn't this the night she'd finally see her best friends, people to whom her outward appearance didn't matter? She flung open her wardrobe and one by one inspected the clothes on their hangers, but found nothing she cared to go out in. She hadn't tried on those clothes for two years, and she'd gained an enormous amount of weight. She would have been the first to admit that their shapes and colors weren't suitable, but what really depressed her, after she had tried on practically all of them, was not being able to button a single one. Finally she came across something that fit, a sack dress that had been fashionable a decade earlier. It had been made for her, a loose black velvet dress with a great white collar, a dress that fell like a cape from her shoulders. The times she wore it outside the house to meet her husband after work, he had said she looked like quite the little girl—implying that she was too old for it. He was particular about what she wore. And Hyeja, who followed new fashions closely, had soon stopped wearing it. She realized now how much heavier she was, for the dress confined her as if she actually were inside a sack. She gathered her long hair in a clasp and then looked in the mirror. The person she saw resembled a silent-movie actress.

The glass door to the veranda rattled open and in came the voice of Hyeja's tenant: "Auntie, I'm going out. Could you please close my coal duct a little later?" Apparently she'd returned while Hyeja had been rummaging through the trunk. Hyeja scowled toward the front gate as she heard it open and shut. The young woman had said she worked at a factory where she had day shift one day and night shift the next, but as far as Hyeja could tell, she'd brought a man home three times in the past week. "That's no good—I should get rid of her," she muttered decisively. "I have better things to do than tend coal for that slut. Ought to tell her I'm selling the house and ask her to vacate, ought to do it right away, tomorrow."

Hyeja waited until five o'clock, then donned her coat and left. Even with the snow slowing down traffic, she could get to the meeting place in thirty or forty minutes. Still, she left hurriedly, as if being ushered out of her empty house by the gathering darkness.

Deposited by the bus on the broad avenue of Chongno with plenty of time to spare, Hyeja descended into the pedestrian underpass that crossed to the other side. The poorly ventilated passage stank, and was slushy with tracked-in snow. The subway rumbled underfoot. To the busy stream of people beneath the pale lights Hyeja gave unguarded looks as she slowly walked along.

The snow had stopped for good, and the darkening streets were windy. At the underpass exit Hyeja took a deep breath and gained her bearings. She hadn't been downtown in a long while, but her mental map was clear. As she set off, she glimpsed the frozen fountain near the clock tower, which read five-forty, and next to the fountain the giant Christmas tree, whose tiny lights were just starting to twinkle. And then, floating hazily in the distance beyond the tree with its coat of pure white were the lights of the Sky Lounge on the thirteenth floor of the Kolon Building. There were no crosswalks, which meant three more underpasses to negotiate. She had more than enough time, though. Should she arrive early and sit there all by herself? No, that wouldn't look good. As she scanned the surroundings for a place to thaw out over coffee, her gaze settled on a brown building across the street and to the left. At that very instant, the Kolon Building, the large tree with its blinking lights, and all the rest were swept from her field of vision. She saw nothing but that fifteen-story building in which every window was lit. Why hadn't she thought of that? It had never occurred to her, when Chŏngok had mentioned the Kolon Building, that her own husband worked across the street. Gently chiding herself, she quickly reentered the underpass. Most likely he was still in his office; he always worked late. And hadn't he always encouraged her to come to him with any problems? For two people who had been closer to each other than anyone else for such a long period of their lives, what could be so bothersome or complicating about sharing a hot cup of coffee on a cold day? If people begrudged each other such simple contacts, what would that say about their lives, and how could they possibly get along with others? What's more, wasn't she off to a fresh start, full of marvelous plans? If she could resume her work right away, perhaps with her teacher, Min, a man who was unrivaled in the world of puppet shows, it would make even her husband a believer.

Her monologue came to an end when the elevator reached the fifth floor and the Yŏng'u Trading Company, which also occupied the sixth and seventh floors. The custodian intercepted her. "What can I do for you, ma'am?" Hyeja hesitated at this unanticipated obstacle, but quickly gathered herself. "I'd like to see the head of the planning office." The custodian picked up the intercom. "Who did you say you were?" he asked while waiting to be connected. "Tell him it's his wife." The young custodian cocked his head skeptically and scrutinized Hyeja, then handed her the receiver. "Manager, planning office." The resounding voice filled the handset, as if the man were right beside her. "Is that . . . you? It's me, Yŏngsŏn's mom," Hyeja stammered, suddenly intimidated by the placid, oddly unfamiliar voice.

"Who's calling? This is the manager of the planning office, but . . . I wonder if it's Manager Yi Kidŏk you're looking for." "Yes, could I have Yi Kidŏk, please? This is his wife." Hyeja's flustered response brought a low exclamation from the other end. "This is Yi Kunho. One moment, please, and I'll be right out." Presently, from the hallway to the left there appeared a tall, slender man. He'd lost a lot of hair and now wore glasses, but Hyeja recognized him at once: Yi Kunho, who'd joined the company at the same time as her husband and was quite close to him. He'd married late, and until then he had always been able to count on a bed at their house if he was too drunk to go home. Hyeja was guided to a small reception room, where two people were talking. They left at once, and the room fell quiet except for the hiss of the steam heat. Sensing in her counterpart an extreme discomfort that perplexed her, Hyeja glanced about the stark room, which contained a table and a few chairs. After requesting coffee over the intercom Yi Kunho finally said, "You look a lot better. How is your health?" Everyone asked about her health. "Is the gunpowder in a safe place?" was how it sounded to her. Hyeja smiled but said nothing. "How are you getting along?" "I've started working." "Well, that's good to hear. May I ask what kind of work?" "Sure. It's related to puppet shows. Also, I'm thinking about moving. I remembered what he told me—you know, about how a change of scenery might be a good thing? But I guess he's not at his desk?" Hyeja ventured a smile. A look of surprise creased Yi's brow. "You didn't know?" A young woman in a short-sleeved sweater arrived with the coffee and set it on the table. Silently Yi added sugar to his cup and began slowly to stir. "Didn't know what?" "He's at the New York office. It's been a month now." Hyeja found her gaze riveted on the scarlet imprint of her lips on the cup from which she had just drank. The room was so hot! Her undergarments were sweaty. And her tight-fitting clothes constricted her, made her feel choked. She unbuttoned her coat and her flesh spilled over the collar of the cramped velvet dress. She produced her handkerchief and dabbed at her face and neck, leaving thick smudges of powder, rouge, and eye shadow on the white cloth. She was embarrassed to admit it, but her makeup was too thick. "He took the children, figures to be there about three years. I'm not quite sure, but maybe he didn't tell you out of concern for opening old wounds." "It's all right. I was on my way somewhere and just . . . stopped by. He said I was always welcome to drop in and talk things over. . . . I'd better be on my way," she said in a dull tone, distracted by the suffocating sensation, the perspiration streaming inside her clothes, and the air in the room, which seemed filthy and stuffy. She rose heavily. "Are you all right? You don't look well," Yi said solicitously, noticing her pale, sweaty face. "I feel kind of hot. Thank you for your time—I know you're busy. And I appreciate your kindness." The elevator door closed on Yi's politely bowing form and she began silently to weep.

The electronic display on the clock tower read seven-twenty. Twenty minutes past the appointed hour and not one familiar face had appeared. From her window seat Hyeja could track the flow of time, second by second, for the clock tower was directly across from her. In the deepening dusk, the Christmas tree lights grew distinct and the lights of the city blossomed in profound splendor. Seven-thirty came and went. The lounge, quiet at first, was now almost full, and with every opening and closing of the door Hyeja shot an anxious look toward the entrance. Was it possible they didn't recognize her? She really did look different from before. So different she scarcely recognized the face imprinted like a negative on the window with its dark background. Desperate for people and the world to forget what she had done, she had worked hard to change her appearance. She had gained weight with the help of the hunger and the hellish sleep that was regularly induced through a regimen of medication and injections, and she had let her hair grow out. Her hair had grown light gray, something Hyeja didn't realize until the woman who shared her sickroom accused her of stealing a hairpin, attacked her, and plucked out a handful. Hyeja moved nearer to the entrance, where she could be seen more easily, and ordered a gin and tonic. An hour had passed. The lounge was well heated and remained warm in its tight glass envelope. Hyeja removed her coat and placed it over a chair, and discreetly undid the buttons at her throat and chest so she could breathe more easily.

A thin slice of lemon and a scarlet cherry floated in the transparent, ice-filled glass in front of her. The drink tasted like sour water, and it made her want to pucker up and spit. The Western saying "Looks good, tastes good" wasn't very apt, she thought as she forlornly watched the floating ice cubes shrink. Presently they melted away and the lemon taste grew suspiciously weak. Her hopes that the others would appear grew fainter. Nine o'clock passed, and as she ordered another gin and tonic she was seized by a doubt that seemed all too real: Had she misunderstood the time and place of the gathering? In her desperation to go out, had she somehow convinced herself that today was the date when in fact it was tomorrow or the day after? It was a lonely business staring at the ice cubes clinking against the glass before disappearing. Staring and waiting. And when ten o'clock arrived and she ordered yet another gin and tonic, the young waiter looked askance at her as if she were a phantom, this obese woman with long, wiry, gray hair tumbling over a broad, white collar that resembled the ribbed semicircle of a folding fan. They weren't coming, she was sure of it. An intense rage came over her. Knowing she would appear at their gathering, they had changed the meeting place—no doubt about it. They were sitting somewhere nearby pointing at her, whispering about her as she sat, all too visible through the window, sick and tired of waiting. "God, she actually called me. She said she tried the rest of you, too. Consider yourselves lucky you missed her." "That man died, and she's running free? But what for? I mean, she's practically an *invalid.*" Hyeja covered her ears, as if actually hearing these voices. "Self-defense, huh? Well, whatever she wants to call it, it happened." "Is it true he divorced her? Well, I can believe it. How could a person live with someone like that? I'd be scared." "Is *that* what you call being loyal to your husband?" "Maybe she lost her head—I'll bet she was terrified." "That's probably why she ended up in a mental hospital." When Hyeja recalled what others had said and then read between the lines, it was always a *man* that was killed, not a burglar. Even her husband. He'd kept trying to find out if the man really was a burglar. Maybe the man didn't have a relationship with her, but wasn't he at least a casual acquaintance? Her husband had been skillfully circuitous but wouldn't give up. "I never saw him before," she had said. "Do you want to know what I was doing? *This* is what I was doing, just like you see here. Now will you please leave me alone? What do you want, anyway?" These thoughts, thousands of times recalled, she repeated to herself, and as she did so she clamped her mouth shut and cried. The fact that she had been wearing only a slip and the man hadn't been armed had left lingering doubts.

Hyeja suddenly realized all was quiet. She looked around. The lounge was deserted except for a couple sitting at a window table, foreheads touching. The waiter produced a great yawn as he leaned against the bar watching Hyeja. The clock on the tower read eleven.

The subway rumbled beneath Hyeja's feet before rolling into the deep of the night. Not much sign of life in the underpasses, just the slush underfoot, and everywhere the stink. The same three underpasses to negotiate, and when

Hyeja rose to the surface she gazed up at the wind-swept heavens. An uncertain number of stars twinkled dimly in the misty air.

Hyeja had just climbed the last step out of the underpass when she bumped her knee against something and lost her balance. Coins clinked and scattered at her feet. The fluorescent light was out and the opening to the underpass was dark. Instinctively she stooped over and looked down. She had tripped over someone hunched up in a blanket and had kicked over a tin bowl. "I'm sorry," she hastened to say. "I've got something on my mind and I just—" Then she realized that the woman beneath the blanket with the sleeping child in her arms was blind. Eyes downcast, chin lifted, the woman extended a hand, groped for the scattered coins, gathered them in. Hyeja bent over to help and managed in the dim light to pick up the coins that had fallen to the steps. She was about to place them in the bowl when the woman's hand shot out and seized her wrist. The strength and tenacity of her grip startled Hyeja. The hand didn't release its painful, lurching hold until the woman was sure every last coin had been shaken free from Hyeja's palm. Hyeja gazed at the woman as she massaged her stinging wrist. The woman curled back into a ball beneath the blanket, perhaps to sleep, perhaps to doze. You thought I was going to take that money? Well, it's mostly my fault, not watching where I was going and walking right into you. The wind buffeted the opening to the underpass with a chill ferocity. Hyeja hunkered down beside the woman. The Christmas tree next to the frozen fountain continued its lonely blinking. The clock tower read eleven-thirty. "Aren't you cold? Have you eaten? Look how sound asleep your baby is! Don't you want to go home now? It's supposed to get colder." The woman gave no reply. "Where are you staying? Why don't I help you across the street? You don't want to go to sleep out here and freeze to death. Especially with your baby . . ." But as Hyeja gently lifted the quilt her hand was slapped. The woman's eyes glared. "Fucking leech—don't you have anything better to do than bother me! Go home, wash your feet, and go to bed, you hen!" Bloodshot eyes gazing furiously at Hyeja, the woman clutched her child, took up her bowl, marched a few steps lower, and plumped herself down. Frightened, Hyeja hurried off.

The wind blew stronger. People raised their collars and scurried along or else chased down taxis. On which side of the street was that taxi stand where she used to catch cabs to her neighborhood? Hyeja had walked only the distance between two bus stops when she noticed that almost everyone was gone. Vehicles sped past. No taxis waited, headlights off, even at the taxi stands. How to get home? She didn't have a clue. But what troubled Hyeja the most was the hunger tearing at her stomach. Only those three watery gin and tonics since lunch, and it was vexing to think that their sourish, puckery taste was stimulating her appetite. As always when she was hungry, Hyeja's mouth watered for a heaping bowl of white rice; seafish swabbed in oil and grilled; piping hot fried scallion cakes; and all the rest. It had been the same at the hospital: perpetual hunger. Once her daughter had brought a warmer full of grilled chicken. How the girl in her dazzling white summer hat had cried as she watched Hyeja devour the food. "Mommy, forgive us. What we did was a crime," she said before offering a short goodbye and leaving. Hyeja hadn't seen her since. But now, if she could just eat something, it didn't matter what . . . If she could just put it in her mouth, just a bite . . . There would be plenty of time later to think about getting home.

Clutching her belly and looking about, Hyeja finally spied a streetside snack-wagon, its canvas curtains brightly lit from inside. She entered. A woman was putting away knives, cutting boards, saucepans.

"Could I have something to eat? Anything you've got—I'm really hungry."

Startled by Hyeja's abruptness, the woman observed her before silently serving up two skewers of fish cakes along with soup.

"That's all there is. I'm out of everything else. I was just about to go home. . . ."

The fish cakes were gone in an instant. The woman ladled out more soup and Hyeja took it in a gulp, then held out her bowl again while wiping her mouth. The woman apologetically waved her hand no. She obviously pitied Hyeja. "All that's left is *soju*—really." The woman uncapped a bottle with her teeth, and Hyeja accepted it, paid, and left.

Hyeja kept to the old palace's stone wall, which angled away from the street. It was like walking in a dream, quiet except for the slow fall of her feet. The alcohol gently warmed her stomach. Unbelievably, her hunger had vanished. With every gust of wind, the ancient trees inside the mossy stone wall threw back their manes and wailed. Hyeja stopped every few steps to let more *soju* trickle into her mouth. She had once tried on thick glasses, and now, as then, the ground seemed to fall away under her feet. "You broke your promise," Hyeja said aloud. These were the heartfelt words she had shouted tearfully in her childhood when she was left all alone by playmates who abandoned her and went home without a word of explanation other than saying that they were tired of playing house; or when they played hide-and-seek and she was "it" and they hid in a place where she couldn't possibly find them and never came out, or else called off the game without telling her.

Again she cursed her liar of a daughter, who had bloomed more lovely with each new day, even when she cried and said, "I can't believe we put you in this place; I can't believe we have to live like this; I wish I were dead." Yes, her husband and children had left her all alone in an empty house and gone their merry way. Just like those faithless little creatures of her childhood.

Where would this street beside the stone wall lead? Her dream of the previous evening suddenly returned to her. Was *this* the street she walked in her dreams? Although she knew there would be a sign for her in a crevice among the crumbling stones, the memory of waking in distress from those dreams made her anxious. Hyeja tilted the bottle of *soju* and the liquid gurgled down her throat. She drank it all at once, as if it were a wonder drug in a dream from which she would never awaken. "You all think I'm a murderer, you're watching for me, you're avoiding me. . . ." She said this in a loud voice and with a grand gesture hurled the empty bottle with all her might. "Anyone else would have done the same thing. What was I supposed to do?" On that day, Hyeja had been making dolls in her basement workshop as she always did after the children left for school. It was a sweltering summer day, she had turned on the hotplate to melt some oxhide glue, and the basement felt like a steamer. The front gate was locked, she expected no visitors, and she was working in her slip. She had finished the complicated process of attaching the sleeping princess's hair and accessories and was intent on adding the finishing touches when she saw the man standing in the doorway. There had been no sound of his entry. What she had seen then was not the man's face but her own nearly naked body. It was pure terror, though, that had caused her to plunge the hot soldering iron into the man's eyes as he approached.

The alcohol made Hyeja feel as if something were blooming from her body as she swayed down the street. Looking straight ahead, she passed her hand along the stone wall, searching the crevices of the crumbling stones for a token of that pledge of love, that hidden, secret promise of her dream. But then she heard a murmuring in her ear: "They've all forgotten you and there's nothing you can do, is there? And even if you hadn't stuck him with that soldering iron, you wouldn't be any better off than you are now." She vaguely realized that the place where this street ended, this street along the stone wall that she had visited in her dreams, was merely the desolate present of wakefulness. But still Hyeja moved, one step at a time, deeper into the darkness, her blossoming body telling her the street would never end.

Translated by Bruce and Ju-Chan Fulton

21. CH'OE YUN

Ch'oe Yun was born in Seoul in 1953. She studied Korean literature at Sogang University in Seoul, obtained a doctorate in French literature at Provence University in France, and then returned to Seoul to teach at Sogang. She began her literary career as a critic and made her fictional debut in 1988 with the novella "Chŏgi sori ŏpshi han chŏm kkonnip i chigo" (trans. 1997–1998 "There a Petal Silently Falls"). She has since published half a dozen volumes of fiction and essays. "Hanak'o nŭn ŏpta" (trans. 1997 "The Last of Hanak'o"), won the 1994 Yi Sang Literature Prize. In addition to her scholarship and creative writing, Ch'oe has partnered Patrick Maurus in a series of well-received translations of contemporary Korean fiction into French.

Ch'oe is a cosmopolitan writer whose stories avoid the tendentiousness of some of her contemporaries in Korea. She writes convincingly from the point of view of both men and women and approaches the upheavals of contemporary Korean history through the eyes of such unconventional protagonists as a riot policeman and an inarticulate laborer. Her characters may unwittingly become involved with political activists or suffer the disastrous results of unswerving devotion to ideology: not just the obvious physical consequences—the deaths, the separation of family members—but also the spiritual losses, the misperceptions bred by absence or silence. In other stories, some of them set as far afield as Venice and Paris, she transcends the historical realities of the post-1945 Korean body politic and comes to grips with the psychological and spiritual state of individual Koreans today.

"The Gray Snowman" (Hoesaek nunsaram) earned her the Tongin Literature Prize in 1992.

THE GRAY SNOWMAN

The events of that period almost twenty years ago have returned to my memory like a stage being lit. I see them first as a somber, bluish green tableau. But then, as if through a window beside the tableau, a warm light emerges. It was a period of confusion. And above all else, suffering. Because it was left unfulfilled? On the other hand, are any of life's stages ever brought to perfection? There are periods in our past that can't be dismissed with a flippant "Oh, *that* time." They may be short, those periods, but they work their influence throughout our lives. Nevertheless, daily life is a powerful healer. Day after day, snow and rain have fallen, flowers have withered and bloomed, and that period has gradually scabbed over, like a wound grown slowly insensible.

We—yes, it's all right now to refer to myself as part of the group—we locked ourselves up evening after evening in that rundown print shop, flush with a fever I didn't understand. It was an ordinary corner print shop on a seedy commercial street on the outskirts of Seoul. We met there every evening for almost three months, they and I tethered to our work, neither of us knowing a thing about the other. Why does the name of that ordinary print shop escape me? It must be selective memory—how else to explain it?

A short article I recently came across in the newspaper has brought back that period to me with the immediacy of yesterday and today. The article was already a couple of days old, and finding it was even more of a coincidence because, sitting in the reference room of the National Library, I was supposed to be looking at the editorial page and not the city pages. I was doing research for a former professor who was writing a book.

I can't say I *read* that short piece. More accurately speaking, my eyes took in the contents, then swept over the words with lightning speed. There, looming huge before me, was my own name. My heart jumped dizzily and for a moment I sat stupefied. As the next shock wave hit, I cautiously scanned my surroundings, but as usual that section of the reference room was nearly vacant. Besides myself there was only the man with glasses who for several days had laid out on the desk before him some sort of statistical data before dozing for half the morning.

And then I read the article in a whisper, my lips moving, as if practicing words of tenderest affection. I read it again and again, as though memorizing a formula that wouldn't register in my mind. This was the article:

> A Korean woman was found dead in New York's Central Park on the 26th. The woman carried a long-expired passport that bore the name Kang Hawŏn, age 41. The Korean Association, however, is questioning her identity. The woman is listed as an illegal alien. An inquest revealed the cause of death to be starvation.

I checked the date of the newspaper, then flipped through the city pages of other dailies. In none of them did I find anything similar. I returned to the page of the newspaper spread out before me. The violent palpitations of my heart eased, and from a place deep inside me there gradually surfaced a peculiar sensation, accompanied by a faint convulsion. At first I felt regret, a long-standing regret, it seemed, for something that could never be repaired. A regret with no concrete object. But nestled in that regret was, paradoxically enough, relief.

If any of the others of us from that period had seen the article, what would his reaction have been? Shouldn't we have been dashing to the telephone and making contact with one another as soon as possible? But perhaps the article had escaped their notice. More likely, I'd long since been forgotten by them. And perhaps, well before the article appeared, they expected that an incident of this sort would happen sooner or later.

In spite of all this, I found myself rummaging quickly through my handbag for my old address book. Their addresses remained, but I had never tried to contact them. In any case, these people's important positions would make it difficult for us to meet, even assuming I could reach them.

With trembling hands I excised the article with the point of my pen, then tucked it away in the address book. I put away the reference materials, packed up my things, and left. The autumn sky was innocently clear.

We were four in number. Why has that word *we* always intimidated and discomfited me? We were not, of course, *we* from the very beginning. And the many people who had known the others in the group would oppose my use of *we*. But I will take the liberty of employing it, regardless of what they think.

What made us *us* was Alexei Astachev's *The Poetics of Violence: Biography of an Unknown Anarchist*. The title of this insignificant book is unimportant, though that title has lingered in my memory. It was a difficult period. I'd completed my first semester at college and was forced by poverty to sell my textbooks in order to buy new books for the following semester. This meant numerous trips to the secondhand bookstores along Ch'ŏnggyech'ŏn. In one of the shops I found this book, whose author I'd never heard of, and obtained it for the price of a meal of instant noodles. That black casebound volume, now dimly distant in my memory, began with a piece of agitation that read something like this: "Comrades, if you have courage, throw away this book that has fettered you; if you are perceptive, read this book and then add it to the fire."

In those days I was intent on collecting banned books that I found at the secondhand bookshops. It gave me the sort of thrill one might get from collecting guns. They were also like money in the bank, something I could sell when I ran out of cash, and because they were fated to leave my rented room someday I read my banned books with a passion. But I was merely an impoverished student during that time, most ordinary and of no account, someone frequenting the secondhand bookshops of Ch'ŏnggyech'ŏn to make ends meet.

I was tormented, in those days, by a fear that someone from my hometown would come and take me back. That would have meant giving up my tiny room, and so I never felt free.

My heart wasn't really in my course work, and because I needed to earn spending money I began tutoring younger children during the day. And till late at night, I would teach older children Korean, English, math—the usual things—and occasionally *"Ich bin, du bist"* or *"Comment allez-vous?"* Though these were languages I'd never studied formally, I'd teach them after a day's brushup; it was a common practice at the time.

I readily took on such jobs as they presented themselves. I knew that I might one day be exposed as incompetent, but my immediate problem was to save up some money. I indulged in only one pleasure: upon returning to my chilly room at night I would smoke, a habit I'd picked up in school.

The following semester I had no luck attracting students to tutor. Even before that semester was over I packed up my texts and walked from my room at the high point of Y Precinct to Ch'ŏnggyech'ŏn. It seemed that money not spent on tutors was not spent on used books either. For there in the corner of one of the shops was a pile of textbooks, unsold, that I had brought in before. It was that very visit that led to my meeting a man I'll simply call An. The bookshop owner gave me a telephone number, saying someone was looking for the book by Alexei Astachev that I had obtained from his shop several months earlier. It was a day of omnipresent gloom, thick as the bottom of a beer bottle. My empty stomach wouldn't sustain me another day, and so I found a pay phone and deposited my last coin.

With certain people it's impossible to tell precisely where they belong, where they come from, what their family background is. . . . I mean those people who pop out of the woodwork right before your eyes, talk nonchalantly about this and that, then disappear from your life. But in contrast with the superficial manner of such people, An introduced himself in more tangible terms. He said he operated a small shop that printed business cards and all sorts of greeting cards, that he enjoyed listening to music, and that Erik Satie was his father. From such particulars I saw nothing in common between us, and I was too burdened by the poverty that was my constant companion to take an interest in his affairs. My knowledge of music was limited to what I heard over the radio, and it took me some two months to realize that the man with the peculiar name whom An had jokingly called his father was actually a French composer. Anyway, I relinquished the book and gained a week's living expenses in return. An slipped the book into his briefcase without even checking the title, then said in a noncommittal tone, "From what I can tell, you're in a tight situation—let's see if there's some work you could do for me."

I wondered what it was that had prompted him to say this. My shabby clothes? My shriveled body, burdened with melancholy since birth? Or perhaps the glint of a thirst hidden deep in my gaze? In those days I could hope for nothing short of a miracle to rescue me, and it didn't matter who the instrument of that miracle might be.

We met again two days later, and from then on I went to his print shop three afternoons a week to do odd jobs. Proofreading, folding printed cards and invitations, and such. From time to time I also delivered orders. Thanks to An I had a place to work and had some variety in my life. But I felt I could never trust a person who said his favorite pastime was listening to music.

Deciding to take the coming semester off, I devoted myself full time to the print shop. Typesetting was added to my odd jobs, and I delivered orders more frequently. There wasn't that much work, and the three other employees left without fail at the end of each workday. By dinnertime I would be wandering the still-unfamiliar streets of Seoul before returning to my room. The coal briquette in my stove had always burned out by the time I got home, which made it a chore to cook. I would take the clothes iron I'd picked up from who knows where, prop it upside down on a few books, toast some cheap bread on it, and make do with that.

There was no doubt in my mind in those days that I would soon be dead. I even imagined the date of my death. I was sure it would be April, maybe in the coming year, maybe in the year after. And since my death would attract no notice, it would be some time before my mother's sister—my only immediately family—was informed. Maybe she would breathe a sigh of relief and say something like, "Poor thing. She runs off with money and look what happens—she couldn't even keep herself alive." When my death approached me in such vivid terms, I looked uneasily about my cramped room but I couldn't bring myself to venture out.

At such moments An's face sometimes appeared. I couldn't help but be startled by this bizarre association. Although it was already several weeks since I'd met An, he rarely appeared at the print shop, and after that first meeting we'd had no opportunity to talk person to person. "You poor kid," I would murmur to myself. "It's because An's the only one who's been kind to you in Seoul." Glancing about the room, I would see on my squat table the thick book written in German by an Italian historian. I had devoted myself to translating it, as if I were composing my last will and testament. A humbling task for someone with no formal training in either Italian or German.

Like the tangled syntax of German, Italian, and Korean, life seemed impossible and unfamiliar to me. My anticipation of death, on the other hand, was quite clear; I could live with it easily enough.

Winter arrived, and the orders for New Year's greeting cards and funeral notices accumulated. I began working late more frequently. A man named Chang, who managed the shop in An's absence, seemed to feel this was a great opportunity to make money by working overtime, but whenever he received a phone call from An he closed the shop at the end of the normal workday and cleared us out. This happened twice or more a week, so to keep up with the orders we had to work on weekends. This was fine with me since I was thankful for a reason to leave my room each day. At work, no one spoke of An, and I couldn't manufacture a way to bring him up in conversation.

The orders for seasonal greeting cards ended, and there followed a winter that was truly difficult to endure. I tried my best to resist the urge to go home and visit my aunt. I felt that once I went back to the countryside, I'd spill out all my bitterness, ask forgiveness, and just plop myself down there. The repetitive work at the print shop was a source of tremendous comfort to me. But when my loneliness became too much to bear, I sought out a friend from back home, a nurse's aide. I found her sick in bed in the very hospital where she worked, and in no condition to ask me how I had been or where I was living. She told me she was recovering from an appendectomy, but as I left the hospital I heard myself mutter, "She's lying; I'll bet she had an abortion." It was then that I realized I had become so impoverished that I believed in no one.

How much of our behavior can be explained logically? It was after ten o'clock by the time I left the hospital, but instead of going home I found myself headed toward the shop. I'd left nothing there, nor did I have work that demanded finishing. The metal screen was down over the front door, but I could see a faint light inside. I grew suspicious, for I distinctly recalled having turned off the light before locking up.

As I approached the back door I heard the sound of a machine. I tugged gently at the small door. The key was in my handbag but I didn't dare try it. Instead, I strained to listen. From the office inside came music and the low-pitched voices of three men. Their murmurs, now muted, now heated, formed a gentle harmony. By listening carefully to the trio I was able to distinguish An's voice, and I forced myself to focus on it. But it wasn't loud enough for me to understand, and its texture was frequently masked by the slightly deeper voice of one of the others.

Needless to say, I didn't knock on the door or call out his name. I just stood there. The steady turning of the printing press, just audible from the front of the shop, sounded like a train approaching from a distance.

It was a month and a half before I was able to sit down with An face to face. He had invited me to dinner, though at the time the invitation seemed more like a summons. It was a simple meal at a Chinese restaurant downtown. The bus we took was packed, making conversation impossible on the way. At the restaurant our surroundings were so noisy and chaotic that I had to shout at the top of my lungs to answer the simplest questions about myself. It was a stunted conversation: at one point An asked where I was from, but I misunderstood the question and in response told him the address of my rented room. Not that I had much to say, but I grew progressively tight-lipped nevertheless, leaving only stupid thoughts such as this to circulate inside my head: *I appreciate your giving me a job, because otherwise I'd have to go back home to my aunt's place branded a thief, and I'd rather die than do that, so there's no telling what kind of trouble you've saved me from.*

The winter air was clear and pure, and cold enough to freeze all the germs in the city. Following An toward the Secret Garden in search of a place where it was easier to talk, I had an urge to tell him things I had never felt before arriving here in Seoul. But as he walked just ahead of me he seemed preoccupied. He is obviously taller, thinner, and older than I am, I thought. But he talks even less. What is there to connect us? I wondered anxiously.

An casually pushed open the door to a bar and entered. What would he tell me? Whatever it is, it'll be a complete shock to me, I thought, something decisive that I'll never forget, something that will change my life all at once. As I followed An through the door it occurred to me that I could simply return to my room. But it was too late. I was enveloped by the warm, dense air inside. So, this is how people forge their destiny, I told myself. Though aware of impending catastrophe, in a momentary lapse people give themselves up passively to some unopposable system, and thereby have the compass of their lives reset. But this passivity is a choice too.

There are certain incongruities to a place that leave their mark in our mind. Take, for example, the beaming face of the actress on the calendar hanging on the wall: she was on the other side of my beer glass, and I couldn't take my eyes from her. Trying to put off the fateful moment I knew was approaching, I watched that empty face until her bright smile looked exaggerated and her gaudy clothes reeked of cheapness. Did people really pin up such photos beside their beds?

"Well, what have you found out so far?" An was so curt I couldn't help flinching at his question. It startled me into silence. "I know you've been checking up on me."

I now understood why An had brought me here. It's true that after that chance nighttime visit to the shop I had gone back, but I had always stayed only long enough to pick out An's voice. I was all the more surprised because I had never been confronted by An or anyone else at that late hour. My face burned with shame. I felt as if I had suddenly bumped into An while lurking in that dark alley outside the shop.

"I'm sorry." My head drooped. The peculiarity of my actions became all too clear to me. I apologized once more.

Arms folded, An solemnly examined my expression.

"Miss Kang, are you sure you can handle the consequences of your curiosity?"

Would he have understood if I had told him that I kept going out at night because death was tempting me, harassing me, that I hovered about the print shop because I had no place else to go, that the sound of his voice from inside the door reassured me? Curiosity was not the issue. But he wouldn't have understood.

"It's . . . not a matter of curiosity," I began.

But I couldn't continue. For some reason I found myself utterly mute. *When you travel at night,* I silently asked, *don't you walk toward light? The light I chose was your shop; why should it be a crime for me to journey there? Don't you sometimes take comfort from something insignificant? Like the sound of someone's voice, or a certain ambience? If I drew a bit of reassurance and comfort from your voice and from envying what you and the others were doing, how could that be a problem for you?* I swallowed, and in doing so swallowed the words that An wouldn't have understood.

His expression still said, "Well?"

"If you want, I'll quit working there."

I looked up at him and for the first time let resentment fill my face. It wasn't hard to imagine how that made him feel, for I had often encountered my twisted visage in the mirror.

"All right, then," he said. Just like that.

Having nothing further to say, I took my handbag and slowly rose.

But before I could leave he added, "Or, maybe you'd like to help us out in the evening?"

I took this as an attempt to lighten the mood. And in fact he was smiling, the whites of his eyes looming large. Some people's eyes are like that, my aunt had told me; I should be careful with such people. An's smile was that of someone who finds himself in a fix. I sat down again.

"Aren't you going to ask what it involves?"

I shook my head. This man wouldn't understand me at all, I kept telling myself.

As we were about to catch the last bus before curfew An handed me a folded sheet of paper.

"Remember the book you sold me? This was inside. I forgot all about it. Better keep an eye on it."

It was a brief note and letter of invitation from my mother, who had left me with my aunt in order to go off to the United States with a man who worked as a chauffeur for the American army. It had arrived after an interval in which there was no word from her. Why the invitation, I don't know. It may have been that the awfulness of the news from our homeland that reached her abroad had reawakened long-dormant maternal sentiments. Or perhaps her living situation had shown a slight improvement. Or else she was being frivolous, well aware I wouldn't be able to go to America. What I had brought with me to Seoul from my hometown were that letter and, unbeknownst to my aunt, the money I had stolen to use for my college tuition. All of that money, to have been used for my uncle's hospital expenses, had come from the sale of family land. The letter had slipped my mind.

It was becoming plainer by the day that school was a pointless luxury. I decided to drop out and be done with it. Having made that decision, I felt more settled. I obtained an application for a leave of absence and gave myself plenty of time to fill it out. There was nothing unusual about this, for me or of course anyone else. It was my second leave of absence from school. Moreover, in the year or more I had been at that school I had met virtually no one. Now, nobody would look for me in the crannies of this huge city of Seoul. Nighttime visits to the print shop became a part of my life, at first irregularly, maybe three or four times a week, and then most every day.

I was still in the habit of aimlessly wandering the streets. That tendency intensified, and I spent the long hours before going to the print shop riding the bus from one end of the line to the other, or else walking most of that distance. I guess this was more a propensity in me than a matter of killing time. It's as if an incurable disease inhabits the rare person who can never settle down in life. I wondered if anyone had walked the ins and outs of Seoul as I had. I felt that by passing a place I'd invested it with a trace of my own life. This city still rebuffed me with the same singular coldness as when I had first stepped off the train here: no matter how I touched, smelled, or desired it, not one person or street accepted me. I seemed to drift over this earth like a spirit with no place to settle. Where had I gone wrong?

But that period of wandering—which appears now through a gloom thick as a liquor bottle's glass bottom—was perhaps the most eventful time of my life. If not for it, there'd really be nothing to say about my life. Because even though it was a period of misunderstanding, uncertainty, and suspicion, for me it was a beginning.

To this day I can't be sure why An invited me to work with him, and without questioning me further. It must have been three months before the disappearance of their Cultural Revolution Association—an underground movement established more than five years earlier—that I decided to join them. I wasn't a confirmed socialist, and although I collected books of that stripe, I wasn't theoretically equipped to comprehend them. Nevertheless, faithful to the employers who provided me my work, I read and proofread the writings they composed and, except for the riskier cases, intermittently took on the chore of distributing them. At a time when any sort of antigovernment movement collapsed as soon as it was uncovered, it was inconceivable to me that their activities had continued for more than five years.

Three people were responsible for the printing: An, Kim, and Chŏng, whom everyone called Scratch Paper because he worked during the day at a precinct office. They mentioned an endless stream of names, but I didn't know and never asked if these were the actual names of real people. An, Chŏng, and Kim existed, and to me that was sufficient. They never tried to exclude me from what they were doing or conceal their methods. We worked together printing and proofreading leaflets that were distributed at demonstration sites and in the countryside. But there was always a distinct distance between me and them. At times I wondered if they felt comfortable with that distance, and I would lose sleep over it for days at a stretch. I made no effort to eliminate that distance between us: life was already more than I could deal with.

One morning in a spasm of activity I rose and sent a letter to my mother in the U.S. There was nothing in particular to occasion this letter. It wasn't that I missed her. But by that particular date I was supposed to complete the application for my passport, something difficult to obtain at the time and possible only if one had a letter of invitation.

> Mother, I turned twenty yesterday. I can't believe it's already twelve years we've been living apart, and four years since you left for America. I hope your work at the stuffed animal factory isn't too difficult. . . .

I had nothing more to write. I didn't give her my address, nor did I mention the passport or what I was doing in Seoul. That evening I silently threw myself into my work at the print shop. The next day I stayed at home. I bundled myself in several layers of thick clothes and spent the entire day in my poorly heated room translating that volume I'd abandoned, the book written in German by an Italian historian. I didn't go to the print shop. More than once, though, I found myself getting up and preparing to go out. Only when the midnight curfew signal was sounded on the radio did I give up. I had not quite three pages of translation to show for my day's work. The night was unusually windy, and for once I wasn't bored by the continual hacking and spitting of the drunks coming up the hill. The more profound the cold, the deeper people seemed to sink into drunkenness.

The following day I went to the print shop a few minutes early and found An waiting alone for his comrades. He immediately demanded to know how he could get in touch with me. My absence the previous evening had held things up, and everyone had been quite worried about me. Something in his tone suggested he wasn't so much worried about me personally as he was slightly mistrustful and anxious. I thought of giving him my landlady's telephone number but didn't want to create problems, and so I gave him my address and left it at that, telling him that since I was a fugitive of sorts he was not, under any circumstances, to pass it on to anyone else. With an expression of disbelief An looked deep into my eyes, trying to interpret my meaning. My situation was very private, I told him. It wasn't important whether he believed me. I guess I wanted to insinuate to these people that in one sense my circumstances were the same as theirs.

Their nightly discussions became gradually lengthier, gradually more intense. I kept my eyes on the proofs and made myself as small as possible in my corner but at the same time listened intently to An and the others. When they vented their impassioned words I tried not to move, often feeling like a piece of needlessly heavy furniture that merely took up a lot of space and was difficult to move around. I tried not to miss a word they said. For the most part they talked about the vulnerability of their group and about their writing.

I knew virtually nothing about their personal lives. From their chats, however, I gradually came to learn various incidentals: Chŏng had recently quit his job at the precinct office, Kim was writing drama criticism, An and Chŏng were from the same province, and An had been expelled from a music school. But that was all. It was only by chance remarks that I learned their ages. An was twenty-seven, Chŏng a year younger, and Kim, who was married with two children, was three years older. There were names they often referred to when problems involving their group came up. Among them was Kim Hŭijin, who seemed to be responsible for a considerable portion of their planning. In fact I had proofread a couple of articles bearing that name on the by-line. Sometime earlier I had developed the habit of trying to imagine the face of the person who had written what I was proofreading. I endowed one person with a long beard, another with a sad, thin face. On rare occasions one or two of these people dropped by the print shop, but of course there was almost never a match with any facet of my imaginings. The rest of the time there were only the four of us at the shop, but my presence doubtless discouraged the others from speaking at length about their private lives.

As I listened to them talk, a slender hope was born inside me, that the business of life didn't have to be as hellish as I made it out to be. I grew more optimistic, thinking I could become one of them by taking a more positive attitude, instead of feeling that with each step I was sinking deeper into quicksand.

Slowly I came to a better understanding of the uses of the printed material with which I worked, and the effects they were meant to achieve. But I was still distant from them, and they were distant from me.

From time to time An would tell me as we left for home, "Miss Kang, you can leave anytime you feel like quitting. I realize we're giving you too much work and not enough compensation." But far from quitting, I would arrive at the print shop before anyone else and keep to my seat until the words "Time to go" dropped from someone's lips. Kim began to tease me with a nickname—The Leech. But none of the three asked me to join them at their meetings. The days passed in this state of uneasy balance.

One day as I returned home late my landlady popped outside all in a tizzy before I could even duck through the small door in the front gate. A policeman had been there, she said. My gaze went to the lock on the wooden door of my kitchen, which gave access to my room, a door I automatically locked before leaving. It didn't seem to have been opened. I sighed with relief and asked the landlady for particulars. All she would tell me was that the policeman would return the following day. With a fearful expression she returned inside, slamming her door.

Should I call An? That might be risky, I decided. I examined my room for anything that might lead someone to the shop. The row of used books against the wall caught my eye. Several of them might attract a policeman's attention, so I hid them in a bundle of clothes in the corner. I checked my watch. Ten minutes until midnight. I gave up on the idea of calling An and plopped myself down on the floor. Since I was away only in the evening, the coal briquettes that heated my floor rarely had time to burn out. I placed my hands and feet beneath my quilt near the firebox and gave myself up to a stream of tears and feelings of fatalism. Lying open on my table was the book that I seemed forever to be translating. Across it crawled a tiny spider.

I took one more look about the room, spread out my bedding, lay down, but couldn't sleep. I tried to think of all the ways my working at the print shop might be discovered. Almost immediately I had to pause. I knew too little about the three who worked there. Weighed down by distrust and regret, I watched the night's layers of darkness present themselves before me. There was no one moment of utter blackness. I saw violet, I saw dark gray. . . . The colors of that anxious night when I awaited the policeman were simply splendid.

To my great surprise, the plainclothes detective who called the next day was merely interested in verifying my identity—part of the process of issuing my long-forgotten passport. Since this was back when authorities would actually interview people when they wanted genuine proof of identity, I took the detective to a hillside tearoom where we could talk. Although I responded calmly enough to his questions, my heart pounded from start to finish. The detective had given my room only a cursory glance, and his questions were routine. I told him I was taking time off from school to visit my mother and was doing occasional tutoring to get by, and that my travel expenses would arrive sooner or later from the U.S. Probably the most unbelievable part of the story, for me, was the idea of actually going to the U.S. to see my mother. But I explained all of this with complete assurance. The detective, neglecting the practice of accepting money for verification of identity, which applied even to persons of spotless reputation, scurried away down the endless slope of the hill.

A month later, passport in hand, I took my mother's letter of invitation and went to the heavily guarded American embassy to complete the visa formalities. Fortunately, because my permanent address was that of my aunt, there was nothing to rouse suspicion, even in the eyes of these officials who were concerned about illegal immigration. And then, as if in revenge for the time and expense I'd wasted, I stuffed the passport into a bundle of odds and ends and returned the banned books to their place against the wall.

Certain nights made me realize that these were dark times for them. Even the theatrical Kim, ordinarily a jokester, would spend the whole evening silent and preoccupied while the others sat around the stove drinking on empty stomachs. Small disagreements developed into arguments, and materials already printed were ripped up. Those were the most difficult moments for me. I could see the others were trying to gauge my reactions, wondering if they could argue openly in my presence. It was an awkward situation: I wouldn't have felt comfortable leaving first when there was nothing to do, and it was impossible for me to ask what was bothering them. Waiting for those tense, anxious moments to pass, I would gaze inattentively at the books I brought to the shop, books I'd been reading in my room to fill the interminable hours of daytime.

Once, Chŏng confronted An about me, suggesting that my participation in their activities put them at risk. An's only reaction was a grin. I wished he had defended me more vigorously, but what could he have said? He knew so little about me.

This was the heyday of government censorship and official investigations, and almost daily the newspapers ran articles about people being arrested and seditious publishing activities being squelched. But only a fraction of these cases were ever reported.

For some time now we had been gathering almost nightly at the print shop to complete a special publication of some three hundred pages. According to the others, two of the authors whose work we had recently typeset had been taken into custody. An urged us on in our work, saying that scarcely a week remained until an absolutely essential conference would be held. Because the work often kept the others at the shop past the midnight curfew, and because someone had to remove any suspicious untidiness by morning, one or two of them regularly spent the night there. Most of the time it was Kim and An. I had never seen them use the phone, but the manuscripts arrived like clockwork nevertheless. After they left my hands as first proofs adorned with my question marks, they returned with corrections and emendations a day or two later, without fail, in a plastic basket.

One night I remained at the print shop after curfew. It seemed the natural thing to do. Chŏng and Kim appeared to have business elsewhere and had turned over their work to me early on. I told An I would finish up and he could leave first, but he replied that he had something to write; he seemed to think it quite normal that I was staying to assist him. I gave the stove a generous helping of coal from the tin bucket. The action seemed so familiar it surprised me: it was as if I were heating a house I had long occupied. An was writing at his metal desk with his back to me. I had been sneaking looks at what he was writing and I wondered how it was developing. I examined his progress with great interest, like someone following the latest episodes of a radio drama. I took the corrected proofs from the plastic basket. The wind whistling beneath the flimsy window had grown colder with the coming of midnight. I opened the stove vent a bit wider, pulled my chair alongside, and sat there with the galley proofs in my lap.

"Miss Kang," he said nonchalantly, without looking up, "don't you think you ought to wash your hands of this work before you get implicated?" For the first time since we'd met a hundred and eleven days ago he was speaking to me in plain speech forms, dropping the polite endings from his verbs.

I looked at him with a blank expression, unsure how to take this. I decided to ignore his remarks and returned to my proofs.

"You ought to resume your studies, find yourself a steady job, and get married."

Perhaps because of the gloom that seemed to emanate from his face I took this banal remark, which I would ordinarily have used as ammunition to put down the speaker, to be a deliberate insult.

"Because once everything blows up, you'll have nothing but trouble ahead of you."

He swiveled around toward me. The stove had just begun to heat up, and I pushed my chair back as I felt the warmth radiate to my face. Was he joking? He didn't seem to be. His exhaustion only served to sharpen the contours of his face. I hardly recognized it. How could the same person's face look so different? I scrutinized him as if he were a stranger I'd encountered late at night.

"Now don't take this the wrong way."

"Mr. An, why are you devoted to something you're so unsure of?"

"It's not me who's unsure. What I mean is, I'm hoping in the near future there will be a lot more people who *are* sure."

We fell silent for a moment. I was of two minds about our rare, whispered conversation. On the one hand I hoped it would long continue, though I didn't care what we talked about, and on the other I wished that gaze, so weary and exhausted, would return to the page in front of him. An stretched his arms, and in a moment everything seemed to return to normal. He turned back to his desk.

"Anyway, once we're done with this particular project, I think it's better if you stay at home until I get in touch with you."

Was this some plan they'd cooked up to get rid of me? True, a girl like me whose background and true colors were uncertain must be troublesome to deal with. But I'd worked faithfully with them until now; what further proof did they need?

"I'll give you a little help with your tuition," he added in a soft tone.

That hurt. Had my life these past few months grown so comfortable that my pride could be injured by this offer of assistance? Even the warmth in his voice seemed to be coming from a cold, calculated distance.

"You don't have to worry about me, Mr. An. I'll soon be leaving the country. I've already arranged for my passport."

My sudden change of tone could well have sounded slightly farcical, but he didn't look up again. Nor did he respond to my words.

Two o'clock passed, and finally An seemed to be done for the night. He turned out the light over his desk, unfolded his army cot, and lay down. I wasn't sleepy. I had work to do, but I didn't want to disturb his sleep, so I added the remaining coal to the stove, narrowed the vent, then lay down on the nearby sofa, which An had left for me because it was more comfortable than the cot. Although I had trouble falling asleep, I tried not to toss and turn or to make noise. I tried to steady my breathing, but this just made me heave great sighs instead. I closed my eyes and imagined I was talking to An: *You don't know a thing about me, Mr. An. I was born in the Ch'ungch'ŏng countryside. We were poor and unhappy. And then my mother went to the city to find work, leaving me with my aunt's family in the country. I guess Mom sent some money for support, but I remained poor and unhappy. I dropped out of middle school, and later took a high school equivalency exam. But none of these stages in my life seems real to me now. Am I the only one who feels this way? That's what I'd like to know. Or do others, even a little? For example, I don't think you feel like this at all—am I right?*

I fell asleep to the sound of An's regular breathing and his tossing and turning. Sometime later I vaguely felt—as if I were dreaming of something from the distant past—the gentle pressure of someone tucking my blanket up to my neck, and then that same person stroking my hollow, emaciated cheek, and I sank briefly into a sound sleep. I seem to remember too that I sobbed as I slept.

For some time there had been more work on weekends than during the week, and so I should have realized that news of a weekend off did not bode well. True, I'd been helping them only slightly more than two months, but during that time I hadn't once spent two consecutive days without working. It's so strange: on the rare occasions that I think back to that time I experience a distortion of my memories. Although we began work around seven in the evening, I harbor the illusion that our labors took place at some dim hour late each night when not just the city but the whole world was asleep. In any case, when they finally gave me a weekend off I convinced myself they had some secret task to do, in which I couldn't be involved. This was the kind of situation where our tacit agreement came into play: I was to help with odd jobs, and was not privy to their internal affairs. And so An gave no explanation. During those two days off I suffered from the doubts and defensiveness that often afflict those who don't belong.

My hillside room was an island threatened by the winter seas, and on that bleak island I waited desperately for a visitor. Only my landlady called. On Saturday evening it snowed, and she knocked at my door, asking me to crush my burned-out coal briquettes and sprinkle the ash on the slippery street. But I had none.

I applied myself to the book I was translating, which lay perpetually open on my table, but before I could finish half a page I was worn out and gave up. I put on my only jacket, stuck my hands in my armpits to keep them warm, and read a book that the three others were always talking about. I don't recall the title or author, but the title of a short piece I wrote after reading it proves that not even a person like me was immune to narcissism: "Reflections on the Non-Historicity of an Alienation Called Poverty." My weekend had gotten off to a slow start. As night set in I started to feel settled. I no longer waited for anyone.

Morning arrived, and I threw off my solitary confinement. To make the time go quickly, I cheerfully cleaned my long-neglected room, then strolled up and down the hilly street, now coated gray with snow, dirt, and ash, whistling as I went. While the faint sunshine sneaked among the clustered plank houses, in a shaded area children with chapped cheeks were making a snowman out of the gray snow. I watched as they made the body, set a round head on top, attached two pieces of rock for eyes, and fashioned a mouth. I thought of the volume we were printing, which was also undergoing finishing touches: early next week we would attach eyes to that book, and a nose. I was seized by a peculiar excitement. Something was missing from the moment. Not people but work. And not just any work, but the work I'd started a few months before. Even though I was an outsider doing odds and ends, I needed the work I did at the print shop, with those three and no one else. When the children had finished the snowman they shouted, "Hurrah!" I removed my muffler and wrapped it around the neck of the gray snowman, who had become quite the stylish fellow with his chopstick mustache. An had given me the muffler one evening when we were short of coal, pulling it from his overcoat and circling it about my neck. I turned away as the children burst out with another "Hurrah!" and I ran all the way up the hill.

I never was able to see that book finished. And I lost forever the opportunity to fit my cherished key in the print shop's worn-out door.

Finally, it was Monday. I left my room even before sundown. I could not show my face at the print shop just anytime I pleased, and so, to pass the hours, I walked the long distance to work. This time I wasn't doing it to save a bus ticket: An and Chŏng were insistent that I avoid encountering those who worked during the day at the print shop, and it wasn't difficult for me to imagine the effect such encounters might have had.

Call it fortune if you will, but I forsook my usual practice of turning down the alley that led to the back door of the print shop. As soon as the entrance came into view in the distance, I saw at once that everything had gone awry. The screen was up, the lights glaring, the glass door wide open. The lower half of the door was shattered; I see it so clearly now, as if in a close-up. People were inside; they looked agitated. Outside the door stood two men in suits, their backs to me, smoking. My heart jumped, then felt like bursting. *Whatever you do,* I told myself, *keep calm and don't bolt away. Don't run, and whatever you do, don't panic; just cross the street. And for heaven's sake, don't look back.* I placed my trembling hands in my pockets, blended with the passersby, and came to a stop at a railroad crossing. The red light seemed to block the way indefinitely. It was already dark, and though I was no longer at risk of being spotted from a distance or pursued, in that short period at the crossing the world seemed to become a den of treacherous informants. At any moment, I felt, someone next to me would cruelly grip my arm and whisper in my ear, "You're Kang Hawŏn, aren't you? Come along, and don't try to resist." I was tempted to look into the faces of those around me, but I managed not to.

I crossed the street, slunk into the nearest alley, and came out on another main street. I reentered an alley . . . and when I had finally convinced myself I was far enough from the print shop I started running. I have no memory of how long I ran or which streets I took. But as I ran I did something I'd never done before: from out of my mouth came something like a prayer, over and over again. "Dear God, let me not be caught here, so that no harm will come to my comrades. I have nothing to lose, but they do. They have much work to do."

In short order I found out from the newspaper that all was lost: the materials we'd been printing for other organizations were confiscated, not to mention the book we'd nearly completed. I read the names of a few of those taken into custody, but there were none I recognized, apart from an author who was familiar from my proofreading. As always with such newspaper articles, this three- or four-line summary of their activities was tucked away where it wouldn't catch most readers' eyes. This did not guarantee that An and the others were safe. But if the names by which I knew them were their real ones, then their capture did not appear in the press.

Anxious days began. My chest pounded at the slightest sound outside my door. It was really very peculiar; it wasn't fear that made my heart pound, but rather the waiting and the longing. More to the point, it was the waiting for An. He was the only person who knew my address. More than that, his appearance one day might mean we could resume our work.

The weather gradually became moderate. I spent several days in bed. I had a temperature but no illness, and there was but one cure—sleep. Now and then my landlady quietly opened the door; she must have been worried. I think she wanted to see if I was dead. I guess I didn't want to disappoint her, for I kept perfectly still whenever she looked in. When my throbbing anticipation turned to resignation, I reached the limits of my suffering. I couldn't bear the certainty that I would never again have the opportunity to work with the others. I felt pangs of guilt and deluded myself into thinking it was my fault that their activities had been thwarted—that I had made a mistake and somehow alerted the authorities.

I roamed the streets. But there was no way I could make contact with them. Nor was there any trace of the few months I had spent with them. Well, there was that used-book shop in Ch'ŏnggyech'ŏn. But it turned out to have changed hands. I also walked by the print shop. But the sign was gone and the shop looked as though it had closed down ages ago and was now off-limits. With no one to make inquiries of, and no place I could phone for information, I ended up back in my room, worn out. But even with a name or a number to call, what could I have done? I was still terrified that through some act of mine they might come to harm. There was no logical possibility of my seeing them again, but stubbornly I waited for one of them to appear.

Several nights later, exhausted though I was from trying to maintain my impoverished body, I woke and rose. I sharpened the blunted feelers of my memory and began to send out signals for anything that could deliver me from despair. But there was no receiver. I opened the notebook on my table and sat down. Mobilizing all of my recollections, I wrote down one by one the titles of the pieces in the book we'd been preparing, essays I'd proofread at least twice. I began to roughly outline their contents, as I remembered them. My memory had mysterious blind spots, but just as often it put on an astonishing display. Occasionally an entire paragraph came back word for word. During that one night I was able to reconstruct three essays, and the preface as well. There were eighteen essays in all, two of them translations. Of those two, I had helped out on one, and I managed to locate a copy of the original in the pile of paper I'd stowed away in a wrapping cloth. It took me all the next day, but I finished that translation. Afraid my resurrected memories would fade, I kept feverishly at my work with scarcely a thought of resting my eyes. A kind of prayer, I guess you could call it. Or perhaps autosuggestion, a superstitious belief that I could signal them as long as my memories were kept fresh.

Perhaps my prayer was answered, even though I was a nonbeliever, for around dinnertime I heard the plank door to my kitchen gently rattle. And then the voice of my landlady, "Student, come out—your cousin's here."

Cousin—my energy drained. I sat still, holding my breath. My landlady's voice, now a murmur, continued from outside. I closed the notebook, then—and I'm not sure why I did this—I fished out my passport from the cloth wrapper and placed it on the table. Inspecting my cramped room, I calmly waited for my visitor to break down the door and enter. Then I heard the voice of a second woman.

"Hawŏn, are you in there?"

The gentle tone almost convinced me that my visitor was a close friend or relative. Still, it was a voice I'd never heard before. I instinctively sensed my visitor was somehow connected with An, the more so since I had no female cousins. I'm not sure what it was about that voice, but I felt as if my last ounce of energy had slipped away. Whether the owner of that voice that had called my name was the bearer of good news or bad, this was no time to hesitate. I opened the door, ushered my visitor inside, and made a show of thanks to my landlady.

"My name is Kim Hŭijin. Mr. An gave me your address and said I should ask your help."

The woman sat down next to me on the floor, gathered her legs to the side, and slumped against the wall. She had with her a good-sized travel bag, and the hand that had set it down looked rough and knotty. That hand spoke of physical and emotional impoverishment. She was pale, but no more so than I. Her face had a chilling beauty that made me feel she had come from a faraway place and would vanish to another. But her expression and general appearance skillfully camouflaged all these things. Her eyes had a feverish glimmer. I could see she was ill, and I placed a pillow behind her back. We observed each other silently. For her this must have been a rare moment of repose. Finally I ventured a question.

"Is everybody safe?"

"Some of them. But our group is pretty much broken up. Everything we were working on was confiscated and everyone's either in custody or a fugitive."

"What about Mr. An?"

Kim Hŭijin's expression turned to utter gloom and she closed her eyes. "I don't know. I just don't know."

In a soft voice she told me about several people she knew. I had met none of them, and most of the names were unfamiliar. I wondered if An had told her anything about me when he gave her my address. But it was enough that he had directed her to me, and almost immediately I felt all of my doubts about him evaporate. In a spirit of deep trust, the kind you would find between longtime friends, she told me of the danger their group was facing. I'm not sure why, but I could not tell her the truth about myself. Instead, I let her believe I had belonged to their group for some time, and at her mention of unfamiliar names or names I had heard only occasionally at best, I put on a concerned look as if they were intimate friends. In fact, in my heart I *was* concerned about them.

After a slight interval I timidly said, "Whenever I heard your name I thought it was a man they were talking about."

This seemed to have reminded her of something.

"Oh, I have a letter for you from Mr. An."

Her tone had a certain uneasiness to it.

From her bag she handed me a thin, sealed envelope with worn edges. Instead of opening it in her presence I impulsively tucked it in my pants pocket and hurried out to the kitchen. The arrival of news, so long in coming, had made me giddy.

I opened the vent to the concrete firebox and put the rice pot on, then cooked stew on the kerosene stove I'd borrowed from my landlady. It seemed an eternity since the aroma of food had last come from my drafty kitchen, and I found myself feeling jumpy. In all the time I had occupied this single room beneath the skies of Seoul, no one had come visiting. I congratulated myself that this first visitor was not my aunt or a relative she had sent. I sat down against the firebox and opened the letter.

Miss Kang,

This will have to be short. I've sent you someone as dear to me as my own self, along with a request for help. For the time being it will be difficult for you and me to meet. To get to the point, I have a very big favor to ask. Could you lend her your passport? It would be a great help. Because of the nature of this re-

quest, I'll understand if you refuse. But I'll say it again: it would be more helpful than anyone could imagine if you agree to it. If you do, I'll leave the rest to you and Kim Hŭijin.

An

Short and to the point—a businesslike letter. I gazed at this letter. Had it really been written by An? It was certainly his handwriting. And did he have the right to ask me such a favor? Yes, he did. Why? But to this I had no answer. Couldn't An have phrased the letter differently? But even if he had, I might very well have been hurt just the same, inconsolably so.

I returned with the meal tray to find Kim Hŭijin half reclining. She sat up and received the tray with trembling arms. We finished the meal in silence. I had eaten meals like this a long, long time ago, silent meals taken late at night, oppression in the air, and I had cautiously observed the weary face across from me. On the other side of the table had been Mom, home from work, her fatigue camouflaged by makeup, and opposite her was myself, no more than eight or nine at the time. But Kim Hŭijin displayed a weariness different from Mother's. Her face had an unusual aura I hadn't recognized till then, an aura I felt she had perseveringly nurtured to resist exhaustion. I wondered if Kim Hŭijin was about as old now as my mother had been back then. No. Kim Hŭijin's face looked much younger. It didn't know how to age.

Whenever I thought of her after that moment, I was seized by a kind of persecution complex. Her face, her bearing, aroused in me something I had to find the words for. And there was nothing so difficult to define as her beauty. She resembled so-and-so, or she looked like such-and-such; no, she had something about her that such comparisons couldn't hope to explain. The only word that occurred to me finally was the simplest of adjectives—*beautiful.* Was this the fantasy of a lonely, immature girl? Certainly it wasn't. Though I hadn't known who was calling me, as soon as I heard the voice outside my door hadn't I produced the passport for her? I would have sheltered her, or anybody else, letter or not. I was sure of it.

"You must have something on your mind, staring at me like that."

I picked up the passport, which I'd pushed to the corner of the table.

"I've been thinking about what to do from now on."

Kim Hŭijin reached across the table toward me. I took her hands without a word. They felt feverish. She gave me a slight squeeze. I released my hands, then enveloped hers with mine. I never asked about her relationship with An.

I sometimes wonder if this thing we call hope is a kind of narcotic. Whatever it is, the person who gets a taste of it ends up unconditionally hooked on it.

Then if her hopes are shattered, she feels the hellish agony addicts experience when the drug wears off. And her anticipation of that agony makes her cling more strongly to her hopes. The day Kim Hŭijin came to my room I watched her weary eyes fall shut and woke up to the fact that I'd long been infected with a hope that was difficult to pinpoint. I knew that in one form or another it would end up guiding me for the rest of my life. Obstinately expectant that my vague hope would be realized, I tended Kim Hŭijin.

She was bedridden from the day she arrived. I nursed her in the evenings and roamed the far reaches of Seoul during the day looking for people who could help her or provide news. But the addresses she gave me were wrong or, with everyone so concerned about the political tensions, I was asked to go away and come by later when things cooled off. There were also times—not so frequent, needless to say—that certain people provided material assistance. In any event, though it was late in the game, I met many people who gave me strength. Through contacting these various people I was able to see Chŏng, who'd been passing anxious days at a tearoom run by a friend of his.

"Who is this! How did you know I was here? Are you by yourself?"

Chŏng looked at me with surprise, more worried than pleased, as if it were my ghost he was seeing. All too clearly I saw in his expression the distrust that can overcome people under these circumstances.

Chŏng's suspicions no longer hurt me, though. What really surprised him was the news that Kim Hŭijin was bedridden in my room. Chŏng too was in seclusion, constantly fearful, and knew absolutely nothing about his friends except that An had escaped to the countryside. I told him the contents of An's letter and Kim Hŭijin's intentions and gave him my passport.

I wasn't sure what connection there was between altering a passport and working at a precinct office, but three days later Chŏng brought the passport back. He'd done a perfect job of replacing my photo with one of Kim Hŭijin. But Chŏng was afraid of handing it over to me and placed it in a drawer instead. We were in a tiny alcove to the rear of the tearoom, and Chŏng was drunk as could be. The hour was late but he kept trying to sit me down so he could rattle on with his griping about An. An had been interested in my passport ever since I started working with them at the print shop, he told me. It had all been planned. Yes it had, I told him—and An and I had done the planning; we'd kept it secret from the start. But Chŏng was too drunk to listen carefully to what I was saying. And he was furious that An was hurrying Kim Hŭijin off to the U.S. so that their problems wouldn't escalate. I waited for him to pass out, and when he started snoring I took the passport from the drawer and started to leave, thankful that he'd obliged me before curfew.

"Hawŏn, I'm sorry!" he called out to my back.

I didn't ask what he was apologizing for and I didn't accept the apology. He'll never understand me and I'll never see him again, I told myself. I felt oddly emotionless.

Kim Hŭijin stayed in my room about three weeks. During that period she slowly recovered and at times she was absorbed in some kind of writing until late at night. When I had time I would sit beside her and continue the job of reconstructing the lost essays.

One night I awakened to a clattering in my kitchen. I opened the door and there she was, scrubbing away at the cupboards and cookstove with a rag. Like a true cousin who from the goodness of her heart had come to help her younger relation clean house, she had rolled up her sleeves and made the kitchen spotless. Hearing me, she turned with a sheepish laugh, like someone caught red-handed in a secret activity. But in that laugh was a hint of a deeper anxiety.

"Don't worry—everything's going to turn out all right," she said.

By then she had returned to a semblance of health. While I made preparations for her trip I vaguely expected An to visit. But that was impossible. The days went by without her ever seeing An or making secret contact with her family in the countryside. The day she left my room, left this city of Seoul, left this nation, she gave me half a dozen letters to mail and her bag, which was full of papers and things.

"Hawŏn, could you take care of this for me? It's some trivial stuff I've written; when the time is right they can see the light of day. I'm sure I'll see you again. And I promise I'll be back."

With the altered passport and the ticket I'd obtained for her she left alone for Kimp'o Airport. For safety's sake I couldn't see her off there.

I spent the days after her departure at home waiting and preparing myself mentally for the arrival of someone, family or otherwise, who would carry me off to the police. But nothing happened to me. I finished reconstructing all the essays and read every last one of the articles Kim Hŭijin had left me, and in all that time no one came knocking at the door of my shabby dwelling. There was no doubt in my mind that Kim Hŭijin had departed safely. Hints of spring were evident, but endless winter was the season of my mind. Not much sunlight reached the neighborhood and the snowman still stood frozen upon the hill. A single postcard arrived, unsigned, bearing no return address:

Miss Kang,
Thank you.

And that was it. Presently I read a rather long article about An's arrest, and then much later an article containing a distorted and exaggerated commentary on the activities of my unnamed colleagues.

I always wanted to write something in the form of a short report about that period, starting out like this: "I can see it now, the gloom of early winter on that endless road. Darkness lay everywhere, like the dense color of a liquor bottle's thick glass bottom, and yet it was during that melancholy journey that I first encountered the word *hope*. . . ." It seems I still hold sacred those thoughts we printed, but I lack the talent to record that period with any precision in writing. More to the point, there's nothing in my existence that could be turned into a story. Who in the world would care about my life, which has been like a bar of the drowsy music An listened to now and then when he worked? An absurd idea.

Even if Kim Hŭijin had tried to make contact with me, it would have been impossible. For I myself left Seoul, telling no one. I dropped out of school once and for all, returned to my aunt's, and for years I helped her with the farm work. At the same time, I ventured into other activities, wanting to share with those around me the color of the hope I had tasted. My life since then has changed little.

Meanwhile, An became well known as a folk artist and activist, speaking out in the media. He gave several lectures in a city not far from the rural area where I live. It's already several years since the one occasion I went to that city, around the time of one of those lectures. I asked the sponsors to give him a bag for me. Although I had highly recommended this lecture to the young people in the village, I returned home once my duty was done. In that bag were the materials Kim Hŭijin had left with me, along with the bundle of articles we'd worked on at the print shop, which I'd managed to reconstruct and hadn't read since. Later I saw some of those pieces in a magazine.

There now remains no physical evidence within my reach that this period of my life ever existed. I take that back. There is one piece of evidence: my unfinished translation of that Italian historian's book written in German. But that translation, my erstwhile remedy for anxiety and solitude, has been stuffed away so long now that the paper has yellowed. And if there's anything to say about that book, it's that perhaps it's been published in a translation by a professional, someone better than I. I've never tried to find out for sure.

After that period I loved a man, the one and only time. But he left me to marry a friend of mine. If I had been him, I would have selected my friend, too. Several years ago I met a professor who had quit teaching and moved to the country to commit his life's work to writing. He was a linguist and said he was preparing a book called *Contemporary Sociolinguistics*. He needed someone who could help him with sources and proofreading, and I went to his house and volunteered. I'm now his assistant, and I go up to Seoul once a week to look up sources for him at the library. But I'm not at all sure when his book will see daylight: the expansive thoughts of this elderly professor only proliferate by the week.

I walked toward the station to catch my train for the countryside. How could the sky in this season be so innocently clear? And how could my suffering during that period be so fresh in my mind? Suffering knows no aging. I guess because our ardent desires to be healed are so fresh and persistent. Shall I gather the neighbor children this winter and build a huge snowman in the fields? We'll fit the head with a long branch, an antenna to send signals to the star of the woman who recently left this world. But wouldn't those children know better than anyone that a person doesn't turn into a star when she dies? Of the person who disappears in pain from our lives, all that is left in the hearts of those of us who knew her is a tiny scar of light.

Translated by Bruce and Ju-Chan Fulton

22. KIM YŎNGHA

Kim Yŏngha was born in 1968 in Seoul and graduated from Yonsei University. His first published work of fiction was "Kŏul e taehan myŏngsang" (1995, Meditation on a mirror). He gained further notice with "Hoch'ul" (1996, Pager), a hit with readers and critics alike and the title story of his first story collection (1997), and with *Na nŭn na rŭl p'agoehal kwŏlli ka itta* (1996, I have the right to destroy myself), his first novel. To date he has published two other story collections and three other novels.

In addition to fiction writing Kim has produced essays and film reviews and is at work on a screenplay. He also hosts a daily radio show devoted to books and authors. He attended the International Writers Workshop at the University of Iowa and has the cosmopolitan, urban outlook of many of his generation. Representative of this outlook are the stories "Sajingwan sarin sakŏn" (1999, trans. 2003 "Photo Shop Murder") and "Ellibeit'ŏ e kkin namja nŭn ŏttŏke toeŏnna" (1999, trans. 2003 "Whatever Happened to the Guy Stuck in the Elevator?"). "Lizard" (Tomabaem) was first published in 1997 in *Hoch'ul.*

LIZARD

I

Kiss the snake on the tongue. If it senses fear it'll devour you instantly. But if you kiss it without fear it'll take you through the garden, through the gate to the other side. Ride the snake to the end of time.

—JIM MORRISON, from the movie *The Doors*

Want to hear the one about the smoke woman? he asks me.

Sure, go ahead.

He's smoking a cigarette. Watching the smoke seep out of his mouth, twist, coil, and drift off.

Okay. One day a man's body turns up. The officer at the scene finds the place littered with cigarette butts. The place reeks of cigarette smoke—it's so strong it covers up the smell of decomposition.

So? . . . I look at him wide-eyed, urging him on.

So how'd he die? Good question. The officer investigates different possibilities. First, he schedules an autopsy. Which is more involved than the usual exam—in an autopsy, you actually cut into the body as well as looking around it for clues. And then the officer discovers something very interesting.

What's that?

The man was naked from the waist down. And there was a large quantity of semen.

I've heard that men ejaculate when they die, I say with a shiver.

He shakes his head.

That's if you're strangled. But there were no signs of strangulation on this guy. If you're strangled, your neck is all black and blue. None of that on him, though.

So? . . .

So the officer starts to suspect there's a woman involved.

He could have been masturbating, you know.

No he couldn't. First of all, nobody dies masturbating. Second, the semen was too spread out. Strange as it all seems.

I know nothing about how men masturbate, but he was so confident in his answer that I had to give in. He's always like that. No doubts about anything. Language seems to come so easy to him. No hesitating, no beating around the bush. Talking to him is like watching a movie or reading a novel. All of a sudden he feels like a stranger. How long has it been since he started coming into my room? How long since he spread himself so naturally over the far corner of my bed? Oh, well. It's all because of the *lizard*. I turned to look at my white walls. They're bare, except for the looming *lizard*.

What are you thinking about? He's noticed I've turned my head.

I look away from the *lizard*.

Nothing.

Men are always asking women what they're thinking. But women don't think the way men do. Men think with their heads, but women think with their bodies. That's why they can't be as articulate as men. Really, it's something that just can't be explained. All I can do is feel the traces of the man and the *lizard*. That's why "Nothing" is the only answer I can come up with.

Go on with the story, I tell him.

But he just offers me a weak smile and shakes his head.

Later.

He dresses and steps out. And off he goes, leaving me with a *lizard*, a dead man, and a large quantity of semen. I have no idea where he's going. He asks no questions, gives no answers.

I first met him in the fall of 1995. It was cold for that time of year, and extremely windy—a street sign blew over on someone's head that day. I was teaching English to junior high kids at a cram school in Kangnam at the time. I was about to photocopy some handouts and in he walked.

Are you still looking for teachers? he asked.

The funny thing was, I'd seen him get out of the elevator and plod up to the door, and still he took me by surprise. Maybe because he didn't look like he had any intention of working at a cram school. What was it about him? He was, after all, wearing the cram-school outfit—navy blue shirt and black pants—so what was it that threw me off?

I guess you could say there was something otherworldly about him. There are people like that. People you bump into on the street and come away feeling like you've bumped into a ghost. People you walk right up to prepared to pass straight through. People who will turn into a heap of ash if you give them a little nudge. You can see them in the subways, too. They look like they've been sitting there for centuries and aren't about to go anywhere.

People who make it seem that the subways will run forever, just for them. There are people like that. And he was one of them.

What do you teach?

Korean.

The way he said it was so awkward it made me doubt for a moment that we even taught it there. Korean . . . Korean . . . I mumbled it over and over on our way to the principal's office. And from that day on he taught Korean.

2

The Indians say the first shaman invented sex. The call him "the one who makes you crazy."

—JIM MORRISON, *The Doors*

You have to transform yourself, he mumbled to me the second time we went drinking. With that, he produced an object wrapped in white paper and placed in on the table.

A present, he said.

I tore the wrapping off, and what I saw made me flinch. A *lizard*. A black metal *lizard*. It was so elaborate that if I hadn't touched it I'd have thought it was real.

Hang it so it looks like it's crawling down your wall. You'll get a rise out of your friends the first time they see it.

I felt a bit leery about all this but put the *lizard* in my handbag nonetheless.

Where'd you buy it?

In the tropics. *Lizards* are as common as ants down there. From the time you're a kid you get used to *lizards* crawling over your belly and your legs. They're everywhere. There's even a *lizard*-worshiping tribe.

Really?

Did you know that a *lizard*'s tail grows back if you cut it off? That's why *lizards* symbolize regeneration and rebirth. People in Europe in the Middle Ages prayed to the salamander. They thought it was a fire-breathing *lizard;* they believed salamanders lived in fire. Chameleons are *lizards* too. *Lizards* have no past. That's what makes them gods. For them there's nothing but the present, an eternal present.

I gave him a long, hard look. I just couldn't figure him out. I'd only been out with him twice, and yet not a word about his past. I couldn't tell you where he'd gone to school, where he was from, or where he'd worked.

We said goodbye and I went home and dutifully studied the walls of my room, which were bare except for a single coat hanger. My friends tell me it doesn't look like a girl's room. Which makes me realize I've never bought anything to decorate it. Not even the standard picture frame. A boring education will do that to you.

I hammered a nail into the wall opposite my bed and hung the *lizard* by the loop in its twisty tail. He was right—it really did look like it was crawling down the wall. And suddenly the wall buzzed with tension.

I saw the *lizard* in my dreams that night. I knew it was supposed to be hanging motionless but there it was crawling down the wall, slow and sinuous, expanding and contracting. The strange thing was, none of this struck me as the least bit extraordinary. It actually made me impatient to see it moving so slowly. I bolted awake and looked at the wall. The *lizard* was hanging there, just where it's supposed to be.

3

The world is a monster of energy, without beginning and without end. This world is a will to power and nothing besides.

—JIM MORRISON, *The Doors*

The *lizard* started coming to me right around the third time he and I went out drinking. I arrived at home that night to discover that the boiler was off and my room was cold. The room looked exactly as it had when I left. When that happens and you live by yourself you lose heart. You come home and open your door hoping for a miracle—but nothing has changed. Then again, it's supposed to be bad luck if you clean your room at night. So I jumped into bed. The alcohol I'd drunk was leaving an uncomfortable path as it spread through my blood vessels. I turned off the lights and stared at the *lizard* hanging on my wall. I played with the idea of giving it a name. But I couldn't come up with anything and in the meantime I drifted off to sleep.

The lizard is creeping down the wall. I can't move. I feel like I'm tied down. I can't make a squeak. There's music. The slow solemn beat of a drum. The rhythm is familiar but I can't place it. The beat is punctuated by a hiss. Is that what it sounds like when the *lizard*'s tongue flickers? I keep my eye on the *lizard*. It's the only thing I can do. The *lizard* is creeping toward my bed. And then he's out of sight. He's entered my blind spot. Now I'm twice as scared. Scared, but excited. The hissing grows louder than the drumbeat. There, the *lizard's* head, at the foot of my bed. Suddenly I'm in a rain forest, still in my bed. There's bright sunlight all around, and birdsong and the distant beating of drums. The lizard has mounted my leg. I feel something I've never felt before, like an electric shock. And then a voice, my father's voice. I can barely hear it. He's speaking very fast. I'm frightened. I've been bad, I tell him. I don't know what I've done but I beg his forgiveness. He's naked and his face is angry as it approaches my bed in the rain forest.

The *lizard* has slithered up my thighs. It's embarrassing having my father there. His face is red with anger. He's going to beat me, I know it. I'm scared. The *lizard* has stopped. Out comes the tongue and it starts licking my thighs. Feels like ice water running down my thighs. Uncomfortably cold, but gently ticklish. In spite of my best intentions the *lizard's* tongue awakens sensations long dormant. Father comes closer, looking back and forth from me to the *lizard*. I can hear my mother's laughter in the distance. She's telling him, See, I told you. I told you she's got spunk. Father doesn't answer.

The *lizard* is moving up. It's reached my vagina. I want to scream. But my father and mother are looking on. Dirty whore. This *lizard* is yours? My father scolds me. I want to defend myself, but the words don't come out. Pleasure overwhelms me.

It's all so strange. Never have I been satisfied by a man. They're either in too much of a hurry or awkward. So sex is always a drag for me. I don't understand how men can be so horny and yet so incapable in bed.

I'm twenty-five and I've slept with three men. The first one was just a boy. He'd kiss like he was trying to suck my tongue out, then tear my clothes off and penetrate me as fast as he could. I guess I should feel grateful he took the time to kiss me. The second one would make a dash for the bathroom to wash himself as soon as he ejaculated. He made me feel as if I had soiled him. And then he'd conk out for the night while the foreign substance was still wiggling inside me. The third one was just plain scared of sex. He'd go through with it, but he obviously wanted to get it over with as soon as possible. He kept asking, did he come too soon, was his penis too small, was I really satisfied? It was so tiresome. No, he never gave me an orgasm, but it would have been worse to disappoint him so I just lied. Oh yes, it was lovely—absolutely wonderful. And then he'd go to sleep. I don't think he really believed me.

But this is different. A sharp wave of pleasure spreads through me. I can't bear it! I don't hear the drumbeat anymore. Can't see Mom or Dad, either. And then I see the face of the man who gave me the *lizard*. He stands there in the dark, a faint shadow, smiling. And then I'm awake. But I still can't move. The sun is coming out. I desperately force my eyes open and stare at the wall. The *lizard* is nowhere in sight. I shake my head violently, trying to clear my head. I feel along the wall for the switch and my eyes return to where the *lizard* should be hanging.

And there it is, exactly where it's supposed to be.

4

I'm a fake hero. A joke that God's played on me.

—JIM MORRISON, *The Doors*

I lost contact with most of my friends the year I taught at the cram school. Most cram school teachers go to work in the afternoon and don't head home until well past midnight. My friends worked different schedules that made it impossible for us to meet. But I was used to odd hours. Father was a minister in a small church, one he had established himself. It was on the third floor in an apartment complex, and none too big—maybe a thousand square feet or so. Mother was busy from sunup to sundown doing the things you would expect a minister's wife to do—keeping in touch with the parishioners, cleaning the sanctuary, helping Father with his sermons, and keeping up with the housework. She was even busier the days there were early-morning and late-night prayer meetings. Father was always somber, Mother was always obedient, I was always bored. We lived in a small room off the sanctuary; I felt like we were surrounded by hymns. Very rarely I'd catch a glimpse of Mother and Father having sex. Father's heavy breathing would wake me and I could hear Mother moaning from somewhere inside the blankets. Her moans sounded like the inarticulate recitations of the parishioners. I never could understand what she was trying to say. Sometimes she'd cry out. When she did that, Father scolded her.

And once in a while he beat her. The house was dirty; or where had she put the sermon? Mother took her beatings silently, the big wooden cross looming over his head.

A large sign hung at the entrance to the sanctuary: *Faith*, *Hope*, *Love*. But neither Mother nor Father seemed to have any hope for me, or faith or love for that matter. I spent my days playing on the swing in the neighborhood playground or poking around the shops nearby. I hated church.

Years went by but Father's church failed to grow. And then Mom disappeared. She left no word, just up and vanished. The parishioners talked about her whenever they could, their gossip revolving about Satan, snakes, and running away. At the time I was in the habit of drawing snakes in my diary. I'd be staring off into space and then realize I'd filled the page with coils of snakes. I'd write *Mommy, I miss you* and decorate the words with writhing reptiles.

Father remarried a churchgoer some ten years his junior and moved the church. I transferred to a university in Seoul, able finally to leave home. I lied to my father when I spoke with him on the phone: Yes, I go to church every day; the minister's sermons are great, they're really inspiring; and I'm in the choir. At school I majored in mathematics. I spent four years struggling with differential calculus and integral calculus. The innocent and straightforward world of mathematics appealed to me. The first midterm I ever took in differential and integral calculus asked me to "prove that 1 is larger than 0." I did it using epsilon and delta. I even managed to produce a complex drawing of a flower as part of a calculus problem. That's how I spent my early twenties, hovering between 1 and 0.

Even now I draw the occasional snake. I was never afraid of them, maybe because I never actually saw one in the flesh. I remember the adults whispering into my young ears that a snake had wrapped itself around my mother. What a joke. I knew what they said was all a lie. I think I was jealous of my mother. I wanted to run away from that church and its oppressive hymns, too. To a place where I wouldn't have a cross looking down on me all the time.

5

The first time I did it, I saw God.

—PAMELA, *The Doors*

The *lizard* entered me a few days after I had that dream. I think it was late in the afternoon and I was sitting in front of the VCR with a cold beer, watching a Hollywood action flick, when I dropped off to sleep.

The dream begins with the *lizard*'s familiar movement. It's darting down the wall. Doesn't scare me one bit. The *lizard* is coming toward the bed. I remember that if you cut off a *lizard's* tail, it starts to grow back right away. I'd like to talk to the *lizard*. The *lizard* climbs onto the bed. Mom is going somewhere. I'm sorry, Mom. I beg her forgiveness, not really knowing what I've done wrong. The *lizard* has climbed up on my foot and it's coming closer. Its tongue is caressing my every curve. Oh, please. I can't move, I bite down hard on my lip, I cry out.

I'm younger now. I'm lying down. I'm wearing a short skirt and there's a ribbon in my hair. The *lizard* is presenting me with an image. I'm a little girl and I'm playing with myself as I gaze at the naked images of Adam and Eve. Excitement rushes over me. The scene changes. I'm in Sunday school, the minister's daughter, touching the penis of one of the boys in my class. I slowly lower his trousers, staring, wanting to put his penis in my mouth. It's suddenly bigger. And the boy is taller—he's an adult. A lush forest of hair rings his penis, and I delight in running my fingers through it. I put his penis in my mouth and feel it harden. My mouth starts to hurt. His penis has turned into a block of wood and I can barely extract it from my mouth. But now it's a neon cross. I kneel piously before this red, glistening cross. My saliva is dribbling from it. I wonder who he is. I raise my head and look into his face. I've never seen him before.

The *lizard* closes this image and proceeds to prowl my crotch, its tongue and tail teasing my vagina and inner thighs. I'm sweating all over. The *lizard*'s head is coming closer and closer. Suddenly my legs are wide open. The *lizard* is gazing at my sex. I'm embarrassed—it's inspecting a part of me that I myself have never examined. He draws his tongue in and starts to enter me. I thought it would hurt but it doesn't. I am wet enough and this knowledge both shames and excites me. I can feel the *lizard* wiggling into me. My head feels like it's going to explode. Now only its tail is visible. Something inside me is trembling violently. It could be the *lizard*, but I'm not really sure.

What are you up to? Mom asks. Suspicious, she examines my bed from the corner of her eye. I pray that she won't see the *lizard*. Deeper, I beg it. She mustn't see its tail. I urge it all the way inside me, but its tail is still showing. Mother hasn't discovered the *lizard* yet. Even with her looking on, my excitement slowly reaches a climax. The ice-cold *lizard* is making its way deeper inside me. I grimace and try to contain my excitement. Mother looks on, dispassionate. Mother. I hurt terribly. She looks like she doesn't believe me.

Mother wants to take the *lizard* away from me, I know she does. I tense my muscles to keep the *lizard* in. The *lizard* crawls deep inside me, so deep that its tail isn't showing anymore. Mom can't see the *lizard* now. The *lizard* is mine, all mine. I grin at my mother as that ice-cold *lizard* wiggles and turns inside me. Mother is grinning back at me. Her grin grows wider. The head of a snake appears at her mouth, and the body slithers out. She bends over to help it out. It looks like she's vomiting. Mommy, I ask her, where's the baby? It died, you know that. I mean, we killed it, don't you remember? Mommy, no. I didn't kill it. I never saw it. The snake that crawled out of my mother has vanished. I awake from my dream and look at the wall. The *lizard* is gone. I shut my eyes again. The dream resumes. The *lizard* starts wiggling inside my belly again. My anus throbs with pain. Please, no. The *lizard* starts to slither out my backside. I want to have a baby. Mother. I'll have your baby for you, Mother. I entreat her, fighting back my pain, but she leaves without listening. The *lizard* exits me. I am overcome with pain and exhaustion. I slowly wake and look at the wall. The *lizard* is nowhere to be seen. Of course not. Because it's still with me, asleep. The phone rings, clearing my head a bit more. Wrong number. I look up again at the wall.

The *lizard* is there, exactly where it's supposed to be.

6

> Lizards *have no past. That's what makes them gods. For them there's nothing but the present, an eternal present.*
>
> —KIM YŎNGHA, "*Lizard*"

Since the *lizard* entered me that first time I've had sex a few times; an old boyfriend got back in touch. But it was business as usual when I slept with him. Which is to say I felt nothing. The whole time we were having sex I kept thinking about the *lizard*. I wish your penis was colder, I told him. He sat up and said, You've really changed. He had a very solemn expression on his face.

That was the end of that. He never came back. Maybe I really had changed, like he said. I snorted. And what if I had? The man who gave me the *lizard* told me I had to transform myself. Well, isn't that what you'd call changing? I remembered his words when I looked at the *lizard*. It was showing up regularly in my dreams. It would enter my anus and exit from my mouth, or enter through my vagina and exit through my eyes. Either way the sensation was almost the same. The days after I had the dream I was too tired to talk. I did feel refreshed and energized, though.

Once in a while at the cram school I'd see the man who had given me the *lizard*. He'd pass by with a mysterious smile. I wondered sometimes if he was there in my dreams, watching. I felt like his eyes could see right through me. Maybe that was why I felt myself blush whenever I spotted the nape of his neck. Why it was the nape of his neck I can't say. But once I saw him in the cram-school cafeteria in the basement. He was all by himself, spooning hot soup and rice to his mouth. I stood at the door, my eyes fixed on his back. He ate silently, his head lowered, while I focused on the nape of his neck. There was a stubborn tenacity in those clenched neck muscles. They made him seem lonely. Something about that neck, I don't know what, reminded me of the *lizard*. I wanted to embrace him. It wasn't even about sex. I just wanted to rush up to him, put my arms around him, and press my lips to the nape of his neck. I couldn't eat at the cafeteria that day.

I often saw him after that. He'd come over to my place once a month or so. We listened to music, shared a drink. He didn't want to have sex. I wasn't interested, either. And so we'd sit together talking quietly and refreshing each other's drink. He said he enjoyed traveling. Working at the cram school was for him an ideal arrangement—no relationships to commit to, and the freedom to leave at any moment.

And here we are. I'm waiting for him to come back and finish the story about the smoke lady. Then again he may never come back. Maybe I'll have to finish the story myself. I even started to imagine that he was back.

Come on, finish the story.

The detective discovers the dead man's diary at the scene.

He starts talking. I light a cigarette for him. The smoke seeps deep into my lungs.

The diary tells of a most captivating woman: Will I see her tonight? She overpowers my senses. I spend the whole day just waiting for this woman.

He goes on with the story.

The detective does some detecting and learns that the man graduated from college but was unemployed and spent his days doing god-knows-what in his room—he was a vagrant, friendless in Seoul. His few acquaintances said they never saw him with a woman. A prostitute, perhaps? He didn't exactly have the means to buy a woman. So who was she?

Didn't you say he scheduled an autopsy? I ask.

He answers: He did, and the result was that the victim had had a fatal heart attack. The detective then resumes his search for evidence, but finds nothing he can connect to the woman. So he gets to thinking. He goes back to the scene, does yet another search, and a second diary turns up. This diary contains the following entry: My one pleasure is making creations out of smoke. Yesterday I made a car and I made an alcoholic beverage. I drank my smoky drink and drove my sporty car. I shut the windows tight to keep the smoke inside my room and to keep the air still. And yet it lasts only a moment. I need a woman. The detective closes the diary and concludes his report. Direct cause of death: heart attack. He rules out homicide and suicide. This was a case of death by natural causes.

I understand now, I say. The man created a woman out of smoke. He was caressed by her, and they had sex. But he's not allowed to touch her. She'll disappear if he does. She slowly drifts down and embraces him. His every sense is overwhelmed.

He nods in agreement. That's right. But the detective keeps that part of the story to himself. Who will believe him? And it makes little difference if no one does.

Cigarette smoke can be very comforting, I say, smoking a cigarette myself. I look up at the *lizard*. It looks bigger than usual today. I crawl into bed, craving sleep. The man keeps his distance as usual. I turn off the lights and drift off to sleep.

As I sleep, I sense someone opening the window to my room and climbing in. I think it's him, but my head is heavy. I hear him taking his clothes off. We've never slept together, and yet he calmly climbs into my bed as if he were my husband. His hands move gently from my feet up my knees and thighs. His hands are cold. I feel goose bumps all over. He climbs on top of me. His cold hard penis pushes inside me. Mustn't shout. I steady myself. And I mustn't touch him. If I do he'll vanish. His penis moves slowly. Violent pleasure explodes inside me. I tremble with a satisfaction I've never felt with a man. A neon cross flashes in the distance. He's thrusting more strongly now. His cold penis slides all over my body. I'm soaked through. I'm afraid his cold penis will pierce me. You must transform yourself, I remember him telling me. His words reverberate. Ahhh, I'm going away—go past the tropical sunshine, through the forest of crosses, and you'll arrive at the playground. I want to scream but nothing comes out. My ears ring with the rhythmical beating of the tribal drums. It feels like his penis is coming out my ears. My eardrums are about to explode.

I'm languishing. He gets up and dresses. And then he's gone, like smoke. Carefully I open my eyes and look toward the wall. The *lizard* is gone. I don't bother to turn the lights on to make sure. I simply close my eyes again. And fall asleep. A most tranquil sleep. I never want to wake up.

Translated by Dafna Zur

SUGGESTIONS FOR FURTHER READING

ANTHOLOGIES

Fulton, Bruce and Ju-Chan, trans., *Wayfarer: New Fiction by Korean Women*. Seattle: Women in Translation, 1997 (hereafter W).

——, *Words of Farewell: Stories by Korean Women Writers*. Seattle: Seal Press, 1989 (hereafter WF).

Kim Chong-un, trans., *Postwar Korean Short Stories*, 2nd ed. Seoul: Seoul National University Press, 1983 (hereafter PKSS).

Kim Chong-un and Bruce Fulton, trans., *A Ready-Made Life: Early Masters of Modern Korean Fiction*. Honolulu: University of Hawai'i Press, 1998 (hereafter RL).

Literature East and West 14, no. 3 (September 1970: Korean literature issue) (hereafter LEW).

O'Rourke, Kevin, trans., *Ten Korean Short Stories*. Seoul: Yonsei University Press, 1973 (hereafter TKSS).

Pihl, Marshall R., ed., *Listening to Korea*. New York: Praeger, 1973 (hereafter LK).

Pihl, Marshall R., and Bruce and Ju-Chan Fulton, trans., *Land of Exile: Contemporary Korean Fiction*. Armonk, N.Y.: M. E. Sharpe, 1993 (hereafter LE).

Stewart, Frank, and Bruce Fulton, eds., *Seeing the Invisible* (*Manoa* 8, no. 2 [1996]: Korea theme issue) (hereafter SI).

Stewart, Frank, and Susie Jie Young Kim, eds., *The Wounded Season* (*Manoa* 11, no. 2 [1999]: Korea theme issue) (hereafter WS).

Suh Ji-moon, trans., *The Golden Phoenix: Seven Contemporary Korean Short Stories*. Boulder, Colo.: Lynne Rienner, 1998 (hereafter GP).

Translation: The Journal of Literary Translation 13 (fall 1984), Korean feature section, pp. 1–129.

AUTHORS REPRESENTED IN THIS VOLUME

1. Hyŏn Chingŏn

"Fire," trans. Lee in *Flowers of Fire: Twentieth-Century Korean Stories*, rev. ed., ed. Peter H. Lee. Honolulu: University of Hawai'i Press, 1986.
"A Society That Drives You to Drink," trans. Kim and Fulton in RL.

2. Kim Tongin

"The Photograph and the Letter," trans. Kim and Fulton in RL.

3. Yi T'aejun

"A Character Sketch," trans. Choe, LEW.
"An Idiot's Delight," trans. Kim and Fulton in RL.

4. Kim Tongni

"A Descendant of the *Hwarang*," trans. Kim and Fulton in RL.
"Father and Son," trans. Kim in PKSS.
"The Flowers," trans. Chu with Pihl in LK.
"Loess Valley," trans. Holstein, *Koreana* (winter 1994).
"The Post Horse Curse," trans. Pihl in LE.
"The Rock," trans. O'Rourke in TKSS.

5. Kim Yujŏng

"The Scorching Heat," trans. Chun, *Korea Journal* (summer 1994).
"Spring, Spring," trans. Skillend, *Koreana* (spring 2001).
"Wife," trans. Kim and Fulton in RL.

6. Yi Sang

"Phantom Illusion," trans. Kim and Fulton in RL.
"Record of a Consummation," trans. Fenkl and Lew, *Muae* (1995).

7. Yi Hyosŏk

"Pig," trans. Yu, LEW.

8. Ch'ae Manshik

"Constable Maeng," trans. Stevenson, *Acta Koreana* 2 (July 1999).
"Mister Pang," trans. Fulton and Fulton, *Asian Pacific Quarterly* (winter 1994).

"Once Upon a Paddy," trans. Armstrong, ed. King and Fulton, in *My Innocent Uncle*, trans. Bruce and Ju-Chan Fulton, Kim Chong-un, and Robert Armstrong. Seoul: Jimoondang, 2003.
Peace Under Heaven, trans. Chun Kyung-Ja. Armonk, N.Y.: M. E. Sharpe, 1993.
"A Ready-Made Life," trans. Kim and Fulton in RL.
"The Wife and Children," trans. Fulton and Fulton in LE.

9. Ch'oe Chŏnghŭi

The Cry of the Harp: Selected Works by Ch'oe Chŏng-hŭi, trans. Genell Poitras. Norwalk, Conn.: EastBridge, 2005.
"The Haunted House," trans. Kim and Fulton in RL.

10. Hwang Sunwŏn

"A Backcountry Village," trans. Fulton and Fulton, *Koreana* (winter 1993).
The Book of Masks, ed. Martin Holman. London: Readers International, 1989.
The Descendants of Cain, trans. Suh Ji-moon and Julie Pickering. Armonk, N.Y.: M. E. Sharpe, 1997.
"Doctor Chang's Situation," trans. Epstein, *Chicago Review* 39, nos. 3 and 4 (1993).
"The Dog of Crossover Village," trans. Fulton and Fulton, *Asian Pacific Quarterly* (spring 1994).
The Drizzle and Other Korean Short Stories, trans. Kim Chong-un et al. Seoul: Si-sa-yong-o-sa, 1983.
The Moving Castle, trans. Bruce and Ju-Chan Fulton. Seoul: Si-sa-yong-o-sa, 1985.
"The Mule," trans. Kim and Fulton in RL.
Shadows of a Sound, ed. Martin Holman. San Francisco: Mercury House, 1990.
The Short Stories of Hwang Sunwŏn, vol. 1, *The Pond*, trans. Bruce and Ju-Chan Fulton. Norwalk, Conn.: EastBridge, 2006.
The Short Stories of Hwang Sunwŏn, vol. 6, *Lost Souls*, trans. Bruce and Ju-Chan Fulton. Norwalk, Conn.: EastBridge, 2006.
"Snow," trans. Fulton and Fulton, *Korean Culture* (fall 2001).
The Stars and Other Korean Short Stories, trans. Edward Poitras. Hong Kong: Heinemann Asia, 1980.
Trees on a Slope, trans. Bruce and Ju-Chan Fulton. Honolulu: University of Hawai'i Press, 2005.

11. Yi Hoch'ŏl

Panmunjŏm and Other Stories by Lee Ho-chul, trans. Theodore Hughes. Norwalk, Conn.: EastBridge, 2005.

Southerners, Northerners, trans. Andrew Killick and Cho Sukyeon. Norwalk, Conn.: EastBridge, 2005.
"The Sultriness of a Cold Evening," trans. Kim in PKSS.

12. Kim Sŭngok

"Record of a Journey to Mujin," trans. O'Rourke in TKSS.

13. Ch'oe Inho

"The Boozer," trans. Pihl in LE.
Deep Blue Night, trans. Bruce and Ju-Chan Fulton. Seoul: Jimoondang, 2002 (contains the title story and "The Poplar Tree").

15. Cho Sehŭi

"City of Machines," trans. Pihl, *Korea Journal* (March 1990).
The Dwarf, trans. Bruce and Ju-Chan Fulton. Honolulu: University of Hawaii Press, 2006.
"A Little Ball Launched by a Dwarf," trans. Fulton and Fulton, *Korean Literature Today* (fall 1998).
"The Möbius Strip," trans. Fulton and Fulton, *Korean Literature Today* (fall 1998).
"We Didn't Know," trans. Choi, *Two Lines* (2004).

17. Yi Ch'ŏngjun

"The Crane," trans. Epstein, *Korea Journal* (June 1990).
"The Falconer," trans. Pickering, *Korean Literature Today* (winter 1996).
The Prophet and Other Stories, trans. Julie Pickering. Ithaca, N.Y.: Cornell University East Asia Program, 1997.
This Paradise of Yours, trans. Chang Wang-rok and Chang Young-hee. Seoul: Korean Literature Foundation, 1986.
"The Wounded," trans. Lee in WS.

18. Yi Munyŏl

"The Golden Phoenix," trans. Suh in GP.
Our Twisted Hero, trans. Kevin O'Rourke. New York: Hyperion, 2001.
The Poet, trans. Chung Chong-wha and Brother Anthony of Taizé. London: Harvill, 1995.

19. Pak Wansŏ

"Camera and Workboots," trans. Fulton and Fulton, *Koreana* (summer 1996).
"The Good Luck Ritual," trans. Epstein, *Korea Times*, November 1, 1990.

"Identical Apartments," trans. Fulton and Fulton in W.
"In the Realm of the Buddha," trans. Fulton and Fulton, *Koreana* (summer 1996).
My Very Last Possession, ed. Chun Kyung-Ja. Armonk, N.Y.: M. E. Sharpe, 1999.
The Naked Tree, trans. Yu Young-nan. Ithaca, N.Y.: Cornell University East Asia Program, 1995.
"Winter Outing," trans. Pihl in LE.

20. *O Chŏnghŭi*

"The Bronze Mirror," trans. Fulton and Fulton in LE.
"Chinatown," trans. Fulton and Fulton in WF.
"Evening Game," trans. Fulton and Fulton in WF.
"Fireworks," trans. Fulton and Fulton, *Asian Pacific Quarterly* (winter 1993).
"Lake P'aro," trans. Fulton and Fulton, *Korean Literature Today* (winter 1998).
"The Monument Intersection," trans. Suh in GP.
"Morning Star," trans. Fulton and Fulton in SI.
"The Party," trans. Sol, *Korea Journal* (October 1983).
"A Portrait of Magnolias," trans. Fulton and Fulton, *Koreana* (summer 1992).
"The Release," trans. Fulton and Fulton, *Arirang* (summer 2003).
"The Toyshop Woman," trans. Fulton and Fulton, *Korea Times*, November 5, 7, 8, 1989.
"The Weaver Woman," trans. Jeon, *Acta Koreana* 6, no. 2 (July 2003).
"Words of Farewell," trans. Fulton and Fulton in WF.

21. *Ch'oe Yun*

"The Flower with Thirteen Fragrances," trans. Suh in GP.
"His Father's Keeper," in *The Rainy Spell and Other Korean Stories*, rev. ed., trans. Suh Ji-moon. Armonk, N.Y.: M. E. Sharpe, 1998.
"The Last of Hanak'o," trans. Fulton and Fulton in W.
"There a Petal Silently Falls," trans. Fulton and Fulton, *Korea Journal* (winter 1997 and spring 1998).

22. *Kim Yŏngha*

Photo Shop Murder, trans. Jason Rhodes. Seoul: Jimoondang, 2003 (contains the title story and "Whatever Happened to the Guy Stuck in the Elevator?").

BIBLIOGRAPHY

Fulton, Bruce. "*Kijich'on* Fiction." In *Nationalism and the Construction of Korean Identity*, ed. Hyung Il Pai and Timothy R. Tangherlini, pp. 198–213. Berkeley: University of California Institute of East Asian Studies, 1998.

——, ed. Korea section of *The Columbia Companion to Modern East Asian Literature*, ed. Joshua Mostow. New York: Columbia University Press, 2003.

Kwon Youngmin. *Hanguk hyŏndae munhak taesajŏn* (Encyclopedia of modern Korean literature). Seoul: Sŏul taehakkyo ch'ulp'anbu, 2004.

Lee, Ann. "Yi Kwangsu and Korean Literature: The Novel *Mujŏng*." *Journal of Korean Studies* 8 (1992): 81–137.

Myers, Brian. *Han Sŏrya and North Korean Literature*. Ithaca, N.Y.: Cornell University East Asia Program, 1994.

O'Rourke, Kevin. "The Korean Short Story of the 1920s and Naturalism." *Korea Journal* 17 (1977): 48–63.

Yi Chae-sŏn. *Hyŏndae Hanguk sosŏl sa* (A history of modern Korean fiction). Seoul: Minŭm sa, 1991.

——. *Hanguk munhak ŭi wŏngŭnbŏp* (Perspectives on Korean literature). Seoul: Minŭm sa, 1996. See especially pp. 13–54.